"So You're
I Hadn't Guessed."

She dared to gaze up at him. The expression on his face stopped her breath. How dark his eyes were, how intense. His lips were solemn, expectant. Her memory of his lips claiming hers started a yearning in the deepest part of her.

He cupped the back of her head; his fingers entangled her hair, disturbing the pins she'd used to secure the thick waves into a semblance of order. His lips touched the widow's peak at her forehead, sending shafts of tingling delight along her spine. With one finger, he outlined the curve of her cheek, then bent to kiss one ear, then touched the tip of her nose.

Her lips parted involuntarily. Fleetingly it crossed her mind that they were not concealed from view here in the moonlight; anyone might come upon them. Her concern melted when he tipped up her chin and flicked her lips with the tip of his tongue.

She was trapped against him, exactly where she wanted to be. Swept into a timeless vortex, she had no lucid thought, only feelings that were carrying her to a place she'd never known. He ended the kiss and held her close, gently now, stroking her and capturing her very soul in his embrace. "My darling Skye," he murmured, "I do believe I'm in love with you."

Much later, after she had stretched out on top of the bed in her cabin, she realized she hadn't done what she'd set out to do tonight. She had not told Kyle Wyndford that she carried the blood of the Lakota Sioux.

SKYE LEGACY

KRISTA JANSSEN

POCKET BOOKS
New York London Toronto Sydney Tokyo Singapore

This book is a work of fiction. Names, characters, places and
incidents are products of the author's imagination or are used
fictitiously. Any resemblance to actual events or locales or persons,
living or dead, is entirely coincidental.

An *Original* Publication of POCKET BOOKS

POCKET BOOKS, a division of Simon & Schuster Inc.
1230 Avenue of the Americas, New York, NY 10020

ISBN: 1-4165-0179-7

This Pocket Books paperback printing May 2004

10 9 8 7 6 5 4 3 2 1

POCKET and colophon are registered trademarks of
Simon & Schuster Inc.

Cover art by Danilo Ducak

Printed in the U.S.A.

For my dear friends, Lois Jarrell and Sylvia Johnson. Thanks for believing in me from the beginning.

With special appreciation to Janice Kitzler and the staff at the Vermillion Public Library in Vermillion, South Dakota, for the wealth of information on the colorful history of the area.

⊰ Chapter 1 ⊱

April 1840 Near Gibraltar

Buried under piles of woolens, with the trunk lid securely closed above her, Skye Mackinnon felt tragedy approaching. She squeezed her eyes tightly shut and took a few quick breaths to keep from fainting. Distant shouts reached her as the ship was suddenly rammed hard enough to force it into a starboard list. Inside her trunk, Skye was pressed against her packed clothing. Uttering a frantic prayer, she curled into a ball as trickles of sweat dampened her body.

The foreign ship had come out of nowhere, slipping through a bank of coastal fog to overtake the Scottish vessel like a sleek eel stalking its prey.

Skye shifted her weight but made no sound. She couldn't believe this was really happening. After all, this was 1840, and pirating was rarely a problem, now that the days of Blackbeard and Drake and Hawkins had passed into history. But here she was, hiding beneath her Scottish tweeds and woolens in a trunk in the ship's hold. Her mother was secreted in a straw trunk nearby, while her father and the crew faced the thieving villains with nothing more than paltry handguns and outdated broadswords.

Every minute seemed an eternity as she awaited the outcome of the encounter. What if the louts sunk the ship— and she drowned in this coffinlike baggage? She was beginning to wonder if she would be better off taking her chances above decks. If only she had MacLard here beside her; but the pup had disappeared when the commotion first began.

She began to feel woozy as her mind drew her into the past, taking her to the windswept Highland moors above her castle home on the Isle of Skye and to the secret cave along the shore where she had played as a child.

1

The evening that had settled her family's destiny played in her thoughts, became a vision deep in her heated brain: the blazing hearth fire, her mother's melodic voice reading a passage from the novel she was currently writing—and then her father's entrance into the grand hall at Strathmor Castle. Skye remembered how her mother's expression had brightened at the sight of her husband, and the stern look in Fletcher Mackinnon's dark face.

"The MacNeils are leaving, Beth, and there's an end to it," Fletcher had announced grimly. "Few of the old families are left to survive on this godforsaken island. Defeated. Same as everyone else. I'm sorry, my love, if I've failed you; I am deeply sorry. But there's no sense in suffering further."

Her mother had looked up at him, her manuscript neglected in her lap. Skye always marveled at the calm strength in her face, no matter what the circumstances. At age forty, Elizabeth was still lovely, her complexion showing few signs of the last twenty years of eking out a living on this Scottish island in the Hebrides. Elizabeth's joy had been her marriage to the half-Scot, half-Lakota warrior who had captured her heart and won her hand. Her sorrow had been the loss of three tiny babes before they saw their first month on earth. And her satisfaction had been seeing her five novels published both in Scotland and England and receiving glowing letters from admirers throughout Great Britain.

On that momentous night, however, everything had been forgotten except the inevitable fate that loomed ahead.

Fletcher had crossed the room and dropped to one knee beside his wife and daughter. He removed his damp wool cap and grasped their hands. "My precious family," he said solemnly, " 'tis all we can do now, or we'll lose what little we have left. It does no good to be the chieftain of a clan that no longer exists except in memory or the laird of a sweet family who cannot count on a decent meal unless the fishermen have a fair catch."

Elizabeth's eyes were sad, but she smiled at Fletcher. "Will not my royalties tide us over for a time? I should have another payment soon."

He smoothed back strands of his shoulder-length hair,

still black as ebony, and shook his head. "Nay, sweet Beth. The castle is crumbling about our ears. We can't afford servants, and our poor lass here is reduced to being both a kitchen maid and stable hand."

Skye had interjected brightly, "I don't mind, Papa, not even a wee bit. I love to garden and harvest and tend the flocks. We can manage, I'm sure."

She would never forget his haunting green eyes when he looked at her at that instant.

"You have courage, my darling, and we named you for our beloved isle. But we've held out as long as possible. A ship will dock at Kylerhae within the month. If we gather our belongings, sell what we can, and take a few head of prime stock, we can start a new life in America. I've heard there are wealthy people in America who might buy a castle such as Strathmor—who would love it as we have and use their funds to save it from ruin. With the money from the sale, we can build a new home—in the West." Fletcher released Skye's hand and cupped her mother's in both of his. Searching his wife's face, he said huskily, "I'm sorry, my sweet Beth. But I will not stay here and see you live like a crofter or starve—not when you once owned a fine estate in England—and gave it up for me."

Skye had watched her mother stroke his face, tracing his prominent cheekbones, then lightly touch his lips that appeared so determinedly sad. "We'll go wherever you say, My Lord Fletcher Mackinnon. My Lakota of the Highlands."

Skye remembered how she felt when she heard her mother's words. She wanted to cry out *nay!* How could she leave the island she loved so much, the only place she'd ever called home, the blue-green sea and the snow-brushed mountains rising at its core? And the castle with its ancient stones and secret hiding places, and her friends from the village school, few in number, but ever so dear? And if she had to give up her horses and her pets, she would surely die.

Somehow, she held her tongue. If there was one thing she had been taught, it was to respect her parents, to obey them in all things, and to trust in their decisions. Never had her powerful father or her quiet, strong-willed mother failed her. They had given her their total love and the best life they possibly could. If they asked this ultimate sacrifice of her, she would have no choice. After all, she was no longer a child. She would soon be nineteen and must learn to deal with whatever difficulties might arise in her future. She had never expected to leave her beloved Scotland, but life had unexpected twists and turns, and this was her first real challenge as an adult.

She folded her hands in her lap and set her chin. "Where will we go?" she asked her father without a trace of the pain that was filling her heart.

"America, where I was born," Fletcher said with scarcely a glance her way. "I know a valley that is the most beautiful in the world. My people—the Lakotas—are there. 'Twas my first home many years ago, though I was forced to leave. I have a plan, but we must be daring for it to succeed."

Elizabeth's lips tilted in a girlish smile. "My fine chieftain, when have we ever lacked daring?"

"Never, Beth."

"And you do recall the motto of the Mackinnons."

"Aye. Fortune assists the daring. We have indeed taken a few chances in our time." The heaviness in his eyes lifted. "And we're not entirely destitute, you know. Are you with me, my love?" He looked now at his daughter. "And you, Skye? Are we a team that will overcome all challenges we must face?"

"Aye, Papa," Skye responded without hesitation. "What is your plan?"

For a time, sitting in the glimmering firelight, her father had explained he intended to go to Gibraltar, then find a ship sailing to Tangier where he would purchase a barb stallion to take to America for breeding. With a barb stud and the two mares, one already in foal to his superb Indian stallion Spirit Dog, who had died during the winter, they would have the foundation for breeding the best horses in the Americas. Skye was fascinated with the idea. It held a real chance for adventure. She decided it would not be as hard to leave Skye as she had expected

Her thoughts of that momentous night two months ago ended abruptly when the ship listed to port. She clung to the

4

clothing packed around her. Everything had gone so well. And now this disaster. All her family's possessions were here in this hold, though there was little of real value except the two prize brood mares. But now, all could be lost, even their very lives.

Husky shouts echoed from above. A door grated open.

Skye cringed inside the trunk, contemplating two dreadful fates: death at the hands of pirates or drowning at the bottom of the ocean while encased in a coffin of clothing.

The lid of the trunk jerked upward. "Skye! Are you all right, lass?"

Skye pushed aside the woolens and gulped the fetid air. Her father was gazing down at her, and he clutched her wriggling black terrier. Across the dingy enclosure, she spotted her mother emerging from her basket. "Papa," she said, gasping, "what happened?" Getting to her knees, she reached for the dog. "MacLard, 'tis safe now," she said soothingly. As the dog raked her chin with his tongue, she stared up at her father. "What happened to the pirates?"

"The rascals made us halt and boarded our ship, but they're Turks, not pirates, though they have the look of it. In fact, 'tis a stroke of luck. I'll be able to sail with them instead of going to Gibraltar. I'll be in Tangier much sooner." He crossed to Elizabeth to embrace her. "Follow me above decks, ladies. I wouldna have sent you into hiding if I'd known the approaching ship was friendly."

Awash with relief, Skye returned her mother's smile and then followed the couple up the stairs. Her knees were still weak, but her breathing was back to normal. The upper deck of the frigate was bustling with activity. She found a spot out of the way and sat holding MacLard while watching a dozen swarthy men haul crates from the Scottish ship to their own waiting vessel.

After a lengthy conversation with the two captains, her father headed her way.

"My bonnie Skye, give me a brave smile before I go."

She gave him the best smile she could manage. He would be all right, she reassured herself. Her father had always been her hero, and she must trust his judgment in this most bizarre circumstance.

He put his large hands on her shoulders and studied her face for several seconds. "I know these are devilish-looking gents with their dark skin and turbans, but they produce the finest horseflesh in the world. I've arranged to go with them to buy our breeding stallion."

"I know, Papa, but . . ." Now that the moment of parting had arrived, her old fears began to surface.

"This is what we planned, isn't it? When we left hearth and home on Skye?"

"Aye, but what if something happens to you? What if—"

"Don't worry, my darling. I'll meet you and your mother in New Orleans as soon as I purchase the animal and find passage. You will now be in charge of your journey."

Skye's courage soared. "Aye, Father. I know what to do. We'll wait for you in New Orleans for two months and try to find a buyer for our castle and lands. If you've not come by then, we must travel to your homeland in the West—to the place of your birth—to Dakota."

Fletcher's green eyes softened as he leaned close. "See to your mother's comfort and safety, lass. My dear wife often lives in a world of her imagination, and I want that world protected always."

A lump formed in Skye's throat, but she smiled again and nodded her agreement. She had witnessed her parents' devotion through good times and bad. As far as she knew, they had never been apart more than a day or two. And she knew how much her mother had come to depend on her husband's common sense and strength. Elizabeth Mackinnon might be a celebrated novelist throughout the British Isles, but when it came to practical matters, she relied entirely on her husband's skill at managing their daily lives. "We'll be fine, Papa. I'll take good care of Mother. And the horses, too."

He gripped her shoulders and touched his lips to her forehead. Then, keeping his eyes on her, he reached behind his neck and untied the thong that suspended the bear-claw necklace at his throat. "If I am delayed, take this to my Lakota homeland. Remember, my name was White Arrow. The old chief is surely dead, but you might find a woman named Ola. She helped raise me after my mother died. Try

6

to locate a well-watered stretch of valley land. Purchase as much as you can. The future of the Mackinnons will rest in your hands if I canna be there." He pressed the necklace into her palms.

Skye forced her words around the growing knot in her throat. "But shouldn't Mother have your necklace?"

After a thoughtful pause, he said, "Nay, Skye. She is the dearest love of my heart—the companion of my soul. But you, my daughter, are flesh of my flesh, blood of my blood. You are Lakota, as I am. As a young warrior, I earned this necklace when I defeated the chief's son in combat." Placing his hand on her shoulder, he said, "If Siyaka still lives, he is the one enemy I have in the land of Dakota. You must avoid him, at all costs. Do you understand, lass?"

"Aye, Father."

"This necklace is your rightful legacy, a symbol of courage and endurance. It will be the proof of your heritage and your protection in America."

Skye felt her father's love and his faith in her as if he had passed a torch to guide her future. She would never fail him. Never. His gift wrapped her spirit in a magic cloud. Rarely had he spoken to her of their Lakota heritage. The Mackinnon ancestry had dominated their lives. After all, Fletcher Mackinnon was now the chief of the ancient Mackinnon clan, the last Mackinnon ruler on the Isle of Skye. But only remnants were left of the glory of the clans. Their past was overwhelmed by the power and ambition of a burgeoning England.

Skye put the Lakota necklace in her skirt pocket. "I'll keep it with me always, Papa, until you join us, and then you will wear it again."

His gratified half-smile showed his pride and satisfaction. "I'm counting on your courage, lass. Remember—if I am delayed, you must claim a parcel of good land and defend it with your life."

"I'll remember."

His smile broadened as he patted her shoulder. When he turned and crossed the deck to embrace his wife, Skye gazed across the stretch of ocean toward the distant rock of Gibraltar, now stark in the morning sun. She wanted her parents to have a bit of privacy in the last moments they would spend together for months—perhaps forever, if things went badly. Her hand closed over the bear-claw amulet in her pocket. A thrill raced along her spine and made her heart somersault. Her father would be fine and soon they would be reunited in America. Then they would make their way west to establish a wonderful new home for themselves and future generations.

The brisk wind teased her hair and cooled her forehead. She was invigorated, challenged, and ever so glad to be young and alive and experiencing the adventure of a lifetime. Her duties were clear, and she relished the new sense of responsibility given her by her father.

"Farewell, my darlings," he called as he boarded the Turkish vessel.

"Good-bye," she cried. Moving to join her mother at the railing, Skye slipped her arm around the diminutive lady's waist. Skye was tall like her father; she had green eyes and raven black hair, like her father. She had been born in Scotland and raised as a Scottish lass, but like her father, she proudly carried the blood of the Lakota Sioux.

⇥ Chapter 2 ⇤

May 1840 New Orleans

Have a cheroot, Kyle, my boy. West Indian tobacco is the best in the world, despite Virginia's claims to the contrary."

Kyle Wyndford selected a large black cigar from the fine-grained walnut humidor his host was extending. He passed it under his nose, inhaling the rich aroma, then slid it into his vest pocket. It was good to relax after the past weeks of travel. Resting an elbow on the mantel, he said, "I'll save it, Mr. Caldwell. I'll enjoy it on my hotel balcony before retiring. There's a fine view of the city from there, especially with a full moon rising."

"Indeed, a favorite sight of mine," agreed Blaine Caldwell, replacing the humidor onto the polished desk that dominated the room.

"Hard to believe the town is so well lighted even after midnight," Kyle said. "Don't the citizens of New Orleans ever go to bed?"

"Most keep late hours. When the Vieux Carré had gaslights installed, the folks took to the city like moths to a flame. Gambling, theater, soirées, restaurants as fine as any in Paris. Ever been to Paris, Kyle?"

"Once. Years ago." Kyle took a sip of brandy from his crystal snifter, then continued. "My parents took the entire family to the Continent just after the war. I was much too young to appreciate it. But my father, the earl, considered a tour quite the thing—and so did my mother."

Caldwell struck a match to his cigar and leisurely puffed it into life. With wisps of smoke wafting around his face, he said, "Your father was a good friend of my family in those early years. The earl used to say he admired my father for leaving his English roots and striking out for America."

"Father always said there were fortunes to be made in America. I'm sure my brother and I were both influenced by his opinion."

"A shame about your brother."

Kyle sipped from his goblet before responding. His brother, Blanton, had preceded him to America and staked the first claim for the Wyndfords in distant Dakota. But two years after establishing Wind River Ranch, Blanton had been tortured and murdered by Indians, leaving behind his desperate young wife and a baby son. Kyle assumed management of the ranch that had been left in equal shares to him and to Blanton's widow. Nine years ago. The years had passed like shooting stars. "Yes, a shame," he muttered, then took another swallow of brandy.

"You've made your family proud, Kyle. Expanded the ranch, improved the stock, looked after your brother's widow and the boy."

Kyle gazed around the sumptuous room, which was

richly paneled and distinctly masculine, with exquisite paintings of sailing ships gracing the walls and a detailed model of a full-rigged schooner displayed on the mantel. The room was a perfect hideaway where the shipping tycoon could plan his next venture to the far corners of the world. Kyle understood and related to an entrepreneur like Blaine Caldwell and counted himself fortunate to be a friend and business associate of the gracious older gentleman.

"Doesn't compare with you, sir," Kyle observed. "The Caldwell fleet travels to every important port on the globe. And your homes—this property and the plantation upriver—are equal to any in Louisiana. Your wife is not only a beauty, but the perkiest little lady I've ever met—and Laurel—well, you know what I think of that delightful young miss."

Blaine Caldwell eased onto the leather sofa and propped an ankle across his knee. "My daughter. Yes, Laurel is a delight, but headstrong as they come. I'd hoped she and you . . . well . . . might consider a liaison, though I'd hate to have my daughter living so far out west."

Kyle sat in the massive leather armchair opposite Caldwell. He had figured the subject of Laurel would arise and he must choose his words carefully. Last year when he'd visited New Orleans, he had escorted Laurel to a barbeque. They had discovered that they enjoyed being friends, but nothing more. Why, he couldn't say. She was a beauty and amazingly intelligent. He guessed she knew as much about running Caldwell shipping as her father. But they had no serious attraction to each other. The feeling was quite mutual and made it easy for them to be comfortable in a relaxed, friendly relationship. "She'll have none of me, Mr. Caldwell, to my dismay," he said magnanimously.

"She has dreams of managing Caldwell Shipping," Blaine said with a hint of pride. "I would much prefer she had more feminine pursuits, but I will give her free rein for now. Do you have marital ambitions, Kyle? Or does possessing a large slice of Dakota keep you too busy for such matters?"

Kyle chuckled. Caldwell was closer to the truth than he knew. Kyle had no interest in settling down with one woman and giving up his independent ways. He was finally enjoying his hard-won success, his financial gains, and the casual affairs with the vivacious and robust ladies in certain houses at outposts along the Missouri. Since taking over his brother's holdings in the most magnificent valley in southern Dakota, he had only one goal, one obsession in life: to build the finest damn ranch ever created, to sell cattle and breed the swiftest thoroughbreds in America. He had everything he had dreamed of, and he had risked his inheritance and his very life to get it. Wind River was a ranch to cause any English lord to turn green with envy. To crown his success, three years earlier he had ordered logs hauled from the western forests and built a house as spacious and comfortable as any English country home in Northamptonshire. His sister-in-law, Melissa, was happy, content to run the household and raise her son there. Their lives had been ideal, until lately. Now, there was this sudden problem of Missy's health.

"So what brings you to New Orleans, Kyle? You didn't say over dinner. I hope you're not worried about your investments?"

Kyle laughed at the idea. "Hardly, sir. We both know your company is as solid as gold in the bank. No, Mr. Caldwell, I never lose any sleep over the running of Caldwell Shipping."

"You've received your profits regularly, I presume," Blaine said.

"Absolutely. Despite the distance and warring Indians along the way. No—it's my sister-in-law, Melissa, who is the primary reason for my journey just now."

"Oh? I remember the lady from years ago. Is she in town with you?" Blaine placed his cigar in the ashtray at his side and leaned forward. "My word, if we've omitted Mrs. Wyndford from our small dinner tonight, I must apologize. Why, Rebecca will skin me for such an oversight."

"No, no. Missy didn't attend because she wasn't able. We just completed our long journey yesterday and she's indisposed."

"She's not well, then?"

"I'm afraid not. The past few months, she has gone from her usual hearty self to a frail shadow of a woman. She's practically skin and bones, and has spells of pain that leave her exhausted and often confined to bed." Kyle tried to shut out the sorrow that his words forced into his heart. "A good woman, Missy," he observed. "Too good for my wayward brother; maybe too good for this world at all."

The door cracked open and a young lady with strawberry-blond curls swept atop her head peaked into the room. "Daddy, are you and Mr. Wyndford finished with your cigars? Miss Shannon has arrived and the three of us are sitting on the back veranda."

"Thank you, Laurel," Blaine said. "I don't believe Mr. Wyndford has met Shannon yet."

Kyle stood simultaneously with Caldwell. "Thank you for the brandy, sir. And the cigar."

After Laurel disappeared, Blaine said in a low tone, "Don't forget—we have a meeting next week with Cheyne Sinclair. The man is rarely here and you may never have another chance to talk to the brigand."

"I'd be delighted. I've always wanted to meet the infamous Falcon face-to-face."

"Some men have—and not lived to tell about it. Cheyne learned the tricks of privateering from Lafitte himself. Those were good days, despite all the uproar and danger. A man needs an escapade once in a while to keep him on his toes, and cobwebs off his brain and sword arm."

Kyle grinned. "I'll keep that in mind when next I encounter the savages out West."

Blaine clapped his hand on Kyle's shoulder. "Remind me to tell you about my stint with old Andy Jackson. Now *there* was an Indian fighter."

The two men strolled outside. The late spring air was balmy, and a breeze from the Mississippi a hundred yards away carried a hint of earthy moisture, as if a shower was approaching.

Laughter reached them before they arrived at the ladies' chairs. In the flickering glow of torches surrounding the veranda, Blaine's wife, Rebecca Caldwell, was shaking her finger under the nose of a stout young woman whose stylishly elegant gown contrasted with the mischief in her eyes. At the woman's shoulder stood Laurel Caldwell, seemingly unable to slip a word edgewise into the lively conversation between the older ladies.

Blaine approached at once and interrupted the chatter. "Shannon, dear, I didn't hear you announced." He leaned to kiss the plump woman on her cheek.

"Blaine," Shannon responded warmly, "I'm so sorry I missed your dinner, but I had a banquet to oversee for nearly a hundred of our most important citizens."

"I know, *cherie,* I was invited, but found excuses to decline. Not my cup of tea, as you know. Much too political."

"I've just been catching up on the gossip with Rebecca."

Rebecca Caldwell grinned across at her husband. "You know, sweetheart, that it's quite the reverse. Shannon is the one who knows all the gossip of New Orleans. Without her update, I would be as uninformed as a muskrat up a tree."

Observing the scene, Kyle hid his amusement at Mrs. Caldwell's charming backwoods expression. He admired the way she made no pretense of being anything other than exactly what she was: a woman of limited education who had grown up in a shanty in the Tennessee hills. She was one of the most highly respected and beloved matrons in New Orleans, and not just because her husband was enormously wealthy and the only son of a distinguished French-Creole mother. Rebecca Caldwell's warmth, courage, and generosity had won everyone's affection. And whoever she befriended was accepted in elite society without the slightest hesitation.

"Please take a chair, Mr. Wyndford. When I think of how far you've come, I am amazed at your endurance. Why, a trip to my old home in Tennessee just wears me to a frazzle."

"And yet I understand you travel abroad."

"Oh yes, to my brother's home in Scotland. His family is in the Sutherland Highlands. We also have cousins in the Hebrides. A Scottish laird, in fact."

As Kyle turned to the second lady, Blaine stepped forward to make introductions. "Shannon, may I introduce Mr. James Kyler Wyndford, son of the earl of Wyndford, and an American land baron rather than an English lord, by his own design. Wyndford, please meet our adopted daughter, Miss Shannon Kildaire, proprietress of Heritage House, the finest hotel in the quarter."

Kyle accepted the lady's hand and bowed. So this was the woman he'd heard so much about—the outrageously independent lady who had been adopted as a ragamuffin right from the city's slums by the distinguished Caldwells. She must have remained a single woman all these years. "What a coincidence," he said. "I'm stopping at your establishment myself. Most elegant. My sister-in-law and I have taken rooms there."

"Pleased to meet you," said Shannon. Her unassuming manner and frank smile won him over at once. He touched his lips to her heavily jeweled fingers. Rumor had it that Shannon Kildaire had inherited Heritage House from an infamous madam, that the place had once been a lavish bordello. One thing a person could always count on at the Caldwell mansion was an intriguing collection of guests, both male and female. "My pleasure entirely," he murmured and returned her smile.

Within minutes, the group was seated and being served a choice of brandy or sherry. Kyle was enjoying himself thoroughly. He lived a lonely life in his majestic valley and had forgotten how much he missed conversation among the worldly and witty. Observing the group, actually a close-knit family, he couldn't help envying them their affection and mutual respect.

When the majordomo appeared unexpectedly, Kyle didn't notice him at first for the laughter ringing in his ears.

"Excuse me," the servant said loudly. "Guests have arrived at the door, Master Caldwell. Two ladies. I told them you were entertaining, but they looked so forlorn, I asked them to wait in the hall."

Still smiling, Blaine cleared his throat and gave the man his attention. "Ladies? Calling at this hour? Without an invitation? Most unusual."

Rebecca scooted to the edge of her chair. "Blaine, darling, you don't suppose . . . you know we've been expecting my cousins from Scotland for days."

A sudden loud yapping erupted from the house. Before

anyone could move, a small black dog, greatly resembling a furry sausage with huge ears and thick hair obliterating its eyes, came tearing across the porch. The creature planted its forepaws on first one pair of knees, then another, and almost upset the table. His barks were high-pitched and wildly excited. His brushy tail slapped the air and tangled skirt hems. When Laurel made a grab for the creature, he evaded her grasp and ran under the nearest settee.

"I'm sorry, ma'am, surely sorry." The servant scrambled to retrieve the pup, but it scooted out the back of the bench and tore off across the manicured lawn.

"Oh no! Oh, for heaven's sake," came a cry from the open door of the house. "MacLard—you stop this minute or I'll have your hide!" A slender young woman ran onto the lawn, her skirts flying and her hat dangling around her neck from its ties. Her stride was impressive for a female, and in seconds, she had disappeared into the stand of magnolias shadowing the river, close on the tracks of the scampering black canine.

Kyle shook his head in amusement and gazed at the startled faces of his friends. Who would appear next at the Caldwell home this rare evening?

⇥ Chapter 3 ⇤

"Dreadful. Absolutely awful."

Skye spoke to her reflection in the full-length mirror. "What must they think of me?"

Her hair was in shambles and her skirt splattered with mud. She stepped out of the skirt and crossed the spacious bedroom to the waiting bowl and pitcher of warm water. Her stockings and petticoats were damp from wading along the riverbank, but her blouse was undamaged except for a smudge left by the squirming MacLard. "At least it was too dark to be seen clearly," she mumbled into the washcloth. "Heavens—Mother must have been mortified."

After scrubbing her face, Skye took a deep breath and gazed at her surroundings. The room was approximately the size of her bedroom at Strathmor Castle, but there the resemblance ended. The furnishings and appointments of the Caldwell mansion's guest suite were luxurious and fashionable. Crystal chandeliers and wall sconces showered the room with light, holding back the thick velvet night beyond the windows. The dominant color in the room was a rich royal blue. Nothing in her past experience had prepared Skye for such lavish living arrangements. Here she was, in exquisite surroundings, and unfortunately she had already disgraced herself. But what else could she have done when MacLard escaped his leash and dashed toward the woods? The poor little dog had been confined aboard ship for so long that he was wild with joy to be scampering on solid ground once more. The river, frogs, crickets, and hundreds of trees had fascinated him. One could hardly blame him for his energetic explorations.

Luckily she had found him before he plunged into danger in the gathering dusk. And then her cousin, Laurel, had arrived to guide her back to the house while avoiding the back porch where refreshments were being served. Laurel had been wonderful, so understanding and sympathetic. She had taken MacLard to the kitchen and arranged for his bath, then led Skye up the back stairs to this lovely suite where Skye could catch her breath and restore her composure.

Skye was extremely grateful that she didn't have to reappear downstairs this evening. She wanted nothing more than to pull on her familiar flannel gown and climb atop the inviting feather bed. Except her gown seemed much too heavy for the humid warmth of the New Orleans night. Perhaps she could sleep in her undergarments. Aye, that was a fine idea. Using the small stepstool leading to the top of the mattress, she climbed onto the bed.

A tap on the door startled her and she slid her feet back to the steps. "Who is it?" she asked tentatively.

"It's Laurel. May I come in?"

"Of course."

Laurel Caldwell entered the room and greeted Skye with a winning smile. "I hope you've had time to freshen up, Skye. Will you be comfortable here?"

Skye felt herself blushing. Here she sat in her lingerie, her clothes scattered on the floor and every light blazing as if she had no shame at all. Facing her in the brightness was the most beautiful young woman she'd ever seen: a fine figure, a flawless complexion, and perfectly arranged hair the color of molten gold. How had Laurel kept her hair in place during their dash across the lawn and into the trees? Returning her cousin's smile, Skye left the bed and scooped up her garments from the floor. "I've made a mess, I'm afraid. But I just had to test that amazing bed."

"It's from Paris," said Laurel warmly. "And please do make yourself completely at home. You must be exhausted after such a long sea journey."

"I must admit I was sick of the wretched ship. Mother enjoyed every minute of the voyage, but MacLard and I . . . well . . ."

"I'm happy to report that Marie is drying your dog this very minute. You can keep him here, if you like."

"Oh, could I? He's very well behaved, but the room is so exquisite. I wouldn't want to impose."

Laurel laughed. "You couldn't possibly. I'm just delighted you're here and we can get acquainted. Let's see—it was more than ten years ago when we met in Scotland—at the Sutherland family reunion."

"Aye. I remember. We met, but we didn't really get to know each other."

Laurel grinned and sank gracefully into one of the tufted armchairs. "Let's be honest, Skye. I was a dreadful snob, ignoring you younger children. But that was my first trip to the British Isles and I was eager to see and do everything."

"And I was a scamp, full of rowdiness and mischief. Laurel, I haven't properly thanked you for rescuing me tonight from complete humiliation. I was so afraid I would lose MacLard in the darkness that I couldn't think of anything else."

"I was glad to help. I could tell you were in no frame of mind after that to suffer through introductions. Tomorrow will be soon enough for you to visit with my parents. Besides, your mother is having a wonderful time getting reacquainted with her cousins. I expect she will be entertaining Mother and Father and Shannon for another hour on the back veranda. Oh, and Mr. Wyndford, too."

"Mother has so looked forward to this visit. But I hope Papa will be along soon. You see, we must head west while the weather is favorable."

"I understand your father has gone to Tangier to search for a breeding stallion."

"Aye. We're convinced that Arabian blood is necessary for the horses we hope to produce."

"And your mother? She will keep writing her novels? I've read several and find them fascinating."

"Writing is her first love . . . well, after her family, of course."

"We welcome such a lady with open arms. So many activities are planned for your visit. Teas, barbeques, the theater. I promise we'll keep both of you occupied until Lord Mackinnon arrives."

Skye had descended from the bed and settled into the chair opposite Laurel. She would have searched out her wrapper, but her trunk sat unpacked in the corner and the evening was incredibly warm. Now, she looked down at her hands folded in her lap. Social activities held no interest for her. She was by nature shy with strangers and preferred the company of a few close friends and her animals. Of course, she had no friends at all here in New Orleans. Just Laurel, and she wouldn't disappoint her for the world. "That sounds very nice," she murmured.

"Now, don't worry about fancy clothes. I've already thought of that."

Increasingly concerned, Skye looked into Laurel's sparkling amber eyes. "You have? But I . . ."

"I know the climate on your Scottish isle is completely different from New Orleans. And of course, you won't need a lavish wardrobe out west. In the meantime, while you're here, I'll loan you a frock or two of mine. We're about the same size, and I've not worn several of the dresses that recently arrived from France. No one has seen them, so you won't be embarrassed as if they were hand-me-downs."

Skye couldn't fathom what Laurel was talking about. Embarrassed? It wasn't her clothing she was concerned about. It was only that she cared nothing for society, hated trying to make conversation about matters that didn't interest her, and despaired of making the right impression for the sake of her family, while feeling certain she was awkward and boring. She wasn't sure why she felt that way, because she found people very interesting, as a rule. Especially if they could converse with some intelligence on animal husbandry or agriculture. Her friends on Skye spoke of little else. Only during her infrequent visits to England did she have the chance to expand her knowledge and her horizons. The fairs and horse races had fascinated her; the museums and libraries captured her imagination. But on the few occasions she had been forced to dress "like a lady" and attend social functions as the daughter of Laird and Lady Mackinnon, she had been dreadfully uncomfortable and stayed on the sidelines as much as possible.

Laurel was studying her. Could her cousin read her thoughts? "Oh, I appreciate the offer, Laurel. But I expect I'll be spending most of my time caring for the horses and preparing for our journey west. You see, my father asked me to begin making the arrangements in his absence."

"My, that's quite a responsibility. I'm truly impressed." Laurel grinned knowingly. "I think we're more alike than you might guess, Skye. As a matter of fact, I'd rather be managing my father's shipping business than socializing. But still, you *must* see some of New Orleans while you're here."

"I do want to, Laurel. Please don't think I'm rude or backward."

"Not in the least," Laurel said, laughing. "You're utterly refreshing, in fact. I'm betting you will have to fend off more than one suitor during your visit."

Skye responded with a shy smile to Laurel's infectious

manner. "I'll have no time for suitors," she said. "Actually, my first concern is the mares we left at your stable when we arrived. They'll need proper exercise. One is in foal, you see."

Laurel cocked her head in thought. Then she brightened. "I have it. Highgrove would be ideal. That's our plantation upriver. It has the very best facilities and a complete staff to care for the livestock. We'll go there in a day or two, after our tea party tomorrow with Melissa Wyndford. Your mother has already accepted Mrs. Wyndford's invitation, assuming the lady is up to entertaining."

Skye was dismayed at the thought of a tea party, but she leaped at Laurel's suggestion about the plantation. "Aye, Highgrove sounds like a splendid idea. Would it be possible for me to stay there, too? I would love to learn the workings of a real Louisiana plantation. Then I'll be better prepared when we establish our own ranch out west."

"Of course. You're welcome to do as you like. But you mustn't spend all your time there. I won't miss this opportunity to show off my darling cousin to the town. And in exchange, I want to learn all about Skye, the Highlands, and Strathmor Castle. Why, I'm green with envy that you've lived in a real castle overlooking the sea. You must describe it in detail, and what life is like there."

"Of course. Oh, by the way, Strathmor is for sale. Maybe you can help us find a buyer."

"For sale? Really? You would part with your ancestral property?"

Skye felt a tug at her heart, but she plunged on. "Aye. We must, you see, in order to establish our new home here in America. 'Tis hard, but we're prepared for the change. And you mustn't forget that my father was born in America, in Dakota. And mother was born in England. So we're not as attached to Scotland as you might think."

"I knew your mother was English, but I thought your father was a Scot. Since he's the clan chieftain, after all."

"Papa's father was a Mackinnon laird. But his mother was a Lakota princess. I'm sure you've heard the story."

Laurel gaped at her. Shock was written in every line of her face.

"You didn't know?" Skye asked, surprised at Laurel's stunned expression.

"No . . . I never heard that. Why, how romantic—how intriguing." Her comment sounded strained and hollow.

Lifting her chin, Skye said proudly, "But don't worry about the matter of legitimacy. My grandfather Mackinnon was married to the princess. The poor girl died in childbirth and later, Finlay Mackinnon went in search of his son and heir—my father."

Laurel covered Skye's hands as she leaned forward. "Please forgive me, Skye. I meant no disparagement of your heritage. I was just surprised that I didn't know this fascinating story." She hesitated as if searching for words. "On the other hand, dear Skye, maybe you shouldn't say too much about it while you're in New Orleans."

"But why not? I'm very proud of my Lakota blood. It's every bit as noble as my Scottish lineage."

"Of course. I entirely agree. But you see . . . well, Indians have been the enemies of the whites for many years. There are hard feelings in some circles—in *most* circles, in fact. I'm not suggesting secrecy exactly, only tact. Choose carefully whom you talk to about your legacy."

"Really? We've heard nothing on Skye about these problems. When my father left America years ago, the Lakotas and the whites were friendly." Skye could see Laurel was truly disturbed. She wouldn't argue with Laurel if she might be upset, but she honestly didn't care who knew of her Lakota blood. In fact, she would be delighted to reveal it to everyone she met. If they were ignorant of the history of her Lakota people, that was their misfortune. Everyone on Skye accepted her father without question as their beloved laird. Why should people in America be any different? Of course, she didn't expect to get well acquainted with anyone in New Orleans, not in the brief month or two her family would be visiting here.

Kyle excused himself at last from the pleasant group on the Caldwell's back veranda. He needed to look in on Missy at the hotel before retiring. Tomorrow while his sister-in-law entertained the ladies at tea, he would have a clandestine meeting with Blaine Caldwell and Cheyne Sinclair. Kyle was eager to meet the Falcon at last and to hear how the rascal's daring adventures at sea were progressing.

Kyle hated the institution of slavery. Three years ago, he had gladly provided funds to help end the practice. In the privacy of Caldwell's dockside office tomorrow, the three of them could discuss Sinclair's latest efforts to relieve slaving ships of their suffering cargo. Kyle realized there was no financial gain and a good deal of risk for all of them. Of course, his risk was nothing compared to that of Mr. Caldwell's. If Caldwell's planter friends knew what was going on, they would ride him out of town on a rail, notwithstanding his vast wealth and Creole connections. After all, the slave trade was vital to the cotton plantations. At least, that was the prevailing view. As for Cheyne Sinclair, the man was putting his very life on the line. Kyle had no hesitation to throw in with Caldwell and Sinclair's efforts and do anything he could to help end slavery.

Jogging his stallion down the moon-splashed river road, he contemplated the fascinating evening he'd just experienced, and anticipated what the morrow would bring.

≈ Chapter 4 ≈

Skye sat stiff as a post in the luxurious carriage. She had never worn a corset, but Laurel had said the contraption was a must if she were to fit into the exquisite gown from Paris. And Skye did want to please Laurel.

Looking across at her mother, she could see she had also pleased *her,* as well. Her mother kept giving her admiring glances, despite the fascinating panorama outside the carriage windows.

Keeping her gloved hands folded in her lap, Skye gazed outside at the sun-splashed afternoon. She had slept till midmorning and awakened quite refreshed. For the next three hours, she had been treated like visiting royalty: breakfast on her private balcony overlooking the garden, Laurel's personal maid helping her select from a succession of beautiful dresses, a seamstress fussing over hems and seams. And finally, a visit from her mother as well as Mrs. Caldwell, who clucked over the transformation of the sprite from Skye into a southern belle. Transformation indeed. Never had she looked so fine—or felt so completely uncomfortable.

Luncheon had been served al fresco on the lower back porch. Over cold slices of ham and fresh fruit and coffee strong enough to hold up a stack of bricks, Rebecca Caldwell explained that her daughter usually spent most of her mornings at the shipping office on Decatur Street. But naturally Laurel would join them for Mrs. Wyndford's tea party.

Skye's mind had drifted during Rebecca Caldwell's explanation of the Wyndfords' background. She was far more interested in surveying Dominique Hall, dwelling on the lushness of the grounds and catching glimpses of the nearby Mississippi River while thinking of its length and how her family would soon be traveling on it toward their western destination. But her ears perked up during Mrs. Caldwell's description of the Wyndfords' vast cattle operation in the southeastern corner of Dakota. She was surprised to learn that Melissa, today's hostess, was a widow with a young boy and was sadly in ill health.

Now, as the coach bumped along the cobbled streets of the Vieux Carré, Skye sat primly in her borrowed dress across from her mother and Rebecca and Laurel Caldwell and tried to concentrate on the sights of the enchanting city.

"More than forty thousand souls," Laurel was explaining. "Growing by leaps and bounds. Caldwell Shipping has an office a few blocks east of the Place d'Armes. Watch now; there on the corner of St. Louis and Royal is our newest hotel, the St. Louis. Would you believe the building cost over a million and a half dollars? Why, everyone is aghast. Shannon was certain she would lose her clientele, but instead, her business at Heritage House has increased."

"Did I understand that Shannon Kildaire is your sister?" Skye inquired politely.

"My adopted sister. But I love her as if she were my own flesh and blood. I worshipped her from the start. No one ever knew who her real parents were—only that she traveled down the Mississippi to New Orleans when she was ten and was rescued from the streets by my mother and father shortly before they married. Shandy was her nickname then, and Mother and Father still call her that sometimes. When she was in her late twenties, a family friend . . ." Laurel's voice fell to a whisper. "Actually, an infamous madam in the old days was so fond of Shannon that when she died, she left Shannon the establishment on Burgundy. Years ago, that area was questionable, but now it's an elegant and exclusive section of the Vieux Carré."

"Vieux Carré?" inquired Skye.

"French for old square. Anyway, Shannon turned the place into a fine hotel. She's an unmarried lady and as free-spirited as a skylark. Dresses to suit herself and runs the business like a bulldog."

"I'm eager to meet her," Skye commented.

"Here we are," Laurel announced. "Heritage House. Now you'll see why Shannon's hotel is the most popular in town."

Skye exited the carriage behind her mother and the Caldwells. Her layers of cotton petticoats and full taffeta skirt tangled around her ankles and made graceful descent impossible. To make matters worse, a pocket book, empty and useless, dangled from her wrist, while from the other hung the requisite silk parasol, unopened and unnecessary for the few steps into the shade of the hotel.

"Hurry along, Skye, my darling," urged her mother. "You're going to enjoy this new experience tremendously. Now, isn't this exciting?"

Skye smiled to acknowledge her mother's encouragement. "Yes, ma'am," she said, smoothing her narrow bodice and attempting to force some air into her restricted lungs.

Moving up the broad steps, she said a silent thank-you for the fashion of low-heeled slippers. Laurel's shoes were soft brocade and fit her perfectly. Catching up with the ladies, Skye prepared herself for the ordeal to come.

As concerned as she was about the situation at hand, Skye was awestruck by the expansive and exquisitely decorated interior of the Heritage House. But before Skye could absorb the scene, Shannon Kildaire appeared and greeted the women with unbridled enthusiasm.

"Welcome, welcome!" Shannon effused, embracing Mrs. Caldwell first, then Laurel. "So nice to see you again, Mrs. Mackinnon. Or should I say Lady Mackinnon? Titles do confound me, but I've heard your husband is a lord."

"Please call me Elizabeth," answered Skye's mother. "I feel like we're friends already. And anyway, we're in America now. Titles are not used here, I understand."

"And this must be Skye," Shannon said, turning toward her. "What a lovely name. And a fetching young lady you are, too."

"Thank you," Skye murmured, feeling some of her shyness fade under Shannon's broad smile.

"Skye—for your island—or for the heavens above? Which is it, dear?"

"The island," Skye responded.

Shannon slipped a plump arm under Skye's elbow and waved toward the sweeping grand stairway leading to upper levels. "Lead the way, Laurel. I'll just hold on to your cousin here so I can get a good look at her. Tell me about that fleet-footed pup of yours, Skye. I thought you'd lost the scamp for good last night."

Skye was blushing, to her annoyance. "You saw me?" she asked.

"Quite a sight. Glad you retrieved him or he'd be swimming in the Mississippi today."

"MacLard is full of vinegar, all right," Skye said, comfortable with this topic of conversation. "He's a terrier from a special breed we have on my island. A Skye terrier.

25

MacLard is smaller than most, but every pound explodes with mischief."

Shannon's rouged cheeks dimpled. "I wish you could have met Pepper, *my* first dog. Big as a pony. Once raced through Andy Jackson's headquarters like he owned the place. Andy said he was part wolfhound, so he could've been from Scotland. Maybe Pepper and MacLard were related—way back in history."

Skye laughed and felt herself relaxing. "Maybe—but that would have been long ago, I'm certain. Considering the size and all."

Shannon released her as they arrived at the second-story landing. "On your right, ladies. Down the hall to number nine. Otherwise, you'll sashay right into the grand ball-room."

Laurel turned toward Skye. "We've had some lovely soirées here, Skye. In fact, we'll be coming here for the masked ball three days from now."

"Oh, how nice," was all Skye could manage over this new revelation. As the door to number nine opened, she wondered again how soon she could escape with her mares to the Caldwells' upriver plantation.

A dark woman wearing a polka-dot dress topped by a crisp white apron showed them into a luxurious sitting room. Armchairs were arranged around a circular tea table, set with linen and silver. A pianoforte sat in one corner beside French doors leading to a tree-shaded balcony.

"Please make yourselves at home, madams," said the maid. "Mrs. Wyndford will be right out."

"I do hope the lady is feeling better today," said Rebecca Caldwell.

"Pert near," answered the soft-spoken servant. "Better than yesterday, though not entirely fit."

Skye was intrigued with her first sight of a female member of the race originating in Africa. This woman was beautiful, with skin like creamed coffee and large almond-shaped eyes that reflected quiet sensitivity. She wondered how these people liked it in the United States. She'd heard there were many who were actually slaves. How could people actually own other people? The idea was strange and repellent.

"Good afternoon, ladies." Melissa Wyndford entered the sitting room and reached for Rebecca's hand. "How lovely to see you again, Mrs. Caldwell."

"We won't stand on formality, Mrs. Wyndford. Do call me Rebecca. You remember my daughter, Laurel Anne. Please meet my cousin, Elizabeth Mackinnon, and her daughter, Skye . . . ah, Skye Eugenia, is that correct?"

"Aye. But Skye will do," Skye said. "I'm happy to meet you, Mrs. Wyndford."

Though pale and extremely thin, Melissa Wyndford had sparkling eyes and an animated expression. Her dress was sage-green silk with leg-o'-mutton sleeves, which were over-large for today's more conservative fashion. On the other hand, the ballooning sleeves and full skirts added weight to her emaciated form. Her graying hair was curled neatly about her face and tucked into a white linen cap. "I'm very much pleased to be informal," she said smiling. "My Christian name is Melissa, but my brother-in-law and my friends out west call me Missy. I'm happy with the shortened version."

"Then Missy it will be," agreed Rebecca. "Now that all of us are on a first-name basis, let's settle down to a good visit. Tell me about your journey, Missy. And then we'll hear from Elizabeth about her trip from Scotland."

Skye was content to be left out of the conversation for the moment. She took a seat beside Laurel on a tufted settee and sat with a fixed smile on her lips. At least today she looked the part of a lady. Now all she had to do was nod and smile and listen to the interesting conversation. Surely it *would* be interesting when the gathering was of such divergent backgrounds. She was especially eager to hear about Melissa Wyndford's experiences out West, of what life was like in that far land, and perhaps to glean some information useful to her own future endeavor.

"As I'm sure Kyle has explained, Rebecca, my health is not as right as it should be. No doubt it's some minor ailment that is only being persistent. But he fusses over me like a mother hen and insisted I see a physician in New Orleans."

"He's a wonderful man," said Rebecca as she accepted a

cup of tea. "My husband always sings his praises." She looked up at Shannon, who was standing by the door. "Won't you sit, darling?"

"I would sure like to, but I have a dozen matters to attend to, with the ball coming up so soon. There's some problem with the orchestra, and the woman who specially prepares my pralines has left an urgent message." She lifted her palms upward. "Ah, the trials of running a hotel. Do excuse me, ladies."

"Naturally," responded Missy. "I hope we can visit another time."

"Surely." Shannon hurried out the door.

"Now, as I was saying," Missy continued, "my health is the main reason for a visit to New Orleans, but not the only one. Kyle wanted to talk business with Mr. Caldwell, something about shipping cattle abroad, if that was financially feasible. We do have an abundance of the beasts, I can attest."

Skye was privately delighted when her mother asked, "Oh? You have a great deal of land, then?"

"Indeed. Enough to summer close to ten thousand head. Winters are very harsh in Dakota, but we keep a sizable herd even then. The rest are trailed to eastern markets."

"The grass is abundant?" inquired Elizabeth.

"Oh my goodness, yes. Kyle says much lusher than the southern ranchers even dream about. Why, our cattle don't even have to bend their necks to nip the tops off prime grass. In autumn, we cut the prairie grass and store it as hay in seven large barns. The hardest job is to get that hay to the animals during the winter snows."

Skye was riveted by Missy's words. This was information she urgently needed, information that could mean failure or success for the Mackinnons, now and in the future.

Rebecca asked, "Doesn't that take lots of workers? Do you use slave labor on your ranch?"

Missy hesitated and gazed into her tea cup. "Uh . . . no. We hire only free men." She looked directly at Rebecca. "Though I mean no disparagement to slave owners. Kyle has explained the necessity of that institution."

Skye caught her breath. Necessity? Necessary for human beings to be slaves? As impressed as she was by Melissa Wyndford, she was getting a less favorable view of Kyle Wyndford, the lady's brother-in-law.

Rebecca looked uneasy for the first time today. "We don't have slaves, either, Missy, but my husband wouldn't dare express opposition in public. Too many of our friends do have slaves, and of course, treat them as family members. Slavery is a subject Mr. Caldwell avoids. Like religion and politics, the matter always stirs up feelings."

Missy nodded in agreement. "You know how men are. Prone to prejudices and temperament. I have respect for the Africans, and the Indians, too, but Kyle sees things differently."

At the mention of Indians, Skye squirmed in her seat. Why shouldn't the Indians, the first occupants of the American lands, have everyone's respect? Before she could stop herself, she blurted, "Indians? Does Mr. Wyndford dislike the native people?"

Again Melissa looked uneasy, but she gave Skye a soft smile. "I admire your question, Skye. And I believe I hear a note of real concern in your voice."

Skye felt her cheeks redden. Now she'd put herself in an awkward spot. She felt Laurel's intense look and remembered Laurel's warning about not revealing her Indian background too quickly. "I . . . was just curious," she muttered, annoyed with herself for some indefinable reason.

"Let me explain," Missy went on. "In Dakota, which belongs now to the United States, there are large numbers of native tribes living all around us. We want to dwell in peace with the Indians, but we do have different views over land ownership. We've had this problem ever since my husband and I went west to find a new home for ourselves."

"When was that, Missy?" asked Elizabeth.

"Ten years ago. My husband, Kyle's brother, did what so many second sons of landed English gentry do—came to America to seek his fortune. I was as eager for the adventure as he. As soon as we married, he took his inheritance and we sailed for New Orleans. Made our way up the Mississippi, the Missouri, and then to Dakota. That was a difficult and dangerous time, but we were young and ready to strike out on our own and claim land for our future."

Skye hung on every word. This was her father's dream, and hers as well, now that the wheels were in motion.

"We found good water and astonishing grasslands near a small settlement called Vermillion. We lived in the village the first year while my husband, Blanton, built a house on the Vermillion River not far away. I had my son the second year, then we moved to our new home, and Blanton worked from dawn till dark establishing the herd. And then . . ."

Rebecca reached out to touch Missy's shoulder. "You needn't go on, dear. Don't bring up sad memories."

Missy gave her a brave smile. "No, it's all right. Blanton was heroic, you see. I want everyone to know what he sacrificed for his family. He was killed by angry Lakotas while he watered his horse at a river twenty miles from home. Kyle found his body later that day."

Skye felt her heart sink. Lakotas. Her father's people. They had *murdered* this sweet lady's husband. And here she sat, Lakota blood running through her veins. She flicked a glance at Laurel, who was looking at her, her delicate eyebrow cocked in warning. Now Skye understood what Laurel had meant by *tact*. She could see the wisdom of keeping silent, at least in the present company. She dared to look at her mother and saw by the set expression on her mother's lips that she had reached the same conclusion.

"How tragic," observed Elizabeth. "Are the natives still a threat?"

"They seem peaceful now. They trade regularly at the posts, but now and then, renegades raid a ranch or attack a riverboat."

Skye found it impossible not to question the lady. "Do you know any Lakotas personally, Missy?"

"Oh, no. Kyle wouldn't approve of such a meeting, even if the Indians were willing, which of course, they are not. Much better that way, I'm sure. Also, Kyle took his brother's murder very hard. He used to speak of tracking the killers, but since that was impossible, he locked away his pain and never mentions it anymore. Sometimes I think he carries more harsh feelings than I. He thinks he needs to avenge Blanton's death, but in lieu of that, he tries to avoid any encounters with the savages."

Skye gasped. "Savages?"

"Savages," Elizabeth echoed. "I've often heard that name used in England. I had hoped the Americans didn't consider the natives to be *savages.*"

Missy shook her head. "As you can imagine, I'm a poor choice to come to their defense. On the other hand, I do understand the Indians' concern over the burgeoning white population in their land. It's my hope someday we can learn to share the vast resources without hostility and blood-shed."

Skye prayed Missy was right. Calming herself, she had to admit the lady was being magnanimous, considering that her husband was slaughtered by the Lakotas. But surely that was an isolated incident. And it had happened years ago.

"Did you live alone on your land after your husband's death?" inquired Rebecca.

"Thank heavens, Kyle left the army and came to America. Blanton wanted his brother and me to own the ranch together. I credit Kyle with saving the ranch for the Wynd-ford family. Kyle has worked every bit as hard as Blanton did. He has built the place into a successful cattle operation, given his constant attention to developing the place. He's as smart as they come, my brother-in-law. A shrewd business-man and tough, despite his elegant looks and manner."

Skye bit hard into her sugar cookie. She didn't believe she liked James Kyler Wyndford, and yet she had never laid eyes on the man. Tough, elegant, prejudiced, and greedy. Not a pretty picture of a man's character. Mr. Wyndford must have a low opinion of the natives—and she herself was part Lakota. Perhaps she wouldn't have to meet the man during her stay in New Orleans. She liked Missy, though. Who wouldn't? The lady was courageous and sweet and amazingly open-minded, despite her use of the term *savages.*

Missy said, "But I've rattled on about myself far too long.

I would like to hear about Scotland, and England, too. My home was on the coast near Liverpool. I've thought of visiting there now that my son is nine years old. I would like for the boy to meet his English relatives. But I don't suppose I will . . . anytime soon . . ."

Elizabeth quickly picked up the conversation. "Why, England is booming with industry now. I visit my old home outside of London every year or so."

Skye's mind wandered as her mother began a long dialogue about her lands and her life. She knew the conversation would soon turn to her novels and their extraordinary success. Gazing across the room, she watched a late-afternoon breeze lift the delicate silk curtain. Outside, the birds were filling the air with their song, and from the street beyond the hotel, she heard the clatter of passing carriages and the call of a street vendor. A city was an exciting thing, she thought. But deep inside, she felt a touch of sadness. She wouldn't want to live in a city, despite its many attractions. She missed the wind blowing free and the sight of horizons stretching endlessly till land met sky. She didn't like wearing a corset and worrying about what to say next. And now she must attend yet another social function. Something called a masked ball. *Hurry, Papa,* she silently urged. *Please come soon, so we can go west to build our new home.*

⇥ Chapter 5 ⇥

Kyle was more than satisfied with his lengthy meeting with Blaine Caldwell. The gentleman was as sharp as when they had first planned their strategy of investment years ago. Kyle had been little more than a youth then, and Caldwell had taken him under his wing as if he were a close relative. Kyle hadn't had much cash, and he had been in a hurry to get to Dakota to see his brother. Caldwell had made him a loan, very businesslike, with contracts in writing and all the details of the payback and profit. But the risk had been great, and both of them knew it. Kyle had paid the debt in full the third year of his cattle operation. Now that his profits were huge, he was glad to "invest" in Caldwell's dangerous and secret efforts to sabotage the slave trade.

Kyle hated slavery as much as Caldwell, and he had been blessed with such good luck, he wanted to do his part for those less fortunate. And who were less fortunate than the poor Africans, dragged from their homes, stuffed in cargo ships, then separated from families and sold into slavery. Americans from the early days had dabbled in the slave trade. In Kyle's mind, slavery was a festering sore in his adopted country. He controlled more acres than any planta- tion owner ever dreamed of, and he had work for thirty men at Wind River. But he paid his hands in cash, and slavery would never have entered his mind. Sadly, this new genera- tion of planters accepted the institution without thinking of the consequences. Kyle was convinced there was trouble ahead, serious trouble.

Walking now at Blaine's shoulder, he inhaled the pungent aromas of the waterfront. Nothing compared with the heady, fragrant atmosphere of New Orleans: dampness from the river, earthiness from the swamps, fresh fish at the wharf intermingled with the smell of spices and chicory coffee drifting from the huge open market near the docks. The effect made him restless, as if he needed something physical, something deep and basic, a woman perhaps, or a rich meal prepared the French way, or maybe an all-night session with a hot deck of cards.

"We'll meet Sinclair in the upstairs room at Gerod's." Caldwell rested one hand on Kyle's shoulder. "Cheyne's barge docked two days ago, but he keeps a low profile for obvious reasons. Jean Lafitte and his band of privateers are not forgotten here. Now that Sinclair is using his fortune to stop slavers on the high seas, he'd be hung in a flash if caught in New Orleans. But we need to rendezvous every now and then. I'm pleased you can be with us tonight."

"I'm looking forward to meeting a man with the courage

of the Falcon. I've heard he makes his home on the Barbary Coast."

"Tangier, yes. The last bastion of the pirates. Cheyne claims no country for his own. You might say he is a country unto himself. The interesting thing is, he can *afford* to be the king of his own domain."

After a short walk though the gathering dusk, Kyle and Blaine arrived at Gerod's. The two-story frame structure was dilapidated and paint peeled from its siding; its small windows facing the street were dark.

"You sure the place is open?" Kyle asked.

"Yes indeed. Plenty of customers inside, despite the look of desertion. We'll go up the outside stairway. I find the place ideal for furtive assignations."

"No doubt," muttered Kyle as he followed his host up the creaky wooden stairs. The contrast between this site and Blaine Caldwell's usual habitat was remarkable. But a man whose compassion for human suffering could endanger the South's basic economy needed extreme secrecy.

Once inside, Blaine lit a dusty lantern and opened the door to the interior hallway. He spoke to someone, then quietly closed the door. "I've ordered a round of the specialty of the house—a famous concoction with a recipe as secret as this meeting. Gerod's bartender inherited the recipe from old Peychaud, who invented it. A combination of cognac and brandy and bitters, measured from a *ko-k-tay,* an egg cup. The drink is called coctay, or cocktail by the Americans. Something new—and it carries a punch, I can attest."

"Sounds delightful."

"Take a seat, Kyle, and tell me about your current cattle crop while we await Sinclair."

Kyle lowered into a flimsy armchair whose springs creaked with his weight. He didn't mind revealing the success of his enterprise to Blaine Caldwell, the man who had believed in him from the beginning, even if it sounded a bit like bragging. "I control half a million acres, give or take a few."

Blaine whistled. "Good God, Wyndford. I had no idea."

"That's open range, of course. I run twenty thousand head on summer range, then trail the four-year-olds to Omaha or sometimes St. Louis, depending on the price of prime beef. On three occasions, I drove the herd all the way to Chicago. Quadrupled my investment on those drives."

"Hell, no wonder your pockets are full."

"It's a booming business. Have you any interest in obtaining stock?"

"Sorry; can't say I have. This is cotton country, Kyle, not cattle country."

At the tap on the door, Blaine called, "Come in." A waiter wearing a dingy apron entered, balancing a tray with three large pewter goblets. "Ah, here we are," Blaine said, tossing a coin to the servant. "A drink fit for Bacchus himself."

Kyle sipped the liquid. He felt the sweet fire all the way into his chest. "Damned fine," he agreed.

"Now, tell me, Kyle, why a handsome devil like you has reached . . . what is it? About thirty? And never taken a wife?"

Kyle chuckled. Caldwell was as nosy as a woman, he thought wryly. "No time. And no appealing women available—since your lovely daughter won't have me. I do have a ladyfriend, though. Lives upriver in Pierre. Scarlet hair, skin like ripe peaches, and amply endowed. Not the type to be the mother of one's children, though."

"I see. But your sister-in-law must have some nice female acquaintances."

"She sees a few women at the church meetings she attends on occasion. Married ladies, every one. Why would an attractive single woman go west, Blaine? No reason, I can think of."

"To find a husband like you is *one* good reason."

Kyle smiled and took another drink, then said, "I'd likely be a rotten husband. A good father, maybe. I'm devoted to Melissa's son. His name is Montgomery, but he's been called Badger since he could crawl. The lad's just turned nine and full of the devil. It takes Missy and I both to keep him out of scrapes. We see him off to the Vermillion school every morning, but we never know if he'll end up there or on some wild adventure instead. Yes, I'd like to have a son of my own." He contemplated his cocktail. "But there's plenty of time for that."

The exterior door swung open and a dark figure pushed inside without benefit of invitation. He ducked beneath the door frame, but the top of his wide-brimmed hat still brushed it. His ankle-length black silk cape enveloped his frame but didn't conceal his large hands, graced with flashing rings of impressive proportion. He tossed back one edge of the cape and held out a hand to Blaine. *"Mon ami,"* he boomed. "Blaine, my old friend, it's wonderful to see you again."

Blaine was instantly on his feet and embraced the newcomer. "Sinclair, you old pirate. I'm delighted, as always."

Sinclair moved to one side and fingered the pistol jammed into his wide belt. A diamond on his finger glittered in the lamplight. "I see you've brought a friend," he said none too happily.

Kyle rose at once and offered a hand in greeting. "Kyler Wyndford, at your service, *monsieur*. I'm a great admirer of yours, Mr. Sinclair."

"Pull up a chair, Cheyne," said Blaine. "Your favorite drink is waiting. You'll enjoy getting acquainted with my good friend, and I assure you he's completely trustworthy. Mr. Wyndford owns an empire in the West and has been putting money into your coffers these past two years. With greatest secrecy, of course."

Sinclair swept off his cloak and laid it over a vacant chair. His demeanor softened as he shook Kyle's hand. "My thanks, then, sir. I welcome any comrade who will join in my fight against the slave trade."

The three men took chairs and hoisted their goblets.

"A toast," offered Blaine. "To the end of slavery."

Kyle downed another large swallow and enjoyed the immediate warming effect. "Here, here," he said. "To the end of slavery and freedom for all Americans."

Cheyne Sinclair turned to Blaine. "Before we discuss business, let me inquire as to your health, sir. You're looking fit as ever."

"A few aches now and then. But can't complain."

"And your wife—and your daughter?"

Kyle thought he caught a special tone at the word *daughter*. He listened closely.

"Rebecca is in glowing health. Laurel, too, and prettier every day. Wish you could meet them personally, and they could meet you."

"Impossible, as you know," Cheyne said. "I must observe them from a distance, and only rarely."

Blaine sat forward in his chair. "I say, that gives me an idea. How long will you be in New Orleans, Cheyne?"

"Goods I ordered from St. Louis have been delayed en route. I must bide my time until it arrives. A week at least."

"Splendid. The spring ball will be held in a few days at Shannon's hotel. A small but very exclusive group in attendance. You must join the party."

"But I couldn't think of—"

"Ah, but it's a *masked* ball, you see. You could take a false name and hide your identity. How long has it been since you've danced in New Orleans?"

Sinclair laughed heartily, his shoulder-length dark hair moving along his collar. "As a boy, I used to attend soirées with Lafitte. Never did any dancing, but I enjoyed the music and swaying skirts and the sight of all that elegance."

"Then you must plan on it. Say you will."

Sinclair chuckled again and nodded. "Why not? But only to see once again the flower of New Orleans society—your fine family, Caldwell."

Kyle would bet his last nickel that this dashing gentleman was wanting to see *Laurel* Caldwell most of all. What surprised him most about the infamous Falcon was the man's youth. Despite sun-browned skin and a few crinkles at the corners of his eyes, Cheyne Sinclair looked no older than thirty or so. Kyle felt a kindred spirit in this man who had carved out a life of adventure and had wealth even greater than his own. But at the mention of Caldwell's family, Kyle had also detected a note of regret. Did the privateer miss respectability? Family? A home in the United States? All in all, a fascinating man.

Abruptly, Blaine turned to Kyle. "And you, as well, sir. You'll attend the ball—and escort our cousin, young Miss Mackinnon."

Kyle was stunned. "What? Oh no, I couldn't—"

"But you must. The ball is the social event of the season following Lent. Laurel is being escorted by one of the Beauregard boys, and she has already invited Miss Mackinnon."

Kyle had an immediate vision of a long-legged chit racing across the lawn after her dog. And *he* was to escort this child to a ball? Unthinkable. "No, I'm sure she wouldn't—"

"Of course she would, Kyle. I realize you're used to more sophisticated types, especially if they're redheads," he added pointedly. "But do me this one favor and I'll be most grateful."

Kyle was trapped. "She's . . . very young," was all he could think to say.

"Nineteen, according to her mother. Not all that young."

Nineteen, mused Kyle. Judging from his fleeting glimpses, he'd guessed closer to twelve. Just his type, a gangling farm girl. But he saw no way out of it. He nodded toward Caldwell. "Naturally, I'd be happy to act as escort to the young lady. May I ask a favor in return?"

"By all means."

"If my sister-in-law is able, perhaps she could be included. I believe the outing would do her good."

"Absolutely. We'll attend to her every comfort. We're all expected for a private party and buffet supper prior to the dancing. The party will be hosted by Shannon in her exclusive suite on the third floor of Heritage House. Then we'll go en masse downstairs to the grand ballroom."

"I'm not sure I should attend the buffet," interjected Sinclair. "Too intimate, too much chance for discovery. Someone might recognize me."

"We'll be wearing masks. But naturally it's your decision," said Blaine. "I hope you can stop by, even for a short time. Shannon's chef is suberb and she promises the best band in town. Now, we'll order more cocktails and get down to serious business. I'm eager to hear about the daring exploits of the Falcon."

⇥ Chapter 6 ⇤

You look lovely, darling. I am so proud of you tonight."

"Thank you, Mother," Skye said affectionately. "So do you. I only wish Papa were here to see us."

Skye smiled at her mother as they strolled into Shannon Kildaire's private drawing room at Heritage House. Gaslights and candelabras illuminated the room. Along one wall, a table laden with silver and crystal displayed a feast that would be the envy of royalty.

Immediately, Shannon Kildaire rushed to greet the arriving Caldwell party. The ladies rustled in their taffeta gowns as they exchanged hugs and excited laughter. Blaine Caldwell, in formal black trousers and frock coat, bowed over his hostess's hand as if she were a titled noble lady. Everyone was wearing a demi-mask, pretending the delightful subterfuge was concealing the identity of close friends and family.

Skye conceded privately that this could all be a great deal of fun, but her nervousness over her approaching rendezvous with the opinionated Mr. Wyndford spoiled her mood. That and the fact that her lungs were crushed by the steellined corset beneath her stylish gown.

As her mother walked away beside Rebecca Caldwell, Skye's eyes drifted around the gathering. Mrs. Melissa Wyndford was occupying a seat of honor beside a coffee table. Beside her stood two tall men whom Skye couldn't identify, even if they had not been wearing black satin masks.

"Have some punch," Laurel offered, handing her a cup and giving her a smile of encouragement.

"Thank you. Now where can I hide?" Skye muttered.

"You mustn't be shy, cousin. Not when you look so

beautiful. Oh, there's Henry Beauregard at the door. I'll have to greet him. Wait here and I'll introduce you. The Beauregards are one of New Orleans' most prominent Creole families."

Skye watched the ebullient Laurel gather her skirts and approach an elegant gentleman in an immaculately tailored gray suit who had just handed his top hat to a serving man. Watching Laurel and Henry Beauregard, she wondered why Laurel was resistant to the fellow. He was quite handsome, obviously cultured and well-to-do, and extremely attentive. But Laurel had said emphatically that Mr. Beauregard would never win her hand.

Skye was uncomfortable standing alone in the middle of the room, and she moved to take up a less obtrusive spot beside an open door leading to a balcony. Removing her mask, she allowed the soft evening breeze to cool her feverish forehead, while offering the illusion of freedom.

This past week had been much nicer than she had expected, so she chastised herself for feeling so annoyed tonight. She had been free to spend mornings at the stable, and had made good use of the small riding arena, exercising her mares and grooming them until they were shining. In the afternoons, Laurel had taken her on endless excursions of sightseeing, shopping, and dining. After a brief rest, they were off again in the evenings, usually with the entire family, to an elegant restaurant or to a musicale or the theater. Skye couldn't deny she had been dazzled by New Orleans, and she appreciated all Laurel was doing to entertain her. Somehow she must muddle through this evening; then tomorrow she would begin preparations for moving to the upriver plantation.

She took a long drink from her cup and turned her attention to the two gentlemen in black. No doubt one of those gents was Melissa's brother-in-law, the man assigned to be her escort for this occasion. Neither one matched the mental image she had of the western cattle baron. Both were perfectly groomed, attired in the current fashion, and apparently enjoying their conversation with each other. With luck, they would stay engrossed for a good while.

Laurel had explained to her what to expect from her

escort. Mr. Wyndford was obligated to stay by her side for a time, bring her refreshments, and dance both the first and final dance with her. Also, in case of an emergency, he was to see to her welfare and safety. She wondered if being a crashing bore might be deemed an emergency. If things became unendurable, she could always plead a headache and return to Dominique Hall. But that might upset everyone, and she would hate to draw attention to herself.

Her breath caught when she saw Shannon Kildaire nod in her direction, then take hold of the arm of one of the gentlemen. So *that* was James Kyler Wyndford. The time had come when she would meet her companion for the soirée. Her early impression of him, thanks to Melissa's remarks, was that he was arrogant and narrow-minded. She would like to set him straight regarding his prejudice toward the Indians, but she wouldn't risk embarrassing the Caldwells. No, she would have to make the best of whatever the evening would hold.

She pretended not to watch Shannon's approach. Angry that her nerves were getting the better of her, she pursed her lips and stared at a point near the ceiling.

"Skye, dear, allow me to introduce Mr. Kyler Wyndford, our friend from Dakota. He has graciously offered to act as your escort this evening. As you can see, you are a very lucky lady. Mr. Wyndford, this is Miss Skye Eugenia Mackinnon."

Skye would gladly have dropped through the floor. Shannon's eyes were twinkling and her pointed remark much too assuming. Skye wondered how she could possibly feel lucky when she'd only just met Mr. Wyndford this instant. She didn't feel lucky; she felt embarrassed and dreadfully out of place.

Reluctantly, she shifted her eyes from Shannon to gaze up at Mr. Wyndford. His lips were set and expressionless beneath his mask. Since she couldn't see his eyes, she had no clue to his thoughts. He might have been attractive with his square jaw and dark brown sideburns, and the broad shoulders evident under his chocolate-colored coat. But she had no interest in his looks. What was more amazing, she had to assume from his prolonged silence and dour scrutiny that he disliked her as much as she disliked him. They had only one thing in common: they were forced against their will to spend this evening together, or at least a portion of it.

Kyle Wyndford inclined his head without changing his expression. "My pleasure, Miss Mackinnon," he said stiffly. "Perhaps I could refill your cup."

"Aye, thank you," she murmured, handing it to him.

Simultaneously, Mr. Wyndford and Shannon turned away and moved to the refreshment table, leaving Skye alone once more.

Grateful for the respite, which was bound to be brief, Skye smoothed her bodice and tried to force air into her lungs. The man disdained her, she was certain. And why not? He was worldly, successful, the creator of an immense empire in the West, and connected to a noble family in England. And what was she? The daughter of a Scottish laird who was practically penniless and had now abandoned lands and title. Instantly, she regretted her disparagement of the father she adored. Fletcher Mackinnon was ten times the man Kyler Wyndford would ever be. And someday, the Mackinnon ranch would equal that of the officious Mr. Wyndford. The Wyndfords had gotten there first, that was all. But the Mackinnons were on their way, and would someday surpass the Wyndfords. After all, she and her father had one major advantage: by blood, they belonged in Dakota. Fate had brought Fletcher Mackinnon back to his home, the place where he had grown up as the renegade warrior, White Arrow. Let Kyler Wyndford top *that,* Skye thought with satisfaction.

After one close look at the exquisite Skye Mackinnon, Kyle was as shaken as he'd ever been in his life. Her cool beauty had taken him completely by surprise. Trailing Miss Kildaire toward the punch bowl, he tried to collect himself.

He had approached the soirée tonight with reluctance. The only good thing he could see coming of it was a pleasant outing for Missy. Until he had encountered Miss Mackinnon, the highlight of the evening had been his visit with Cheyne Sinclair.

"My name is *Hammond Brown,*" Cheyne had said pointedly.

"Of course, Mr. *Brown,* I'd almost forgotten—my apologies," Kyle had replied with a knowing smile. "New in town, are you?"

"You could say that," quipped Sinclair. "I'm a business acquaintance of Mr. Caldwell's. I'm engaged in maritime enterprises," he added with a grin.

For the next several minutes, Kyle had thoroughly enjoyed his private conversation with "Hammond Brown." Then Shannon Kildaire abruptly took his arm.

"Pardon me, Mr. Wyndford, but I must introduce you to Miss Mackinnon. I fear she's been ignored much too long."

Kyle had excused himself and prepared to meet his companion for the evening, the peculiar waif from Scotland.

With Shannon's hand hooked through the crook of his elbow, he had moved across the room where a slender young woman wearing a frothy mist-green cotton dress stood alone beside the balcony door. She seemed ethereal as he approached, with the breeze ruffling the lace trim along her low-cut bodice and slightly lifting the raven curls beside her small ears, set with tiny emerald earbobs. She was not looking at him but gazing toward the ceiling. Surely this vision of feminine loveliness was not the scampering girl he'd seen at Caldwell's party. Impossible.

Indeed, she was one and the same. Miss Skye Eugenia Mackinnon was pure delight. He had been thunderstruck as he watched this enchanting creature slowly move her amazing green eyes along the level of his cravat, across his lips, and upward to his mask. Feeling like an idiot wearing a mask when she wore none, he absorbed her careful appraisal and returned it. Her full lips were haughty, condescending, challenging. Her eyes were guarded and inquisitive. He'd seen such a look before in a year-old thoroughbred filly he was about to halter. And he knew a thoroughbred when he encountered one. Yes, he had entirely underestimated young Miss Mackinnon. But he had the evening to correct his mistake.

At the punch bowl, he balanced the two cups while Miss Kildaire filled them.

"A fetching lass, eh, Mr. Wyndford?" whispered Shannon. "I knew she had possibilities."

"I am surprised, Miss Kildaire. You may recall I saw her galloping across the Caldwells' lawn like a headstrong yearling."

"From what her mother tells me, she is *mighty* headstrong. Independent and self-sufficient. Has worked beside her father on the Isle of Skye and is expert at farming and horse breeding."

"She appears as delicate as a daisy tonight. But—yes, she has a certain look in her eyes. Green eyes. Amazing green eyes."

Shannon lifted her eyebrows at his tone. "I can see your interest is piqued, sir. Here are your drinks. Go attend the lady and we'll see what develops."

Kyle was only too happy to comply. He quickly rejoined Miss Mackinnon.

"Thank you," she murmured, accepting her cup and raising it to her lips.

He studied the smooth skin of her arm above the edge of her white kid glove. He noticed the long lashes brushing her cheeks as she closed her eyes while sipping from her cup. Her coloring was unique. He'd never seen any woman with such rich skin tones. Most ladies of his acquaintance valued the look of alabaster whiteness, protecting their delicacy from the sun and dabbing rice powder on their faces to create a fragile appearance. Some of the women out west were dark, but he knew they had sacrificed their looks to work beside their husbands in the harsh sun. Either that, or they had Indian or Mexican blood. Like the wives of some of his hired hands. But Skye Mackinnon was the daughter of a Scottish laird and a gently born English lady. Where had she come by such exquisite coloring? A gift, perhaps, from some distant ancestor.

They both spoke at once.

"Miss Mackinnon, I was—"

"Mr. Wyndford, did you—"

An awkward silence fell like a stone between them.

Kyle cleared his throat and wondered why he felt like a lad of thirteen speaking to his school-boy idol. Hell, he was eleven years older than Miss Mackinnon and had seen the world. He'd soldiered for the king and carved out an empire. He'd dallied with ladies at the royal court and tumbled his share of doves in the American West. But for some reason, this girl's combination of fire and innocence captured his fancy like no woman had before.

"I understand you and my sister-in-law are becoming fast friends," he managed at last. A perfect opening. He should have thought of it sooner. He saw the girl relax a bit and the suggestion of a smile grace those adorable lips.

"Aye. Mrs. Wyndford and I have had several nice visits. I hope there will be more."

Thank God, she *smiled.* Kyle figured he had made a good beginning. "You have a charming lilt to your speech, if I may say so, Miss Mackinnon. But not as Scottish as I expected for one raised in that land."

"My mother is English," she responded somewhat curtly.

Damn, he'd said the wrong thing. He saw the cool veil return to her eyes. "Of course. I find your mother delightful. I must read one of her books someday."

"You wouldn't care for them," she said icily. "They're very romantic."

"Then you think romance is only for females?" he ventured.

"How can I say," she responded airily, "since I am not a man?"

"I wouldn't argue that fact."

She glared at him as if he had insulted her. This conversation had definitely taken a wrong turn.

Laurel arrived with a gentleman at her side. "Skye, I would like you to meet Henry Beauregard, an old and dear family friend."

"You make me sound as if I've one foot in the grave, Laurel," Beauregard said, while lifting Skye's free hand to his lips. "Where have you been hiding this astonishing cousin of yours?"

"She has just arrived from Scotland, Henry. Also, meet Mr. Kyle Wyndford, who is visiting from his home in Dakota."

Kyle was strangely annoyed at the interruption of his conversation with Skye Mackinnon. He was further annoyed to see Skye gift Mr. Beauregard with a winsome smile. Maybe this Southern dandy was the type she preferred. If so, he figured he was wasting his time trying to impress her. He took a drink of the insipid punch and listened to Beauregard ramble on in that thick accent typical of the local planters. *So coated with honey it must stick in their throats,* he thought, then realized he hadn't minded the drawl until just now, when Beauregard arrived on the scene.

Since Kyle found himself totally ignored, he used the time to study Miss Mackinnon. She was animated now as she conversed with Laurel Caldwell and Mr. Beauregard. He could see she had a lively personality and plenty of intelligence beneath that youthful and most attractive veneer of delicate femininity. It was also plain she had no intention of sharing any of her charms with *him.* What had he done to cause such immediate hostility? All he had done was say good evening and bring her a glass of punch.

"We must fill our plates now," Laurel suggested pleasantly. "Shall we find seating together?"

"By all means," simpered Beauregard. "Miss Kildaire has outdone herself with the feast. We can enjoy her repast and get better acquainted before the dance."

Kyle had not the slightest interest in getting better acquainted with Henry Beauregard. Feeling like an unwanted intruder, he extended his elbow toward Miss Mackinnon so she had no choice but to grasp it. "Allow me," he said, and was disgruntled at his grumpy tone.

The girl barely glanced at him as she took his arm and walked beside him to the table. As soon as possible, she withdrew her hand and replaced her mask. He moved behind her while she made her selection from the table, then he put a few items on his own plate. Where the hell was Sinclair? He might enjoy himself more if he were in male company.

He spotted Cheyne Sinclaire occupied across the room, deep in conversation with Blaine Caldwell. As he looked at the two, Sinclair glanced up and caught his eye. Immediately, Kyle excused himself and joined the men.

"I'm going to the bar downstairs," Sinclair said under his breath. "A man could die of thirst trying to drink that pink stuff in the punch bowl."

"I envy you your freedom of choice," answered Kyle. "As you can see, I'm required to accompany the lady, see to her needs. Not that she needs a damn thing except to be rid of me."

"What's this? Rejection already?"

Kyle smiled crookedly. "Rejection would be a step *up* from where I am. *Invisible* is more like it."

"We're two of a kind then," Sinclair noted with a glance at Laurel Caldwell seated beside Henry Beauregard.

"You have an eye for Miss Caldwell?" asked Kyle.

"An eye, yes. For years. But I must worship from afar. I've seen her grow from a gangly toddler into a woman of rare beauty and substance. And believe me, I've known some interesting women in my time."

"No doubt. Does she know how you feel?"

"Bloody saints, no. Do you think a rascal, a pirate, a blackguard like me would reach for such a jewel?"

"You've stolen jewels before, I'll warrant." Kyle saw a glint of humor behind Sinclair's mask.

"That I have. But only to use them for my greedy pleasures." Cheyne looked again toward Laurel. "Nay, I'll not think of dragging that exquisite creature into my evil nest. A dance later tonight, that's all. To hold her once, to receive her smile, for Hammond Brown, but never for Cheyne Sinclair."

"She has no idea of your true identity?"

"None. She was no more than five when I left New Orleans to learn my trade from the master, Lafitte. I've seen her occasionally these past twenty years, but she's never recognized me."

"Unrequited love. And someone has just implied to me that men are not romantic."

"We're fools," growled Sinclair. "Every damn one of us."

"I agree with that," said Kyle. "If you'll excuse me, I must take up my post in that empty chair beside Miss Mackinnon. Watch closely and you'll see her turn her back to me as soon as I'm seated. She appears fascinated with Beauregard."

"Then I'm off to the bar. But I will return to the dance— briefly. I'll be sufficiently fortified with good brandy before I take Miss Caldwell in my arms, then graciously let her go, once and for all. The lady is ripe to marry. I'm certain she'll make her choice before my next visit to New Orleans."

Kyle had never experienced female rejection. With his looks, money and connections, he had taken his pick of the ladies and enjoyed the dalliances. Maybe his pride was hurt, he told himself. Whatever the reason, he felt a stab of pain when he sat beside Miss Mackinnon and she immediately turned away and engaged Beauregard in close conversation. Just as he'd predicted. But it annoyed the hell out of him.

⊰ Chapter 7 ⊱

Skye did not want to feel what she was feeling. Not at this point in her life, not about any man, and certainly not about Mr. James Kyler Wyndford. When exactly had it happened? That peculiar fluttering under her ribs, that sudden pleasurable desire, that awakening curiosity that made her follow him with her eyes when he wasn't looking.

She decided it was when he made that remark about men and romance. It was not so much the words, but the way he shaped them with his lips, the low-toned suggestion of challenge, the residue of his English accent, and perhaps most of all, the way he had focused on her as if she were the only thing that mattered in the world. He had accomplished all that while wearing a mask over his eyes.

Laurel's arrival with Mr. Beauregard had helped immensely to distract her from her sudden fascination with the gentleman. For the next half hour, Skye had managed to visit with her cousin and Laurel's talkative escort and eat two platefuls of delicious, though unidentifiable, offerings from the table.

But now that the party had moved into the spacious ballroom and the orchestra was tuning its instruments, she could no longer avoid looking at—and even being held by—the disturbing Mr. Wyndford.

"The first dance is a waltz, Miss Mackinnon. May I have the honor?"

She wanted to say, *Naturally you must do your duty, after all—and I must politely respond, despite my extreme hesitancy.* Instead she murmured, "Of course, sir. I'm delighted."

He led her onto the dance floor where other couples were beginning to revolve. She was grateful now for her own mask. Otherwise, her eyes might give away her rush of feeling when he slipped one hand to press her waist. Her nerves were on edge, and she knew her lack of skill with dancing was not the only culprit. He did have the devil's own charm, and his commanding figure and lithe grace set her pulses racing. She wore low-heeled slippers; her eyes were staring directly at the ruby stickpin piercing his cravat. Fixing on its brilliance, she set her lips and concentrated on the one-two-three of the swaying rhythm.

Her right hand was locked into his left, her right arm extended and stiff as if carved in marble. Her left hand, encased in its white glove, sat on his shoulder, gripping it to help her keep her balance and indicate the direction she was supposed to go. The dances on Skye had been relaxed, informal, and often lively, accompanied by fiddles, bagpipes, and drums. But the soaring strains of the dozen stringed instruments, flutes, and harpsichord provided by Miss Kildaire for the ball filled the room, enveloped the dancers, and made Skye as tense as if she were performing a solo on a London stage. At least she didn't have to look into her partner's face or struggle for conversation.

She was trying so hard not to make a mistake that she

clipped his boot with her toe and stumbled. She felt her face flame in embarrassment as his arm tightened around her, holding her against his length for a heartbeat, then relaxing again so her feet could follow in time to the music. Gnawing her lip, she tried desperately to flow smoothly in response to his strong lead. But she couldn't flow; she didn't know how, and this was one lesson Laurel had neglected. Humiliation washed over her and she prayed for deliverance from this agony.

"Would you care for a breath of air, Miss Mackinnon? And perhaps a drink of something other than pink fluff?" Still holding her firmly, Mr. Wyndford revolved them toward a row of French doors, open to the night. "Wine is being served, or maybe you would prefer sherry?"

She thought a large mug of Scottish ale would be just perfect, but anything would do, not just to moisten her dry throat, but to rescue her from Mr. Wyndford's arms.

Her breathing rapid, she halted by the door and stepped away from him. But then she made the mistake of looking directly into his face. One edge of his lip was crooked upward, a touch of moisture had appeared along his temples, and an errant lock of dark hair had fallen across the top of his mask. He could be taunting her with that look, or merely laughing silently at her ineptness on the dance floor. But somehow she knew he wasn't doing either of those things. He was feeling sorry for her. Absolutely. He sensed her mortification and sympathized with her. He knew how she felt and he had ended the dance and saved her from further discomfort. Unfortunately, the awareness of his pity made her more miserable than ever. She shouldn't have come, she raged at herself. She never should have gotten into such a predicament.

"What will it be, lass. Wine or sherry?"

Lass. He had said *lass*—just like her father. She heard her father's gentle voice across distance and time, comforting her over some minor injury. This man had no right to speak in a fatherly fashion to her. "Wine, please!" she snapped, and swirled away to walk onto the veranda beyond the doors.

* * *

Miss Mackinnon just needed to relax, Kyle decided as he filled two wine goblets. The wine would help, and he would try to find some topic of conversation of mutual interest. He was out of practice making small talk with ladies, but surely it wouldn't take him long to retrieve his old skill.

He found her on the shadowy porch, gazing below at the interior courtyard of the hotel. She looked even more enchanting in the soft glow spilling from the doorway. The fragrance of lilacs and gardenias drifted upward from the gardens. Behind them, the orchestra began another gentle melody.

"Your wine, Miss Mackinnon."

"Thank you," she responded, accepting the goblet without looking into his eyes.

He pulled off his mask and laid it on the railing. "Damnable things," he said. "The French do like their fanciful games."

She glanced up at him, then lowered her eyes. "I believe we're not to unmask till later. Those were my instructions."

"My guess is a lively girl like you doesn't always follow instructions. Am I right?"

She took a swallow of wine before she responded. "Not always. But I'm a guest of the Caldwells' and I try to do what's proper."

"Of course." He cleared his throat. "Tell me, Miss Mackinnon, what are your impressions of New Orleans so far? Do you like America?"

Her gaze moved back to his face. For the first time, her eyes held his. "I do like America. And New Orleans is an amazing city. So different from London. But you see, I'm quite eager to travel west, to find our new home before winter."

"Very wise. I understand you await the arrival of your father."

"Aye. He'll be here soon with a stallion from the Barbary Coast."

"Is that so? A stallion. Does he disparage the stallions of America?"

Her eyebrow cocked. A shaft of light highlighted the tip of her nose, which supported the lacy edge of her demi-mask.

He had hoped she would remove the thing so he could once more enjoy those compelling green eyes.

"We've little knowledge of American horses," she said with an authoritative tone. "But we have excellent mares from Skye that must be bred to quality animals. We're looking for size and speed to add to the stamina and heart of our Indian . . ." She paused.

"Go on, please. Fascinating." At last she was showing enthusiasm for visiting with him. They were on common ground with the subject of horse breeding. "I have strong interest in animal breeding myself."

"Do you? You have a breeding program on your ranch?"

"It's just getting underway. I'm trying to line-breed my thoroughbreds."

"Thoroughbreds. Aye, I'm familiar with them, but also with their limitations."

Kyle was dumbstruck. This little chit of a girl deigned to instruct him regarding the limitations of thoroughbreds? When everyone knew a thoroughbred was the finest horse-flesh in the world? "Pardon, miss, but I must dispute the use of the term *limitation*. Surely you aren't suggesting the great English thoroughbred has some fault."

She cocked her chin. "As I said, Mr. Wyndford, I'm rather unfamiliar with the breed. All I'm saying is that for certain purposes, my horses from Skye are superior to any in existence. We hope to enhance their qualities by out-breeding to the famous barbs."

Damned, she was something. Never had he seen such stanchness in a lady, a mere child really, and regarding a subject on which he was a proven expert. "Your horses must be very special. I've heard of the ponies from the Scottish isles—the Shetlands, for example. Actually small draft animals, I understand. Is this what you're breeding?"

Her mouth dropped and she stared at him as if he had taken leave of his senses. "Draft horses? You're jesting, of course. Oh, I know the type of ponies you refer to, but I hardly consider them equal to a riding mount."

"My apologies," he hastened. He'd almost forgotten his newfound purpose—to win the lady's trust and admiration.

"I can see we have much to talk about—a great deal in common with our interest in horseflesh."

Her eyes roved toward the garden below. "Perhaps. Actually, I have greater interest in your ranch out west. You see, my family will soon be going to that area; I believe you call it Dakota."

Excellent, he thought. Another subject to bind their interests. "Wind River is the center of my life. Has been, ever since I came from England, then stayed to help my brother's widow."

She looked back at him. "Then I'm sure you understand my deep interest in your project, your apparent success. I would like to know more about—"

"So here you two are!" interrupted a feminine voice. Laurel rushed onto the veranda, trailed by Mr. Beauregard. "Skye, your mother has need of you. A hanky is all, but you have disappeared with hers, she complains. She's seated across the room with Melissa Wyndford."

Laurel drew Skye into the ballroom, accompanied by Henry Beauregard, who was sipping a toddy.

Kyle bowed them away, then stood in the door frame, watching them maneuver through the guests toward the seating area. He had difficulty taking his eyes from Skye. His first impression had been correct. She was as feisty as an unbroken filly. Skittish, fiery, and full of youthful confidence. He must give her plenty of rope, then gradually lead her to his way of thinking. About breeding horses, about a woman's place in relation to a man, generally speaking, and more specifically, about his own favorable qualities. At this point, he wasn't sure where all this might lead, but he was pretty certain he could make the right impression on the young lady, if he set his mind to it.

"Mon ami."

He pivoted to see Cheyne Sinclair climbing the exterior steps from the garden.

"I thought I heard your voice, Wyndford," Cheyne said, joining him.

"So you've come back to claim your dance with Laurel Caldwell."

"I have. And I can recommend the bar next door to

Heritage House. Serves as fine a whiskey as any I've sampled. Is Miss Caldwell about?"

"She just left here in the company of Miss Mackinnon and Mr. Beauregard."

"Beauregard," said Sinclair with a snort. "A worthless dandy, if I ever saw one."

Kyle chuckled. "Most gents are, compared to you, sir. If I were you, I would dare to capture the lady's fancy. You *could* I'll warrant, with minimum effort."

"Nay, I'm born to roam, a rogue sea lion, if ever there was one. Only in a weak moment or two am I tempted by such a paragon of a woman. Even if I succeeded with the lady, I would regret it in a fortnight."

"Then take your turn around the dance floor with her. Looks like Beauregard is stationed at the brandy table."

He watched with interest as the mildly intoxicated Sinclair squared his shoulders, adjusted his mask, and marched toward where Miss Caldwell stood with the other ladies. The man had enormous presence and was turning heads as he walked. If he had hoped for anonymity, he was defeated before he began.

Sinclair bowed before Laurel Caldwell. Kyle smiled at the startled look on her face that even her mask couldn't conceal. She accepted Sinclair's hand and accompanied him to the dance floor, where a reel was about to begin. Moving gracefully among the couples, the young woman appeared astonished that this stranger had appeared from out of nowhere to capture her for the dance. It was a lengthy execution. Each couple moved through the intricate maneuvers, changing partners, exchanging sidelong glances, gliding, then returning to the original squire. Kyle was impressed that Cheyne Sinclair was expert in the movements. If Sinclair was inebriated, he gave no sign of it.

When the dance ended, Cheyne escorted Miss Caldwell back to the ladies and headed toward Kyle's secluded spot.

"Done," said Sinclair.

"Magnificently," noted Kyle.

"Now I must leave. Miss Caldwell may be curious about Hammond Brown, but her curiosity will go unanswered. Forever."

"A cruel thing to do to a lovely lady," Kyle said.

"If she suffers, her pain will be infinitely less than my own. Farewell, Mr. Wyndford. And my deepest thanks for your assistance in our mutual endeavor."

"Are you sailing, then?"

"Along the southern coast for now. Galveston Bay, then back here to restock before returning to my home. I'll make a sweep of the Atlantic as I go. Lay in wait like a vulture off the African mainland. With luck, I'll sink a slaver or two and return the Africans to their own shore."

"Best of luck, Mr. Sinclair. Oh, and the secret of your identity is safe with me. No matter what efforts Miss Caldwell employs to learn the truth."

"She won't pressure you, I'm sure. I'm forgotten already. *Au revoir,* my friend. Until we meet again."

Kyle watched the man disappear down the steps, then turned back to observe Laurel Caldwell. The lady was staring in his direction, ignoring the dialogue going on around her. He was sure Sinclair had completely underestimated his impact on her. From what he could see in her expression, she was longing to know more about Hammond Brown.

Such was the heartbreak of love, Kyle mused. Then he searched the room for his own new interest. There she was, dancing with a gentleman in a blue satin jacket. He could tell she was uncomfortable as she attempted another waltz. She had natural grace, though, and he knew she would soon be as expert as any of the locals. It occurred to him he would better play his hand if he gave his attention to some other lady. There were many to choose from. In minutes, he had a new partner, one with auburn hair and a teasing smile. He had a penchant for redheads. On the other hand, the sable locks of Miss Mackinnon held enormous attraction.

The pace of the evening increased. The orchestra was encouraged to perform several classical numbers to demonstrate its versatility. Then more dancing was followed by more food, which was followed by livelier dances, including a fandango. As the stronger spirits flowed, the crowd grew ever more boisterous and uninhibited. At the stroke of midnight, the revelers flung aside their masks and circled the room, laughing and visiting as if they had just discovered a roomful of dear friends they hadn't seen in years.

Skye was enjoying herself much more than she'd expected. She knew the continuous filling of her wine goblet had made her slightly giddy, but this had happened in Scotland at especially pleasant parties, and she had no concern over the matter. She had overcome her earlier shyness and had danced with any number of partners, several repeatedly. She refused to worry over the fact that she had not danced again with Mr. Wyndford. After all, he had done his duty by supplying her with refreshment and opening the ball with her as his first partner. On the other hand, she couldn't help watching him with other ladies, moving in perfect rhythm around the dance floor, engaging them in friendly conversation, causing them to titter and laugh, and even giggle at some private remark. He was indeed at ease with the fairer sex, she concluded. Why hadn't such a man found a wife by now? Maybe he preferred to dally with many rather than settle for one. His nature might be quite loose and independent. No doubt it was. Why should she care? she chastised herself. She had no intention of falling under his spell.

The last dance was announced, and violins began a melody with the distinct haunting quality of a gypsy serenade. *Sensuous* was the only word for it. Couples filled the floor, holding each other much closer than earlier in the evening.

"May I have the final dance, Miss Mackinnon?"

Skye took Mr. Wyndford's outstretched hand. So here was the obligatory closing dance described by Laurel. He must ask her, and she must accept.

He swept her into his embrace, taking her breath as he pressed her against his body. Stiffening, she tried to keep space between them, but found it impossible with his strong arm around her back and his hand firmly grasping hers.

"Relax and enjoy the music," he whispered above her ear. "Don't worry about steps. This is a dance of invitation. Allow your spirit to soar with emotion."

Invitation, she thought wildly. *To what?* At first, she

fought his suggestion, then found herself giving in to the beating of her heart against his chest and the heady rhythm pounding through her veins. The two moved as one, swaying slightly, revolving slowly, as their bodies shared the romance and the passion of the gypsy violins.

Skye had never felt such sensations. Her head was swirling, her body liquid; she was aware only of the man who held her with such commanding strength. Her cheek rested against the smooth lapel of his coat. So intimate she should be shocked, but she was not. The world around her dissolved, and she wanted the magic to last forever.

When the musicians played their last note, the music echoed in her ears and she continued to grasp Mr. Wyndford's hand.

He carefully stepped away, but kept her hand in his. Then he leaned near. "I request permission to call upon you, Miss Mackinnon. At your earliest convenience."

Permission to call? She blinked herself into reality. "I . . . no, I don't think so, sir." Her voice was annoyingly tremulous. "I'll be leaving soon for Highgrove Plantation. I must keep my horses there until we move west."

He released her hand, and smiled down at her. Hadn't he heard her refusal?

"I don't suppose you would object if I visit you at Highgrove—to see this breed of horses you're so fond of. I'm always interested in learning something new about animals. You could instruct me."

"Why . . . I suppose so," she stammered, unable to think of any reason he should not.

"Excellent. I'll see you again once you're settled. Will your mother accompany you?"

"I'm not sure. She's welcome, of course, but she may prefer her accomodations at Dominique Hall. *I'm* in charge of the livestock, you see. While she is the writer in the family."

He smiled at her and she felt it to the tips of her toes. His eyes were light brown, with amber flecks. And his deeply tanned skin looked exotic and rugged; fine lines crinkled at the corner of his eyes. This was no callow youth standing before her. For the first time, she could see him at Wind

River Ranch, gazing at endless horizons, riding across open plains as he kept watch over his cattle. Did he actually do those things? she wondered. Or did he hire others to do the work? Suddenly she was more than pleased she would see him again. She had so many questions. So much to learn. She returned his smile. "Yes, please do call at Highgrove. I would like that very much."

≈ *Chapter 8* ≈

Sometime between one and two in the morning, Skye left her room and tapped on her mother's door. She had seen a soft glow from the transom and knew her mother was still awake. She herself had found sleep impossible.

"Come in," Elizabeth called.

Skye entered the room and crossed to the bed, where her mother was sitting in her nightcap, writing in her journal.

"I couldn't sleep, Mother. So much is happening."

Elizabeth laid aside her pen. "Then sit for a spell, darling, and share your thoughts with me." She patted the quilt at her knee and Skye settled beside her.

"This past week seems like a dream," Skye said. "New Orleans is amazing; America is so much bigger than I imagined."

"You're right. We're on a new continent, and 'tis huge indeed. Before long, we'll be seeing a great deal more of it."

"I know. I'm so eager to travel west. I hope we'll like it there."

"Your father thought about it long and hard, I promise you. We had no future on Skye. If the land of Dakota is like he remembers, we'll find all we need to start a new life."

Skye leaned against the pillow propped at her mother's shoulder. "Mother . . . what does it feel like to fall in love?"

For several seconds, her mother didn't respond. Then she said, "My darling girl, when it happens, you will know. It may be sudden, or grow slowly in your heart. But when it arrives, you will feel its power like no other in your life. Why, dearest? Have you met someone special?"

Had she? Mr. Wyndford had sent her senses reeling, but that couldn't be love. Not like the love her parents had shared all these years. On the other hand, maybe that was the beginning. "I'm just curious. I know how important it is to continue our journey and find our land. Nothing must interfere with that."

Elizabeth stroked her hair. "Be patient. I'm sure there must be interesting young men out west. But if they don't please you, we'll look elsewhere. I hear there's a fine city on the river, St. Louis by name. We'll visit it on our way to Dakota."

Skye decided to broach a question that had occurred to her lately. "What if I fell in love with an Indian, a Lakota like Papa? What would happen then?"

"Then you would marry the man. We must be fair and respectful to the native people of America, Skye. I know you're thinking about Missy Wyndford's comments about the Indians, of what she said about Mr. Wyndford's disliking them. But he has reason to hate them, since they killed his brother. Where there is a lack of knowledge and understanding, there is anger and violence. When we settle in Dakota, we will get acquainted with the indigenous people. We'll learn about their lives and their traditions. I know they will be quite different from people we've known, but we won't let the prejudices of others influence our thinking."

A knock came on the door, startling both of them.

"Who is it?" Elizabeth asked in a low voice.

"Laurel Caldwell. I saw the light. Is everything all right, Mrs. Mackinnon?"

"Please come in, Laurel. We might as well have a lady's tête-à-tête."

Laurel slipped in the door. She wore a luxurious robe but was barefoot. "My goodness, here's Skye. Are you sure I'm not interrupting?"

"Not a bit," said Skye. "I'm glad you're here so I can tell you again how much I enjoyed the ball."

Laurel pulled up a chair beside the bed. "It was exciting, wasn't it," she said enthusiastically. "The gowns were lovely, and masking is such fun. Only . . ."

"What, Laurel?"

"Only I wish one certain gentleman had *not* been wearing a mask. I would have liked very much to see his eyes."

"But everyone unmasked at midnight," observed Skye.

"He was gone by then. He just disappeared."

"You must mean the tall gentleman whom none of us met," Elizabeth said. "We were all curious, but he was never introduced."

"That's the one," said Laurel. "I don't know why Father didn't introduce him at Shannon's party. I expected him to, but suddenly the man left. He reappeared at the ball, danced once with me, then disappeared again. Very odd, don't you think?"

Skye nodded. "Aye. Very odd. But surely your father knows who he is."

"He does. I insisted he tell me, and he said the man's name is Hammond Brown."

"Well, there you are. Mystery solved," said Elizabeth.

"Not really," Laurel responded. "Father has some slight business connection with Mr. Brown, but the man is from overseas and making only a brief stop in New Orleans for supplies."

"He was extremely attractive," said Skye, then watched Laurel closely for her reaction.

Laurel's eyes grew dreamy. "I know. I've never met anyone quite like him. He looked at me from behind his mask and I felt shivers up and down my spine. I had the strangest feeling that I've met him before, but that would be impossible."

"Did he frighten you?" asked Elizabeth.

"No, not at all. Just the opposite. I was drawn to him as if he had some magical power over me." She shook her head as if to rid herself of an unseen force. "I'm sure I'll never see him again, but I can't get him out of my mind."

Skye reached out to touch her arm. "Maybe there was elfin dust in the punch. I had a very similar experience."

"With Mr. Brown?" asked a startled Laurel.

Skye laughed. "Oh no. I caught only a glimpse of your Mr. Brown. I'm speaking of Mr. Wyndford. I didn't want to find him fascinating, but I did." She looked sideways at her mother. "He has asked to call on me when I'm established at Highgrove."

"Skye Eugenia!" said her mother. "Did you agree?"

"I told him he could. He asked if you would be there, but I wasn't sure. Have you decided yet, Mother?"

"As a matter of fact, I've decided to stay here at Dominique Hall. I'm sure 'tis much too soon for your father to arrive, but I want to be on hand when he does. Also, I promised Missy Wyndford another visit, maybe several. I'm sure she's lonely, and she must see several doctors. I'm afraid she's dangerously ill."

"I'm sorry about that. She is so very sweet and gentle," Skye said softly. "Mr. Wyndford looks very worried when he speaks of her."

"You may go to Highgrove, at any rate, Skye. I know you want to make sure the mares are properly pastured and exercised. I assume there is a staff there to see to your needs."

"Naturally," Laurel interjected. "Much more complete than here at Dominique Hall. Highgrove has an overseer and field hands and a wonderful stable manager. Our housekeeper, Mrs. Dubois, is a French Canadian who is like a second mother to me and acts as chaparone when I visit, which is quite often."

"In that case, Skye, lass, you may receive Mr. Wyndford. We all know him to be a gentleman in good standing with the Caldwells—that's all the recommendation I need."

"It's growing late," said Laurel, "but as long as we're here together, I'd like to bring up a most important matter."

"Of course," replied Elizabeth.

"I've been thinking about your castle and lands on Skye. I would like to purchase them immediately, if you're sure you want to sell."

* * *

61

On a marshy flat on the west bank of the Missouri River, Loup Leveque sat slumped on his pony. Moored at the river bank was a steamer, the *Western Queen*. Loup had ridden two weeks, all the way from the Dakota badlands, then trailed the Missouri River to this secluded spot along its shores. His horse was lame, and he was in a rotten mood. But he was here, and the ship was here, exactly where he had been told it would be. Plying between Pierre and St. Louis, the *Western Queen* hauled freight and passengers through endless miles of unsettled wilderness, a single avenue connecting the white man's cities to their far-flung outposts in the West. The *Queen* made a regular stop at this bend in the river to allow the crew to find firewood for the boilers.

Loup was tired, hungry, and eager to get aboard.

He rode his exhausted horse into the shallows and swung out of the saddle. Then he pulled off the saddle and bridle and carried them up the plank.

Loup was met by a uniformed boatman.

"You gotta have a ticket, mister. How far you goin'?"

"St. Louis," grunted Loup.

The man looked at Leveque's horse. "What about your mount? Gonna bring him aboard?"

"He's lame. No good anymore."

"You can't just leave him there. The wolves'll have him for supper."

"So? Not your business, is it? Here's my passage." Loup pulled a coin from the pouch at his belt and flipped it to the man. The boatman caught it but shook his head. "This'll buy you a cot with the crew. Passenger cabins cost more."

"A cot will do. Don't plan to sleep much."

"Here's your ticket. But I don't take to cruelty to dumb animals, even horses. At least put the creature out of his misery before the wolves bring him down."

Leveque pointed a richly carved black walking stick at the boatman's chest. *"You* do it," he snarled, then walked toward the steps leading to the crew's quarters.

"Hold up, there, mister. I need your name for the passenger list."

Leveque paused, but didn't look back. "Name's Loup Leveque."

"Leveque. French, ain't it? Don't Loup mean *wolf* in Frenchy?"

Loup didn't answer. As he made his way into the bunk room, he heard a pistol shot. *White men are fools,* he thought. *Wasting bullets on nonsense.* But because the whites were fools, he expected to do well at the poker tables on the trip to St. Louis. In St. Louis, his journey would end in a white man's death.

Loup stashed his tack beneath a cot and located the salon where men were seated at round tables. Passengers. Passengers who had money he could acquire with little effort. *The wolf will eat the chickens,* he thought, sure that he would soon have the pokes of the white gamblers traveling on the *Queen.* His mother had taught him all the tricks of the gambling saloons of Quebec before she died. "You are a half-breed," she often reminded him. "You must be cunning, my little wolf, my little Loup." He was expert; he was fast; his cheating was never detected and his looks were intimidating. In the past, he had worn a bandanna over the puckered scar slashed through the corner of his left eye. But when he switched from fur trapping to gambling, he used the ugly disfigurement to his advantage. No one questioned his play. No one dared. Loup was large for a half-breed. His Lakota father had given him his size, but not his name. His name had come from the French whore who spawned him.

He headed toward an empty seat and plunked his money pouch on the table. The four men looked up at him, then nodded for him to join them. He saw disgust in their eyes, but he was used to that. He had inherited the best traits of both his parents: his mother's ambition and brains, his father's courage and hatred of the invading whites. Loup had one goal in life: to kill a man, a *particular* man who needed killing. In the name of his Lakota people, he would take this great coup, and then he would be accepted by the tribe. His father, Siyaka, had been rejected by the Lakota long ago. Now, as Siyaka's son, he would reclaim his rights as a Lakota Sioux. His French blood had dominated long enough. His hatred for the white man had grown the more he encountered them. Now the time had come to take his place among his father's people—as soon as he counted coup with his walking stick and killed the English intruder—James Kyler Wyndford.

Loup touched one of the twisted braids hanging along his shoulders. He knew the whites disliked gambling with Indians, but he also knew they were impressed with his fat pouch of coins. Money always ruled the Americans. He would take theirs before morning, then use it in St. Louis, where he would attend the horse fair and find Wyndford. Wyndford always went there to buy horses in June, he had learned. And it was better to kill him far way from his ranch in Dakota. Afterward, Loup would return to the Lakota village and show Wyndford's scalp to Chief Red Hawk. Loup would be a great hero, and no one could deny him the right to participate in the Sun Dance and obtain elevated status among his father's people.

"Deal," he growled. "Haven't you ever seen a half-breed play poker?"

ᵈᴵ Chapter 9 ᵇ⁼

Skye sat astride Spirit Lady and collected the reins. The day was brilliant, pristine, and she basked in the warm sun and cloudless morning sky. She had adjusted quickly to the warmth of Louisiana after the uncertain climate on Skye, and she enjoyed the luxury of knowing she could count on daily outings with her mares.

Putting Lady into an easy canter, Skye crossed the broad riding arena, then halted in a cloud of dust. One tug on the reins and Lady pivoted to the left; a second tug turned the mare in a tight circle to the right.

"Good girl," Skye said, patting the broad neck. "Now we'll do the same without the reins. You remember, like you learned on Skye."

She dropped the reins and used the pressure of her knees to put Lady through identical circular maneuvers. Then she kicked her into a sudden burst of speed to cross the arena to a spot shaded by a spreading magnolia in full bloom. It was her special pleasure to imitate her father's astounding horsemanship, though she was not yet his equal.

Catching her breath, Skye gazed at the idyllic setting and smiled to herself. Highgrove Plantation was a dream come true. The stark white two-story house, sitting on expansive grounds above the river, made a breathtaking picture of serene elegance. In distant pastures, horses grazed with their noses in knee-high grass. Mrs. Dubois and the house servants treated her like a princess, and the stable manager and groom took such excellent care of Lady and Legacy that the mares were bound to be permanently spoiled.

Skye pushed back her wide-brimmed hat, a necessary item in the Southern sun, Laurel had explained, and scratched Lady beneath her lush flowing mane. The light chestnut mare responded with a satisfied whinny. So Laurel Caldwell would be the new owner of Strathmor Castle. If Laurel married, her husband might one day petition the queen for the title of laird. Skye was delighted that Laurel would own the property. The day before she had came to Highgrove, she had signed a binding agreement with Laurel at the attorney's office. Laurel hadn't quibbled a bit over the price, and had paid the exact sum that Fletcher Mackinnon had indicated was fair. Skye knew her father would be proud of his daughter's business acumen and relieved that funds were in the bank for their journey west. The step was a major one for the Mackinnons. Their ties to the old world were now completely severed.

Laurel Caldwell had been pleased as punch to own a castle of her own. Mr. Caldwell placed the title in Laurel's name, as sole owner, and Laurel had glowed with excitement and hugged her father till he gasped for air. Then she had said in a very businesslike tone that the property would be her northern port in the British Isles. Perfect for shipping goods into Scotland without having to stop on English shores.

Whatever Laurel's reasons, Skye was happy that her cousin now owned the Mackinnon estates on the Isle of Skye.

Skye's musing was interrupted by the sound of approaching hoofbeats. Twisting in her saddle, she saw a lone male rider traveling at a canter along the path leading from the river road. Could it be—? Aye, it was Mr. Wyndford. All week, she had anticipated his visit, but now that he was here, she felt as unprepared as she was thrilled.

"Good morning," he called, doffing his felt planter's hat and guiding his stallion toward the railing. "A lovely day, and a lovely sight you are, Miss Mackinnon. My timing appears perfect to witness a display of superb horsemanship."

Skye rode toward where Mr. Wyndford waited, his horse snorting and tossing its dark, full mane. The sight of Kyler Wyndford mounted on his tall black horse sent her pulse racing. Must he always have this affect on her? she wondered. She must remind herself that he was not as perfect as he appeared. His character was flawed by racial prejudice and an unforgiving nature. Who knew what arrogance and cunning might lie behind that remarkably handsome face?

She was forced to look up at him because of the height of his mount. Sixteen hands, for certain. His clothing intrigued her, as well. He wore a leather sleeveless vest over a billowing white shirt open at the neck. Extremely informal for calling on a lady. The shirt was tucked into skin-tight breeches that disappeared into knee-high black boots. The effect was enormously appealing. She decided she preferred it to any male attire she'd seen to date in New Orleans.

"I'm using Spanish-style tack today. What do you think of it?"

"I'm not sure. Is the saddle comfortable?"

"Very. We're adopting quite a few ideas from the Mexican vaqueros in California. These are popular in Texas, too."

California. Texas. Exotic names of faraway places. Skye shifted her weight in her own English-style saddle. "Then the tack must have merit. Is this the thoroughbred you described?"

"Indeed he is. Meet Raven Duke, progeny of Herod, the most famous stud in England. Raven's full brother resides at Wind River."

She studied the animal's sleek conformation. "Built for speed, looks like. Did he ever race at Newmarket?"

"Never raced at all. Except after a stray calf or toward the barn after a day on the range."

"A fine animal, that's plain." She captured his eyes. "But limited in some respects, I'm betting."

She enjoyed his predictable reaction to her comment. His eyebrows raised, and he gave her a disbelieving look.

"Miss Mackinnon, I must pursue your peculiar observation. What is it about Raven Duke that inspires such a remark?"

"No offense intended, sir. But he has the blood of the best racer ever born. Would he care to race my mare—say, to that distant oak and back?"

Wyndford threw back his head and laughed heartily. Raven danced nervously under his hands. "Race? Please don't misunderstand me, but that very attractive little mare wouldn't stand a chance against Raven. Surely you're joking."

Smiling at how quickly the sophisticated Mr. Wyndford had fallen into her trap, she reined the horse along the rail to the opening and left the arena. Approaching Wyndford in the slow gait so natural to her half–Indian pony, half–Irish racer, she smiled winningly and pointed toward a starting place approximately a hundred yards from the oak.

Laughing again, Mr. Wyndford trotted past her toward the indicated spot. "We race from here?" he called.

"Aye. As soon as I'm even with you, we'll start. But we must turn at the tree. First one back is the winner."

"Done. The loser owes a lemonade to the victor. Agreed?"

She could see he was pleased and utterly confident. "Agreed," she responded. Loosing her reins, she allowed Lady to slip into a collected canter. In seconds, she drew next to Wyndford, then released the reins and whistled shrilly to the mare. She felt the horse gather beneath her and leap forward, then pound the earth with flying hoofs. Already, Wyndford was two lengths behind.

Leaning close to the horse's neck, she felt the surge of straining muscle as the animal flew along the turf. A glance showed her Wyndford gaining now as they passed the halfway mark. The long-legged thoroughbred had hit its stride and was fighting hard to overtake her.

Wyndford and Raven drew beside her, then inched past just as they reached the tree.

"Ho!" cried Skye, gripping with her thighs and putting the short-coupled mare into a tight pivot. This was the moment the race would be won or lost.

Skye gave Lady her head and laid close behind the thrashing mane as they flew toward the finish. She had heard Wyndford curse back at the tree as his thoroughbred swung wide before turning for home. With Lady running full out, and with four solid lengths lead, no horse could possibly catch her in such a short distance.

Lady crossed the finish line one length ahead of a frustrated Raven Duke.

Skye didn't stop but cantered toward the house. Wyndford followed and gradually, they eased into a walk. Only then did she dare look at her defeated adversary.

He was grinning as he touched the brim of his hat in salute. "My compliments," he called. "The day is yours, Miss Mackinnon. I would have bet my ranch on the outcome and lost all that I own."

"Too bad I didn't think of that beforehand," she said gaily. "Then I would have nothing to do when I got out west but move into my new house and start feeding my cows."

"Cows," he chuckled. "Let me be the first to suggest you refer to your stock as cattle—or beeves."

"Very well," she responded. *"Cattle.* How does that sound?"

"Perfect," he said, halting at the railing in front of the mansion. "My only concern now is how and when I pay my debt to you. One lemonade, am I right?" His lopsided smile as he swung from his saddle revealed no trace of annoyance or dismay at his loss. "Allow me." He reached up to assist her to dismount.

She didn't need help, but she gladly took his hand and stepped to the ground. "You're a good sport, Mr. Wyndford. I'm afraid I took advantage of you."

He cupped her elbow and guided her up the broad steps to the front porch. "No, I'd say you outsmarted me—and taught me a lesson about short-coupled horses. Let's see if I got it right." He gently turned her to face him. His expression was relaxed, friendly, rather admiring, if she guessed correctly. He did have looks to melt a mountain of granite.

"Across a short distance," he began, "with a tight turn to be managed, a sturdy, short-coupled horse with a well-muscled chest and massive rump—such as your mare—will win every time. Is that my lesson for today?"

She blushed under his plain words and close scrutiny. "Exactly," she said with a smile. "But in honor of the occasion, *I'll* supply the lemonade. Especially since you don't have access just now to a kitchen—and I do."

"I'd be obliged, Miss Mackinnon. Losing a horse race is hot, thirsty work. May I wait for you in one of those inviting rockers?"

"Please make yourself at home. I'll speak to Mrs. Dubois and be back shortly."

Kyle observed the retreat of the petite young lady as she strode into the house. Then, making his way to the waiting chairs, he shook his head in amazement. The defeat of his horse had set his vanity in the dust, but he clearly saw the reason for it. Served him right for being so cocksure and arrogant. In another three lengths, Raven would have easily overtaken the little mare, but he didn't have three lengths, and Miss Mackinnon had planned that from the start. More interesting was the way her pony had spun in its tracks, after galloping at full speed a split second earlier, then bounded forward and gained momentum before a person could blink. The animal had possibilities he'd never considered. Possibilities for enormous success in rounding up cattle on his enormous, far-flung range.

As for Miss Mackinnon herself, she damn well took his breath away.

With her small boot heels clicking on the brick, Skye Mackinnon returned to the porch.

Kyle stood and held her chair, while she smiled coyly at him. Her eyes were as green as the grass beyond the porch, and they were made all the more astonishing by the tawny tones of her flawless complexion. Her coloring was unique, as if alabaster had been underpainted with liquid bronze. Equally as unique was the expression behind her eyes. As open and unassuming as a child's. Innocent, but perceptive. He felt she was defying him to trick her, challenging him to test her intelligence against his own. How unlike the veiled glances and subtle wit of the ladies of New Orleans. And how enormously refreshing.

"Tell me, sir, *everything* about your ranch in the West."

He tore his mind from her seductive beauty to give thought to her inquiry. "Well now, that's as big a question as I've ever heard. I'm not sure where to begin."

"At the beginning would be perfect. You have a successful ranching business in a place called Dakota. 'Tis what my family will have someday. I would like any information you could offer on how we can achieve that."

"Oh, is that all? Ten years of back-breaking, bone-chilling, God-awful hard work. Nothing to it."

He could see she didn't care for his response. But he was telling her the absolute truth.

"We have money to buy land. That should be a beginning," she suggested.

"No. You can't buy land."

Her eyes widened. "What? But we must. . . . I don't understand."

"Not yet anyway. Let me explain. The land called Dakota is a vast wilderness, only recently explored by white men. All the land was acquired from France in the Louisiana Purchase. It is known as the public domain. The United States feels some obligation to negotiate with the nomadic Indian tribe for pasture, but once that's done, then I expect the land will be offered to white settlers. For now, the land is not for sale."

She looked stricken. "But we must have it. We must have it for our horses and cows—I mean, our *cattle*."

"That's entirely feasible. When you arrive with your livestock, the land is there waiting for you. Just turn the creatures out. There is no one to stop you."

"No one? No one at all?"

"So far, that is the case. Eventually, of course, that will change. As I said, the first settlers will have first claim. The United States is eager for ranchers and farmers to develop the land as soon as possible. But for now, Miss Mackinnon, the man facing you is the only rancher in Dakota. I have the entire place to myself. Except for primitive Indians—Sioux mostly."

She was so absorbed by his words, she didn't see the servant bringing lemonade until he arrived beside them.

"Thank you, Paul. Return soon; we may need another. Goodness, Mr. Wyndford, I had no idea the area was so sparsely populated."

"Sparse is an insufficient description. *Empty* is more like it. The beaver are trapped out and the trappers are gone. Soon the ranchers and farmers will come, but at the present, I have only a handful of neighbors at Vermillion, a few more upriver at Fort Pierre, a settlement or two in between—and the redskins, of course."

He saw her intake of breath. He hadn't wanted to frighten her. "Opportunity is there, Miss Mackinnon. But I have wondered why you chose Dakota. There's been more interest in the Texas Republic of late. Much milder winters, though not such abundant grass."

She placed her glass on the table and looked him squarely in the eye. No, he hadn't frightened her, though for a minute he saw a fleeting look of alarm.

"I must explain that my grandfather, Finlay Mackinnon, was a trapper, the type referred to as a mountain man."

"Your grandfather? In Dakota?" It was Kyle's turn for surprise.

"Aye. He lived there for several years and knew the country well."

"So that's where your family's interest came from. Quite a few Scots spent time in Dakota in the early days. I suppose your grandfather told glowing tales of Dakota, and now you're ready to make your home there."

The girl looked uncomfortable for the first time today. She stared at her hands in her lap. He thought she might be about to share some secret, but she finally said, "Aye. We know all about the rich land and good water." She looked up, and he saw a challenge in her exquisite eyes. "But we didn't know the land is free for the taking. Do the *Indians,* such as the Lakotas, agree with that view?"

⊰ Chapter 10 ⊱

The Lakota Sioux? The savages?"

Skye felt her heart thrubbing under Mr. Wyndford's steady gaze. His eyebrows knitted as he considered her question. She knew that his response was far more significant than he could possibly realize. With every effort to appear nonchalant, she took a sip of her lemonade.

"I have no love for the natives," he said finally. "As you may have heard, they murdered my brother, Missy's husband. I have no way to bring the culprits to justice. I choose instead to avoid the red devils as much as possible." His voice was tight, barely concealing deep emotion.

She chose her words carefully. "I'm deeply sorry about that. But don't you think there are good and bad people in every race? Can you judge all by only a handful of evil-doers?"

"I don't have to judge—if I have minimal contact with them."

"But you said there are many Indians nearby. How can you avoid them when you have so much land?"

"Their permanent villages are well away from the forts, though they set up tepees near Vermillion in summer to trade their goods. Occasionally, I glimpse small bands crossing my range. I assume they are as content to keep their distance from me as I am from them." His tone was cool and carefully controlled.

Skye thought of her mother's advice that ignorance brought danger and violence. How sad that Mr. Wyndford based his view of the natives on one bad experience. "I have heard a great deal about the Indians from family members. My mother toured America when she was thirteen. She saw the native people and found them intriguing."

"Forgive me, but your family's views are not based on realistic and current information. I can understand how renegade savages could kill a white man, especially years ago when they had little knowledge of our race. But what they did to Blanton was unforgivable. My sister has no idea what her husband endured before he died, and she will never know."

So his hatred ran deep, Skye thought with a sinking heart. She couldn't resist one more observation. "Cruelty is not exclusive to the American natives. Even the English have been known to be brutal beyond belief. My own father was once condemned by the king. He barely escaped death, and the manner of his execution would have equaled any torture the Indians could devise."

Wyndford's slight smile held no humor. "A point well taken. Man's treatment of his fellows has a shameful history, on every continent and in every society. But I insist that my position is a wise one. Live and let live is the best policy when surrounded by primitives."

"And you view *half-breeds* the same way?" She bit her lip, but the question was out.

"Worse, if possible. Completely untrustworthy. Too cunning by half. Some are scouts for the soldiers, but I would find them quite unreliable."

She looked away to hide her dismay at his words. "How unfortunate," she murmured. "I do think you should at least give them a chance to be friends." She wanted to tell him that she was one-quarter Lakota—and extremely proud of her heritage. She would have liked nothing better than to challenge his views at once, but he was still practically a stranger to her and a close friend of the Caldwells. There was plenty of time for revelations, especially once he met her father, whose Indian blood was evident in every line of his sculptured face and in his coloring, which she herself had inherited. In fact, she was surprised Mr. Wyndford hadn't already observed that *she* had Indian blood. When he learned the truth, would he choose to ignore her existence as he did the natives of Dakota? How disappointing, when she had hoped they could be friends and he might lend some assistance in the enormous undertaking facing her family.

"Have I upset you, Miss Mackinnon?" he asked gently. "My deep apologies, if I have. And on so fine a day. Let me make a suggestion."

She gave him a tentative smile. "Please do."

"You have aptly demonstrated the prowess of your mare. Next week at the Eclipse racing track in New Orleans, a match race is scheduled between two outstanding thoroughbred racers. Would you attend with me?"

"Aye. That would be very pleasant." Her best effort went into the cordial tone of her response. "I'm sure the horses are magnificent. You mustn't think I disparage them in any way."

He set aside his glass. "Excellent. Then I'll be going. When do you expect to return to Dominique Hall?"

"Six days hence. My mother is expecting me. And I would like to call on your sister again. Also, 'tis possible my father will be arriving soon."

He stood and bowed over her hand. "I anticipate the honor of meeting the laird in person. Now that his daughter has so enchanted me."

Did all Americans exude such charm? she wondered. Then she reminded herself that Mr. Wyndford was not an American, but English. Could his smooth demeanor be only a polite veneer that went no deeper than his skin? She held her hand stiffly as he brushed her fingertips with his lips, then watched as he walked across the porch and mounted his stallion. He touched the brim of his hat in salute, then rode swiftly down the path toward the river. As elegant and dashing a gentleman as she'd ever encountered. But bitter and prejudiced, as she'd learned first from Missy Wyndford and now from the man himself. Was there any way to change those feelings, or was he doomed to carry them to his grave?

Kyle made his way through a misty morning toward Blaine Caldwell's office. Raven's shod hooves clattered on the cobbled street as the stallion trotted briskly, tossing his head and sniffing the cool air off the river.

Kyle's spirits were high as he anticipated the afternoon he had arranged with Miss Skye Mackinnon. With her family's approval and with Shannon Kildaire as token chaparone, he expected a most interesting few hours at the local track. For six days, he'd kept himself busy obtaining supplies he would take back to Wind River. The balance of his time he'd spent with Missy, taking her to several doctors, who promised a diagnosis before long. He was optimistic that the new medicines were all she needed for complete recovery.

After securing Raven in front of the low-slung stucco building on Decatur Street, Kyle let himself into the office. Plain, with two small dust-covered windows and a wide-planked wooden floor, the office appeared hardly suitable for Blaine Caldwell's worldwide shipping enterprise.

Caldwell rose from behind his cluttered oak desk and extended his hand. "Good to see you again, Kyle."

"Good morning, sir."

"Pull up a chair. I won't keep you a minute. I understand you're having an outing at the track today with Miss Mackinnon. An astonishing young lady, I must say. Capable and bright under those feminine frocks. A great deal like my daughter. The two have become fast friends."

"So I've heard. I wouldn't want to match wits with either of them, much less the two together."

Caldwell chuckled and sat again at his desk. "No indeed. You're right about that." His smile faded. "I asked you to come today so we could have a private conversation. I've had disconcerting news. My concern also includes Miss Mackinnon."

"Oh?" Kyle leaned forward.

"I'm afraid she may have to call on every bit of strength

she owns, perhaps more than it's possible for a girl her age to muster."

"Why? What has happened?"

"You remember Cheyne Sinclair. Well, the gentleman docked in New Orleans last night. We met at Gerod's."

"Of course I remember Sinclair—and Gerod's."

"I assume you know that Mr. Mackinnon, Skye's father, sailed to the Barbary Coast last month to purchase a stallion to use for breeding."

"Yes. I've heard the story."

"That coast is where Sinclair makes his home. He has received news there's been an uprising there among the native people. Mass murders have taken place, and the government, such as it is, is in turmoil. Ships have been burned in the harbor at Tangier and foreigners have been murdered in their beds."

"Dear God—you don't think Mackinnon—"

"I don't know. Sinclair doesn't know. But it's a very dangerous situation."

"Have you told Mrs. Mackinnon?"

"No, and I don't plan to until I get more definite information. Cheyne is even now sailing toward Tangier to ascertain the situation. He knows the horse traders in the area and will begin making inquiries as soon as he arrives. But that will take time, as you can imagine. And it will be even longer before he can report back to New Orleans, once he learns something."

"What do you suggest?"

"I'm going to strongly advise Mrs. Mackinnon that if her husband doesn't appear soon, she should forget her plans to go west. I don't want to alarm her, but I feel it my duty to save her and her daughter from a serious mistake."

Kyle nodded. "I couldn't agree more. At best, Dakota is a tough place to build a home and secure a livelihood. The settlers heading west are thinking not of themselves, but of future generations. For two women alone, the enterprise would be virtually impossible. I would help in any way I could, of course, but their long-term survival would be very doubtful."

"I'm sure that's true. I'm prepared to offer the two ladies

residence under my roof as long as they like. Mrs. Mackinnon is a quiet woman, keeps mostly to her room and her writing. If her husband is lost, I believe she could be persuaded to continue her life as a member of my wife's family, here in New Orleans. But her daughter is another matter. Laurel tells me the girl is born to the land and speaks of nothing else but heading west. She has no concept of the struggle, but only fanciful dreams of adventure."

"She told me her grandfather was a trapper in Dakota years ago."

"He was. But he died before Skye was born, so her stories of the place are secondhand and bound to be sketchy."

"I verify that. She lectured me last week on my feelings toward the Indians—said I should make *friends* with them. I got the impression she would entertain them at a soirée as soon as she set foot in Dakota."

"No doubt. Well, I won't keep you, but I wanted to apprise you of the situation in Tangier. If Fletcher Mackinnon doesn't show up soon, I may need your help to dissuade the ladies from traveling west."

Kyle rose and replaced his hat. "I'd be glad to do that. Though naturally I'll be disappointed at not having the Mackinnons for neighbors."

Later, as Kyle rode toward Dominique Hall, where he would meet the ladies, he felt his earlier high spirits wane, despite the fact that brilliant sunshine had replaced the gloom of the morning. It would be a tragedy if Mackinnon had been killed. From all reports, his wife and daughter were devoted to him, and he sounded just the type to carve out a successful ranch in Dakota. What's more, that would put an end to any future relationship with Mackinnon's delightful daughter.

He thought of how the girl's face glowed when she spoke of her plans to go west. He admitted he had been extraordinarily pleased at the prospect of having her close by. Poor Missy had been ecstatic at the idea of being near such a nice family in their vast and lonely land. Still, there was hope Mackinnon had escaped the uprising and might arrive soon in New Orleans. Kyle vowed to conceal his worries during today's outing.

⊰ *Chapter 11* ⊱

The day of the highly touted horse race began with a heavy, overcast sky and threatening showers, but by noon, the summer sun had obliterated the gray atmosphere and the temperature began to soar.

Skye was struggling once more with the fastenings of the dreadful corset. Only Laurel's lively conversation kept her from complaining as her cousin pulled hard against the strings.

"Your figure is superb, Skye. There now, just look at that tiny waist. Why, Mr. Wyndford will ache to put his hands around it. Very discreetly, and with your permission, of course."

"As I said, Laurel, I find Mr. Wyndford extremely attractive, but we will be friends, and that's the end of it."

"I hear your words, cousin, but your eyes say otherwise."

"I'm sure he wouldn't want any serious connection with a woman of Indian blood."

"But you might overcome his prejudice in time. If you're determined to go to Dakota, just think how much trouble you would save by marrying a successful rancher instead of starting from scratch."

"But I want to start from scratch. That's the fun of it."

"You won't find it fun when you've worked your hands to the bone scrubbing and hauling, or broiled your pretty skin. You may be required to pull calves out of a snowdrift when the temperature is twenty below zero."

"We'll have to hire help, of course. And I expect we'll live at the settlement nearest our ranch for a year or two. If Melissa Wyndford can make a go of it, so can I."

"Yes, and think of poor Melissa. Looks twice her age, and

possibly dying." Laurel gave Skye a sudden tight squeeze. "I just hate to see you take such chances, Skye. And I'll rarely get to see you."

Skye was flooded with warmth at Laurel's affectionate gesture. She had always wondered what it would be like to have a sister, and now she had found this wonderful cousin to fill that need. "We'll visit, Laurel. That's a promise. In winter, we'll come to New Orleans. In summers, you will come to Dakota."

Laurel plopped on the bed beside a snoozing MacLard. "I hope so. But remember, I have Caldwell Shipping to think about. My father depends on me more than he realizes."

"I'm sure he does. And my father depends on me. Not that he isn't vigorous and hard-working, but he only has two hands and two arms and one back. I'm like the son he never had, I suppose. That suits me just fine."

Laurel paused and stroked the dog's ear. "Skye . . ."

"What is it?" Skye fastened the tiny pearl buttons down the front of her organdy bodice.

"Are you sure your father will arrive safely in New Orleans? I think he took an awful chance going alone to Tangier. That's one port our ships avoid like the plague."

"Of course, he will," Skye hastened. "But it may take longer than he thought. In that case, Mother and I will go on to Vermillion and wait there. We must get Spirit Legacy to safe haven before she foals. I plan to find good land and water and claim it before anyone else does. I gather that's how it's done in America."

Laurel sighed and shook her head. "I don't know . . . the trip is long and could be dangerous."

"But the steamboats provide safe travel. First to St. Louis, and then up the Missouri to Dakota. We should be quite comfortable."

"Is there any chance Mr. Wyndford and Missy will be traveling with you?"

This possibility hadn't occurred to Skye. "I never thought of it. I suppose they might. That would certainly be pleasant." Her heart skittered at the idea. How romantic it would be to share the riverboat journey with such an interesting man. She might even have the opportunity to change his thinking about the Lakotas. Immediately she chastised herself. Her mother was the romantic, not she. "On second thought, I doubt very much if we would travel together. We'll be leaving as soon as Papa arrives and has a chance to catch his breath. The Wyndfords will certainly want to continue their visit in New Orleans for some time yet."

Laurel's expression saddened. "I'm truly worried about Mrs. Wyndford. I don't think she tells her brother about half her discomforts. Yesterday, when our mothers called on her, she had to leave the room. She was . . . hemorrhaging."

"Oh, I'm grieved to hear it," Skye said with sincere sympathy. "I'll call on her tomorrow if she feels like having company. I've been remiss in staying so long at Highgrove." She fastened the sash around her waist.

"Would you like for Marie to help you finish dressing? I'll call her right away."

She didn't need Marie, Skye thought. She'd never had a lady's maid, and saw no reason for such pampering now. "Thank you, but I'm ready. I just have to put on my hat. I can't wait to see the races."

Laurel rushed to peer out the window. "He's here!" she cried. "The top is down on his buggy. You'll certainly need a hat and gloves and a parasol."

"Where is Miss Kildaire?" Skye said with a sudden attack of nerves.

"She brought her own carriage and will follow the two of you. Don't worry about Shannon. She will only observe the proprieties, then sit in her own box nearby."

Skye cocked her chin and pulled the satin ribbons into a bow. "We don't know much about proprieties on Skye. And I've never had a chaparone."

"But this is New Orleans, cousin. We do play such silly little games."

Kyle found he had no difficulty at all giving Skye Mackinnon his complete attention. She looked so winsome in her frothy, rose-colored dress and beribboned straw bonnet that he couldn't take his eyes from her. Her charm was increased by the obvious fact that she was unaware of her haunting beauty. A lady who was as unspoiled as she was lovely. She captivated him, but unfortunately, he did not seem to have the same effect on her.

Her glance had been decidedly cool when he assisted her to and from the carriage.

During the ride to the Eclipse Racetrack, she had barely looked at him. Her enthusiastic comments were reserved for the passing scenery, for the numbers of conveyances making their way toward the track, and for the elegant double-tiered grandstand already overflowing with racing fans.

As they made their way through the crowd with Miss Kildaire in their wake, Skye kept her parasol balanced above her head, effectively blocking his view of her face, her dark ringlets, and her wide-brimmed hat. He had the feeling she was using it to keep her distance from him, though they were necessarily forced close by the crush of people.

He escorted her to their box, a private one he had obtained only by bribing track officials, using the Caldwell name as leverage. Every racing fan in Louisiana and several surrounding states was on hand today for the match race between the two top thoroughbreds in the South.

Once they were in their box seats, Skye lowered her parasol and waved at Shannon, who had met friends at her own exclusive box one row away. "My, how exciting!" she exclaimed, turning in a circle to absorb the sights.

At last she was impressed, he saw with satisfaction. Her color was high and her eyes glowing.

"Our timing is perfect. I'll place a small wager and have sherry delivered. By then, the horses should be on the track. I've heard the winner's purse is $20,000. Both the animals are stallions and will command thousands more in stud fees, win or lose this race." He knew most ladies of New Orleans would blush at his outspoken observation, but not Skye. She nodded vigorously, fully knowledgeable of the value of a stallion's potent legacy to its offspring.

He excused himself to go place his bet. When he returned, two glasses of sherry sat on the table in their box. The enclosure was small and open to view by other box-holders, but it was overlooking the finish line, a prime spot from which to see the race.

Skye looked up at him with sparkling eyes. He hoped this meant he had gained her favor at last.

"I've never seen anything so wonderful," she bubbled. "What is the purpose of that gazebo across the track? How far will the horses race? Where does it begin? What will—"

"Hold on, Miss Mackinnon." He grinned at her and took the chair at her side. "I'll explain everything. That gazebo is the judges' stand. The horses will race twice around the track; that's four miles. And the race will start at that spot down the track where you see the rope stretched across. A standing start, this time, I believe, though some races are running starts."

Her eyes grew wide as saucers. "Four miles! Astonishing! Are you sure they will survive running such a distance?"

"Absolutely. Their endurance is what I wanted you to see—the stamina and speed of thoroughbred horses. Not your ordinary animals, by any means."

Her attention flew to the track as the two gleaming stallions, one bay and one chestnut, were ridden onto the turf. The crowd was on its feet and cheering wildly. The horses tossed their heads; the bay sidestepped, but his jockey rose and took him under firm rein and began the turn back to the starting post.

In minutes, the starting pistol fired, and the two magnificent horses pounded side by side along the track, until they passed the box seats and headed into the first turn.

Kyle stood back and relished the sight of Skye Mackinnon's breathless excitement as she leaned forward and shouted her encouragement. The noise around them was deafening, making conversation impossible.

Kyle laughed at Skye, now standing on tiptoe, applauding and shouting along with everyone around them. On their left, the box-holders screamed for the bay; on their right, the fans shouted even louder for the chestnut.

When the two straining horses rounded the far curve for the second time and headed for the finish, the screams swelled, and genteel ladies and gentlemen lost all dignity as they cheered for their favorite.

The chestnut from the state of Louisiana edged out the bay by half a length.

With the uproar beyond control, Skye turned to stare at Kyle. Her face was flushed and her emerald eyes dancing. She mouthed a word or two of delight, then abruptly threw her arms around him and gave him a hug. Beside and behind them, others were doing the same. Sheer pandemonium erupted as fans who had chosen the winner celebrated and anticipated their winnings.

Kyle would have loved to return Skye's embrace, but the gesture ended so quickly, he was left standing with his arms at his sides. A furtive glance toward Shannon Kildaire revealed she was busy with her own celebration rather than attending to chaperone duties. He grinned into Skye's upturned face and waited for the hullabaloo to lessen.

Finally, he heard her shouting, "Did you win? Did you pick the chestnut?"

He nodded. "I had a fifty-fifty chance, after all," he called back. "My lucky day!" he said, thinking privately he was extraordinarily lucky to be sharing the fun with Miss Mackinnon.

After a time, the crowd began to thin and the noise abated. Kyle suggested they sit and enjoy their sherry. Another race appeared to be on the schedule this afternoon.

Skye's hat was askew, but she ignored it. With her cheeks still glowing, she took her seat and drank from her glass as if the liquid were punch. "Another race? Why, this is the most exciting afternoon of my life," she said unabashedly.

He leaned near. "And what do you think of the thoroughbred now? Has the breed redeemed itself, Miss Mackinnon?"

"The horses are astounding," she said breathlessly. "I can see why you're so keen on them. They must cost a fortune, though," she added with Scottish pragmatism.

"Indeed they do. Certainly those two are worth their weight in gold."

He didn't want to take his eyes from her, but she turned to watch the approach of the next two racehorses. Smaller, less showy, but extremely muscular, the animals walked along the rail, then were guided back toward the starting post.

"Are they thoroughbreds?" asked Skye. "They're built entirely different from the first two racers."

Kyle pulled out his program and studied it. "No. This is a breed developed in Virginia. I've heard about it, but didn't see much value to it. Called quarter racing horses. The horses race only a quarter mile. Over in a flash. I do believe it's a passing fancy."

Reluctantly, he took his gaze from Skye's shining face and observed the start of the race. Then he watched her once more as she jumped to her feet and cheered the horses with as much excitement as the first race.

A sudden silence fell over the crowd. One racer pounded past—but only one.

Kyle rose to peer down the track and saw the second animal limping along the rail.

"Oh no," Skye cried. "Oh, poor thing. He's injured himself."

"Too bad," said Kyle. "Does happen, though."

He felt her hand grasp his sleeve. Her face was etched with concern. "He's favoring his right front leg. What will happen to him now?" The worry in her eyes when she looked at him stabbed straight to his heart.

"I don't know. Depends on how serious the injury is—and the value of the horse to its owner."

"He must be very valuable to be in a race," she commented.

"I know nothing about these quarter racers or their worth."

The grandstand was emptying as the unchallenged horse jogged to the winner's circle to receive his award in a silent anticlimax to the race.

"Look, Mr. Wyndford. The losing horse is being led away. He looks so sad, so embarrassed. He must know he has failed. He's limping badly." She gazed at Kyle with stricken eyes. "Is there anything we can do?"

"I rather doubt it. The track will have a veterinarian attend his injury. The rest is up to the owner."

"The rest? What are you suggesting?"

He hesitated before answering, but decided to be frank. "The animal's owner will weigh the cost of the horse's recovery against his potential earnings—as a racer, or as a stud. If the cost is too great—"

"What?" she demanded.

He could see he had jumped into deep water. "Well, the owner may decide it's better all around if the horse is destroyed."

As he expected, Skye's mouth dropped and she gaped at him in horror. "But he's beautiful. He did his best. Surely it isn't his fault that he came up lame and couldn't continue the race. I pray, Mr. Wyndford, that we discover his fate. I won't sleep a wink unless we do."

What could he do? He couldn't refuse such a heartfelt request. Realizing he could be getting into a very sticky situation, he said, "We must explain our absence to Miss Kildaire. We'll arrange to meet her at the front entrance after we visit the barn. Hopefully the injury is only a temporary setback and the animal will be back on the track soon."

She looped her hand around his elbow and scooped up her skirts. "I'm much obliged, sir. Much obliged, indeed."

At the last minute, he retrieved her forgotten parasol and tucked it under his arm.

⊰ Chapter 12 ⊱

Skye stood in one corner of the stable, clinging to Mr. Wyndford's arm and watching intently as a veterinarian ran his hands along the horse's right leg. Close by, two well-dressed gentlemen observed the examination, one smoking a pipe, the other appearing distinctly bored as he lounged against a post.

After several minutes, the veterinarian rose and dusted his hands. "Don't think anything's broken, Mr. Deveraux. Got a splint, though, about halfway between the knee and the fetlock joint."

Skye breathed a sigh of relief. So the injury wasn't too serious. She'd had horses with this problem and healed them in a few weeks with proper treatment. Serious cases could require surgery, but that was not usually necessary. She eased her tense grip on Mr. Wyndford's arm and smiled up at him. "We can go now, if you like. The horse will be fine."

He nodded and they were almost out the door when she heard one of the men speak.

"Put the horse down, Mr. Hale. An injection or a bullet. Whichever is quickest and cheapest. Dispose of him in the usual way."

Stunned, Skye whirled around. The man with the pipe was striking out the ashes against his palm and preparing to leave.

Churning inside, she marched over to the gentleman and slammed her fists into her waist. "Pardon me, sir, but surely I didn't hear right. You can't destroy that horse. You can't do it."

The heavyset man poked his pipe in his pocket and placed his top hat on his balding head. "He's *my* horse, madam. I'll do as I please with him."

"But his injury sounds like a minor one. He'll be good as new in a few weeks."

The man's thick eyebrows leaped upward. "Full of it, aren't you, lady? Excuse us, but our carriage is waiting. My day has been disappointing enough without encountering some high-handed female."

Wyndford approached from his place by the door. "You may apologize to the lady, sir. No need for rudeness, though I'm sure you're distraught over the injury to your horse."

The man stared in surprise, then doffed his hat. "Sorry. Now we'll be on our way."

"No! Wait!" Skye pleaded. "I beg you not to destroy your

horse. Look at him. He's beautiful, and fit, and . . ." She knew she was making an awful scene and intruding into other people's business, but she was desperate. "I have a lot of experience with horse injuries. I'm sure your physician is skilled, but a splint injury is rarely fatal. The horse can recover and race again soon."

The man looked at the veterinarian. "Assuming what the lady says is correct, what is the cost, Mr. Hale?"

The veterinarian thought a minute. "He'll have to be boarded nearby. I wouldn't recommend any long journeys with a sore leg. Then, depending on the severity of the injury: medicine, blistering if necessary, my fees, and a stablehand to tend him . . . around three to five hundred dollars, I'm guessing."

The man snorted. "Put the animal down. I have other fine prospects in my stable. Faster runners, younger, with good prospects. Diamond Dust has had his day."

Skye couldn't believe her ears. How could anyone be so cruel as to kill a beautiful creature like this horse, when he could easily be saved? "But sir," she cried, "surely you must have some use for him. He's a stallion, isn't he? He could stand at stud and make far more than a few hundred dollars in fees."

She felt Mr. Wyndford touch her shoulder. No doubt he was embarrassed and upset by her boldness, but she ignored him and continued. "Think about it, sir. Think what fine foals he could produce. He's a blue roan, as pretty as any I've seen. His conformation is . . . is . . ." She turned to look at the animal. "Sturdy, barrel-chested, high-rumped. Bet he can turn on a dime. He doesn't look so old to me."

The man chuckled. "Sounds like we have a female expert here. You have a good eye, little lady. In his prime, Dusty won over ten thousand dollars on Virginia quarter-mile tracks. But he's nine years old, and runs slower in every race. I had hoped he'd win one more big one and then I'd sell him before he broke down completely. As for using him at stud, his bloodlines are not outstanding. Might pair him to the mare down the road for a few bucks, but it would never be enough to justify all this expense." He gave her a long look. "Now, if you'd like to buy him . . . you'd have to pay the horse doctor here, but since you seem set on getting him healed . . ."

Skye gnawed her lip. Then she looked at the horse, who was watching the proceedings with his nose almost to the floor. She knew he was in pain. And no one was doing anything but standing around gabbing while he suffered. "What . . . what price would you ask for him, sir? If I were willing to take him off your hands."

"Miss Mackinnon," Wyndford said gently. "Don't be hasty."

She looked the owner squarely in the eye. "I repeat, sir: what do you want for the horse?"

"Three thousand dollars," he answered sharply.

Her breath caught. No horse could be worth that. Maybe one of the thoroughbreds, but no ordinary horse, and certainly not a horse that was lame. "You can't be serious, Mr. . . ."

"Deveraux. From Richmond. I also own the bay thoroughbred who lost today, so you can see I'm in no mood to bargain. I'm tired, disappointed, and my friend and I are late for a party in town. This quarter horse is of no further use to me."

She covered her mouth to hide her sorrow and dismay. Never in a million years could she justify spending so much on a horse. Every penny her family had was committed toward their new life in Dakota. Including the money she'd received for Strathmor. She turned to look at the horse. His dark, round eyes, set in his steel-gray head, studied her from across the room. The animal had earned so much money for his owner, and now he would be killed without mercy. It was so unfair. But—three thousand dollars. A veritable fortune. She knew tears were filling her eyes, and she would soon make more of a fool of herself than she had already. She was vaguely aware of murmured conversation behind her between Mr. Wyndford and Mr. Deveraux, but her mind was enveloped by the pain in her heart.

"Excuse me, madam."

She faced the greedy, heartless man who would do such a thing.

"I've been thinking this over. What *would* you pay for Diamond Dust?"

She swallowed the knot in her throat. "I couldn't pay more than . . . more than five hundred, sir. I have other obligations, you see."

"Sold. But you'll have to settle up with the track and the doc there."

She couldn't believe her ears. He had reduced the price by such a huge amount, she thought he must be joking. She spun to look at Diamond Dust, wondering if he might have collapsed when she wasn't watching. But there he stood, staring dolefully at her the same as before.

She walked over to Mr. Deveraux. "We have a deal then?"

He laughed at her, then threw a glance at Wyndford. "Quite a feisty one, aren't you, madam?"

"Deveraux—" Wyndford growled.

"Never you mind, sir, I'll apologize again to the lady. But I'll wager every man present would agree with me."

"You needn't apologize," Skye interjected. "Just give me possession of the horse. You will have to accept my note of payment until I go to the bank tomorrow."

Wyndford stepped up. "Miss Mackinnon, allow me to pay off the scoundrel and send him on his way. We'll make arrangements between us after that."

"But I couldn't—"

"Only a loan until tomorrow. I'd prefer we not have further dealings with Mr. Deveraux beyond the next five minutes."

"If you're certain."

"Quite certain." Wyndford pulled a roll of money from his vest and counted out five one-hundred-dollar bills, then handed them to Deveraux. "We would like the animal's papers, sir. His title of ownership and his lineage, if you please."

"The track officials have them. Consider them yours." Deveraux stuffed the money into his pocket and gave Wyndford a surprisingly satisfied smile. "Good day, sir, madam." He replaced his hat, nodded to his companion, and the two strode toward the door.

"By the way," called Wyndford, "it's never good practice to *smoke* in a barn."

Deveraux slammed the door without a backward glance.

Skye was ecstatic. She didn't know who to hug first: Mr. Wyndford, the veterinarian, or Diamond Dust. She decided on Mr. Wyndford. Rushing to him, she moved into his embrace and let his arms settle around her shoulders. No doubt she was spotting his lapel with her tears, but she was weak with relief and thrilled at the outcome of the episode. She was extremely grateful to Mr. Wyndford for his support and encouragement, and she wanted to express herself in the best way she knew how. Hugs were a tradition among friends on Skye, and Mr. Wyndford had proven he was her friend.

Smiling through moist lashes, she moved away and gazed up at him. His tender expression, the feel of his hands encircling her waist tripped her heartbeat and flooded her with startling new sensations. "'Tis a miracle," she whispered.

"Yes, lass. A miracle."

She decided she liked the way he referred to her as lass after all. The word caressed her and sheltered her and made her feel cared for. Collecting herself, she turned to address the veterinarian. "I would like you to make Diamond Dust as comfortable as possible for tonight. Naturally, you'll be paid for your services. I will consult with you in the morning." She looked back at Wyndford. "What time does the bank open tomorrow, Mr. Wyndford?"

"Ten o'clock. But there's no rush—"

"Then I'll be here at eleven o'clock sharp, Mr. Hale. We will discuss the horse's injury, and then I will transfer him elsewhere. I'll have to arrange accommodations close by, as you recommended. Until he's able to travel a longer distance. I assume your examination proved him to be a stallion—intact, that is?" Her voice held no sign of shyness over the question.

"He is a stallion, ma'am."

"Fine. I do intend to breed him eventually."

"Good idea. If his offspring inherit that shade of silver

blue, you'll have fine-looking animals. And with the depth of that chest, he must have a large heart."

She stroked the damp, silvery hide, ruffled the black mane. Of course he had a large heart. She adored him already. But another horse to take to Dakota. What would her father say? The five hundred dollars she must pay tomorrow to reimburse Mr. Wyndford was a great deal of money, even if Mr. Deveraux thought it was a bargain. And there would be further expenses to heal the horse and transport him on the steamship. Still, she felt her father would be pleased with the purchase. With Diamond Dust and the new barb, and the two mares out of Fletcher's famous Indian horse, Spirit Dog, the Mackinnon's foundation herd of quality horses would be established.

The animal lifted its nose and whinnied softly.

"There's a good boy," she said, patting him again. "No harm will come to you now. This gentleman will look after you tonight, and tomorrow you'll meet new friends."

Mr. Hale addressed her. "What if he needs blistering? He might, you know."

"I've done the procedure many times."

He shook his head and smiled. "Such a capable little lady. Forgive me if I'm surprised."

"This little lady is full of surprises," Wyndford commented. "But she looks a bit worn just now. I believe we'll be on our way, if you guarantee us the horse will receive immediate care."

"I assure you he will, sir. I'm delighted you rescued this fine animal from the jaws of the grave."

Skye had to agree with Mr. Wyndford that she was feeling a wee bit tired. The afternoon, the sherry, and the drama of saving and purchasing the horse had taken its toll on her energy. "I'm ready to go, Mr. Wyndford," she said, smiling at him.

He took her elbow and headed toward the door. "Your parasol, Miss Mackinnon."

"Thank you again for your patience," she murmured. He had truly been kind to her, more understanding than she could have imagined.

He leaned near as he escorted her outside. "Miss Kildaire must be growing impatient. What a shame if she's abandoned us."

She laughed gaily, feeling slightly giddy as they strolled through the gathering twilight.

"Miss Mackinnon, would you feel comfortable addressing me as Kyle? Formality is losing fashion in the West. Besides, I feel we're on friendly terms, now that we've weathered this crisis together."

She wasn't sure if such familiarity was proper, but she really didn't care. She already addressed his sister as Missy. Why not do as he suggested? "I will. But only when we're alone. I wouldn't want the Caldwells to think I have no breeding. And you must call me Skye."

He laughed deep in his throat as they headed toward the track entrance.

Kyle and Skye gave their apologies to Shannon, then Kyle assisted the lady into her carriage. The two hurried to their own conveyance as enormous drops of rain began to splatter around them.

"Perfect timing," laughed Kyle as he quickly aided their driver to raise the top, then settled into the seat beside her.

Grinning across at him, Skye brushed raindrops from her skirt and untied the ribbons of her hat. Her upswept coiffure had loosened somewhat, dropping soot-black tendrils to curl around her ears and along the back of her graceful neck. A few drops of moisture dotted her cheeks, a happy change from her tears of the past hour.

Kyle was smitten. He could hardly believe the way his usually well-controlled emotions were running rampant under the onslaught of that trusting smile and those merry, intelligent green eyes. Whatever her earlier reservations about him might have been, he was certain he had won her over, and their relationship would proceed in the most favorable manner. There was no need for her to ever know he had slipped Deveraux the additional twenty-five hundred dollars for her blue roan stallion. In fact, he was certain she would be appalled and resent the indebtedness, considering her independent nature. He regretted she had to pay even five hundred, but if he had tried to pay the entire three thousand, she might have prevented the purchase. He was pleased for Skye to have her quarter racing horse, and his own coffers wouldn't suffer in the least. He had thought Deveraux disgusting and hated to fatten the man's purse, but there had been no time to negotiate with him. No, he was satisfied to have saved Skye from despair, and also to have acquired another common interest, a blue roan named Diamond Dust.

He pulled a small basket from under the seat. "I have a small surprise arranged by Miss Kildaire in her kitchen at Heritage House."

"Oh? A snack? I am truly starving."

He opened the basket and drew out two napkins and offered her one.

"A picnic in a carriage," she effused. "How very elegant."

Next he withdrew two crystal wineglasses and a silver flask. "French champagne," he explained. "We can drink a toast to Diamond Dust."

"How wonderful. I've heard much about it, but never tasted it."

"Then tonight will be special for you, Skye." He savored the sound of her name on his lips. How well it suited the heavenly miss. He thought it carried an insinuation not only of lofty beauty but also of endless possibilities. The fact that she allowed him to use her Christian name was a very positive sign.

Skye nibbled on a small frosted cake. "I'm astonished at the food in Louisiana," she said between bites. "It's a wonder every person isn't the size of a draft horse."

He smiled and lifted his goblet. "To Diamond Dust. May he recover rapidly and be everything a stallion should be."

He relished the way her full lips tilted at the corners, creating one tiny dimple in her right cheek. She was possibly the most seductive woman he'd ever met, but her innocent smile and unassuming manner prevented any thought of ungentlemanly behavior. The honest joy of a child shone from her eyes; her feelings were easily discerned in her open expression. One thing was certain, he would always know where he stood with the young lass. Whether it was favorable or not.

Her eyes held his as she sipped the champagne. "My, this *is* tasty," she said, touching the tip of her tongue to her upper lip.

"The wine merchants of Champagne Province would thrill to your description."

"Tell me more about Dakota, Kyle. I want to learn as much as possible, so I'll know how to plan."

"The settlement at Vermillion sits on a bluff overlooking the Missouri River," he began as the rain pelted on their roof and the carriage slowed. "It once was merely a fur trading post, but now some militia are on hand, and the post caters to a handful of military personal and their wives who live in cottages enclosed by a stockade. Beyond the walls, the Indians set up their tepees during the summer. There's a chapel and a teacher for five or six children. Missy reports there is hope of a minister and his family moving out next year. Not much of a town, Skye, but that will change when more ranchers discover the exceptional grazing land to be had for nothing. Large numbers of buffalo drift across the range, but they're harmless."

"Buffalo! I can't wait to see one!"

He knew Skye's enthusiasm was a solid asset to her endeavors, but in fairness, he wanted her to know what difficulties she faced. "I must honestly warn you that the life is hard. The steamships owned by the fur companies arrive in the spring and ply the river during the summer months. But the winters are long and harsh. Are you certain you want to build your home in Dakota? Many other places would be easier."

For the first time, her eyes became veiled. She twisted her goblet and stared at its contents. "As I said, my grandfather spent time in the American West. My father, too, and he is set on going back. He believes Dakota is the most beautiful place on earth, and he is sure we'll be able to make a success there, now that the country belongs to the United States."

He was satisfied with her response. By warning her of the difficulties, he had eased his conscience and was now ready to make her an offer. "Very well then, I wish to give you and your family my complete support. Although there is housing at the fort, you might find my home more comfortable your first winter. The house is large, and you could use my barn and stables for your livestock. During the coldest months, I could spend time with your father, showing him what must be done to survive and prosper. You and your mother and Missy could pass many a pleasant hour in front of the fire in my parlor. I know Missy would be delighted— and so would I."

Her soft look of pleasure melted his heart. "Perhaps we could," she murmured. "I'm very much obliged for your offer. But naturally, that will be up to my father when we arrive in Dakota."

Kyle mulled over her words. She was so sure her father would appear. He couldn't bring himself to upset her with the disconcerting news from Tangier. What if Fletcher Mackinnon was dead? What if he never came?

⇥ *Chapter 13* ⇤

Skye relaxed as her cheeks took on a warm glow. Considering that Kyle had been her champion during the horse crisis and had provided this wonderfully romantic picnic, she found herself viewing him in a new and more favorable light. His most generous offer of his home in Dakota proved he truly wanted to be helpful, and she was deeply touched by his kindness. But would he still feel the same when he learned her father was a half-breed Lakota? Kyle appeared to be compassionate and reasonable. Surely there was some way to overcome his prejudice toward the Indians. Once he met her father, he would know for certain that not all Indians were bloodthirsty killers, nor all half-breeds untrustworthy souls. Sitting in such close proximity to Kyle, she felt her fascination growing by leaps and bounds.

As she handed him her empty glass, she shivered in the suddenly cool air.

"I should have suggested you bring a wrap," he said softly. "Evening squalls are common this time of year."

"I'm not cold," she said, feeling the warmth in his tone enfold her.

He replaced the glasses and put away the basket. "Lovely little lass," he whispered, cupping her chin and raising her face to his. "I find you completely irresistible."

She knew he was certain to kiss her if she would allow it. She shouldn't, of course. But she wanted him to, a real kiss from a man who attracted her as if he had power over her very soul. They were wrapped in their own private bower, sheltered by the patter of the rain, the moist fragrance, the clip-clop of the horse's hooves on the cobbles. She could just make out Kyle's features in the dimness. Somewhere deep in her mind, she blamed the champagne for her whirling senses, but her emotions had taken control of her thoughts.

His lips brushed her forehead. They were firm and heated.

She waited—but only for a heartbeat. He wrapped one arm around her back and drew her to him, finding her lips, pressing them, teasing them, then abruptly lifting away. She opened her eyes, but his face was a blur in the shadows. She could feel his breathing, his strength, his intensity. Instinctively, her hands moved along his sleeves until they rested on his shoulders. She couldn't stop herself. She was actually embracing this man, here in the afternoon, alone, willing him to kiss her once more.

He obliged her at once. Holding her against him, he forced her lips into submission, parted them with his tongue, and invaded the recesses of her mouth. She was swept into such a tumult of sensation that she was suspended in time, whirled into spiraling delight, charged with a craving deep inside that demanded some indefinable fulfillment.

He released her, and her fingers moved to her lips. Swollen and moist, they tingled from his kiss. She had been kissed, seriously, by someone who was experienced in the art—and she adored it. She would never forget this moment but would cherish it forever.

His voice seemed to come from far away. "You're a wonder, little lass. Thank God I found you."

She felt the power of his presence surrounding her. And she was absolutely positive his thoughts also lingered on the kiss. Nothing would be the same between them again. A few seconds, and her life was changed forever. Whatever else would happen in the future, she had been thoroughly kissed, and had felt the first stirrings of a woman's passion. No wonder her mother wrote books of such poignancy, such heart-wrenching beauty, such glory and tragedy. For that was what love was about. She knew it now, and felt helplessly caught up in the romance of it all. For surely she was in love with James Kyler Wyndford.

Abruptly, the carriage jolted to a halt. Skye was thrown back against the cushion.

Kyle cracked the door and called to the driver. "What happened?"

"Sorry, sir. Someone jumped in front of us. Could've been a runaway slave, by the looks of him."

"He's gone now?"

"Yes, sir. He took off down Royal Street."

Kyle shut the door and covered her hand. "Nothing to worry about." The coach lurched forward.

"Slavery is so very evil. Don't you agree?" Skye idly spoke her thoughts.

She was surprised when Kyle didn't respond at once. She stared at him in the watery light. The romantic mist of a moment ago slipped away. "You *do* agree, don't you, that slavery should be outlawed?"

He cleared his throat. "My opinion hardly counts. I don't own slaves, but then I don't own a cotton plantation, either."

She felt her heart stop. She had hoped to surmount his negative attitude toward Indians, but now he seemed to be defending the horrible institution of slavery. "Are you saying that if you grew cotton, you would own slaves?"

"I'd rather not discuss it."

"Please, Mr. Wyndford, please answer me. I must know where you stand on the issue of slavery."

She felt her throat go dry as she studied his face. His prejudice toward the Indians, as dreadful as it was, was one thing she could understand, considering his brother's murder. But if he approved of slavery, of buying and selling human beings, all was lost. She could never have affection for such a man.

"I'm not especially taken with the idea," he said defensively. "But I stay out of matters that are none of my business. I'm an Englishman who came to America to make my fortune. The laws of this land allow slavery. I'm in no position to sit in judgment on the founders of this nation or the people who govern it."

She was appalled at his weak excuse for avoiding a stance. "I'm sorry, sir, but I don't see how you can hold such a view. Laws can be changed. Slavery has long been abolished in the British Isles. I would think you would feel strongly that it is an abhorrent practice."

"Skye . . . don't press me on this. I do have an opinion, but I wish to keep my opinions to myself."

"I would prefer you address me as *Miss Mackinnon,*" she said tightly. " 'Tis plain I've allowed far too many liberties. I don't know you nearly as well as I thought."

"As you wish." His tone was as stiff as her own.

She was so disappointed she wanted to cry, but she was too angry for tears. How could she have so completely misjudged the man? She had been given warning signs weeks ago by his own sister, but she had ignored them, not wanting to believe anyone so handsome and charming could have such a dark side, a *cowardly* side to his nature. Her first instincts about the man had been right after all. And she had fallen under his spell, become indebted to him, and even allowed him to kiss her. What should have been a beautiful memory now caused her cheeks to burn with embarrassment, her mind to rage with regret. Well, she couldn't undo the past, but she could control the future. Staring through the oval window at the rain-shrouded night, she made every effort to pretend Kyle Wyndford was invisible.

When the coach halted in front of Dominique Hall, she turned and fixed her eyes on his chin. "I'm appreciative, Mr. Wyndford, for a most entertaining afternoon. And naturally, for your help with Diamond Dust."

"My pleasure entirely."

"I believe we have an appointment tomorrow. Would you prefer to meet at your bank or at the track?"

"Whichever is most convenient for you. I would be happy to help with the horse—"

"That won't be necessary, thank you. I'll arrange with the Caldwells' stablehand to do whatever is required. If I need a conveyance to move the horse, I'm sure Mr. Caldwell will make one available."

His silence told her she had made her point. The pain she was feeling would soon go away, she was sure. It was better if Kyle Wyndford understood clearly that he was no longer held in her esteem.

Finally he said, "Mr. Caldwell will be completely accommodating, as always."

She glanced around. "I'm sure Miss Kildaire is waiting behind us until I'm safely inside. Please excuse me now."

Without responding, Kyle exited the carriage and hurried to open her door. She avoided his eyes when he took her hand and escorted her quickly to the shelter of the veranda.

Immediately the butler opened the door, and Kyle bowed himself away with a brief murmured farewell. The second coach, with a waving Shannon Kildaire peeking from inside, moved down the drive.

Skye set her lips against the misery spreading through her, hurried to her room, and tore off her hat and gloves. She had learned a good lesson today, she told herself hotly. She would get over Mr. Wyndford, forget he existed. Unfortunately, that might prove difficult in Dakota, where he would be the only person of her acquaintance within hundreds of miles.

Kyle ordered the coach to take him directly to the waterfront. One way he might take his mind off Skye Mackinnon's dismissal was to indulge in an all-night game of poker aboard the floating gambling palace, The Mississippi Star. Within the hour, he was settled in the smoke-filled salon, a double bourbon at his elbow and an expensive cheroot crooked between his fingers.

He stared at the cards, a possible winning hand, and his mind drifted to the sight of Skye's sweet, upturned face, her parted lips inviting his kiss. She had enjoyed it thoroughly—both his first tentative exploration and then the second kiss that had set his own passions soaring. She was a woman with latent desire just waiting to be stoked into a raging fire. Like a rosebud under the power of a summer sun, she was on the verge of bursting into full bloom. Tonight he had wanted nothing more than to possess her loveliness, her dewy freshness, her awakening passion. But instead, he had awakened only her Scottish ire, laid himself bare to her scorn.

He couldn't blame her for responding as she did to his weak excuse for accepting the existence of slavery. He would have felt exactly the same way about a person who would condone such a travesty. But he had given his solemn oath to Caldwell to never disparage slavery to anyone. In fact, Caldwell had exacted a promise from him to uphold slavery whenever possible. He had longed to reveal his true feelings to Skye, but an oath was an oath. If he told Skye how he felt about slavery, she might innocently repeat his words to Caldwell, thereby costing him Caldwell's trust. He knew his own risk was the least, involving only money. If the planters threatened him, he would merely escape to his remote ranch in Dakota. But Caldwell could be ruined, if not imprisoned, and Sinclair would be hung from the tallest tree. Even to win Skye's affection, he wouldn't dare take such a gamble with other men's lives. Once they were in Dakota, he might safely explain his views to the lass.

"I'll hold. And raise two hundred, sir."

What would he do about the lady? he asked himself. Under their present circumstances, Skye was finished with him. But still, he could be a great help to her. There was the chance Fletcher Mackinnon would never appear; Skye and her mother could settle permanently in New Orleans, have a comfortable life here. No doubt that was the wise choice. But if Mackinnon did arrive with his stallion, the laird would take charge of his family and make whatever decisions had to be made. Now that Kyle considered the matter, he wasn't nearly as valuable to the Mackinnons as he'd thought or wished or hoped. His vanity had swelled his sense of self-importance beyond reality. But damn it, he was attracted to Skye beyond all reason. Could he forget her and get on with his life? He might have no choice. What irony that he should lose her for a reason that was false and be forced to silently approve her decision to reject him. He was trapped in a lie, an important lie with lives at stake. For now, there wasn't a thing he could do about it. He couldn't even try to change the lady's mind.

"You lose, Mr. Wyndford. Sorry."

He shoved the money across the table toward his opponent, gave the man a sardonic smile, then tossed down a hefty swallow of straight bourbon.

⇥ Chapter 14 ⇤

Easy, boy, easy. You're so much improved, Dusty, I'll soon have a saddle on you."

Skye ran her hand along Diamond Dust's lower leg, which was devoid of hair in one spot where she'd used the blistering compound a week ago.

"We won't have to apply any more ointment. Aren't you glad, boy?" Rising, she stroked the velvet muzzle, then patted the stallion solidly on its broad shoulder. The horse shook his head and sniffed, as if agreeing that the worst was over.

Skye untied the lead rope from the post and led Dusty out of the stable into the bright June morning. Jogging around the paddock with the horse beside her, she reminded herself how fortunate she was to be here at Dominique Hall, how nice everyone had been to her and to her mother, and how lucky she was to have Diamond Dust almost fit to ride.

But her heart was heavy. She hadn't been able to shake off the depression that had taken hold of her since her disappointment over Kyle. In the company of Blaine Caldwell and the stable manager, she had met Kyle at the bank the next morning. She had carefully counted five one-hundred-dollar bills into his palm, thanked him for the loan, and hurried outside before anything other than polite conversation could take place. She had refused to look him directly in the eye, fearing that the memory of his kisses would be reflected there. Her own eyes had been bleak after a restless night with little sleep. She had done her best to hide the dark circles with rice powder, but she succeeded only in appearing more wan than before.

On the positive side, she had found Diamond Dust much more comfortable than she'd last seen him, and he was docile and patient when she and the stable manager had inspected his wound. She had paid the balance of what she owed and taken the horse to Dominique Hall. That very afternoon, she had blistered the wound, closely watching the resulting hair loss and swelling, then made the horse comfortable in the airy and spotless stall provided by Mr. Caldwell.

During the following week, Skye had continued her chats with Melissa Wyndford. She had never known a more likable or courageous woman. During her last visit to Missy's suite, the two had spent an hour pouring over maps of the Dakota area and discussing foodstuffs, clothing, basic furnishing, dozens of items that Skye must acquire before she could make her home at a wilderness outpost. Since Missy never echoed Mr. Wyndford's offer of their home, Skye assumed the subject had not been discussed between them. In fact, Skye carefully avoided any mention of Kyle, except of the most perfunctory kind. Not once had Skye seen or heard from Kyle Wyndford. She was quite sure he had no further interest in her, other than as a passing acquaintance.

"Skye! Skye, you have a message."

Skye looked up to see her mother walking down the path

toward the paddock. Halting Dusty, she flipped the rope over a railing.

"Mother, 'tis good to see you out." She ducked under the rail and hurried to embrace her.

"I do apologize, sweetheart, for closeting myself in my room for so long. But my novel is nearly complete. I hope to mail the manuscript to London before we leave for Dakota."

Looking at her mother, Skye thought again how different they were. It wasn't just that she was three inches taller and brunette while Elizabeth was golden blond, but she was consumed with energy, driven by a restless spirit, while her mother exuded a serenity that was unflappable whatever the circumstances. Of course, Skye knew that a youthful Elizabeth had once used her writing in a dangerous effort to challenge the power of the English throne and the decadent court of George IV. Perhaps her mother's inner strength came from the consuming love she had for her husband, returned by him with passion and loyalty throughout all the years of their marriage.

"This message just arrived, Skye darling. I believe it's from Melissa Wyndford."

"I hope she's all right," Skye said, glancing at the folded paper. "Let's sit on the bench in the shade, Mother. I need to discuss several pressing matters with you."

The two settled under the branches of an ancient cottonwood and Skye opened the note. "Mrs. Wyndford has asked me to come see her—this afternoon at two o'clock. I wonder if she has a report from her doctor."

"I pray the news is good, though I'm not optimistic," murmured Elizabeth. "She must want a private conversation, since neither I nor Rebecca Caldwell received an invitation."

"I assume 'tis important. We completed our work yesterday on my lists of supplies for the trip. Unless she thought of something necessary to add to it."

"I'll be waiting until your return, praying for good news."

Skye gazed through the humid sunshine at Diamond Dust, who was standing quietly inside the paddock. Maybe this was as good a time as any to broach the subject that was causing her increasing concern. "Mother, we've not had any word from Papa. I'm worried about him and about our journey."

Elizabeth smiled and patted Skye's knee. "He's fine, I'm sure. I expect him any day now."

"No doubt you're right, but . . . but . . ."

"What is it, Skye? Surely you don't think something has gone wrong."

"I'm guessing he's been delayed, that's all." She hoped her voice didn't betray her growing uneasiness. "He gave me strict instructions about what to do in that event."

Her mother looked surprised. "Oh? What did he suggest you do?"

"He did not *suggest*. He *insisted* we proceed to Dakota if he didn't appear in New Orleans within two months. He said we *must* be there with the mares by midsummer or we risked both Legacy's foal and the chance of not being situated before winter. Winter comes early in Dakota, he told me, and it is dreadfully harsh."

Elizabeth gave her a stiff look. "I understand, dear, but I will not go without him. I won't even think of it."

"But, Mother, we can't stay in New Orleans an entire year. We must go within two weeks, or we might not have another chance until next spring. Papa didn't intend for us to wait here indefinitely. He was very clear about that."

"You mean he thought we should go to Dakota and make a home there without his guidance?" Her tone carried shock and denial.

"No. He will come, I'm sure of it. But he anticipated possible delays. Anything could cause that—trouble finding a suitable stud, finding passage to New Orleans, bad weather at sea—any number of unexpected complications. He made me promise to go upriver no later than June fifteenth. Only ten days from now. I must make the final arrangements for us and our supplies and the livestock. *Three* horses, now, and MacLard."

Elizabeth appeared barely ruffled as she said, "I won't budge from New Orleans until Fletcher Mackinnon arrives. That is final, Skye Eugenia. If he is annoyed that we disobeyed his instructions, I will take full responsibility. If the delay is lengthy, we'll just have to make other living arrangements for the winter. I wouldn't think of imposing on the Caldwells for such a long time. But, my dear child, I will *not* go north without your father."

Breathing a sigh, Skye nodded reluctantly. "I can see you have made up your mind, but this puts me in a difficult position. I have never broken a promise to Papa. I don't know how I shall deal with that."

Elizabeth stood and gave her a benign smile. "We'll talk about it later. But be assured, I am immovable on the subject."

Skye watched her mother walk briskly back to the house. This was a problem she hadn't considered or hadn't wanted to think about: the possibility that her father might not come at all and that her mother would refuse to go without him. What if something dreadful had happened to him in Tangier? She hadn't liked the look of those men who took him aboard their ship. As strong and gallant as he was, he couldn't fight an entire shipload of brigands. She walked slowly back to a waiting Diamond Dust. *I must take one day at a time,* she told herself. *One day at a time, and hope for the best.*

Skye knew the minute she walked into the room that Melissa's news was not good. She laid aside her parasol, pulled off her gloves, and drew up a chair as close as possible to her friend.

"Thank you for coming," Melissa began. Her voice was hoarse and she appeared weaker than Skye had ever seen her.

"Dear Missy, what has happened? Yesterday you looked so well."

Melissa reached for her hand. "I'm just having a bad day. Tomorrow I'll be much improved." She attempted a smile.

Skye was moved by the lady's courage, but she felt a lump in her throat when she studied the thin face. Melissa was only in her late thirties, but she could be twenty years older, the way she looked today. Skye remembered Laurel's warning about life in the wilderness. Would she herself look like this in a few years? Or was it some terrible illness that ravaged Missy's body? "I'm sure you'll be fine, Missy," she murmured through tight lips.

Melissa looked into her eyes, absorbing them, scrutinizing her as if she weighed some serious decision. "I must share a secret with you, dear Skye. Are you able to keep secrets?"

She clasped Missy's delicate hand in both of hers. "I'm very good at it indeed, Missy. I give you my solemn promise." She forced her lips into a curve of reassurance.

"I managed to speak privately with my doctor yesterday. I begged him for the truth, because I must make plans—"

"Oh, no. Don't talk like that. You'll be well—"

"Shh," Melissa said with a sad smile. "My time is short, Skye. For everyone else, especially Kyle, I must keep up a brave front, hide the truth. But I've known for some time I was seriously ill. The doctor has confirmed it."

Skye couldn't speak. Her throat contracted and she blinked hard to keep tears from spilling into her eyes. "I'm so very sorry, Missy." Leaning forward, she put her arms tenderly around the lady's shoulders and held her for a minute or two. When she moved away, her lashes were wet and she was forced to sniff and touch her cheeks with the back of her hand. She saw tears welling in Missy's eyes despite her attempt to control them.

"Thank you for caring, dear. I wanted us to have this time together because from now on, we will pretend all is well. I have new medicine, and the doctor is willing to release me to go home."

"Home? To Dakota? Are you able to make the trip?"

"I have to try. I want more than anything to die in my own home. And I must see my son before I leave this earth." Her chin trembled as she struggled to control her emotions. "He's only nine, you know. Such a darling boy, and so full of joy, a zest for life. Into mischief much of the time, but Kyle has spoiled him. And so has Reyes, our ranch foreman. When I'm gone, Badger will be without parents to guide him. The burden will fall on Kyle, and he has already taken on many burdens for me."

"Your brother told me about his nephew," Skye said

quickly. "He obviously adores him. I'm sure you'll have no concerns from that quarter."

"He will do his best, of course. But running a huge ranch is a consuming life. Kyle hasn't had time to marry or start a family of his own. I had hoped . . ." Her voice trailed and she reached for a handkerchief.

Skye was sick at heart. She herself loved life so much, she couldn't imagine how anyone could face dying, giving up all the glories of life, and especially saying good-bye forever to one's child. But Melissa Wyndford had no choice. "What can I do, Missy?" she whispered. "How can I help you?"

Melissa dabbed her eyes and gazed at her. "You told me yesterday that you and your mother plan to go right away to Dakota, even if your father hasn't appeared. We must leave, too, as soon as Kyle can make arrangements. Would it be possible for us to travel together? On the same boat, at any rate? I don't want to hire a nurse who would only be a nuisance most of the time. But occasionally, I need a bit of help, things only a woman understands. The journey to St. Louis usually takes a week. With my new medicine, I should be strong enough to manage without any problem. Then we'll take a Missouri steamer to Vermillion. If I must stay abed most of the time, that is quite all right. But . . . if I knew you were near, I would feel so much better."

Skye couldn't think of refusing. Not if there was any way possible to grant the dear lady's wish. "Of course I would be happy—honored—to travel with you. But in all honesty, Missy, my mother is refusing to go until my father is safely here. We had a discussion about it this very morning."

Melissa mused several seconds, then said. "Very well. My illness may be a blessing in disguise. If your father hasn't arrived by the time we're ready, your mother could stay in New Orleans. With her permission, and if you're agreeable, you can travel with me as my companion. You'll have our protection, and I will certainly pay your passage as well as provide additional funds for your pocketbook."

"I couldn't think of accepting pay, Missy. No, I won't hear of it."

"Then you *will* consider going? You could stay at Wind

River until your parents come out. You can look over the country and think about obtaining land. Communications between Dakota and New Orleans are time-consuming, but letters do get through. If Elizabeth was unable to come to Dakota before winter, she could let you know, then you could decide whether to stay or return here to be with her. At least you would have seen the area and would be able to make a decision."

Skye saw the sense of the plan. She would have an opportunity to see firsthand the country where they planned to start a new life. Perhaps her father's memories had grown rosier with the passing of the years. Maybe Dakota wouldn't do at all for what they had in mind. Despite the fact he had grown up there and that he might have a desire to go home to his Lakota people, the northern wilderness might be too harsh for them to successfully establish their ranch. Kyle had mentioned Texas. Aye, it might be a very good idea for her to scout the area before they made a final decision.

"I'll do it, Missy. Assuming my mother and Mr. Wyndford approve of our arrangement."

"Kyle won't object, I'm positive of that."

Skye stared at her hands folded in her lap. She wasn't positive, at all. Not after what had happened between them, not after she had cut him cold and he had accepted her rebuff without protest. She mulled over the situation, then made a daring decision.

"Missy, you spoke of keeping secrets. I give you my word, yours is safe with me. Now I must share mine with you. I wouldn't feel right if I didn't. It really isn't a secret, but something that you and Mr. Wyndford might not know."

"What is that, Skye, darling?"

"My father chose to move to Dakota because he was born there. He grew up there, lived in Dakota until he was eighteen. You see, his mother was a member of the Lakota Sioux Indian tribe. A princess, in fact. His father, Finlay Mackinnon, married her in an Indian ceremony when he was a fur trapper in the early days. When she died in childbirth, he left his son to be raised by the Lakotas."

Melissa's eyes grew wide. "An Indian? Your father is a Sioux Indian?"

"A half-blood. Or half-breed, I've heard it called. But when my grandfather Mackinnon went home to the Isle of Skye, he didn't marry again or have children, so he decided to return to America to find his son. By that time, my father, who was called White Arrow, had become a renegade because of his mixed blood. He had no real home, even though he received some education at an English fort."

"My goodness. What a story."

"I won't go into all the details, but my mother plans to write a book about it someday. When White Arrow became Fletcher Mackinnon, he was educated in Edinburgh, then fell in love with my mother. They married and he became the new chieftain and laird of Mackinnon." She paused to let all this sink in. The main point was yet to come. "So you see, Missy, *I* am one quarter Lakota Sioux. Part Indian. And I am very proud to be so."

Missy smiled softly. "Of course you are. You should be."

"Then—you don't hate me because of what happened to your husband?"

"That wasn't your fault, my dear. Not in the least."

Skye grasped Missy's hand. "I'm so glad. You see, Laurel was worried about my mixed blood. She suggested I not reveal it to just anyone I might meet in New Orleans."

"I understand her concern. There has been much hatred and conflict here between the whites and the native people. I fear it will only worsen unless both sides try very hard to increase their understanding of each other. Why, three years ago, most of the Indians from the southern part of the United States were forced to give up their lands and their homes, the places they have lived for generations, and move to a place called Indian Territory."

"How terrible. I had no idea—"

"Skye, dear." Melissa fixed her attention on Skye's face. "I believe we should follow Laurel's advice on this matter for now. Once your father arrives, he will know how to deal with it. But I must warn you that Indians are hated by many whites out West. Hated and feared. So far, there hasn't been much bloodshed in Dakota because there are so few white settlers. But I feel in my bones that it will come. You are the best of both worlds. Maybe you will find a way to help bring about understanding between the two races."

"I would like to help, but I don't fancy myself a crusader. I just want to establish a home for my family, for now and for future generations."

"Don't worry about it, child. But remember my words. The day may come when you will have a chance to make a difference."

"What about Mr. Wyndford?" Skye dared ask. "I'm afraid he despises Indians. After what they did to his brother."

Melissa sank back in her chair. "It's sad, I admit, that he carries such anger in his heart. Sometimes I think his pain has eased, but he won't discuss it with me. He's bitter because he has never been able to bring the killers to justice."

Skye considered Kyle's emotional dilemma. How could she condemn him when she herself had never experienced anything like his tragic loss? She would need time to consider the matter before she formed a final opinion of his character. "We agree, then: 'tis best not to reveal my heritage to Kyle or anyone else. Not just now. As you said, when my father arrives, he can handle the situation. Besides, if Kyle finds out about my Indian blood, he might object to my traveling as your companion—and I would like very much to go with you to Dakota."

≈ *Chapter 15* ≈

Loup Leveque stood by the rail of the *Western Queen* watching the crew toss thick ropes to waiting hands on the dock. No fanfare had greeted the boat's arrival in St. Louis. These small Missouri steamers docked at weekly intervals during the summer months and carried nothing of particular interest to the citizens of the town. Just stacks of buffalo hides, a few crates of fur and Indian trade goods, and a dozen or so tired, dirty, and unimportant travelers from the upper reaches of the Missouri.

In the growing dusk, Leveque studied the first sizable community he'd seen since leaving Quebec. Beyond the docks and warehouses, lights were flickering on in cottages where the hill rose above the wide bend of the river. He would sleep on the ground tonight, then go to the fairgrounds tomorrow. He had two matters to deal with before he could relax and wait for his prey to fall into his trap. First, he must learn the arrival schedule of all steamboats coming upriver from New Orleans. Next, he must acquire a horse. Not just any horse, but a carefully chosen animal that was young, and strong, and capable of running until its heart burst within it. If he had not needed to be so particular, he could easily steal a mount. But he couldn't risk making his escape on a beast that might not have the courage and stamina to carry him swiftly to safety, back to the land of his father's people, the Teton Lakota Sioux. This meant he would have to pay for the horse with the white man's coins. And despite winning the pouches of the men on the boat, he had not yet acquired enough for the purchase.

The passengers were leaving the boat, making their way down the lowered gangplank. Leveque picked up his saddle and hoisted it over his shoulder. Waiting to disembark, he spotted the boatman who had taken his fare a week ago. The man was not young, he noticed, and was limping as he approached from across the deck.

"Here, mister, I took this rope off your dead horse," the boatman said. "Saw it was finely braided, probably of value. It's yours, I reckon."

Loup took the coiled rope and put it around his shoulder. *"Merci,"* he muttered. "I heard the shot."

"Hated doing it, but better that then letting the horse be torn apart by a wolfpack."

"You live in St. Louis?" asked Loup.

"All my life. Got a wife here, grown daughter and grandson. Anxious to see 'em as soon as I'm relieved of duty."

"Where is the horse fair usually held?" Loup asked, as the seed of an idea began to take root.

"Downriver, 'bout half a mile. Barns, stockyards, big arena there. Fair and auction held once a month in summer. That where you headed?"

"Oui." Loup put his plan into action. "Want to gamble tonight? You didn't join us during the trip."

"Cap'n don't like for the crew to gamble. Besides, got nothing to gamble with till we get paid."

"You get paid tonight? We could deal a few hands afterward."

"Yes, but I can't afford to gamble, Mr. Leveque. Not when I got a family to look after. Son-in-law got killed upriver last summer. Drowned in the rapids. It's up to me now to provide."

"Too bad," mumbled Loup, thinking how quickly the fish had taken the bait. Without further conversation, he left the man on the deck and walked down to the dock. A few gaslights had been lit along the main unloading area. Half a dozen men were taking boxes from the boat.

Loup drifted toward a wooden building and moved into the shadows behind one corner. He shoved his saddle under a bench and settled in a spot where he could see the boat without being seen.

Patiently, he waited for over an hour. At last, he saw the crew walk down the plank and head for the nearest building by the dock. He eased out of his hiding place and hurried silently toward the office where the men had gone after leaving the boat. He heard laughter and muffled voices as he leaned his back against the wall, then peeked inside the lighted room. The old boatman was there, in line with the others. The man wasn't laughing, though, but stood quietly, fatigue etched in his heavily lined face beneath his knit cap.

Loup moved away and stood behind a post supporting the overhanging roof. When the boatman came out, Loup watched him walk along the riverfront, then turn down the street at the end of the pier.

Stealthily, Loup padded behind him, being careful to avoid the lamplight. Walking thus, he kept the man in sight as he crossed a broad, stone-paved street, made his way across the grounds of the imposing cathedral, and then limped his way down an alley and made a sharp right turn into a twisting street between rows of clapboard shanties.

Loup slipped his black cane from his belt, twisted the top, and pulled a foot-long dagger from inside it. Soundlessly, he moved closer to the boatman.

"Grampa! Grampa! You're here!" came a child's happy greeting.

Loup halted and ducked into the shadows. From the opposite end of the street, a young boy was running full tilt, his arms outstretched, rushing to fling himself into the boatman's welcoming embrace.

The old man scooped up the child, hugged him, then set him back on his feet. He began fishing in the pocket of his coat. "Got a present for you, Teddy. Lookee here."

Loup saw his chance.

He dashed forward and grabbed the boy around his small chest, then stepped back and pointed the dagger at the child's heart.

"My God!" shouted the boatman. "No! Let him go! What the hell do you want?"

"Your purse," said Loup calmly, tightening his grip around the squirming youngster. "Your purse or your grandson! You choose, *monsieur.*"

Immediately, the old man jerked a pouch from his coat and held it out. His hands were shaking so hard that he dropped it to the street.

"Is all your pay in that?" growled Loup.

"Have pity, Leveque. I worked two months for my money. I must have it or my family will starve. My purse there has coins, even the coin you gave me for shooting your horse. Take it. But please let my boy go. Leave us some money for food. I beg you."

The old man stumbled forward, his hands reaching for the child.

So swift it was invisible, Loup's dagger left the boy and

pierced the boatman's chest. It slid through the cloth jacket and the flesh beneath, penetrating the heart, then was as swiftly withdrawn.

Loup curled his lip in pleasure, the pleasure he always had when he killed a white man. He gazed at the boatman's gaping eyes. The man was dead and didn't know it, he thought.

Nor did the boy know what had happened. Loup waited for the boatman to crumple, then squatted over the body. Quickly, he found the envelope bulging with two months' salary from the American Fur Company Steamboat Line, enough to buy several good horses if he needed them.

The child began to kick and gasp for breath.

Loup put down his dagger and reached for the skinning knife he kept in his boot. "Be still. I won't hurt you," he soothed, placing the boy on his feet. Instantly, he grasped a handful of the child's hair and jerked back his head. Before he could draw the knife blade across the pale, narrow throat, a woman's scream ripped the air. She was bearing down on him, only yards away, and she carried a pistol.

Releasing the boy, he picked up the dagger and ran down the street, heading for the darkness and squalor of the waterfront shacks he'd seen earlier. He knew without doubt the woman would first stop to see about her child, then she would discover the old man's body and take time to see if she could help him. By then, Loup would be well away and safe.

He slowed to a trot and slid the slender dagger back into the cane. The rich white Englishman who had once owned it should be proud that the instrument had been used with such skill, he thought wryly. Then he stuffed the purse and the envelope into his pocket.

Turning toward the dock, he strode toward the place where he'd hidden his saddle. *I'm a rich man,* he thought with satisfaction. *I won't sleep on the ground after all. I'll visit a brothel, buy a bottle of good whiskey, and take a room in a hotel. I'll enjoy myself in St. Louis while I await the arrival of Kyler Wyndford. And then, my vision of the white man's death will be fulfilled.*

⚞ Chapter 16 ⚟

Kyle leaned near Melissa's ear. "Are you comfortable, Missy? Can I get you anything? We'll be leaving soon."

"I'm comfy as can be," she answered, her eyes bright and her cheeks showing the first pink Kyle had seen in weeks. Maybe the doctor was right. With her new medicine beginning to take effect, all she needed now was to go home, recuperate in the surroundings she loved, and spend time with her rascally son.

He looked up to see Skye Mackinnon coming in through the open cabin door of the steamship. His heart skipped at the sight of her freshness and grace—as it was prone to do whenever she appeared unexpectedly.

Kyle had spent the past ten days preparing for the journey. All the items he had purchased had to be boxed and taken to the warehouse to await loading. He had secured the most spacious cabin available for Missy and an adjoining room for Skye. His feelings about Skye Mackinnon's joining them fluctuated between satisfaction that she was going with them to Dakota and concern over the strain that had developed between them. Missy did need a companion, and Skye would be ideal, he had to agree. And the thought of her proximity on the voyage gave him pleasure that he couldn't deny. But her coolness toward him was hard to accept. Keeping their distance during the next few weeks, when they were bound to be thrown together, could prove difficult, if not downright painful. She had refused any further assistance from him as she made her own preparations. He knew, of course, that Blaine Caldwell had made himself available to help the girl, making sure she had all she needed and that her animals were safely on board, settled in stalls next to Raven Duke in the cargo deck. Once they reached the Missouri, the horses would have to be transferred to a freighter for the final leg of their journey.

MacLard bounded into the cabin and barked vigorously before rushing to every corner of the room to sniff out unwanted intruders.

"Behave yourself, MacLard," Skye said, watching the thrashing tail with a look of resigned affection. "I hope he won't be a nuisance." She smiled at Melissa, but she didn't glance in Kyle's direction.

"He's adorable," responded Melissa, returning the smile. "I hope he spends as much time in my room as you'll allow."

As if he understood, MacLard ended his guard-dog duties and scampered to the seated lady and leaped uninvited into her lap. Melissa laughed gaily and hugged him to her.

Kyle cleared his throat. "Excuse me, Miss Mackinnon— is there anything I can do for you before we depart? We'll be leaving very soon."

"No, thank you," she said coolly. She looked again at Melissa. "You have visitors, Missy. My mother and the Caldwells would like to say their farewells."

"By all means. Have them come in."

Skye stepped outside the door and crooked her finger. Immediately, Laurel rushed inside and leaned over to peck Melissa's cheek. "Take care of yourself, Missy. And our Skye, too." Rebecca Caldwell and Elizabeth Mackinnon entered the cabin, followed by Blaine Caldwell, smiling and dapper as always and holding his top hat in his hand.

The little room was suddenly crowded to overflowing. The ladies were chattering, doing their best to conceal whatever their private concerns might be over this leave-taking. Kyle didn't want to eavesdrop on private conversations, but he was trapped in his corner. He heard Skye speaking to her mother.

"If I don't have word from you and Papa by the first week in September, I will start back to New Orleans, no matter what."

"Yes, Skye darling. I suppose that's the best plan, just in case . . ."

"Papa's fine, I'm sure," Skye said reassuringly, "but I won't take any chances on your being alone in New Orleans this winter. Nor my being detained in Dakota. I'll just make certain that Missy is safe and comfortable; I'll scout the countryside for a few weeks, and make sure Legacy foals safely—then I'm returning, unless we've received word you're on your way."

"Yes, lass. I understand."

Elizabeth Mackinnon turned to Kyle and held out both hands. "God go with you, Mr. Wyndford. I'm sure we'll meet again soon."

He took her hands in his. "We will, indeed, Mrs. Mackinnon. And you may rest assured your daughter will be well looked after. You must know how much Melissa and I appreciate what she's doing for us."

Elizabeth smiled at Skye, who was gazing at her with a trace of tears. "I know how impatient she's been to make this journey. I believe this is a very satisfactory arrangement for us all." Turning back to him, she added, "My husband will be pleased as well, I'm quite sure. We'll take the first steamboat available after he arrives in New Orleans."

Her optimism touched his heart. He prayed Fletcher Mackinnon would soon be reunited with his gracious and talented wife.

The sudden bellow from the steamboat's whistle warned that it was time for all guests to leave.

With MacLard's excited barks as accompaniment, Mr. and Mrs. Caldwell and Elizabeth Mackinnon exchanged hugs and kisses with Missy and Skye and left the cabin. Only Laurel remained.

The ship's whistle sounded three warning blasts.

"I must go," whispered Laurel, quickly squeezing everyone's hand in turn. "Bon voyage, my dears. Until we meet again." She whirled from the cabin, her emotions plainly out of control.

Kyle saw Melissa reach for her handkerchief. He couldn't

prevent the ache that gripped him at the sight of her effort to conceal her feelings. Thank God she would soon be well. He loved her as if she were his own flesh and blood.

Another long, throaty whistle filled the air.

"We're leaving!" Skye cried at no one in particular. She patted MacLard to calm his latest round of barking.

"Shall we go outside, ladies?" suggested Kyle. "We can watch New Orleans disappear before our very eyes."

"Aye," said Skye breathlessly, looking directly at him for the first time. "I would like to see the shoreline."

He rewarded her with a sincere smile, then turned to Missy. "Up you go, my love. You don't want to miss this." Lifting her frail body, he crossed to the door and went out on deck where she would have a good view from the security of his arms. In moments, with MacLard scampering at her feet, Skye arrived at Kyle's side. Although she didn't look at him again, he felt one small stone of the wall she had erected between them slip away. Someday, sometime, somehow, he would regain her trust, if not her affection. This small beginning surely held promise for the future.

After the first few minutes when her good-byes still tugged at her heart, Skye was as elated and thrilled as she'd ever been in her life. At last she was on her way west, traveling on the most beautiful boat she'd ever imagined, on a day made in heaven, and in the company of a sweet and courageous woman whom she had come to love dearly. She would not let her concerns over Kyle Wyndford spoil her adventure.

With her elbows on the railing, she watched the city of New Orleans fade around the bend. The Mississippi River stretched a glittering silver welcome, a broad path to her future—hers and her family's. Watching the passing shoreline, lush green and dotted with private docks, small settlements, and the occasional mansion looking down from a knoll above the river, she was overwhelmed with joy and anticipation. She was barely aware when Kyle excused himself to take Melissa back to her cabin.

She arranged the brim of her hat and placed a hand over her skirt as it billowed in the sweet Southern breeze. She was happy to be wearing her own clothes again, and especially happy to be rid of the horrible corsets she'd endured the past two months. Not that she didn't appreciate Laurel's wonderful generosity in loaning her so many items from her own wardrobe, but she felt much more at home in her simple Scottish cottons and plaids. She had been warned by Laurel that she must dress for dinner on the *Mississippi Belle,* and she was prepared to do that when required. She had purchased several simple frocks from Laurel's dressmaker, disappointing the talented seamstress by insisting on a dearth of laces and frills. She had two gingham dresses for warm days, two light wool dresses for cooler climes, and one warm wool dress that would do for winter if she stayed in Dakota.

Staring absently at the drifting clouds in a turquoise sky, she let her thoughts dwell on Kyle. How good he was to Missy. How gentle, how caring. Today he had looked so incredibly handsome in his immaculately tailored chocolate-brown suit and wide-brimmed hat, she had found herself giving him sidelong glances like a schoolgirl with a crush on her teacher. Luckily, he never saw them. And when he carried Missy to the rail to view their departure, she had felt an undeniable tug at her heart. How terrible that Missy would never see New Orleans again. But *Kyle* didn't know that. She shook her head sadly. How could someone so intelligent and so thoughtful support the dreadful institution of slavery? It just didn't make sense. But he hadn't denied it when accused, stating that slavery was not his concern. She had been in New Orleans long enough to know that slavery was a serious issue in this country. Skye didn't care what anyone thought; slavery was wrong, and she would state her views to anyone who would listen.

Gradually, Skye became aware that the sun was dropping low beyond the far hills and the air was rapidly cooling. She must see how Missy was doing. After all, that was her most important responsibility.

When she entered Melissa's room, she saw that the lady was dozing after the excitement of the afternoon. Missy stirred when Skye leaned near.

"Could I bring you a dinner tray?" Skye asked. "Or would

you like to go to the dining salon? I'll find Kyle. I'm sure he would be happy to carry you, if you don't feel like walking."

"A tray would be ideal, sweetheart."

"Then I'll arrange for two. I'm rather tired myself and would love to dine here with you. I'm planning on going to bed early as well. Maybe we can read a few chapters from *Pride and Prejudice* before we retire." She saw how grateful Melissa was at her suggestion. The poor dear looked absolutely exhausted.

"I believe my brother-in-law has discovered the gaming tables on the upper deck," Melissa noted with a smile. "He fancies himself an expert at poker, and no doubt he's quite correct in that assumption. I've never heard him admit to losing, at any rate."

"Then 'tis settled. We'll spend a quiet evening, just the two of us. I do believe you'll adore Jane Austen's novel."

⊰ *Chapter 17* ⊱

For two blissful days, Skye was content to stay near her room, within earshot of Melissa. She arranged chairs outside the cabin doors and spent hours there, either alone or with Missy dozing at her side and MacLard asleep under the seat; she was happy to watch the ever-changing scenery along the banks of the Mississippi.

As for Kyle Wyndford, she saw him only briefly, once each morning when he came to check on Missy, then again each afternoon and evening. Melissa encouraged her to join Kyle and the other guests for dinner in the Grand Salon. Skye thought she might do that one evening, just for the rare experience, but she was in no rush to spend time trying to make small talk with a man who had no interest in her, despite the embarrassing fact that she'd allowed him far more liberties than she should have. Besides, there was always the possibility the topic of the slave trade would arise, and she would certainly lose her temper again and cause a quarrel, which would cause greater tension between them that might be detected by Melissa.

On the third morning, however, when she was sitting on her bed giving MacLard a vigorous brushing, a knock came on her door. "Are you in, Miss Mackinnon?" came the unmistakable voice of Kyle Wyndford.

Shushing MacLard before he could bark an alarm, she scooted off the bed and took a quick peek in her mirror. Tweaking her cheeks and smoothing her hair while chastising herself for caring what Mr. Wyndford thought of her appearance, she paused, then casually opened the door.

"Good morning, Skye." His voice held a note of sarcasm as he rested his weight on his palm against the door frame. He gave her a lazy smile that implied a far more friendly relationship than existed between them.

Skye had no intention of reverting to the use of their Christian names. That had been a mistake and she wanted to avoid inviting familiarity of any sort.

"Good morning, Mr. Wyndford," she said crisply. "I believe Melissa is having her morning nap. I looked in on her a few minutes ago."

"I'm sure she's fine. You've been doing an excellent job of looking after her. I appreciate that immensely, but I thought you deserved a respite from your duties."

"I don't consider being with Missy any sort of duty."

"Nevertheless, you've been confined to this area far too long. Melissa is well enough to spare you for an hour or so—and I think you have other responsibilities that need your attention."

"Oh? What would they be?"

"Have you forgotten about your two mares and Diamond Dust?"

"Forgotten? No, but I thought they were well attended. I've looked in on them each day, and they were clean and well fed in their quarters."

"Yes, but they might enjoy an outing. Some exercise, don't you agree?"

Skye hadn't thought that was possible. She knew the boat had been moored below a protective sandbar for the past hour, but this was a regular occurrence, she'd been told. Stops were necessary to do some cleaning, make small repairs, and take on a few fresh supplies. But she'd never considered removing the horses from their stalls.

"The captain tells me we'll be here for several more hours. He'll allow us to exercise the horses, but we must take an armed crewman as guard."

The idea was exhilarating. "I would love that. But why must we have a guard?"

"Just a precaution. I argued the matter, since I carry my own pistol at such times, but the captain said it is a hard and fast rule. No passengers can go ashore in the wilderness areas without a crewman to protect them. He mentioned wild animals, but I'm guessing the real fear is Indians. There is a great deal of hostility felt by the few that are left in the area—ever since the majority were forced to move out."

Her annoyance at the disparagement in his voice when he spoke of Indians almost made her decline to go, but she couldn't resist the thought of riding one of the horses through the glorious woods she saw along the shore. "I have absolutely no concern about *Indians*," she snapped. "Give me a moment to change into riding clothes and I'll meet you at the stalls."

She saw his expression register mild surprise at her brusqueness, but she merely closed the door and hurried to her trunk. Which horse should she ride? Legacy was better off in her stall during her advanced pregnancy. Lady had been ridden often during the last few days in New Orleans. But Dusty had recovered from his injury and needed to get better acquainted with his new owner. Aye, Dusty was her choice.

In minutes, she raced down the steps to the bottom deck where cargo was stored along with the animals. Six horses, two goats, and a crate of cats were making the trip upriver with their owners.

Kyle was waiting beside a saddled Raven Duke. Raven

pawed the floorboards and showed signs of impatience when she approached.

"I'll saddle Diamond Dust," she announced.

"Have you ridden him since you bought him?"

"Several times. He has amazing strength, but he's as manageable as the mares. A very sweet horse."

"Sweet stallions are rare," he pointed out.

"Nevertheless, he is *sweet*." She would not let Kyle lecture her on the nature of horses. She had lived closely with the creatures since before she could walk and knew all there was to know about them.

Kyle put his hand under her elbow to assist her to mount. Without meeting his eyes, she murmured a thank-you. Then he swung onto the elegant Spanish saddle she had admired at Highgrove. Wordlessly, they walked their horses across the planks leading from the cargo deck to the firm ground on the shore.

"Wait a minute, you two!"

"Damn," Kyle cursed under his breath. "Thought we'd escaped the fellow."

A heavyset man in rough clothing was chasing after them. He carried a rifle in one hand and a leather pouch slung over one shoulder. "You know the rules. You'll get us in a heap of trouble if you ride out there and get et by a bear."

Skye clamped her lips to keep from laughing. Somehow, getting eaten by a bear on such a lovely day seemed extremely unlikely.

Kyle wheeled a prancing Raven and kept him on a tight rein. "What are we supposed to do, sir—stroll along with you? Or do you plan to gallop through the woods with us?"

"As I recollect, there's a clearing just beyond those trees. I'll stand and watch and you kin race them ponies up and down as much as you like. Just don't get out of my sight or I'll start firing my rifle until help comes to hunt you down."

Skye was disappointed they wouldn't be free to ride along a woodsy path, and she could see that Kyle was seriously annoyed. She watched in wry amusement as he struggled to control his temper. Taking orders must go against his grain, she mused.

"Come on, *Miss Mackinnon,*" he said hotly. "We'll have to make the best of it, I suppose."

Putting Dusty into an easy jog, she marveled again at the horse's gentle temperament. Privately, she had to agree with Kyle that the stallion was most unusual, a willing goer who would leap at the lightest touch of her heels but was ready to obey the slightest tug of the bit. Securing the strings of her broad-brimmed hat, she followed Kyle and Raven through a ring of oaks and into a wide clearing. Riding astride, as was always her preference, she put the horse into a canter and felt the massive muscles expand as the ground flew beneath his feet. She had traveled a hundred yards before she could catch her breath.

Keeping an eye on Kyle, who was cantering Raven toward the opposite side of the field, she almost missed seeing the face peering from behind a low-growing shrub a few feet in front of her. When she saw the ebony skin and large round eyes, she screamed before she could stop herself. Dusty shied and sidestepped away from the brush.

She turned him in a circle to calm him, then looked again toward the thick shrubbery. Had she really seen a face? Or had that talk about Indians and bears caused her imagination to work overtime?

She didn't see a thing now. But to her embarrassment, Kyle was racing toward her and the grumpy guard was running at top speed behind him.

Kyle reached her well ahead of the guard and halted Raven in a cloud of dirt and uprooted grass. "Did you see something?" he called.

"I thought I saw a face. But I might have been mistaken."

Kyle pulled a pistol from his belt and rode into the brush, standing in his stirrups to peer into the shadows.

He was out of sight for several seconds, and then she heard him speaking to someone. Obviously the face hadn't been in her imagination.

"What's going on?!" yelled the guard, who was fast approaching.

Kyle reappeared, leading his horse. Beside him, clad in rags and with no shoes at all, walked an African man with his head bowed in exhaustion and defeat. The man appeared almost too weak to walk. Skye was aghast to see he had an iron collar around his neck and his shirt showed signs of bloodstains.

She leaned forward in her saddle. "Who is he?" she whispered. "Where did he come from?"

Kyle looked at her, his eyes narrow, his brow knitted, his lip curled in disgust. He glanced at the guard, who was nearly upon them. "An escaped slave," he said tightly. "Guess this is the end for him."

What happened next stunned Skye so completely that the event was burned forever in her memory. Kyle grasped the slave's arm and hoisted him atop Raven Duke. "Ride like hell," he ordered the man, who appeared too startled to put his feet in the stirrups or pick up the reins.

"Ride north," rasped Kyle. "The horse is rested and will go all day and all night. Get out of here fast!" He shoved the reins into the man's hands and clapped Raven hard on his rear. "His name's Raven," he shouted. The animal leaped forward, almost tumbling his rider from the saddle. Just in time, the desperate Negro grabbed the saddle horn and leaned forward, took up the reins, and raced across the open field toward the protection of the trees.

The guard halted and took aim.

Skye screamed.

Kyle turned, just as the rifle exploded.

⇥ *Chapter 18* ⇤

Kyle fought the whirling darkness just beyond his eyes. Then, with the clarity of consciousness, came intense pain in his left shoulder.

He focused instantly on the guard. Pulling his Colt

revolver from his belt, he leveled it at the man who was reloading his rifle.

"Drop your gun, mister. *Now*—if you'll indulge me, sir."

He sat back on the heel of his boot and rested his right forearm on his knee, aiming the pistol at the guard's shoulder. Thankful for clear vision and a steady hand, he watched the man lower the rifle, then drop it to the ground.

Skye rushed toward him and fell to her knees at his side. Her face was pale, her green eyes wide with shocked concern.

"Kyle . . . Kyle—you're hit . . . the blood." She started to reach for his arm.

"I'm all right," he said sternly, without taking his eyes from the guard. "Go back and get Diamond Dust before he runs off. Do it now." He wanted her out of the line of fire in case the guard made a grab for the rifle. He wasn't sure if the man had been able to shove another cartridge into the chamber.

"But, Kyle, you're bleeding badly. Tell me—"

"Do as I say, Skye Mackinnon. If you lose *your* horse, we'll both be without mounts when we get to St. Louis."

She studied him for several seconds before jumping up to obey his command.

Now he was free to concentrate on the guard. "I don't know if you made a good shot or a bad one. What's your name, sir?"

"Gordon" was the gruff reply.

"Very well, Mr. Gordon, I want you to know I have no hard feelings toward you for shooting me. Done in the line of duty, I expect."

"Right. That's it. Didn't mean to shoot you. Was aiming at the—"

"Slave? Naturally. All in a day's work. Shooting an unarmed man trying to make a dash for freedom."

"It's the law," grumbled the guard.

"I fully understand. That's why I won't have you hung for shooting *me* instead of him. You merely fired at an escaping slave who happened to be stealing my prize stallion. I got in the way. Right, Gordon?"

"Looked to me like you giv him the hor—"

"No. You only *thought* that's what happened."

"But I saw you hand him the reins."

"Mr. Gordon, you're missing the point here. I am Kyler Wyndford, a successful and highly respected rancher from Dakota. Why would I help an escaping slave? No court in the land would take your word against mine, now would they?"

"Court? Oh." Gordon's voice fell as he understood his predicament. "Guess I git your meaning."

"Sit down, Mr. Gordon. Let's have a little visit. Where're you from, sir? Your name sounds Scottish."

From the corner of his eye, Kyle watched Skye tie a nervous Diamond Dust to a tree limb. She ran back to kneel by his side. Her face flushed with color, she said breathlessly, "Kyle, we have to get back to the boat, find a doctor—"

"Nay, Miss Mackinnon, we'll rest here awhile." He flashed her a pointed look but could tell she missed what he was trying to do. Under his breath, keeping an eye on Gordon, he said, "Sit down. We've got to give the African time . . ." A sudden spell of dizziness interrupted his explanation.

"I see," she murmured, her voice sounding far away.

He clinched his teeth and waited until his vision cleared. "Don't suppose you have a handkerchief with you?"

"Aye." She whipped a lacy white handkerchief from her pocket.

"If you have the courage to do so, please tie it as tightly as you can over the wound. I'll buy you a new one in St. Louis. I'd like to stay here as long as possible."

Biting her lip, she concentrated on the task.

He clamped his jaw as fiery shafts burned along his arm and into his shoulder. When he could speak, he addressed the guard, who was sitting on the ground thirty yards away. "The lady here is a Scot, in case you didn't know. From the Isle of Skye. Ever been there, Mr. Gordon?" he asked as if he chatted at a tea party.

"No."

"Too bad. Nor have I. But I expect you have some distant relatives in the Scottish Highlands."

"Kyle, I don't think the bleeding has stopped. My handkerchief is soaked."

"Thank you for trying, Miss Mackinnon."

"You don't have to call me Miss Mackinnon. I was just angry before, because you said you supported slavery." Her voice shook as she worried over the binding.

"Did I?" He began to realize his assistance to the Negro slave had a bonus. His only thought at the time had been to save the poor man's life, but his actions had apparently impressed Skye.

"You . . . gave him your fine stallion." Her words held awe verging on adoration.

"Did you think so ill of me that you assumed I would place the value of a horse above that of human life?"

"No . . . yes . . . maybe. I don't know. But you didn't, and that proves you care deeply about people, whatever their race or circumstances."

He realized he was enjoying this sudden burst of hero worship. It helped offset the agony in his shoulder and the loss of Raven Duke.

"I'm pleased you've adjusted your opinion of me, Skye."

"I have, most definitely. But my opinions will make little difference if we sit here much longer. You could die from loss of blood."

"Your medical expertise extends to people as well as animals?"

"Same principle, I expect."

He was indeed having peculiar wavy sensations in his head and in his stomach. "Mr. Gordon," he said loudly, "are the unfortunate events of the past few minutes clear in your mind?"

"Yes, sir. I shot at a runaway slave who had just stolen your horse. Accidentally winged you, by mistake. But you won't press charges because I was only doing my duty, trying to help."

"Perfect," said Kyle. "Miss Mackinnon is a witness to it, so there's no mistake. Now, if you'll come over here and lend me a hand, we'll see if we can make our way back to the boat."

Gordon reached for the rifle. "I'll fire a shot for help."

"No! Leave the gun where it is. The lady will retrieve it while you assist me."

He watched Gordon stand and head in his direction. When the figure blurred, he handed his pistol toward Skye with a shaking hand.

She took it at once. "I have it, Kyle. Don't worry. I'll get the rifle, too."

"Clever girl," he muttered. Gordon bent over him and helped him to his feet. Kyle knew he would never get to the boat without the strong arm of the guard. Damn, he didn't want to pass out. He managed to walk across the field before his strength failed him completely. He sagged and felt himself being lowered to the ground.

He heard Skye's authoritative voice, her enchanting brogue, tempered by careful English tutoring. "Go to the boat for help, Mr. Gordon. We'll wait here. Go quickly, if you please."

Then he heard the rifle fire into the air.

Skye was beside him again as he drifted into a strange gray place that was damp and cold like a swamp in winter. Her warm fingers stroked his forehead. Her hand clasped his and squeezed it.

"You did a wonderful thing, Kyle Wyndford. I won't ever forget it. Don't you dare die, do you hear me? Melissa needs you. And so does her son."

He heard Skye's words and wanted to respond. He was feeling better, the pain was less, but he couldn't see her, and his lips refused to form any sound.

She stroked his cheek, moved her hand along his arm. If he died, he thought fuzzily, heaven couldn't be any nicer than what he had right here.

He was surprised to find himself riding Raven Duke across his rangeland in Dakota. A storm was coming, a blizzard in fact, and he wasn't wearing a coat. He pushed the horse harder and harder, until they were flying over the level prairie as if there was no ground at all beneath

Raven's hooves. The flailing ice bore down on them; he was shaking, freezing, and the house was nowhere in sight. He was lost, he realized, engulfed in white, moving now like a wraith caught in a gale. He was doomed, he knew. Too soon, too soon. He wasn't ready to die. People he loved depended on him. He heard a feminine voice calling from inside his head. Skye Mackinnon's face appeared and he knew it was her voice he heard. She was holding back the bitter cold, forcing him to look at her, see her face, her vivid coloring, her blue-black hair thrashing in the wintry blast. If he could reach her, he would be warm again. Safe. Home. A woman offering safety was something he'd never experienced. A man should offer safety to a woman, not the reverse. He reached for her hand and grasped it. He held it tightly, aware now of the agony in his arm. He heard a moan, but the sound drifted from somewhere else. And then the blinding whiteness became a black abyss.

After the doctor left Kyle's cabin, Skye pulled up a chair and tried to relax. The doctor had been very positive about Kyle's chances of recovery, assuring both her and Melissa that Mr. Wyndford was not in danger of death.

Skye had kept up a brave front for Melissa's sake. The poor lady had abandoned her sickbed and refused to leave her brother-in-law's side until he regained consciousness. Kyle had insisted he would rest better if he knew Missy was taking care of herself rather than fussing over his own minor flesh wound. He said two hysterical women fluttering about was more than he could stand, and Skye was better trained in nursing than Melissa. He actually smiled at Skye when he said that, causing in her such a surge of emotion she almost burst into tears.

The cabin was peaceful as the light faded toward the west. The *Mississippi Belle* was underway once more, with the passengers in a dither of gossip and excitement over the shooting of their most illustrious passenger, Kyler Wyndford, by some imbecilic crewman who was aiming at a runaway slave. One of the men suggested that Wyndford had gone to great lengths to stay away from the poker table, thereby ensuring he would keep his impressive winnings in his pocket. Two single ladies, who had made Mr. Wyndford's acquaintance in the dining salon, ordered the chef to prepare special broth and a plump peach pie to tempt his appetite.

Alone with Kyle at last, Skye allowed herself the luxury of studying the face on the pillow: pale but still rugged and enormously appealing. Nor could she keep her eyes from straying along his throat to his bare chest above the sheet and admiring the sight of his well-muscled arms. The lads on Skye occasionally went bare-chested in the summer or when swimming along the shore, but she'd never seen a mature man in a state of undress at close range. Kyle was wonderfully put together, she decided. Her curiosity about what was *below* the sheet was titillated by the outline of long legs reaching to the end of the bed.

Of course, she had not been allowed in the room when Kyle's bloody clothing had been removed and his wound tended by the doctor. But she had stayed close by outside the door, waiting for news. Thank heaven that when it came, the news was good. The bullet had passed cleanly through the flesh, so there was no need for probing or surgery. A lucky man, the physician had said. The greatest danger had been the loss of blood, and that couldn't be helped since the accident happened at such a distance from any medical facilities.

Skye knew that wasn't the entire story. Kyle had taken an awful chance when he delayed seeking medical help to keep news of the runaway slave from reaching the authorities. Even if he had acted instinctively when he handed over his horse, his decision to aid the man's escape by sitting on the ground talking with his assailant was tantamount to risking his own life. Not to mention the additional suffering he'd endured in the process. Kyle was more than vindicated in her eyes; he was an extraordinary hero. The fact that she alone knew of his courage and sacrifice made it even more special. She held the secret of what he had done inside her heart like a precious jewel. Sitting there, watching the slow rise and fall of his broad chest with its feathering of golden-brown hair, she knew without doubt she was hopelessly in love with him. She wanted to know everything there was to know about him: his childhood, his parents, his years with the army. She wondered what he liked to eat, what made him laugh, and what filled his dreams at night. Her fantasy drew her down beside him, placed her head on his pillow with her lips close to his, slipped her legs under the sheets, wrapped him protectively in her arms . . . if only she could . . .

"Skye, you're still here."

She jumped at the sound of his voice. She must have dozed. The room was shadowy and growing cool. At once, she leaned near the bed.

His eyes held a tenderness she'd never seen before. He seemed so vulnerable lying there, a slight smile playing across his lips, a hint of a day's growth on his chin.

"Are you in pain?" she murmured, barely trusting her own voice to remain steady.

"Not much. A little, perhaps. I'll soon be good as new."

"Your soup has grown cold. If you like, I'll get you something hot from the kitchen."

"I believe it's called a galley aboard ship," he quipped. "But I'm not hungry. As I recall, I stuffed myself a short time ago when Melissa was poking spoonful after spoonful down my throat. How is she doing, by the way? I hope she isn't unduly alarmed."

She detected a weakness in his voice, and his concern over his sister-in-law at such a time touched her deeply. "She's doing well, now that you're out of danger. But it was hours ago when you ate the soup."

"I don't think I was ever in danger."

"You were. From loss of blood. You shouldn't have taken such a risk."

"The man got away; that's the important thing."

She sat again in her chair. "Kyle Wyndford, why did you lead me to believe you supported the slave trade? I must chastise you for that."

He took a deep breath before answering. "Because I took a solemn oath not to reveal my true opinions. To do so would put certain people in danger."

"I think I can guess who, but I won't ask you to break your word. Still, knowing you're against slavery means a great deal to me."

"Thank God the matter's cleared up. I hated for you to believe I supported the cruel practice. I'd like to do my part to stop it."

She touched his hand. "I'm proud of that. I promise I won't reveal to anyone how you feel, but I will express my own views whenever I get the chance."

"No doubt," he said wryly. "I wouldn't have expected otherwise." He ran his hand over the bulky bandage swathing his left shoulder.

Her love for him brought her to the edge of tears. "I'm deeply sorry you lost Raven Duke. I understand the need, but your sacrifice was very great. I know what a valuable animal he was."

"I'll miss him. But I do have his full brother in my stable at home. Horses are replaceable. A man's life is not. I'll try to buy a decent mount at the horse auction in St. Louis."

She thought a minute. "I have an idea. Why don't you buy Diamond Dust? I don't need three horses, and you could arrange some sort of stud service for me if things work out in Dakota." She had no sooner said the words when her face flamed with embarrassment. Of course, she hadn't meant to imply any sort of physical union between the two of them, but her words could have been interpreted that way. Rather than ignoring her unfortunate remark, she stupidly stuttered, "I . . . mean . . . I didn't mean—the horse could—well, service Lady . . ."

He reached to take her hand. "Skye Eugenia, we're friends, and friends speak their minds to each other. I know *exactly* what you mean. Diamond Dust would make a great sire. He has qualities I've never seen in any other horse, qualities that could be developed and put to fine use in the cattle business."

She appreciated the way he put her at ease. Picking up the thread of the conversation, she said, "Actually I would be glad to *give* him to you. In exchange for a breeding with Spirit Lady."

"That's a fine idea. But I insist on paying for him. I'll give you six hundred dollars. Does that seem fair?"

"Not fair at all. We both know I only paid five hundred two weeks ago."

"But he was lame then. You healed him and turned him from racehorse to saddle horse with great skill. You must collect a bonus for your effort."

She saw him flinch as he shifted his position on the bed. Carefully, she withdrew her hand. "I'm going to the *galley* now. While we talk of horses, you're losing your strength. You need to eat if you're to be well when we reach St. Louis next Sunday."

He sighed and relaxed on his pillow. "Very well, Nurse Mackinnon. It's amazing how women believe everything can be mended with food."

"Usually they can," she said lightly. "By the way, the doctor has arranged for one of the kitchen boys to sleep here on a cot tonight."

"What? I won't have it. I like my privacy."

"For one night only. He insists, I'm afraid. If you care to climb out of bed and argue the matter, you may do so and see how far you get. I might add that Melissa and I are much in favor of the idea."

"Hell, I can't fight a committee. Send the food and the boy. I hope he knows how to use a razor. Tomorrow I expect to be shaved, dressed, and back at the poker table."

She laughed with pleasure and relief. She would have a favorable report for Missy when she returned to her cabin. "I pray your expectations will be fulfilled on the morrow. I'm going now to order your dinner, then I'll visit Melissa. Rest well."

"Skye—"

His low voice stopped her as she headed toward the door. "I was proud of you today. You kept your head, did all the right things. While I was acting like a newborn colt trying to get my legs under me, you were my strength, my partner in a dangerous subterfuge. I want you to know that I admire you greatly."

She glowed under his praise. Admiration was good, very

good. Perhaps it would eventually become something more. She lowered her head to hide the extraordinary thrill his compliment had given her. "Thank you," she said softly. "I was glad to oblige."

⊰ *Chapter 19* ⊱

I'm taking a stroll with Kyle," Skye said to Melissa as she placed a dinner tray at her friend's elbow. "Are you sure you don't feel like joining us?"

"You're sweet to ask me, but I'm content right here with my tray on my knees. After I eat, I'll step outside for a breath of air, then curl up with my novel. Go along and enjoy your outing with Kyle."

Skye knew Melissa was pleased that she and Kyle were getting along so well after the recent strain on their relationship. Tonight would be Kyle's first time to venture from his room since the shooting. Despite the careful attention of the doctor and both ladies, Kyle had been forced to remain quiet for several days. His wound was healing well and after the first day, he'd had no fever, but the loss of so much blood had drained him of strength. Yesterday, he had dressed in casual clothing, finally getting his left arm into a sleeve. He had stayed out of bed most of the day, but by nightfall, he had been exhausted.

"You look lovely, Skye, darling," Melissa observed. "I'm happy you and Kyle will have this evening alone together. I believe you've taken a fancy to each other."

Skye felt the joy in her heart send an irrepressible smile to her lips. "I do think highly of Mr. Wyndford. He's quite dashing, of course, but more than that, he is a fair-minded gentleman."

"There was more to the shooting than I was told, wasn't there?" Melissa said. "I don't like to pry, but I've been curious about what really happened in the woods."

Skye settled on the edge of the bed. "I'm sure Kyle wouldn't object to your knowing what happened."

"He told me he helped a runaway slave to escape. He gave the man his stallion, Raven Duke."

"Then you already know most of the story, Missy. Did he tell you the shooting was no accident? The African was out of sight when the guard reached our side of the field, but I'm sure he saw what Mr. Wyndford did to help the man escape. The guard raised his gun and fired directly at Mr. Wyndford."

Melissa shook her head. "Then praise the Lord, Kyle wasn't killed. I'm surprised he didn't shoot the beastly fellow."

"He could have, easily. He drew his pistol while the guard was reloading his rifle, but he only forced him to sit awhile. That gave the slave extra time to ride away. I was astounded at the way Mr. Wyndford handled the situation, especially since he was in pain and bleeding badly."

"I must say I've never seen my brother-in-law lose his head completely, even the day he came home with my husband's body across his horse. Kyle had been visiting us after his service in the military. I thanked God he was with us that day. He was extremely distraught, just as I was. Very tight-lipped. He had a deadly calm about him, took care of all the necessary arrangements. He knew, of course, the hopelessness of searching out the Indians who killed Blanton. I sometimes wonder if he would have felt better in the long run if he had vented his fury rather than holding it all inside."

"Melissa," Skye ventured, "does he know yet about my Indian heritage?"

"Oh my, no. I never told him."

"Then I must do it soon. Now that I know his true feelings of sympathy toward the African slaves, I'm sure he'll be reasonable about my being Lakota."

Skye was surprised when Melissa didn't immediately agree.

"I'm sure Kyle will temper his feelings because he cares for you," Missy said finally. "But his first reaction may be unpleasant. I speak frankly, Skye. The fact that I will soon die gives me that privilege."

"Don't say that, Missy," Skye said quickly. "You're much improved, growing stronger every day."

"The medicine frees me of pain, and I'm grateful. But my time is short, dear, and there's no pretending otherwise."

"Oh, Missy . . ."

"But we won't speak of that now. What I want to say is that I've longed to see Kyle happily married with a family of his own. And frankly, Badger is going to need a mother. Taking on an independent and extremely self-confident man, a man like Kyle who is used to having his own way, plus a spunky nine-year-old, is asking a great deal of any woman. But I believe you have all the qualities needed for the task."

"Are you saying you've chosen *me* to be Kyle's wife?" Skye's heart stopped beating. As infatuated with the man as she was, she hadn't thought seriously of marriage—and certainly not of acquiring a young boy to raise. She had the Mackinnon family to consider, first of all. She was just beginning that adventure with all its challenges and dangers.

"I have," Melissa said emphatically. "You're perfect for him, and I won't pretend to play coy little games about the matter. I don't have time."

"But 'tis much too soon to consider such a serious step. I admit I find him enormously attractive, but I have no idea what he feels for me. Not in the deepest sense."

"I've seen him look at you when you weren't aware. He's never looked at a woman with such fondness. It may take patience and a few feminine wiles, but I believe you could win him if you tried." She sat up in her chair. "You wouldn't be sorry, Skye. He's a good man, though a bit untamed at the moment. And he is a builder, an empire builder, if you will. You two have that trait in common; I've seen it in your eyes, and in his, when you speak of land and cattle and the future of the West."

Skye's head was spinning. The idea of becoming the wife

of the most handsome cattle baron in Dakota was exhilarating. She knew she was in love with Kyle, and the next logical step was that he would love her and make her his own. "I'll have to think about it, Missy. I guess I'm overwhelmed." She reached out to touch Melissa's arm. "But there's one thing for sure, I'm enormously complimented you would select me. I know how you love your brother-in-law. I'm sure you want his happiness. But I must have time to think things through, to search my heart and determine his true feelings."

Melissa sank back in her chair. "Not *too* much time, dear. I will die happy if you and Kyle are husband and wife."

Skye stroked the skeletal arm beneath the silk dressing gown. "Then I will tell him tonight about my father being half Lakota Sioux. His reaction could make all the difference. If Mr. Wyndford is going to hate me, we might as well know it as soon as possible. I wouldn't want to buoy our hopes and dreams if they are doomed from the start."

Skye's hand was resting on Kyle's right forearm as they walked along the deck, though she was careful not to put any weight on him. Despite his dapper appearance, clean-shaven and immaculately dressed in a fashionable black suit, Skye knew he was not yet up to full strength. His step was confident but not brisk. His touch was firm but not strong. His voice still held an occasional hint of weakness.

Skye felt she looked her best tonight, despite the fact that her dress was simple cotton and her only jewels were pearl earrings, a slender gold bracelet that had been a gift to her mother from Queen Caroline of England, and a brooch displaying the crest of the Clan Mackinnon of Skye.

Kyle could barely take his eyes from her. Other guests passed by and smiled and nodded, plainly intrigued to see the heroic Mr. Wyndford abroad with his lady friend. Skye shyly kept her eyes lowered, but she was happy to share in the tribute to Kyle. She hoped that later they might have a chance to be alone.

"I'm astounded I've caused such a stir," Kyle remarked. "All I did was lose my horse and get myself shot by an officer doing his lawful duty. Hardly a heroic act. If these nice people knew I had aided a criminal to escape, they would be singing a different song, I can swear."

"Shh. They might hear you. No use enlightening them, do you think?"

"Not if I might end up in jail for my honesty. Wonder what happened to Gordon?"

"I heard he left the boat at Columbus. Dismissed by the captain."

"For his questionable marksmanship, no doubt." He took her arm and motioned her toward a secluded area near the smoke stack. Relieved to be off center stage, she observed the churning paddle wheel toss water in the moonlight like dancing diamonds. From their gingerbread perch three levels high, Skye marveled at the splendor of her surroundings. With every sense satiated, she wondered if life could ever be sweeter than this. How glorious to share such a romantic setting with the man she adored. Was it possible they were meant for each other, destined to be husband and wife? When his arm slipped around her waist, she allowed the intimacy, welcomed it, knew she had been expecting it.

"Beautiful," he murmured. "The air is as light as a butterfly's wing, caressing. The fragrance is summer at its zenith."

"So you're a poet, sir. I hadn't guessed." She dared to gaze up at him. The expression on his face stopped her breath. How dark his eyes were, how intense. His lips were solemn, expectant. Her memory of his lips claiming hers started a yearning in the deepest part of her. "You have many wonderful qualities, Kyle," she whispered. "You have important virtues like courage and caring. Forgive me for being so outspoken, but I don't have the gift of subtlety."

"You credit me with more goodness than I possess, lass," he responded. "But I consider myself extremely fortunate you feel that way, and I happen to admire your frankness. Don't ever change, Skye. Don't ever let disappointment destroy your happy, trusting nature."

His hand moved along her back, touched her nape, and lingered there.

Resting her hands on his shoulders, she was careful not to press against the bandage beneath his jacket.

He cupped the back of her head; his fingers entangled her hair, disturbing the pins she'd used to secure the thick waves into a semblance of order. His lips touched the widow's peak at her forehead, sending shafts of tingling delight along her spine. With one finger, he outlined the curve of her cheek, then bent to kiss first one ear, then touched the tip of her nose.

Her lips parted involuntarily. Fleetingly, it crossed her mind that they were not concealed from view here in the moonlight; anyone might come upon them. Her concern melted when he tipped up her chin and flicked her lips with the tip of his tongue.

His arm encircled her back, forcing her against his chest. She had doubted his strength, but now felt the flow of his power underneath her hands, along her body, and penetrating the depths of her being. His lips covered hers, heated, demanding, insisting on a response. She complied by wrapping her hands around his neck and drawing his tongue into her mouth. It was as natural as taking her next breath, and as life-giving.

She was trapped against him, exactly where she wanted to be. She was on tiptoe, every fiber of her being reaching out to him. Swept into a timeless vortex, she had no lucid thought, only feelings that were carrying her to a place she'd never known. He ended the kiss and held her close, gently now, stroking her and capturing her very soul in his embrace. "My darling Skye," he murmured. "I do believe I'm in love with you."

Her heartbeat raced at his words. Was it possible this astonishing man could love her, an ordinary girl who had none of a grand lady's charm and sophistication? Moving from his arms, she tried to muster some defense against the dangerous whirlwind of her emotions. But when she gazed up at him, she knew he was giving her the greatest gift a man could give. He did love her. The truth was written in his eyes. Wilting under the onslaught of this sudden awareness, she gave herself up to joy.

"I love you, too, Kyle. I've never known a man such as you."

Voices erupted from the door of the salon. Guests were leaving, walking along the deck in their direction.

He put his arm around her waist and led her toward the cabins. "We'll speak more about this later," he said in a low voice.

Arriving at her door, he stopped in the shadows and raised her hand to his lips. He kissed the back of it, then carefully unfolded it to brush his lips across the palm.

Her eyes searched for his through the darkness. At last, she managed to say, "Thank you, Kyle, for a lovely walk." Her voice was a whisper and she heard the adulation in her tone.

"There will be others. Many others, if I have my way. We should be docking in a couple of days at St. Louis. Tomorrow night is the captain's dinner, followed by the segregation of men and women for private parties. A poor plan, in my mind, but popular among the married travelers. We may not be alone again until we arrive. I hope you will remember my words tonight, Skye. I, too, am outspoken. And I have a habit of saying exactly what I mean."

"I'll remember," she said softly.

"Sleep well, little one. I fear my own sleep will be long in coming."

She smiled at him, though she knew he couldn't see her.

He bent to kiss her cheek, then walked away toward his quarters.

Quietly, Skye opened her door and floated inside. A taper was burning low on her nightstand, and her gown had been laid across the bed by the chambermaid. MacLard gave her a sleepy glance, then put his head back on his paws. Slowly, she turned in a circle, hugging her arms around her. Love. This was love. Her mother had told her she would know—and she *did* know. With absolute certainty.

Later, after she washed her face and put on her gown, she stretched out on top of the cool satin bedspread and listened to the rhythmical splash of the paddle wheel. Only then did she realize she hadn't done what she'd set out to do tonight, what she had told Melissa she would do. She had not told Kyle that she carried the blood of the Lakota Sioux.

⊰ Chapter 20 ⊱

St. Louis was a sparkling jewel in the midst of an endless landscape of green and blue. Thousands of points of light dotted the land and decorated the hill above the indigo river at dusk on the evening of July fourth when the *Mississippi Belle* docked near the broad boulevard separating the rows of building from the water's edge.

One long blast, followed by two short ones, announced the arrival of this floating palace of the Mississippi. Strollers in the city park stopped to gaze through twilight's last glow at the graceful ship. A band was playing in a nearby gazebo. Youngsters paused in their games to gape at the white multitiered boat, then continued their play, since such arrivals were commonplace throughout the summer.

Nothing about the occasion was commonplace to Skye Mackinnon. St. Louis appeared like a mirage in the wilderness. She leaned against the railing and marveled at the hundreds of people milling along the mile or so of riverfront. Looking at Kyle, who puffed a cheroot as he lounged at her side, she asked breathlessly, "What do all these people do? So isolated here in the forest? What made the town grow? What are all those buildings? I'm amazed at the . . . the liveliness of the place."

"Well, it is Independence Day, you recall. I expect the citizens have been celebrating with their families. The town was French in the early days—still is mostly—though it's part of the United States now."

Her excitement leaped again when she saw a large permanent sign on the side of a building that read: WELCOME TO ST. LOUIS, GATEWAY TO THE WEST.

"We're here, Kyle. This is the West at last," she effused.

He chuckled and gave her an affectionate smile. "Only the *gate,* little lass. Upriver several miles, the Missouri joins the Mississippi. When you travel Old Misery, you'll know you've reached the West. Until now, you've been pampered by civilization. I assure you that will soon end."

"Old Misery?"

"An experienced traveler's name for the Missouri. The Mississippi is a grand lady, willing and able to move mankind through the length of the countryside. The Missouri is a wildcat. You have to tie her down and fight her every inch of the way or she'll eat you alive. We'll be traveling on one of those small boats you see over there at the next landing."

In the shimmering gaslight along the water, Skye could make out several small, squatty boats moored along the wharf. Quite a different sort of craft than the luxurious sternwheeler they had been enjoying.

"I see what you mean. But they are run by steam, are they not?"

"Missouri packets. Steam, yes. Or sail, or poles manned by passengers."

"What?"

"I exaggerate, but not by much. The Missouri is shallow upriver and full of sandbars, which constantly shift their location. A boat pilot on the Missouri has got to be the best in the world to get his craft to its destination. Most of those boats belong to the American Fur Company, owned by easterners. We'll book passage on one and leave St. Louis as soon as Missy has a few days' rest."

"I should see about Melissa now. Her clothes are packed and she's saying good-bye to the chambermaid who's been so sweet to her."

"We'll take rooms at the Louis Hotel across from the church." Kyle flipped his cigar over the side and grasped her elbow. "Maybe you would like to take a walk once Missy is settled. We haven't had a moment alone lately."

"I would like that very much," she said guilelessly. "But we have to take care of the animals, too. Stable the horses.

And MacLard is having fits after being confined so long. I'm afraid I have my own little wildcat to deal with."

"Then we'd better get started."

Two hours later, with the air still warm from the hours of intense summer sun, Kyle walked beside Skye along the riverside in city park. He shook his head at MacLard's frantic explorations of everything in sight. The grassy boulevard was paradise for a pup long cooped up in a ship's cabin. But MacLard seemed to have learned his lesson about dashing far afield after his close call at Dominique Hall.

Kyle felt much stronger and had only an occasional dull ache in his shoulder. All things considered, he decided the shooting episode had been a lucky break, not just for the African, but for him as well. He had won Skye Mackinnon's admiration—even her love. These past years, he had never considered marriage; he had too much to deal with without complicating his life with a wife and children. Besides, Missy ran the house, and he had Badger to raise as if he were his own son. He had concluded this arrangement would probably be permanent. A man who chose to raise cattle in virgin territory had little chance to meet many women. Some of the Texas ranchers had married Mexican women; one had married an Indian. Trappers often wed native women, in fact, but personally he'd never met a woman of any race who tempted him toward the altar. That is, until he met the Scottish beauty who had captivated him with her exotic looks, her tomboyish manner, and her challenging intellect. He must proceed with caution, he told himself, though he would greatly prefer to do the opposite. The girl was committed to founding a ranch for her family. If her father appeared, that would take precedence for a few months, at least. Maybe a year or more. If it turned out Mackinnon had been killed, Kyle would then step in and make himself available to the lass, in whatever capacity she would agree to.

Could he wait a year to possess this winsome lady? Watching her walk beside him, her small gloved hand tucked into the crook of his arm, the ribbon on her bonnet bouncing with every jubilant step, he had strong doubts about delaying the match. What would he do if her family didn't appear and she returned to New Orleans in the fall? Could he leave home and escort her back to Louisiana? Autumn was an extremely busy time at Wind River. He'd been gone more than a month already and knew how much he was needed at the ranch. One of his first duties would be to hire a woman full time to stay with Missy when he was away from home; he wouldn't leave her alone, even though she was obviously recovering from her illness. And he wanted to relieve Skye of any further responsibility for his sister-in-law. The girl wasn't a nurse or a lady's maid, for God's sake. She was the daughter of a laird and had been raised in a castle in Scotland. Besides, he wanted to show her his valley, surely equal in beauty and majesty to any place on earth. He needed to scout for land for the Mackinnons. Already he had a locale in mind to show her: a well-watered place with level acreage that stretched to the farthest horizon, closer to Vermillion than Wind River and less than an hour's ride from his headquarters. Why not establish the Mackinnons there? It would be both pleasant and handy for all concerned if his closest neighbors were also his in-laws.

He was jerked from his contemplation by pops and explosions near the bandstand.

A yapping MacLard came at a run and was scooped into Skye's arms. She laughed up at Kyle. " 'Tis a celebration," she said gaily. "The fourth of July, remember?"

"Of course. We must toast the occasion. Should we search out a restaurant?"

"We had luncheon so late that I'm not the slightest bit hungry. Oh—look!"

The sky erupted in a canopy of colored fireworks. A shower of red, white, and blue burst over the river. In the distance, a band began to play the "Star-Spangled Banner."

"What a thrilling song," said Skye, hugging a trembling MacLard.

"It's the national anthem of the United States. Written, so I've been told, during America's second war—the *final* war, I hope—with Mother England."

"You know, I keep forgetting you're an Englishman."

"I forget I'm English. That's easy enough since I've made my living in the American wilderness for the past nine years."

She put down MacLard. The dog stayed close to her skirts as they strolled toward a bench facing the river. "Kyle, tell me about your family. Missy has described your brother, Blanton, and his dream to come to the New World to create an empire. Was that also your dream?"

"Not at first. Our eldest brother inherited the property at Northamptonshire, the title of earl, and all that goes with it. Blanton was the second son and I was son number three. I entered the military once I finished my stint at Cambridge. I was in Africa for a while, and then France. I didn't like the discipline of army life, I'm afraid, but I liked seeing the world. Blanton struck out for America as a ship's cabin boy. He found Wind River valley and saw the possibilities in a country full of youthful energy."

"When did he marry Melissa?"

"Eleven years ago. He met her when he was visiting England." He shook his head. "They were extremely happy and well suited. She was the daughter of a country squire, but she didn't hesitate to leave hearth and home to be with her husband in a harsh land."

"My mother was a squire's daughter, too."

"So I was told. You come by your penchant for farming quite naturally."

Skye sat on the bench and gazed toward the dark band of river. "My mother's father owned property outside of London. My Scottish grandfather, of course, had the land on Skye. My father . . . my father . . ." She gazed at him, a strange, almost frightened expression in her eyes.

He sat beside her, trying hard to listen to her words rather than lose himself in her loveliness.

"I know about your father," he said. "He was the laird of Mackinnon. I've heard the story from Missy, who heard it from Laurel, who I presume heard it from your mother."

"You've . . . heard the story?" She looked startled.

"Why . . . yes. I don't suppose it's a great secret anymore, after all these years."

Skye rested her hand on his sleeve. "Then you know? You've known all along?"

"Of your father's enormous courage? Of how he was accused of poisoning Queen Caroline of Brunswick when she died mysteriously? And of how he was to be hung but was rescued when he stood in the shadow of the noose? Yes, I've heard all that. A fascinating story, I must say. I understand your mother intends to write a book about it someday."

Skye was staring at him, her eyes wide.

He took her hand. "It's nothing to be ashamed of, lass. You must be extremely proud of your father—and your mother."

"Of course. I adore them both. But I thought you were going to say something else. There is something you *don't* know."

He waited, mildly curious about what could be so unsettling, more dramatic than the true story of Fletcher Mackinnon and his close brush with death.

A sudden blast nearly shook them from the bench. MacLard yelped and leaped from Skye's arms and scampered away.

"Damn fireworks," Kyle muttered. "I'll catch the dog," he said, jumping up to go after the fleeing pup. "MacLard, you rascal. Stay!"

The terrier halted, almost tumbling head over paws, then crouched in the grass.

Kyle picked him up and scratched behind his feathery ears. "That's better, little guy. The noise will soon be ended."

Skye arrived and took the dog from his arms. Looking gratefully at Kyle, she said, "I'm so sorry. I know he's a nuisance, but I couldn't leave him on Skye, not when we're so attached."

"Dogs are among my favorite things," he said. "Next to cattle, and horses—and perhaps a certain young lady whose acquaintance I've made recently. Speaking of horses, we'll go to the fair tomorrow. St. Louis is packed for the holiday, and the auction will be a lively one."

They began to walk slowly toward the center of town. "I

thought you intended to buy Diamond Dust," Skye observed.

"I would like to, if you're still willing to sell. But we shouldn't miss the fair, at any rate. It's quite a sight, even if you're not in the market for a horse."

"I'd enjoy it," she said. "Maybe Missy will go with us."

"I hope so, though she's seen it several times and complains of the dust and some of the raucous behavior of the bidders. She might prefer a buggy ride around the town later in the day. Then dinner at a good restaurant. I want her to gain some weight. She's far too thin."

Skye was silent for a time.

"Skye, you were about to tell me something about your father, I believe."

"Aye. But I suppose it can wait. We're nearly at the hotel and I do want to look in on Missy."

Something had been bothering her these past few minutes, but he couldn't figure what had happened. In the light of the street lamp the face beneath the perky bonnet had taken on a veiled, uneasy expression. As he studied her, she gnawed her lip as if struggling with some weighty subject, or maybe indecision. She had abruptly withdrawn from him in a way he couldn't understand. She was generally so cheerful, so open, speaking what was on her mind. This was a new and different Skye he hadn't seen before. He hoped whatever was disturbing her would soon be resolved.

They entered the hotel foyer and climbed the steps to Missy's third-floor suite. Skye tucked MacLard under one arm and pulled out a key. She whispered, "Missy told me to peek in when we returned. If she's sleeping, I'm to let her rest." She carefully opened the door and looked inside for several seconds. Then she closed it without making a sound, and gave him a reassuring nod. "She's sound asleep."

"Good. Now may I suggest you get some rest yourself. I'll call on you at eight o'clock sharp. Is that agreeable?"

"Fine. I'll be ready."

He saw her safely inside, then headed toward the street. He had noticed a gambling hall near the hotel and had a pocketful of winnings from the *Mississippi Belle* to lay on the line. No doubt Skye was just tired after the trip. The bloody fireworks had probably started her headache. Tomorrow she would be her usual vivacious self, he was sure. They would start planning the last leg of their journey west, nine hundred and fifty miles on the Missouri to Vermillion—and home.

Loup Leveque left his squalid backwater hotel shortly before dawn and headed toward the fairgrounds. He rode an old horse that had little life left in it. He had bought the sorry beast from a peddler for ten dollars; too much, but he needed something to ride until he purchased a quality animal at the auction.

Today would be the most important day of his life. By the time he left St. Louis, he would be the greatest hero the Lakota people had ever known. Not the first to kill a white man, but the first to count coup, then rid Dakota of the worst threat from foreigners since Blanton Wyndford arrived ten years ago.

James Kyler Wyndford was that threat—and others like him who would be inspired by his success. Loup knew the story of the Wyndfords by heart, had heard it at the campfires as soon as he returned to the badlands from Quebec. It had become a legend, outlasting the lives of the five Lakotas who had killed the first Wyndford nine years ago. The Sioux had made an example of that Wyndford. They had made certain no person could look upon Wyndford's mutilated body without fear, without knowing for certain the Sioux would never tolerate the white man in their land. Loup hadn't been around to participate in that killing, but now he would establish his place in the tribe when he murdered Wyndford's younger brother.

Loup kicked his horse, merging into the stream of people headed toward the fair. Plodding through the crowd, he thought of the how the Dakotas, the Yanktons, and the Yanktonais who lived near the Missouri allowed boats to pass unscathed. Loup considered them traitors. Being half white, he understood the white man's lust for land, once they pierced the wilderness. If he could cleanse himself of white blood, he would do it. He would rid the land forever of the white ranchers who seduced the Indian people into giving up their pride, their land, their way of life. It would begin *today,* because James Kyler Wyndford had arrived last night on the paddle wheeler from New Orleans. Wyndford would be at the auction. This would be the last day of James Wyndford's life.

⇥ *Chapter 21* ⇤

Skye was dressed and ready several minutes before eight o'clock. She had looked in on Missy and found her comfortable and looking forward to a morning of leisure, a bath provided by the hotel maid, and in the afternoon, the carriage ride promised by Kyle. After a brief chat, Skye bid her good-bye and returned to her own room to await Kyle's arrival.

Sitting in the room's single chair, Skye slowly pulled on her kid gloves. She wished she had told Kyle about her Indian blood when she'd had the opportunity. She would have done it if the fireworks hadn't exploded and caused a delay. Later, she had lost her nerve, which annoyed her greatly. She must put her faith in his good sense and fairness. If he loved her, as he'd told her several days ago, he wouldn't think twice about her being part Lakota. Maybe she could show him how it might be an advantage to have connections to these people who had lived on the land for so many years. They would be neighbors and, she hoped, friends. Of course there were cultural differences, but all it would take to bridge them was wisdom, understanding, and mutual respect. The country out west was enormous beyond belief. There would surely be land and water for everyone in this bountiful land. On the other hand, Kyle could just as easily be appalled, so she should be prepared for the worst.

When the knock came, she adjusted her wide-brimmed straw hat and opened the door. Kyle grinned down at her. His tanned, rugged good looks increased the tempo of her heart, as it always did. Today he looked unusually handsome in western garb. Under a tan broadcloth jacket, he wore a white linen shirt, topped by a maroon neckerchief in place of a cravat. His belted trousers were tucked into dun-colored boots. At her appearance, he swept his black felt slouch hat from his head and gave her a slight bow. *Dashing* was an understatement for the way he looked; *devastating* was a more accurate description.

"Good morning, Miss Mackinnon," he said as he held his hat over his chest. "I hope you're well rested."

"I'm happy to say I am, thank you," she responded. "Have you seen Missy?"

"I have. She is eating a hearty breakfast, though she must share tidbits with MacLard. She has a first-class seat overlooking the street and says she will be ready to tour the city with us this afternoon." He reached in his coat pocket and held up three tickets. "I've been to the steamship office, and we're set to travel on the *Royal Eagle* tomorrow afternoon. Our horses and supplies will be on a freighter following in our wake. And I have received correspondence from Reyes Pacheco, my ranch foreman. He knows I always stay at the Louis Hotel, and he was kind enough to have a letter waiting for me."

"Really? News from your home." Skye took Kyle's arm and accompanied him down the hall. Her spirits were bright this morning. She felt rested and ready for whatever the day might hold. One thing for certain, she would tell Kyle about her heritage as soon as possible. Her attraction to him was boundless, and she must get this matter settled before she was so in love she had no way to manage a retreat—if that should become necessary. The possibility he might totally reject her was unthinkable. And yet, deep inside, she knew that could happen. She had to muster her courage and tell him the truth this very day.

"Good news. Reyes reports the grasses are thriving and the yearlings weigh pounds more than this time last year. Reyes will meet us at Vermillion when we dock there. And so far this summer, there's been no problems with the Indians."

There it was again. That tone Kyle used when he spoke of Indians. "Indian problems? What sort of trouble would you expect?" She kept her voice casual and pleasant as she preceded him down the stairs and out to the bustling, sun-dappled street.

"None that a hundred miles of prairie wouldn't take care of. Distance; that's the key to peace and harmony."

"I see," she responded. She was in no mood to argue with him now, and after all, she had no personal experience in dealing with the Lakotas in their own land. She climbed into a hired carriage, and popped open her parasol. She could hear Laurel's voice reminding her that the Missouri sun was just as damaging to a lady's skin as the sun in Louisiana.

Kyle climbed in beside her and ordered the driver to take them to the fairgrounds.

"Don't you have *any* Indian friends, Kyle? Native families in the neighborhood?"

His smile, while warm, was definitely patronizing. "There are no *neighborhoods* in the Wind River valley, little lass. We have trading posts; we have native villages, which are temporary settlements; and we have *one* ranch head-quarters—mine. The Indians hunt buffalo across vast areas and sell the hides to traders along the river. I assure you, the natives give Wind River Ranch a wide berth."

She gazed at the passing scenery as they traveled along the streets toward the river road. This was not a good beginning for the conversation she had in mind. "You mean you never see them? Ever?"

"I see them. When I go into town. Badger has some breeds in his school at Vermillion."

Breeds. What a disparaging term. She fought back an angry remark. Her voice was frosty when she said, "Oh? Then I suppose Badger has Indian playmates."

"Not if I can prevent it," Kyle said sharply. "I've told him to be polite but keep his distance."

"Distance. You use that word often when referring to the native people."

"Trust me on this, Skye. *Distance* is the best way of handling the matter."

You don't keep distance between yourself and me, and I *am a breed,* she wanted to say hotly, but clamped her lips instead. She reminded herself that he had no idea she carried the blood of the Lakota Sioux. She must tell him—now. Taking a deep breath, she turned to him. "Kyle—"

"There it is—where all the flags are waving from the top of the barn."

Turning, she left her words unspoken. She had expected the ride to be longer, but the fairgrounds was only a short distance from the center of town. Her revelation would have to wait until after the auction. But then she would tell him, no matter what.

Loup located the horse he wanted within minutes of arriving at the pens. He knew prime horseflesh when he saw it, and the tall black stallion was a rare prize. Luckily for him, he had killed the old boatman and stolen the man's earnings. A horse like the black would cost plenty. It was good the stallion was underweight and not well groomed like most of the others going up for sale. Where had the auctioneer acquired such an animal? Sometimes a horse could be purchased before the start of the auction if a top price was offered.

He tugged on his eyepatch and headed toward the sales office.

A few minutes later, he emerged and headed for the pen. "Greedy white bastard," he mumbled under his breath. "Should have gotten the horse for one-fifty. The bastard put half the money in his own dirty pocket." Hooking a lead rope to the surprisingly fine bridle the stallion was wearing, he led him to a shade tree where his former mount stood swatting flies. He switched his tack to the back of the slender stallion and took him to a spot within view of the barn's main entrance. He noted with satisfaction that the animal was young enough to have plenty of stamina. It would soon have a chance to race its guts out.

Loup had been watching the crowd for over thirty minutes when he saw a well-dressed couple arrive in a carriage and make their way toward the barn's entrance. The man exactly fit the description he had of James Kyler Wyndford: tall, well-built, light brown hair, a commanding presence in any assemblage. Loup had to be completely sure, though, before he took the man's scalp and left for Dakota. He inched through the dozens of people waiting to gain entry to the auction and slipped in behind the couple, who were deep in conversation.

"What if we see a horse we want to buy?" the girl was asking. She was a beauty, Loup noted. One glance told him she probably had Indian blood.

"We will buy it," said the man. "If you see a horse that appeals to your expert eye, I would be a fool not to take your advice."

"You flatter me, Kyle. I'm no expert when it comes to the new American cross-breeds."

Kyle. All the proof Loup needed. Wyndford had arrived on the boat, and now he was here at the horse auction, just as Loup had known he would be. Loup hadn't counted on the lady, though. Not that it mattered. When the time was ripe, Wyndford would die.

Loup trailed the couple, memorizing the man's features. The crowded fair was not the best choice of a place to pierce Wyndford's heart and take his scalp. Escape would be easier if the location was more secluded. After the auction, perhaps. When Wyndford returned to town, maybe he would leave the lady somewhere, then walk alone to his next destination. If dark had fallen, so much the better. The temptation to reach out his hand at once and count coup by touching his adversary was hard to resist. That much, at least, he could do. Loup wasn't sure if he would reap less glory if the adversary didn't put up a fight, but he figured he could embellish the event when he told the story to the tribal council. He stretched out his hand toward Wyndford's shoulder.

Wyndford took an abrupt turn to his right, inadvertently moving away from Loup's grasp. "I'll be damned!"

"Kyle, what is it?" The girl stopped walking and looked where Wyndford was staring.

"I think that's Raven Duke over by that tree."

"No! Really? Where?"

Loup dropped his arm and backed up a step, following Wyndford's gaze. The man was staring at the black stallion.

"We must see!" the girl exclaimed, starting toward the horse with Wyndford at her side.

Loup followed the couple, uncertain as to how to deal with this new development.

Wyndford stood directly in front of the black horse and rubbed its muzzle. The animal tossed its head and whinnied, almost as if it were glad to see him. "I'll be—it *is* Raven." Wyndford looped his arm around the horse's neck and patted him. "Hey, old boy, I never thought I'd see you again." He glowed with pleasure.

Loup approached. *"Monsieur,* you know this horse? I just bought him from the auctioneer. He's a fine one. Cost me five hundred dollars."

Wyndford looked him in the eye, staring at him as if trying to size up the situation. "You just bought him today—here?" he asked.

"Oui, monsieur." Loup pulled out the receipt he'd been given, grateful that the price he'd paid was not written on it. "A fine bit of horseflesh, you'll agree. I hope you'll be as fortunate at today's sale."

The girl grasped Wyndford's arm. "You must try to buy him back. Explain he was once your horse."

Loup narrowed his eyes and gazed at the lady. The sight of her catlike green eyes, the full lips, and the petite waist with a generous swelling above started a surge in his loins. He'd like to have her, if there was any way he could manage it.

"I'll explain, sir," Wyndford was saying to him.

Loup wanted to laugh at the rich white rancher calling him—Loup Leveque, son of Siyaka—*sir.* He liked the sound of it. He stroked a braid along his shoulder and waited for Wyndford to offer his explanation, not that he gave a damn about hearing anything from this man whose heart he would soon pierce with his concealed blade.

"This horse was stolen from me not five days ago," Wyndford explained. "I was transporting the animal on the steamboat *Mississippi Belle*. I took him for a ride in the woods near the river, and a runaway slave stole him. Shot me in the process."

Loup stared hard at Wyndford. He was most fortunate, if this story were true, that Wyndford hadn't been killed before he could do it himself. That would have ruined all his plans. "Not my concern," he muttered. "I bought the horse today with no questions asked. The stallion is mine."

"Mr. Wyndford—" The girl looked stricken. Loup wondered idly why she should care so much about the horse.

"Look, Mr. . . ." Wyndford began.

"Leveque."

"Look, Mr. Leveque, I'd like to buy the horse from you. I bred this horse myself and was very upset when I lost him. I'll pay you whatever you're out, and an additional one hundred dollars."

Loup liked the way this was going. "You know he's part thoroughbred, then."

"Yes. I know that."

Loup wanted to laugh at Wyndford's stupid admission, but he kept his lips tight and acted as if he were considering the offer.

"You said you paid five hundred," commented Wyndford. "I'll pay that plus a hundred-dollar bonus. The stallion's not a racehorse, but I do have an attachment to him."

Loup was secretly delighted. This was a very lucky day. He'd prefer the animal had been a racer, but everyone knew these thorougbreds were built for speed. His plan of action was clear. "I'll sell you the horse, but not now, not here. We'll meet in town to make the deal."

Wyndford nodded. "I have no problem with that. In fact, I'll need to get additional funds at my hotel. We can go immediately, if you like."

"Oui. I will ride the horse back to town where my other mount is stabled. I will meet you in front of the cathedral within the hour."

Wyndford turned to the girl. "Miss Mackinnon, we'll have to delay our visit to the auction. I apologize."

"But I'm thrilled you found Raven. The auction isn't important."

Facing Loup, he said, "One hour. I will be at St. Louis Cathedral near the river."

"And I will bring the horse," Loup replied.

Wyndford reached out his hand. "Then we have a deal."

Loup allowed himself to grin. He took Wyndford's hand and shook it in the white man's foolish way. This gesture was like counting coup, he thought with satisfaction. A touch, or a handshake. It was the same—once he sliced the scalp from Wyndford's head.

Loup rode the stallion back toward town, pleased to find the horse was all he had hoped and more. As expert a horseman as he was, Loup found he had his hands full with the powerful animal beneath him. He looked forward to the moment he could unleash that power and ride like the wind toward Dakota.

As he rode, he thought of Wyndford, of his good looks and condescending manner. How easy it was to despise such a man. Then he thought of the girl. He would like to possess her. She would scream and struggle if he forced her to his will. He yanked the eyepatch from his forehead. Next time he saw her, he would enjoy tormenting her with his own shocking visage. He mulled over her name—Mackinnon. It was a name he'd heard somewhere long ago. He reined up the horse at a cheap bar at the edge of the city. Time for one drink and then he'd head for the cathedral. Mackinnon. He knew that name for sure. As he slid to the ground and fastened the stallion's reins to a post, an old memory slid into his thoughts. His father, Siyaka, was telling him the story of his banishment from the Lakotas. *I watched as the braves prepared to kill the half-breed renegade who had defeated me in combat,* Siyaka had said. *A Scottish trapper appeared suddenly and claimed that the renegade was his son by an Indian princess. He bought him from the chief, and I was not allowed to save face by taking White Arrow's life. I left the land of the Lakota to search for the Scot and his son. But I never found them. Their name was Mackinnon.*

Loup frowned as he envisioned the girl and the color of her skin. Light as fresh cream, but with undertones of golden bronze. Mackinnon. Had he stumbled into the most remarkable find of his life? Could the girl be related to the Scot who had destroyed his father's life? Taken away his honor? He would give all he possessed to know: the black stallion, the gentleman's fancy walking stick with the hidden knife—anything, except the chance to kill James Kyler Wyndford. He would study her closely when they met at the cathedral. If she was part Lakota, she must surely be related to the Scottish trapper and thus to White Arrow, the two men he hated most in the world, besides James Wyndford. A new idea exploded in his brain. He could kill Wyndford and take the girl to Dakota. If she was related to White Arrow, he would take revenge in ways that would know no limits of pleasure and satisfaction. Entering the dark, pungent bar, he grinned at the prospect and thanked whatever gods existed for this golden opportunity.

⊰ Chapter 22 ⊱

With mixed emotions, Kyle watched Leveque canter away from the fairgrounds. He knew that finding the horse was a miracle, but Leveque was disgusting and dangerous. He felt the man's evil like a coiled snake ready to strike. But he didn't want to frighten Skye.

Skye gave him an excited grin as he joined her in the carriage. Her lovely eyes were sparkling. "It's wonderful, Kyle. Think of it. You've found Raven. He's fated to be your horse, 'tis certain."

Staring again down the river road, Kyle noted Leveque

was almost out of sight. The half-breed had given Skye a lecherous appraisal, and the thought of what was in the man's mind sickened him. Kyle was grateful Skye hadn't been aware of the man's lewd thoughts.

"I assume the escaping slave made it safely away. At least, I hope so."

"I'm delighted," she said perkily. "You see, Kyle, you did the right thing, and now all will end well. But—"

"Yes?"

"But I will be quite relieved when you have Raven back in your possession. That Mr. Leveque doesn't look too trustworthy."

Kyle leaned against the cushion as they traveled toward town. "You guessed right about that. Besides being uglier than sin, I'm sure he lied about what he paid for the horse. He's entitled to a profit, but I'm betting he more than tripled the price."

"My goodness, maybe you should point that out when you meet him. Tell him he must adjust the amount, or he's not being fair."

What a charming innocent she was, he thought. He loved her all the more for her occasional naïveté and was pleased he was around to guard her from any charlatans who might try to take advantage of her. "Leveque—fair? I doubt if he knows the meaning of the word. Typical half-breed, you see."

He was surprised to see annoyance flit behind her eyes.

Lifting her chin, she said, "I've known a few Scots who could bargain with the devil and win. And I expect the English do their share of horse trading, on occasion."

He laughed at her feisty tone, though why she would be riled over his comment about Leveque escaped him. What a handful she was going to be; how interesting she would make the long winter nights in Dakota with her high spirits and startling observations. Looking at her in the morning sun, her heart-shaped face shaded by the lacy umbrella, he decided he would have to propose marriage soon, whether or not her family moved to Dakota. If she insisted on returning to New Orleans, he would simply have to accompany her. It was time he looked after his own future happiness; Reyes could manage the ranch this fall. He wanted this bonnie Scottish lass at his side, now and for all the seasons of their lives.

In minutes, the carriage pulled up to the Hotel Louis, and Skye allowed Kyle to assist her to alight. She chastised herself for almost losing her temper again, but she had only herself to blame. Kyle would be more careful with his remarks once he learned she had Indian blood. She must convince him his prejudice was wrong and doing him more harm than good. Otherwise, his hatred could destroy any hope for their future together.

As they entered the cool interior of the hotel lobby, he gazed at her while she lowered her parasol. "Would you prefer to wait here while I go to the cathedral? I don't imagine you care to encounter our friend, Leveque, any more than necessary."

"He's distasteful, but I would like to go with you, if you have no objection."

"Of course not. I intend to avoid trouble with the man— just give him his inflated price and take the horse. To be honest, Raven Duke is worth more to me than I'm paying. Much more."

"I'll change into my riding clothes. And Kyle, there is something we *must* discuss once this is done, something important I've been wanting to tell you. I do hope we'll have time for a serious discussion."

He nodded solemnly, almost too solemnly. It crossed her mind that he was again being patronizing. Did he think a youngish female couldn't manage a serious discussion? Just wait till he heard her news. Their talk could be more than serious; it might be fatal for their relationship.

He followed her up the thickly carpeted steps. "While you change, I'll say hello to Missy and tell her about Raven."

"Aye. She'll be thrilled." Skye let herself into her room. She was still elated over the discovery of Kyle's horse, but every time she thought of telling him her secret, she felt her heart quicken and her stomach fill with butterflies. How would she begin?

You see, Kyle, my father is one-half Lakota Sioux. If my

arithmetic is correct, that makes me a quarter-breed Indian. Is there a name for such a creature? Or is every such person simply called a breed by the white man?

Or she could say, *By the way, sir, my grandmother was a Lakota princess from this very land you call home. That makes me royal, I suppose. You may address me as Your Highness, if you like, since your father was merely an earl.*

Or perhaps, *I'm aware your brother was brutally murdered by Lakotas, but I must tell you I carry Lakota blood in my veins. You may, therefore, take your revenge on me, if you like. But if you go too far, my father, who is a half-breed, will take his revenge on you.*

Indeed, any way she said it, it was sure to create shock at the least—maybe even revulsion. Kyle was definitely disgusted by Mr. Leveque, but she could forgive him for that, considering the man's unpleasant face and blatant lies. It was fortunate for all concerned that Kyle hadn't noticed the rude look that Leveque had given her. She had felt shivers along her spine and had been forced to fix her smile in place to hide the queer feeling in the pit of her stomach. Leveque was a half-breed, but so was her father. That just proved that people of similar heritage could be entirely different from each other. She had pointed out to Kyle that there were bad and good people in all races. Surely here was proof of her words.

She pulled on her riding skirt, a simple cotton blouse, and a lightweight jacket. The day was growing steamier by the minute. She was looking forward to riding Spirit Lady and seeing more of the town of St. Louis. She hoped the purchase of Raven Duke would go smoothly and they would soon be on their way.

Kyle was elated as he rode beside Skye on the way to the cathedral. What fantastic luck to have found Raven Duke. He hoped fervently that Leveque would be on time and be grateful enough for his profit to get the matter settled quickly. Kyle wanted Raven out of the man's grasp. And he knew he couldn't tolerate any more insulting looks thrown at Skye Mackinnon.

He noticed she was suddenly quiet. He was sorry he

hadn't insisted she remain at the hotel until this transaction was complete. But she had been eager to come along, and he couldn't think of any good reason to refuse her. No doubt he was overreacting to the man's scarred, grizzled face, the eyepatch, and the greasy braids dangling around his ears. After all, ugliness was not a crime, or half the people he knew might be spending time in jail. Folks out west didn't concern themselves too much with good looks. They were too busy trying to survive to worry about such frivolous matters.

He rode the easy-gaited Diamond Dust across the broad square in front of the St. Louis Cathedral, new and imposing and the centerpiece of the community. With relief, he saw Raven tied just outside the cathedral door. His fears that Leveque might somehow disappear had been for naught.

"There's Raven Duke!" cried Skye, reining her mare toward the waiting horse. "But where is Mr. Leveque?"

"Not far, you can bet," Kyle noted. "He's not going to miss making such a profitable deal."

"Then you'll pay him what he asked?"

"We shook hands on it. That's the same as giving one's word. Besides, I'm glad to pay any price to get Raven back."

They halted near Raven, who greeted them with a nervous toss of his black mane, which was matted and dirty but thickly luxuriant.

Kyle dismounted and patted the muscled chest. "Well, Raven, you've had quite an adventure. Meet your new stable mate, Diamond Dust."

The black rolled his eyes toward the stallion several yards away and cocked his ears forward.

"I know, I know," said Kyle. "You think this big blue roan is a rival for the girls. Well, he just might be before the summer is through. But I'll make sure there are plenty of pretty fillies for both of you." Looking at Skye, he gave her a rather apologetic look for his suggestive speech, then a slow wink of mutual understanding. She grinned back at him, and before he could assist her, she stepped gracefully from her saddle.

"You're full of promises, Kyle. I hope you own mares as

attractive as my Spirit Lady. Otherwise, you might have two very disappointed stallions." Her eyes twinkled in shared merriment.

Kyle turned his attention to Raven while Skye began securing Lady to the hitching rail. Suddenly he felt something sharp pressing into his lower back.

"We meet again, James Kyler Wyndford," was the low voice near his ear. He hadn't seen the light-footed Leveque emerge from the nearby shrubbery.

Kyle started to turn, but he felt the sharp object begin to prick his flesh at a spot just below his belt next to his spine. "What in hell—" he said in a low tone.

"Don't turn around. Not yet. I have something to say to you."

"What've you got poking into my back, Leveque? I'm ready to make our deal."

"The knife you feel is a very clever instrument of death. I took it from an Englishman in Quebec years ago—a very *dead* Englishman who had the stupidity to cheat me at cards."

Kyle sucked in his breath but couldn't dislodge the knifepoint. He knew the thing must have penetrated his clothing to be causing such a burning sensation. Leveque was crazier than he was ugly. The man was indeed treacherous; he'd felt it from the moment he looked into Leveque's devilish face. He must try to keep him talking.

"All right, Leveque. What's on your mind? I've got the gold on me. It's yours. Why don't you take it and enjoy yourself in the town with all that wealth? You don't know me, and I don't know you. Get your weapon out of my back, and we'll complete our deal and go our separate ways."

"But I *do* know you, Mr. James Kyler Wyndford. And I believe I know your lady there, the woman named Mackinnon."

Kyle's blood ran cold when Leveque spoke Skye's name. He had to keep his head, keep his thoughts collected and his temper under control. "It's possible you've met *me* somewhere, Leveque. But I can assure you, you've never laid eyes on Miss Mackinnon. The lady is from Scotland. Her grandfather visited Dakota years ago, but she's never been in

America, not until this spring. She's been in New Orleans ever since she arrived. She's traveling with my family—under *my* protection."

To his surprise, Leveque began to laugh, the sound deep in his chest, then erupting from his throat like some half-mad animal. "So her grandfather was the Scot trapper named Mackinnon. Her father was White Arrow, the half-breed. I guessed right." Leveque leaned near, keeping the pressure of the knifepoint against Kyle's back.

"You're crazy, Leveque."

"What going on, Kyle?" Skye asked as she walked toward them, wearing a puzzled expression on her face.

Kyle knew he must warn her to get away. If this madman intended murder and robbery, he must make certain Skye escaped. He might find a chance to jump Leveque, but if he failed, he knew the villain's knife would swiftly find its way to his heart.

Leveque stopped laughing and called to the girl. "Miss *Mackinnon*—from Scotland, is it true?"

"Aye. My home was the Isle of Skye." She stopped, her eyes locked on Kyle.

Kyle knew she suspected something was wrong, but she was courageous enough to stand by until she knew what was happening. As much as he admired her courage, he had to give her a chance to escape. Then he could try to get Leveque. "Miss Mackinnon," he called, an edge to his voice, "you must go to the hotel—*now*. Leveque and I have business, more complicated than I thought. Now mount your horse and leave us alone." His voice was as gruff as he could make it.

"No," snarled Leveque. "I want her here."

Kyle felt the pain increase as the blade pressed his flesh. Leveque laughed again.

"Listen, Leveque. I don't know what you're trying to pull, but if you've got some grudge against me, let's discuss it, man to man. Let the lady leave. She's a complete stranger to you."

"No, *mon ami*. She is my destiny, delivered to me by avenging gods."

So—the man wanted *Skye* and would kill to have her.

Maybe that was what he had intended from the first. "Skye, get the hell out of here!" Kyle's tone was harsh and demanding. He was rewarded by the knife's piercing the flesh under his coat. He winced but kept his eyes focused on Skye. She had to understand, had to leave now, before it was too late.

She didn't budge. "What do you want, Mr. Leveque?" she asked in a clear, calm voice.

"Many things, Lakota woman. I want your friend's money, his horse . . . his *squaw*, and maybe his life."

Huskily, Kyle said, "Take the gold; take the horse. Hell, push that blade home, if you must. But you've got the lady mixed up with someone else. She isn't Lakota and certainly not a *squaw!* She's from Scotland and has never set foot in the West."

Leveque's laugh was a gurgle of pleasure deep in his throat. "Tell your friend, Miss Mackinnon," he shouted to her. "Tell him you are a Lakota *breed*. Tell him about your father and grandfather—and maybe I will decide to spare his life so he can think about what pleasure I'm having with you—in my Lakota lodge, every night, until you begin to bore me."

⇥ Chapter 23 ⇤

Leveque's shouted remarks hit Skye like a physical blow, almost making her knees buckle.

Leveque must be Lakota, and somehow he knew about her. He had revealed everything. Her mouth went dry as she stared at Kyle and saw shock and disbelief written plainly in his face. She was dizzy with regret. She should have told him the truth long ago, when they'd first met. No matter what she said now, he might never trust her again. Would he dismiss her from his life like a mongrel dog that had overstepped its boundaries?

She had too much pride to let tears of humiliation and anger slip into her eyes. It was a great mystery where Mr. Leveque got his information about her private past. But he knew, and he was calling her a Lakota, a squaw. She was Scottish, of course, but not entirely, and her Lakota blood was something she couldn't deny, didn't want to deny, and had taken pride in for as long as she could remember.

"Skye, will you for God's sake go back to the hotel!"

She couldn't imagine what was in Kyle's mind, but the time for truth had arrived. "Kyle, what Mr. Leveque says is true. I intended to tell you this afternoon. I know I should have done so sooner . . ." She stopped as she saw Kyle wince and grit his teeth. As critical as her speech was, she suddenly realized something else was going on. She would swear Kyle was in physical pain and trying hard to conceal it.

"The girl isn't going anywhere," Leveque said in a loud voice. "Except with me."

Leveque's words didn't register. She stared hard at Kyle, but he was looking at her with tight lips. "Kyle—"

"Don't move," snapped Leveque. "I have a knife at his back and if you don't cooperate, I'll kill him."

Horror spread through her. She was frozen in place.

A shout came from the cathedral doorway.

"You're here! At last! We've been watching for your arrival." Two priests hurried forward, one small and middle-aged, the other young and burly.

The smaller priest rushed up to her and grasped her arm. His kindly face was wreathed in smiles; his eyes crinkled in excitement.

"Everything's ready, so please come with us. I'm Father Aumont and this is Brother Paul."

Her mind whirled. She didn't care who the newcomers were, only that someone was here who might be of help. She grabbed the priest's sleeve. "Aye. We're ready. Shall we go inside?"

"Wait!" snarled Leveque. "We're not going anywhere."

Father Aumont moved toward Kyle and Leveque, with

Brother Paul close beside him. "I assume you're the groom," he said directly to Kyle. "I'm sorry Father Lenoir couldn't be here for the wedding. He had to rush to the bedside of a dying parishioner. Death takes precedence, you know," the little priest said gaily. "We haven't met, but I assure you, I can conduct the service as well as Father Lenoir. I'm new in St. Louis, but I'll soon be acquainted with everyone."

Skye watched Kyle struggle with uncertainty, knowing he was weighing the possibilities of rescue.

She hurried up to him. "Kyle, my guess is Father Aumont is expecting a wedding party. You and Mr. Leveque should stop quarreling so we can go inside."

The priest turned to her. "You *are* the bride, are you not?"

"Uh . . . yes. I'm the bride." She couldn't believe her own words, but anything was better than standing helplessly by, watching Kyle be killed.

Kyle squared his shoulders. "Yes, she is the bride, but we've called the whole thing off. Now she's leaving—aren't you, Skye?"

Ignoring his commanding tone, she said, "Not until we've talked things over—inside the good father's office."

The priest rung his hands. "Surely this is a case of last-minute nerves. I have everything ready. The papers are prepared for your signatures. Your clothing is in the dressing room and flowers are in the chapel." He looked at Leveque. "If you're their friend, sir, I implore you to help them settle their differences."

Leveque glared in stony silence.

Father Aumont took charge. "We won't stand out here arguing. Will you please all come into the church."

Kyle stepped forward and took Skye's arm. "We'll go through with the *wedding,* as planned—if that's your wish, Skye, darling."

Leveque hovered near with a look of pure hatred on his face.

"I'm sure the good father knows what's best," Kyle said. "We'll follow him inside. Agreed?"

Skye saw that Leveque had one hand inside his jacket,

presumably concealing his weapon. She also caught a glimpse of blood on Kyle's coat.

"You may leave, Leveque," Kyle said fiercely.

"No. I'll stay here. I still have the upper hand."

Kyle frowned and squeezed Skye's arm. "Then we'll go inside with the priest."

Father Aumont led them into the foyer of the cathedral. Skye held onto Kyle, aware that Leveque was only a step behind them. Behind Leveque came Brother Paul.

Once inside the church office, Father Aumont pointed to papers on his desk. "You'll need to sign these documents before the ceremony. My, you'll be a beautiful bride," he simpered. "Just glowing. Now don't be nervous, young lady. Do you have any attendants?"

"I'm sorry, no." She looked over her shoulder at Leveque and gulped at the terrible visage, annoyance and determination etched in every line of his face, his eyepatch gone to reveal a puckered eye, half obscured by a jagged scar from his forehead to his cheekbone.

Woodenly, she picked up the stylus and signed her name in the space indicated.

"Now you, sir. What was the name again?"

"Wyndford. James Kyler Wyndford."

"Sign right there, Mr. Wyndford. For some reason, I thought a Mr. Morgan reserved the church."

"Yes, Morgan's a close acquaintance," said Kyle.

Skye was amazed at how smoothly Kyle had fallen into their scheme. His cool manner settled her nerves. Surely Leveque would soon give up and leave them alone.

"Congratulations, you are now legally wed," announced Father Aumont. "In the eyes of the state, but not of the church, of course." The father pointed to a closed door. "Your dress and veil were delivered this morning by your seamstress, my dear. Your suit is there, too, sir, in an adjoining room," he said to Kyle. "I'll leave you now—"

"No, don't go," Kyle snapped. "Uh, we may need you close by to consult with us—regarding this serious step we're about to take. If you'll wait outside the dressing room for a few minutes, Miss Mackinnon and I will go inside and discuss a few private matters."

"Yes, I understand. Whatever you prefer," answered the priest. "I'll wait right here and say a prayer for you to resolve your differences. I can see you're perfectly suited. Such a charming couple mustn't allow a few minor problems to spoil a lifetime of love." He clasped his hands under his chin as he contemplated the joys of matrimony.

"Thank you, Father. Please remain near enough for us to summon you." Kyle spoke so emphatically, he sounded like he was issuing an order rather than making a request.

"Yes. I'll be within earshot. I don't believe I've met your friend. I assume he's a member of the wedding party." Aumont indicated Leveque with a brief glance.

"If he chooses," muttered Kyle.

Leveque glared at husky Brother Paul beside him, then grunted and folded his arms over his chest.

Kyle revolved to squarely face Leveque. "Unless, of course, Mr. Leveque decides to keep that urgent appointment he was so concerned about. The one in the *next county*. We don't want to *detain* you, Mr. Leveque." He pulled a leather coin purse from inside his coat and held it toward the half-breed.

Leveque looked daggers at Kyle, then snatched the money from his hand. "I'll take that, but I'm not going anywhere— not until I get what I came for."

Kyle opened the door the priest had indicated and ushered Skye inside. He closed it quickly behind them.

"Kyle," she whispered and embraced him.

He held her tightly, steadying her until her heartbeat slowed a bit. "It's all right, lass," he whispered. "We're going to be all right now."

She moved back and gazed up at him. "How badly are you hurt?"

"I'm all right."

"I saw blood on your coat. Please let me see what he's done to you."

He pulled off his coat and turned his back toward her. The back of his shirt was stained with blood.

"Dear heaven, you need help. We must—"

"It's not serious," he said, facing her. "Only a cut where he kept jabbing me with some sort of knife—a stiletto, maybe. The lucky arrival of the priest and your quick thinking saved our lives." He gave her an admiring smile.

"Leveque is insane."

"I'm sure he is. I thought I could get him to leave if I gave him the money, but the man's as tenacious as a starving wolf."

"Kyle, he knows who I am. And now, so do you. I started to tell you several times, but—"

"I understand. We can discuss all that later. What matters now is getting rid of Leveque without his harming us or anyone else. If I could somehow alert Brother Paul, we'd have a stout ally."

"Maybe we can slip out of here," she suggested.

He glanced around the small, windowless room, whitewashed and lighted by several tapers. Two chairs and a table were the only furnishings, the only decoration a large painting of the Virgin Mary hanging on one wall. From a hook on the opposite wall hung a man's formal suit of clothing, complete with ruffled shirt and a black cravat draped over the shoulder. A closed door occupied the fourth wall. Kyle threw it open and entered the adjoining room.

"No way out," he said, reappearing quickly. "There's a window in there, but it's sealed with glass and barred from the outside."

"Do you think Leveque really intends to kill us?"

"He intends to kill me. You, he plans to kidnap."

"Oh." Her hand covered her throat as her stomach contracted violently. "Then he'll have to kill me, too."

Kyle crossed to her and rested his hand gently on her shoulder. "I expected that to be your choice. We'll have to go along with this wedding scheme for a while longer. If Leveque doesn't get discouraged and leave, I'll have to find a chance to jump him."

"Oh, Kyle, please be careful."

"We'll put on these wedding clothes and keep up our pretense until I see an opening."

She stared at him as her fear escalated once more.

"Your wedding dress is in the next room. Put it on quickly, and I'll see if I can fit into that suit." He gave her a wry smile. "We may look like fools, but the subterfuge could save our lives."

Wordlessly, she nodded and hurried into the adjoining room. An exquisite wedding gown created from yards of creamy satin and lace was displayed on a wooden bench. A veil of sheer white tulle rested across it. On the floor were white kid slippers with hosiery folded over them. *Some lady's wedding ensemble,* she thought sadly, *about to be badly misused.* She prayed the dress would come close to fitting her.

A tap came at the door. "I hate to rush you, but we can't stall too long. The real wedding party might arrive and I'd prefer no one else is put at risk. Please hurry, Skye."

"Aye, of course. I'll just be a minute."

She tossed away her hat and stripped off her riding attire. She grabbed the dress and pulled it over her head. Though it was several sizes too large, it would do if she cinched in the waist. She could use a stocking for that and no one would be the wiser. Tiny pearl buttons started at the neck and traveled down the bodice past the waist. She wouldn't need to button all of them, since the veil would cover her from her head to the hem of the skirt.

Her fingers were shaking so badly she wondered if she could get any of the delicate buttons into their loops. She fastened just enough to keep the gown from falling off her shoulders. For a fraction of a second, she thought of the unfortunate bride whose gown would now be secondhand, but she couldn't waste time feeling guilty—not with her life and Kyle's at stake. She picked up one of the stockings and twisted it around her waist. Glancing at the shoes, she decided they were unnecessary since her skirt ballooned over her riding boots. She snatched up the veil and tossed it over her head. It shimmered around her, settling softly over her shoulders and drifting toward the hem. Then she called through the door. "I'm ready, Kyle. Are you?"

"I suppose. Come in."

She walked into the room and stared at him. If the situation hadn't been so dangerous, she would have laughed. The suit was definitely made for a smaller man.

The trousers were no problem, since they were tucked into Kyle's boots and the waist hidden beneath the coat. The shirt was also passable, with its frilly lace from throat to lapel. But the coat was stretched to the breaking point across Kyle's broad shoulders and muscular forearms, and the sleeves were three inches above his wrists.

Kyle frowned at her. "My tailor is totally inept, I fear."

Someone pounded on the door. "If you don't come out, I'll have to come in," came Leveque's unmistakable voice. His patience was plainly wearing thin.

Kyle held out an arm and Skye slid into it. "Here we go. Courage, lass."

Her throat knotted; she smiled wanly.

"Priest!" Kyle shouted. "Father Aumont, are you there? We're ready for the wedding."

Her knees were shaking as they waited for the priest to appear. Kyle held her tightly, then gave her a half-smile touched with regret. "I'm sorry, Skye, for getting you into this."

She looked intently into his dark eyes. "I got myself into it, as you recall. Just please be careful. I'll help if I can."

"No. You must stay out of the way. Promise me you won't interfere, no matter what happens."

She knew his officious tone was meant for her safety. Nodding, she took a deep breath. The door opened to admit Father Aumont.

⊰ Chapter 24 ⊱

Come with me, please," the priest graciously requested.

With his arm around Skye's shoulders, Kyle entered the foyer. He had held out hope that Leveque might have changed his mind and fled. But of course, that hadn't happened, and Leveque was guarding the door, waiting like an animal stalking its prey. Amazingly, the priests were totally unaware of the tension and the maneuvering going on under their noses. Father Aumont was as happy as a sunbeam, doing his best to make the wedding a delightful fait accompli.

"Ah . . . lovely, lovely," Aumont effused over the bride. "Flowers have just been delivered. If you will all come with me—" He flicked a glance at Leveque. "Follow me to the chapel of Our Lady of the Waters, where I will conduct the ceremony."

"Excuse me, Father," Kyle said. "I understand you have a rule against anyone's taking weapons into the sanctuary."

"Weapons? Oh my goodness, yes. No weapons allowed in God's house. Isn't that right, Brother Paul?"

"That's right. No weapons allowed," Brother Paul echoed.

Kyle looked pointedly at Leveque. "Guess you'll have to hand over that knife, Leveque."

From his impressive height, Brother Paul faced Leveque. "No weapons in the church, sir," he said firmly. "You can leave whatever you have with me for safekeeping."

Leveque hesitated.

Kyle said a silent prayer.

"Damn you, Wyndford," shouted Leveque. He lifted his fist in the air. "Watch for me, white man. Behind every hill and bush. You haven't seen the last of Loup Leveque." He ran out the open door, crashed through the shrubbery, and disappeared toward the waterfront.

Father Aumont and Brother Paul gaped in surprise.

"He's gone," Skye cried in relief. She flung her arms around Kyle and accepted his tight hug.

"Yes, he's gone, my love. Thank God, we're all safe."

"But he threatened us. He might lie in wait somewhere."

"You overestimate the man's talents, I'm sure," he said soothingly. "My bet is he's long gone. He's got a pocketful of gold and I figure he'll head toward the wilderness."

"I hope so," she murmured, apparently accepting his reassuring lies.

Father Aumont marched forward, hands on hips. "What happened? What's going on?"

"That man was holding a knife on me," Kyle explained, "threatening to kill me and kidnap the lady."

The priest crossed himself. "I had no idea. Oh my, then God was merciful. You poor children. Shall we call the authorities?"

"It wouldn't do any good, though you might make a report. He's got a solid head start and plenty of gold to buy transportation."

"I'm surprised he didn't take one of our horses," observed Skye as she moved from Kyle's embrace.

"He figured I'd be on him before he got it untied. And he'd be right. There was no way I would've let him ride out of here on Raven or Diamond Dust."

Skye tossed back her veil and tugged at the neck of her dress. Suddenly she burst into jittery laughter. "Look at us, Kyle. Aren't we a sight?"

He joined in her laughter as their eyes met.

"We should change and get on our way," she suggested.

"Just one minute," interjected Father Aumont. "You are legally married. Or should we draw up annullment papers right away?"

"I'd forgotten we signed the papers," Skye said, wiping tears of mirth from her eyes. "Yes, we'd better get the marriage annulled."

Abruptly, Kyle drew her down the hall into the rainbow tinted shadows of a stained glass window. "Skye, a few minutes ago, I thought we had lost all hope for the future and maybe even our lives. I've learned something from my brush with death. We must take happiness when it comes our way, and I know my happiness is with you. You saved my life today with your clever ploy, and I guess that means you can lay claim to it."

"What are you suggesting?"

"We've signed the papers. We're legally wed. Why not accept this event as a blessing in disguise? I love you, my sweet, brave lass. Will you be my wife?"

* * *

Skye couldn't believe her ears. For a long moment, she was too stunned to respond. Then she whispered, "Kyle, I love you, too. But I have to know how you feel about my Indian blood. You've only just learned that my father is half Lakota, and we both know that Lakotas murdered your brother."

He lifted her chin with his fingers. "Skye, I don't care whose blood runs in your veins. I don't care if you're the daughter of my worst enemy and have the blood of a she-wolf. I know what you are inside. I accept you for what you are and love you for it."

His face blurred in front of her.

"Now—will you remain my wife?"

She swallowed and said softly, "Of course I will. I love you with all my heart."

"It's settled, then." He put his hands on her waist, pulled her to him, and covered her mouth. One arm encircled her, pressing her close, as his lips sent lightning streaking through her body.

Abruptly he released her, leaving her senses exploding in mindless joy. He led her back to where Father Aumont waited by the cathedral door. "We will stay married, Father. But we have no need for a ceremony in the chapel."

A woman's scream split the air.

An hysterical woman rushed up to Skye and grabbed her arm, pulling her around to face her. "You've ruined my dress," the matronly woman howled. "And my veil. Who are you, you wicked witch?"

"Calm yourself!" Skye shouted, as if the woman must be deaf as well as blind.

Abruptly, they were confronted by a steaming bride-groom.

Kyle held out his hand. "Mr. Morgan, I presume."

The plump bride-to-be sagged into her fiancé's arms.

Father Aumont rushed to help lower the lady to the floor, where she revived with sobs and moans.

"I demand to know what's going on," Morgan shouted. "Look at my poor little fiancée. I want an immediate explanation." He verged on apoplexy.

"My deepest apologies, Mr. Morgan. We've had a near

tragedy during the past few minutes," Kyle answered smoothly. "We had to borrow your wedding attire in order to survive a crisis."

"Do you think she'll be all right?" Skye asked, leaning near the weeping woman.

"Her color is returning. I believe she'll soon come around," the priest observed.

Brother Paul offered the lady a glass of water. She took several swallows before once again sobbing loudly.

Morgan stood beside her, his face a rigid mask of annoyance.

The two priests helped the lady to stand.

Skye said, "I'm deeply sorry, mistress. But I do believe the dress can be salvaged. There are just a few spots here and there and—"

"Salvaged!" screeched the woman. "Are you suggesting that the bride of the most prominent banker in Memphis should be married in a *salvaged* wedding gown? I've come all this way to be married in the cathedral and my guests will be arriving any minute." Her voice rose shrilly. "What am I to do?"

Mr. Morgan huffed. "You are fortunate, my dear. Look at *my* wedding attire."

Skye took his suggestion and almost giggled, though the sight was hardly amusing. The black suit into which Kyle had forced his large frame had ripped apart across the shoulders and one pants leg had a jagged tear over Kyle's large calf. Kyle's face was a picture of remorse.

"Again, my apologies, Mr. Morgan," he said in a voice overly laden with regret. "Naturally I'll buy you a new suit of clothes. And a dress for your bride, as well. You will have to take my IOU, however. I'm staying at the Louis Hotel and my funds are there." He cocked an eyebrow at Skye and added under his breath, "Those funds that are left after today's fiasco."

She shook her head and pursed her lips.

"Mr. Morgan," the woman interjected, finding something approaching her normal voice. "I'm going home. We'll just have to reschedule our wedding at a later date."

"But sweetheart," Morgan crooned, bending near her, "we have our reservations on the *Mississippi Belle,* leaving tomorrow for New Orleans."

Sweetheart's mouth twisted and tears flowed anew.

Father Aumont rose to the occasion. "I must take some responsibility for these unfortunate events, though I believe I was misled by the Wyndfords." He included both Kyle and Skye in a look of chastisement. "I realize they were in rather desperate circumstances, however, so both I and the Lord will surely be able to forgive them their subterfuge. Let me suggest, Mr. Morgan, that you reschedule your ceremony for tomorrow at 10:00 A.M. I'll make certain the occasion is lovely. Then you can leave on your honeymoon as planned. I believe the boat is due to depart around four o'clock in the afternoon."

"I don't have a wedding dress!" cried the desolate woman.

Mr. Morgan touched her shoulder. "Doesn't Hattie keep samples in her shop, my dear? Perhaps she could quickly alter one to suit you. I am extremely eager to make you my wife, little lady."

Skye was impressed with Mr. Morgan's silken manner. *Little* lady was hardly an accurate description of the buxom matron, but she saw that the woman was responsive to his soothing words.

The lady stared through watery eyes at her groom-to-be. "I'll go at once. Hattie does work miracles, it's true." She glared at Skye, then at Kyle. "I might also say Hattie's bill will be exorbitant. You can count on it." She marched from the office.

Mr. Morgan walked over to Kyle. He pulled a key from his pocket and held it out. "Take this, sir. It's the key to the bridal suite at the Louis Hotel. You'll also find the hotel bill *extremely* exorbitant! I'll stop by the Louis within the hour to present *my* bill to you for the cost of this debacle."

"That's fine, Mr. Morgan. Whatever you say. Leave it at the hotel desk and I will have the funds there by midafternoon. You see, my wife and sister-in-law and I are traveling on tomorrow's packet up the Missouri."

After making cursory farewells to the priests and placing their own clothing into a sack, the newlyweds walked out into the sunshine.

"Wait one minute." Kyle crossed to a rosebush exploding with white blooms and picked the largest one in sight. His expression was tender as he handed her the flower. "Skye, I had intended to propose to you when we reached Dakota. I wanted you to see my country and my home and not be pressured into a decision until you were satisfied you wanted to spend your life there. I do love you. I believe you love me. I realize this was not the wedding you would have preferred, but the important thing is . . . we love each other."

She held the fragrant blossom, entranced by his eyes, his lips, the emotion in his tone.

"Skye Eugenia Mackinnon, you are the loveliest bride I've ever seen."

Full realization of his love swept over her like a warm tide and found its way to her heart. Even though he knew now about her Indian blood, he still loved her and wanted her to be his wife.

Kyle chuckled at Skye's wide-eyed, rapt expression as they rode in the decorated carriage through the streets of St. Louis. The open-air conveyance, draped with white ribbons and dotted with white paper rosettes, had arrived at the front door of the cathedral just as Skye and Kyle exited. Arranged, of course, by Mr. Morgan for himself and his bride to accomodate the brief but momentous journey from the church to the hotel. Tethered behind the carriage jogged Spirit Lady, Diamond Dust, and Raven Duke.

Skye's hair was in complete disarray, but he liked the look. As far as he was concerned, he wanted her disheveled, preferably from a lengthy night's tumble in his bed. Her happiness moved him deeply. She was like a little girl he could adore and spoil and pamper while knowing she possessed the heart of a woman of intelligence and courage and passion. The fact that she was part Lakota was certainly a surprise, but it was nothing he couldn't deal with in time. His prejudice toward the natives had deep roots, but through the years, his initial hatred had mellowed. The prejudices of other whites could be a problem, but he would deal with that whenever it became necessary. For now, he was content to worship the lady seated beside him.

The only flaw in his joy was his concern over Loup Leveque. His reassuring words had been for Skye's benefit. The man was evil and determined to cause trouble.

"Kyle, look! The people are smiling and applauding us. I feel so—so foolish, but I love it, too. I feel just like a princess."

"You deserve their accolades, my darling. That's small compensation for such a peculiar wedding."

She smiled broadly, holding the white rose to her cheek. "Most weddings are unforgettable. Ours certainly was. I only hope my mother isn't too disappointed to have missed it."

He laughed heartily. "You are amazing, lass. I'm relieved your mother missed the experience. She would have declared it a poor substitute for the romantic event a wedding is supposed to be."

Her cheeks turning pink, Skye lifted her hand to acknowledge more applause from well-wishers.

"My concern is Melissa," he said lightly. "If she should see us in these tattered wedding clothes, she would think we had lost our senses."

"Kyle, I'll tell you a secret."

He touched a loose tendril at her shoulder. "What is it, my darling?" he murmured, distracted by the sight of the curl resting on the smooth ivory flesh of Skye's shoulder where the over-sized wedding dress had begun to slip.

"Missy wanted us to marry. She told me so a few days ago."

"Um. I'm not surprised. She's urged me to settle down, discontinue my wayward behavior, as she puts it. But you can be complimented that she approved of you. She was bound to be very selective."

"That's exactly what I told her. That I was deeply flattered."

He lifted an eyebrow. "So you accepted my proposal just to please Missy, not because of my sterling qualities."

She giggled and passed the rose over her lips. "I had doubts, I admit."

"Doubts about me? I'm astonished."

"No. Doubts that . . . that you would still love me after you knew all about my background."

He caught the hand holding the rose and moved it away from her lips. "I know all I need to know, Skye Eugenia. And I love you with all my heart." He gave her a fleeting kiss, not trusting himself to linger on those lips, which were far more exquisite than any rose.

After he moved away, she said, "But you need to know one more thing, my husband."

"What's that?" he murmured.

"I hate the name Eugenia."

Kyle ordered the driver to take them to the back stairs of the hotel, then arranged for the horses to be stabled. "I don't think we want to be seen in these clothes," he said to Skye with a grin. "If we sneak up the back way, we'll avoid any questions from the desk clerk about the sudden switch in Mr. Morgan's identity."

Holding her hand and the sack containing their clothing, he guided her up the wooden steps outside the structure and into the upstairs hallway. At this hour, the hotel was quiet and deserted, unoccupied in the time between departing and arriving guests.

Kyle found the number on the door matching the one on the key. He unlocked it and turned to Skye. "Allow me, Mrs. Wyndford." Lifting her in his arms, he carried her into the expansive bridal suite.

She was looking at him with absolute adoration. Carrying her around the two-room suite, he kept his impatience in check. She was his; there was no need to rush. He wanted her to enjoy every single minute of what he had in mind for the two of them. Everything had happened so quickly. He must consider her feelings and allow her plenty of time to get used to the idea that she was now his wife.

He strolled through the lavishly furnished bedroom with the full tester bed swagged with satin and netting to protect against mosquitoes. One peek into the bathing room showed a large footed tub and a porcelain basin and water pitcher on a stand supplied with white fluffy towels. He hurriedly returned to the parlor, revolved once so she could absorb it all, then set her on her feet.

"So, lass, will this do?"

Her glowing expression was his answer.

"Shall I order champagne?"

"That would be wonderful," she said happily. "Kyle, is this a dream?"

"If it is, I don't want to wake," he answered softly. He reached for her and drew her into his embrace. Her willing response to the touch of his lips filled him with tender affection at the same time it set desire pulsing through his body. Drawing on every ounce of self-control he owned, he released her and located the bell cord to summon someone from downstairs to take their order.

While she explored the room, running her fingers over the brocade chair cushions, drawing back the drapes to peer at the view toward the river, then lingering by the carved mahogany desk to locate paper and pen, he pulled off the torn coat and limp cravat. The back of his shirt was sticky with blood. He was looking at blood on his fingers when she turned.

"Kyle! My goodness, I'm stupid as a stump. I'd forgotten your wound entirely."

"I told you it's nothing serious." He pulled his shirttail from the trousers, noticing that the waist was gaping and two buttons down the front were missing.

"Turn around, please, and let me see your back," she said crisply. "Oh my, look at the blood. Some dried, but some still damp. The least I can do is wash it for you. Though I do think some ointment would be helpful."

He pulled a straight-backed chair from the table in the middle of the room and straddled it with his back toward her.

"Take off your shirt, Kyle. This is no time for modesty."

He couldn't have agreed more and quickly obeyed her command.

She hurried to the bathing room and returned with a wet towel. Her soft hands on his flesh and her gentle ministrations were almost his undoing. The ache in his groin far surpassed the stinging in his back.

"There. That should feel a bit better until we can get some medicine. I have some ointments in my trunk downstairs." She walked around the chair to face him. "We will need our things soon. I don't care to venture out in *this*." Her hand fluttered over the half-buttoned bodice and the flowing skirt secured by a lady's stocking. "Or the crumpled garments in there." She indicated the sack.

He gave her a slow smile. "You may wear many lovely garments in your lifetime, Skye, but none will become you more than the wedding dress belonging to Mr. Morgan's fiancée."

She tilted her head. "So say *you*, Mr. Wyndford. But I don't believe anyone in St. Louis would agree."

A knock interrupted his reply, and he rose and cracked the door. "Champagne, your very best," he said to the hotel porter. "And please deliver any messages that arrive at the front desk. My name is Wyndford."

He closed the door and turned back to Skye. "Excuse me while I rinse off. It's the least I can do, since I'm doomed to wear these breeches for a while longer."

"Of course. But I hope we can have our own things brought up soon. Remember we're to take Missy riding this afternoon."

"I haven't forgotten. I thought around four o'clock. I'll send her a message when the porter returns."

"Kyle, don't tell her yet about the wedding. I would like to make the announcement in person."

"Naturally," he said as he entered the washroom and closed the door. A look in the mirror showed him that a little soap and water would improve his condition and enhance the pleasure of the slow seduction he had in mind for his adorable wife. A glass or two of champagne, closed drapes to soften the afternoon sun filtering into the room, a luxurious feather bed for their comfort. Yes indeed, he intended to make the next couple of hours supremely enjoyable.

⚜ Chapter 25 ⚜

Skye watched Kyle stroll into the room. She found his appearance as titillating as it was amusing: he was shirtless, and his torn trousers allowed occasional peeks at the rippling muscles of his long legs. He reminded her of a pirate returning from a fight on an enemy galleon or of a Viking warrior intending to claim forbidden treasure after a ferocious battle.

A knock on the door jarred her wild imaginings.

"Your champagne," came the young voice from the hallway.

Kyle winked at her, sending fireflies dancing under her ribs. "Watch the lad's face when I open the door," he said softly.

Peeking from under her lashes and suppressing a grin, she watched the young man enter pushing a cart laid with fine white linen and crystal and displaying an etched silver bucket holding the bottle of champagne.

The boy gaped at Kyle, then ducked his head, his face turning fiery red. He dared a glance toward Skye, then buried his chin quickly in his shirt collar and mumbled something indiscernible.

"What's that, lad? Speak up," Kyle prompted with a chuckle.

"Two messages, sir." He spun toward the door, bumping the table and rattling the long-stemmed goblets in his hasty retreat.

Kyle followed him to the door and handed him some coins. "Thank you, young man. I'll warrant you'll be on your own honeymoon, ere long." Laughing, Kyle shut the door and picked up two envelopes from the table.

Wearing a happy smile, Skye moved to his side.

"An outrageous bill, as expected, from Mr. Morgan." He put the paper aside. "And a note from Missy, addressed to my old room. I suppose Mr. Morgan has notified the desk clerk of the change." He read the message aloud. "Dear Kyle, I am more tired than I realized. Please allow me to delay our tour until our next visit to St. Louis. Go on without me, and I will plan to join you for dinner. Missy."

"I hope she's all right," said Skye.

"I expect she's only tired." As Kyle poured two glasses of champagne, Skye studied his lithe, muscular body at close range. She'd seen him without his shirt before when he had been wounded and abed, but then, her observation had been shy and secretive. Now she relished the sight of him, this man who was her husband, this man who loved her and who had made her his partner for life.

Silently, they lifted the goblets and clicked the edges, making them ring. Holding his eyes as she sipped the sparkling liquid, Skye knew he didn't regret having to cancel the afternoon tour with Melissa, assuming the lady wasn't ill, which apparently she was not. He was focused totally on his bride, his thoughts consuming and heated, his desire for her written in his face.

She was hardly ignorant of sexual union, of the basics of how this was performed between male and female creatures, but she had no idea what might transpire between humans who added fierce emotion to the physical needs of their bodies. Until this minute, she had half expected they would fetch new clothes and go sight-seeing around the town until nightfall. But now, she knew that would definitely not be the case. Her husband was impatient, and she gloried in that impatience. Just looking at him in the shafts of noonday sun, seeing his masculine beauty, tripped her heart and started a throbbing deep inside her.

She had emptied her glass before she knew it. He refilled her goblet, then tipped back his head to drain his own. Over the rim of her goblet, she saw the play of light and shadow across his bare shoulders and noticed briefly the red welt that was all that was visible of the gunshot wound. His chest was broad and golden, and the springy, light-colored patch of hair was shaped like an hourglass that disappeared below the waist of his ill-fitting trousers. The waistband of his pants was pulled open at the top; his navel and a few inches of the flat planes of his stomach were visible. She allowed herself only the most fleeting glance below that, for his arousal was quite evident beneath the tight fabric of Mr. Morgan's wedding breeches.

He put down his glass, reached for hers, and set it on the table. Placing his hand on the nape of her neck, he stood motionless, gazing at her without flicking an eyelash, while his eyes scoured her face, dropped to her bodice, then returned to fix her with a look of heated power. She felt a current of fire course along her neck, down her spine, and explode between her thighs. If his mere touch was so devastating, so overwhelming, what would it be like to be dominated by his manhood, to become a woman fulfilled by his mastery of her?

Eager to learn this most profound of lessons, she rested her hands on his shoulders and lifted her face to his.

Kyle was overwhelmed with love. This exquisite, courageous, graceful woman was his very own. He saw the gift of acquiescence in her eyes, soft now and as deep green as the ocean awaiting a coming storm. She was, of course, a virgin, but there was the knowledge of a sorceress lurking behind her youthful innocence. She trembled as he studied her, but he knew she held no fear, only anticipation and the dawning of passion.

He cupped her chin and touched her lips with painful gentleness. They were warm and softly parted. He moved his mouth carefully over them, finally lingering to claim them, tease them open to invade the moist recesses of her mouth.

Her hands on his bare shoulders caressed him as her body responded to his kiss. He was only too happy to possess her at once, but he had the experience and the mature self-control to keep his need under control to magnify her pleasure.

Lightly he kissed her cheek, then eased his hand under her knees and swept her into his arms. Her head lolled against his shoulder as he carried her into the bedroom. He laid her across the satin coverlet and stepped to the window to close the drapes, sheltering them from the intruding glare of the midsummer sun. As he moved to sit beside her, a breeze lifted the drapery, allowing filtered light to move in luminescent waves across the bed and along the brocaded wallpaper of the elegant room.

"My darling lass. My sweet wife." He lifted her hand and held it to his lips while gazing at her with a heart bursting with love.

She smiled and touched his wounded shoulder with delicate fingertips. "My husband," she echoed the sound of his words. "Surely I am dreaming."

"No. As I will soon prove, sweetheart." He pulled a large square pillow from under the coverlet and placed it behind her back. Then he carefully untied the gauzy stocking from around her waist and eased the pearl buttons, one by one, from their loops.

At one point, she raised her hand to assist him, but he caught it and placed it back beside her.

"Allow me," he whispered. "I will enjoy the task immensely."

He felt her relax under his fingers. "We'll go very slowly, my love. At least in the beginning."

The adoration and trust in her eyes were more revealing than anything she could have said, and it moved him deeply.

When the voluminous dress was open down the front, he discovered a lacy barrier over her breasts, but it was a fragile barrier indeed, with one tiny blue bow securing the opening. One tug and a creamy breast was exposed to his view, enticing his touch. Aching now, he enclosed the globe with one hand, hoping his work-hardened fingers wouldn't chafe the silky smoothness of her skin.

She moaned and laid her head back and closed her eyes. Keeping his hand on her breast, he rubbed the nipple with his thumb and bent to kiss her slender neck near the hollow of her throat, flicking his tongue and moving gradually to the lobe of her ear.

Her fingers dug into his bare back as she pressed her breast into his hand. He thought she murmured his name, but the sound was lost in the pulsing in his own ears.

Slowly, he reminded himself. She must be given as much pleasure as possible before he caused her pain.

He slipped an arm behind her back and drew the upper part of the dress from her shoulders. Then he raised her hips, removed the bulky skirt and tossed it aside. To his tender amusement, he found she was wearing pink cotton underdrawers, edged with lace and ending just above her ankles. He could understand why she had opted for this charming fashion rather than a corset. Incongruous with the feminine undergarment were her leather riding boots. Smiling, he crooked her knees and pulled off first one boot, then the other.

When he looked back at her, she had propped herself on one elbow and was gazing at him with an expression that stirred his emotions to the depths of his heart. She loved him; no, he saw worship in her eyes, however unrealistic were such feelings. She was granting him princelike qualities that he did not possess, a beauty his soul did not own, and a status he could only pray to someday earn.

The drapery billowed as he observed her dark loveliness, the play of light streaking her with gold and shadow, making him think of a jungle cat reclining beneath a sheltering tree, its branches wafting in the wind. His physical need for her was driving him to distraction.

He pulled the pillow from beneath her; she stretched out on her back and raised her arms to welcome him.

Her trust wrenched his heart. "Are you . . . aware of what I will do?" he managed to say, moving over her, continuing his gentle circular massaging of her breasts.

One side of her lip tilted up as she held his eyes. "I am. At least, I believe so."

Her courage in the face of his onslaught made him her willing slave. "There will be pain this first time."

"Oh?" She looked rather surprised, he thought. He was

glad he had forewarned her. He would prepare her the best he could.

He bent to suckle the bud peaked at her breast. Without raising his head, he moved his hand to the ribbon at the waist of the underdrawers and pulled it loose, splayed his fingers across the giving flesh of her stomach, then searched below until he found the feathery softness.

He felt her intake of breath but didn't withdraw his pilfering fingertips. When her thighs tightened, he parted them and enclosed her cusp, imprisoning her most intimate place as if guarding it from his own invasion.

Despite his desperate desire, he held her intimately for longer than a minute, every second throbbing through him like a sledgehammer inside his chest.

She groaned and twisted under him, not as if she resisted but as if she urged him onward.

He felt her moisture now, but she was still tense. Perhaps there was no way this first time for her to ease that virginal tension. In this respect, he was as inexperienced as she. He'd never taken a woman's maidenhead. He prayed he could possess Skye with enough love and compassion to outweigh any pain for her. He knew that swiftness would be the kindest way. And he could wait no longer.

Quickly, he maneuvered the pillow under her hips. She seemed reluctant to move her eyes from his, but when he smiled at her and gently urged her backward, she lay quiet and waited for him to proceed.

He stripped off his boots and pants, and placed a knee at either side of her legs. Her feminine beauty, the soft mounds of her breasts above her narrow waist, the contours of her hips, the dark triangle, the smooth, pliant thighs and well-formed calves, all bathed in the shimmer of dancing ribbons of sunlight, stopped his breath. Was this woman real? This golden-skinned goddess whose hands even now grasped his upper arms while she awaited fulfillment?

"My darling Skye," he murmured and lowered to claim her mouth once more. Her arms slipped around his neck as her hips moved instinctively in answer to the natural hunger of a woman's body.

Massaging again her sweetness, he knew she was as ready as a virgin could be.

"God alone knows how much I love you," he whispered. Then he entered her, clamping his teeth, feeling sweat start along his brow with the effort to control his assault.

He felt her sudden resistance, her legs try to close.

Hating this necessary cruelty, he unleashed his passion and pierced her in one quick thrust. Flooded with an agony of longing, he rocked into her, again and again, mindless now of anything but their union, driven by uncontrollable spasms of release.

He gradually became aware of the hands digging into his back near his shoulder blades, of her trembling beneath him, of the small choking sounds in her arched throat. Gasping, he lifted above her, fear penetrating his passion. "Skye, Skye, my love," he choked. "I've hurt you—I've—"

She raised her head to look at him. Tears had moistened her lashes and filled the corners of her eyes, but she smiled at him and stroked his cheek, brushing back the displaced hair from his temple. "Not much, my darling, only a little. And now I am yours—and you are mine."

He hadn't wept since he was four, but he came close to it at that instant. He inhaled deeply and leaned near her, supporting his weight on an elbow while stroking her cheek with the back of his hand. "I do love you so, my precious lass. From now on, there will be only pleasure between us, I swear to you."

"There is already pleasure," she answered. "Your pleasure in me, and mine in giving pleasure to you."

He covered her lips and felt her gentle smile, knowing without doubt that she was speaking the absolute truth. He adored her, and already he was needing her again.

The second time he possessed her, he found he had an eager partner, a delicious woman who followed his lead and surprised him with her own instinctive innovations. What a sublime future awaited them. Years of love and laughter, children surely, and this physical bond invented by a gracious God as a gift to delight and preserve humankind.

Later, with the warm afternoon breeze lifting the edges of the curtain and the muffled sounds of a town going about its business outside their window, Kyle pulled a sheet over the two of them and held her tucked in his embrace until they both slept.

Skye stirred and wondered momentarily where she was. Then, before she opened her eyes, she smiled and reached out her hand toward Kyle.

He wasn't there.

She sat up, holding the sheet over her bare breasts. The shadows in the room were long and the heat was oppressive. She felt damp in all sorts of places. She swung her feet to the floor. Since the door to the sitting room was closed, she concluded Kyle must have slipped in there while she was sleeping. She found her underdrawers and her chemise beside the bed and carried them to the adjoining bathing room. As soon as she was refreshed and into her lingerie, she walked boldly into the parlor.

The room was deserted.

For a second, she was puzzled, but then she saw her trunk sitting beside the window. A note was propped on the table against an empty champagne glass.

As she read Kyle's note, she relaxed and smiled.

> *My darling Skye, you'll find your belongings close by. I looked in and saw you asleep, looking like the angel you are. You are as lovely in repose as you are when your exquisite eyes meet mine. So that you won't be disturbed, I have gone to my former room to bathe and change into clothing more suitable than Mr. Morgan's hand-me-downs. I'll return shortly.*
>
> *Your adoring husband,*
> *Kyle*

She was filled with a pleasant languor. Humming a tune, she stood for a time gazing out the window at the street below, recalling every wonderful moment of her afternoon with Kyle. She had been nervous at first, but his gentleness, coupled with her growing desire, had carried them to heights she'd never dreamed existed. No wonder her mother often wore a secret smile of pleasure after long, cold nights on the Isle of Skye. The wonders of the bedroom far surpassed anything Skye could possibly have imagined. Giving herself to the man she loved, holding all that power in her arms, feeling it unleashed and flowing into her—the experience was awesome and profound. She was a fulfilled woman and she would never be the same again. Her satisfaction and delight were boundless.

After a time, she crossed to her trunk and opened the lid. What would she wear on this momentous occasion? With pleasure, she anticipated Missy's response to the announcement of her marriage to Kyle. She and Missy would be sisters. For now, she would refuse to think of Missy's illness or how their relationship might be cut short. For tonight, at least, she would allow herself only unbridled happiness.

The first item she noticed inside the trunk was her most valuable possession, her father's bear-claw necklace wrapped in a linen cloth. The necklace would be the key to proving her heritage to the Lakota Indians. She looked forward to the day she could return it to her father. Opening the cloth, she fingered the black shining claw on its leather thong. Her mother had told her how White Arrow had won the amulet by great prowess with bow and arrow, had actually killed a bear in a terrible fight to the death. But even that story had paled next to the one about White Arrow's mounted battle against Siyaka, son of the Lakota chief. Siyaka had been evil and greedy and jealous of White Arrow. Siyaka had lost the fight, and in so doing, lost his prestige in the tribe. Embittered, he had convinced his father to make a sacrifice of the halfbreed, White Arrow. Only the intervention of Finlay Mackinnon had saved White Arrow from burning at the stake.

Skye lifted the bear claw and tied it around her neck. Turning toward the wall mirror, she admired the look of the amulet along her throat. Hardly feminine, but impressive against her smooth, golden-bronze skin above her lacy bodice. She was fingering it, contemplating the effect, when the door opened behind her.

"Skye—you're awake."

She revolved to greet her husband and give him her warmest smile.

"What have we here?" he said, his eyes falling on the necklace.

"'Tis my father's. You must agree, it is quite impressive."

"Indeed it is."

"I thought since you knew about my Lakota blood, you might enjoy seeing it." She saw a strained look cross his face. "But you haven't heard the whole story. I'd love to share it with you."

Kyle looked somewhere beyond her. "Some other time, perhaps."

Suddenly uneasy, she realized Kyle was not entirely comfortable with the subject of her Indian blood. "Kyle, are you *sure* you can accept my being part Lakota?" Her question hung in the air between them.

Kyle rubbed his hand across his forehead. "Of course. I told you it makes no difference to me. But the fact is, it could make a difference to others. Some people have strong feelings against the natives."

"So I've learned," she said. "I'm sure Leveque's revelation was quite a shock to you." She was abruptly defensive.

"I didn't believe him. I thought he'd made up some crazy story to add insult to injury."

"Insult? Then you consider it an insult to be called Lakota?"

Kyle's expression softened and he moved toward her. Placing his hands on her shoulders, he held her eyes in a look of great intensity. "Skye, my darling, it makes not the slightest difference. Not one bit. I admit I had hard feelings toward the Lakotas after some of their people murdered my brother. You know about that tragedy, of course."

"Aye. Missy told me in New Orleans. She also told me about your prejudice toward the Lakotas, how you ignore the Indians of your land. Even Laurel suggested that I take care with whom I shared the knowledge of my legacy. She said many people truly dislike the native people." She shook her head. "'Tis such a shame and so unfair. I was afraid *you* were like that until you saved the African slave. After that, I decided you were fair-minded after all, and I intended to tell you about my father, but we were always interrupted."

Kyle's voice was deep with emotion when he responded. "My precious girl, you should have trusted me. It's *you* I love and will always love. But Leveque is not as crazy as I first thought. I hope we've seen the last of him, but he might still be a threat. Also, other settlers will be prejudiced against you and against your father. Your Indian blood doesn't change my feelings for you, but it does complicate things."

She studied his face, searching for the look of total adoration he had given her earlier. She didn't see it now. His pledge of love was smooth and sounded sincere, but she saw confusion and concern in his eyes. Her euphoria disappeared in the cold light of reality. "Maybe we acted in haste. Maybe this does change things between us."

"No." He stroked her hair, but his frown deepened. "Not between us. But I *am* concerned about your family's move into Dakota. Your father's being a half-breed could cause difficulties."

She stiffened at the term *half-breed*. "Aye. I've heard that description used more often than I care to here in *civilized* America."

"My darling Skye, I apologize with all my heart. But Laurel was right to warn you about prejudices that exist. They extend from the ordinary settlers to the heads of the government. Frankly, I'm not at all sure what the laws are regarding Indians owning property, taking possession of land, running a business—"

"Such as a cattle ranch?" Skye felt her temper start to boil.

"Now, Skye . . ."

With the utmost effort to conceal her dismay, she stared at him. "Then, sir, since I am Indian, and my father is Indian, what do you suggest we do in this wonderful land of America? This land of freedom and opportunity?"

"You, Skye, are my *wife*. You will stay at my side and I'll kill the man who dares insult you. But your father . . . well, he may want to reconsider this idea of returning to the place of his birth. He doesn't understand the changes taking place, the prevailing views toward the native population."

She took a deep breath and moved out of his grasp. "I see. Now I will explain something to you, Kyle Wyndford. Before I met you, I took a solemn pledge to my father to look for land in Dakota, to prepare the way, if he were delayed. Even though I'm your wife, we must remember I have a duty to my family." She rested her hand on the bear claw.

"Yes. I remember. I'm prepared to help in any way I can."

Despite his words, she couldn't help feeling he was hiding feelings of disparagement toward her and her father. The idea he might think himself superior was deeply upsetting. "I can't expect you to risk your reputation and be called upon to defend my honor for the rest of your life. How would you explain to your white neighbors that the man you've helped establish in Dakota, your father-in-law, is actually a Lakota warrior, a *half-breed* scorned by all white Americans? And what about our children, Kyle? How would you explain their dark skin and hair, their mixed-blood heritage?"

Kyle's face was stormy when he answered. "You're being completely unreasonable. I've told you how I feel."

"Words are easily spoken. I'm asking you now about your feelings toward my father and his people, the Lakotas."

His hesitation broke her heart.

"I . . . I don't feel anything. That's the truth of it," he finally muttered.

"They killed your brother. You must feel something."

"Damn it, Skye. You ask too much. I hated the people who did such a thing. Who wouldn't? Since then, I've simply kept my distance from the natives. I told you that already."

"A mistake, in my view."

He stared at her, his annoyance and frustration written in every line of his face.

"Kyle, I'm deeply sorry we didn't have time to discuss this before we married. But that's entirely my fault. I believe we should keep our marriage a secret and continue our journey as if the wedding never took place."

His jaw worked before he answered. "If that's what you want."

"I think it's best. Besides, I need to stay close to Missy, travel in her cabin so I can be near her. I'm sure we can sort this out when we get to Dakota. In the meantime, I need time to do some thinking."

"Would you prefer to return to New Orleans? I'm sure I could make other arrangements for Missy."

His cold suggestion stiffened her resolve. "Not on your life, Mr. Wyndford. Regardless of the circumstances, I am going to Dakota."

"Then I'll say good evening. You and Missy can order dinner sent to your rooms, if you like—or you can keep the bridal suite until we leave tomorrow. I'm going out."

Unnerved by his vehemence, she said, "Oh? Where will you go?"

"To the nearest saloon. I need a drink, probably several. This has been one hell of a strange day." He spun on his heels and slammed out the door.

≈ Chapter 26 ≈

Are you sure you don't want to stay in St. Louis, Missy? I'll stay with you, if you like, until you're feeling better." Skye gazed with concern at Melissa's drawn face. Their coach was moving slowly through the crowded street toward the waterfront.

Missy smiled wanly. "I must get to Dakota. I'll be all right once I'm at home."

Skye doubted that very much. Last night when she'd

dined with Melissa in her room, she had seen a definite downturn in the lady's usual spirits. Missy's face had lost its color, and she was almost too weak to pick up her fork. She herself had been in a gloomy mood and had made the evening brief, keeping inside her any news of the extraordinary events of the afternoon.

This morning, Skye had finished packing and had written her mother a letter. She had described the journey on the *Mississippi Belle* and had urged her mother and father to come as soon as possible to Dakota. She couldn't imagine how she would explain to them she was now Mrs. Kyle Wyndford, if indeed the announcement had not been made public before their arrival.

The carriage halted at the smallest of the St. Louis docks, and Skye emerged to take her first look at their paddlewheeler. MacLard leaped out and danced around her slippers. Staring at the rustic craft, she thought there must be some mistake. Surely that small boat with a single rickety sternwheel couldn't be the *Royal Eagle,* which would take them to Dakota. The vessel was one quarter the size of the *Mississippi Belle* and was shaped like an elongated rowboat with a double tier of boxlike cabins stacked in the middle. The paddlewheel at the stern appeared badly in need of repair, and faded white paint was peeling from every inch of the boat's wooden frame. But as she gazed at the forlorn, dilapidated packet, she saw ROYAL EAGLE emblazoned in letters along the bow.

"What's wrong, Skye?" Missy asked as she put a foot on the carriage step.

Skye forced a confident smile to her lips. "I was sizing up our ship, Missy. I'm afraid 'tis smaller than I expected, but sturdy, I'm sure."

Missy was using her full concentration to exit the carriage.

Skye reached a hand toward her but was stopped by a deep, authoritative voice.

"I'll carry Melissa," Kyle said, stepping forward. "Follow me, if you please, *Miss* Mackinnon."

Skye marched behind the briskly moving Kyle as he

carried Missy across the gangplank and onto the *Royal Eagle*. MacLard scampered in her wake. She knew Kyle was angry at her insistence they keep their marriage a secret. But she had to keep her distance from him until she pulled herself together. Keeping a distance from anyone would be difficult on this small conveyance. The passenger area was scarcely larger than their suite at the hotel—and far less luxurious. She and Kyle couldn't help being forced to live daily in close proximity.

Skye followed him up a flight of flimsy wooden steps to the upper deck, then trailed behind as he shouldered open a door and placed Missy on a bed in a room the size of a large closet. The enclosure held two narrow beds and a washbasin. Windows a foot square on opposite walls let in the only light. The place smelled like fish and coal oil and something else Skye refused to identify. The terrier jumped onto the bed beside Missy and settled with his chin across her ankle, a spot he had grown accustomed to lately.

As Skye watched, Kyle took Missy's hand and smiled down at her. "We'll soon be home, my dear. A week and a day, the captain predicts. Naturally, we could have the usual delays."

Skye was about to comment on the possibility they couldn't survive these dreadful surroundings for an entire week when she noticed Missy's brave smile. The lady was looking fondly at Kyle and squeezing his hand. Melissa's courage made Skye ashamed of her own uppity attitude.

"We'll be fine, Kyle," Missy said with a show of vigor. "Won't we, Skye?"

"Absolutely," Skye hastened. She followed Kyle out of the room to the narrow deck beyond.

"Excuse me, Mr. Wyndford; I'd like a word with you, if I may."

He stopped and slowly revolved toward her. His eyes were veiled and cool, his expression unreadable. He didn't speak, but waited for her to continue.

"I must tell you I don't believe Missy is as well as she has been lately. I'm worried about her making this journey."

His eyes narrowed. "My sister-in-law and I have made the

passage several times in past years. It's not easy, but she knows what to expect, I believe. I've made sure she has everything she needs. If you're worried about your own comfort, let me assure you this is not the *Mississippi Belle*. And the Missouri River is not the Mississippi."

She simmered under his condescending gaze. "I am not concerned for myself, sir," she snapped. "I merely want to know where Melissa's things are—her trunk and medicines and books. My *sole* interest from this point until we reach Dakota is to see to her comfort and safety."

"I'm much obliged, Miss Mackinnon. Let me say emphatically that my goal is the same. Melissa's trunks, and yours, will be placed in your cabin. Also a box of fresh fruit, which you should eat sparingly during the journey. I fear the menu on the *Royal Eagle* is extremely limited."

"Where will we take our meals?" Skye inquired.

"You have three choices: in your cabin, at a makeshift table somewhere on the upper deck, or on shore."

"Shore?"

"I've never made this voyage without spending a great deal of time on the banks of the river—looking for firewood for the boiler, hunting game, or passing time while the river rises and lifts the boat off a sandbar."

"Oh. I see." She met his explanation with a lift of one eyebrow. "And won't there be danger from the attack of wild beasts—or *savage* Indians?"

"Probably. Along with the other men, I'll stay armed at all times."

She watched his hand slide over the butt of his pistol. He was dressed as a westerner: a rough, hand-woven shirt under a black leather vest, open at the neck; thigh-hugging leather breeches trimmed with fringe at the sides and tucked into knee-high chunky brown boots; and a broad-brimmed slouch hat set at a rakish angle. Unfortunately, she found the outfit incredibly masculine and attractive. The low-slung pistol only added to his air of authority.

"I am an excellent shot," she said, tossing her head. "Perhaps I should carry a weapon."

"Perhaps. What do you prefer?"

"Oh—a bow and arrow," she said crisply. "Wouldn't you think that suitable?" She spun on her heels and marched back into the cabin, where Melissa was reclining on her bed.

"Your cheeks are unnaturally rosy, Skye dear. Has my difficult brother-in-law been rude to you again?"

She dropped to the bed opposite Melissa. "Aye . . . well, not really. 'Tis not his words but his attitude toward the Indians I find hard to accept."

"Please be patient, Skye. He will change, if we don't give up on him. We just need to break through his wall of pain over his brother's death."

Skye rose to open a window. "I know. But his stubborn prejudice toward my father's people has been so unexpected. After Kyle helped the slave escape, I had hoped he would be fair toward the Indians."

She heard Missy sigh and ceased her complaining. Gazing out the window, her attention was drawn to a commotion behind the boat. A flat-bottomed barge was moored there, and freight was being loaded by husky stevedores.

"Missy, they're bringing the livestock to the barge next to us. Kyle is leading Raven Duke; another man has my mares."

"Go along and see about it," Missy said, closing her eyes and resting on her pillow. "I'll snooze a bit. Once we get started, sleep is almost impossible."

Without asking why that was so, Skye hurried outside and down the steps. She ran across the gangplank and arrived at the barge just in time to see Kyle lead Raven on board. She confronted a bearded man who was leading Legacy and Lady. "Excuse me. I'll help with that mare," she said, reaching for the rope. "This is Lady," she explained. "Will you be traveling on the barge with the horses?"

"Yes'm," the man answered, his twinkling brown eyes barely visible as he squinted in the bright sun. "All the way to Fort Benton," he added.

"Is that beyond Vermillion?" she inquired.

"Vermillion's less than halfway to Fort Benton. Is that your destination? Vermillion?"

She nodded. She liked the look in the man's eyes. He was

unkempt, with his shaggy, shoulder-length hair; his full black beard streaked with gray and stained at one corner; his baggy, well-worn clothing and ragged straw hat. But he had a lilt in his voice and she detected friendliness without seeing his camouflaged smile. She might need a friend before this trip was done, and she could enlist this gent to give special attention to her horses.

"I'm Miss Mackinnon," she said, patting Lady's nose. "Do you carry any treats for the horses? Like carrots and such?"

"Sure do, ma'am. Fine-looking animals you got. Looks like one of the mares is about to be a mama."

"The other mare is Spirit Legacy," she explained. "She's in foal to a wonderful stallion from the Isle of Skye in Scotland. My former home."

"I thought I heard a bit of a Scot's twang," the grizzled man observed.

"Could I ask your name, sir? I understand our two boats will be traveling together."

"Name's Garwin. Buck. From Buckhart, Tennessee. Ever been there?"

"I'm sorry to say I haven't, Mr. Garwin."

"Call me Buck, young lady. And don't worry none—I'll keep a close eye on the mares. The stallions, too. Good-looking stud, that blue roan. Is he yours?"

"He's—" She threw a glance toward where Kyle was securing Raven next to Diamond Dust in the center of the barge beneath a canvas canopy. "He's mine, at the moment. I've offered him for sale to Mr. Wyndford."

Buck crooked his finger to draw her near and whispered. "Don't sell 'im, Miss Mackinnon. Breed 'im to your mares and you'll have the finest cowhorses in the West. I guarantee it."

"Really?" she feigned surprise. "Then you're a horse breeder, Buck?"

"Done my share in Tennessee. I know good blood when I see it."

"I'll consider your advice; thank you very much." She turned when Diamond Dust raised a commotion, stamping vigorously on the wooden floor of the barge. "Stallions do get restless, Buck. Will Dusty have a chance to exercise along the way?"

"Plenty, I reckon, ma'am. There's good grass along the riverbanks. 'Course, there's Injuns, too."

The term startled her. "Injuns? You mean Indians?"

"Yeh. Injuns. Generally they keep to themselves unless they get hungry and cain't bring down a buffalo soon enough to suit 'em. You never know what mood those red devils are in. Could be wanting to trade or could be on the warpath. Better to shoot first and ask questions later."

She stared at the lovable fellow in disbelief. "Shoot first? Kill them without finding out if they're friendly, or only hungry?"

He rolled his eyes and pulled his beard. "I had a pal once't who waited to find out what the 'skins had in mind. Have you ever seen a man scalped, Miss Mackinnon?"

She swallowed hard. "No, fortunately I haven't."

"Doesn't always kill a man, you know. The savages use knives traded from the whites and slice the skin clean as a onion. Takes the top right off to the skullbone."

She began to feel queasy. "I'd rather not—"

"Plenty o' blood oozin' all over his face and neck, but he lives sometimes." The leathery old fellow chuckled. "Wears his hat after that, I can swear. Don't want his brains falling out." He laughed heartily.

Skye pressed her hand against her stomach. "I'd better put up the mares, Buck," she said through clenched teeth. "Where do you want them?"

"On the side away from the stallion," he said, collecting himself. "Here, ma'am, let me take Spirit Legacy. Small, ain't she, but built like a bulldog."

Skye might have taken exception to that description if she hadn't been mildly lightheaded over Buck's description of Indian brutality. As it was, she merely nodded and led Lady toward the boat.

Kyle came face-to-face with her as she arrived at the gangplank. "I put the stallions in the middle," he said. "The steadiest part of the boat. You can put the mares over there by that stack of hay."

"Thank you, but I've already taken my instructions from

Buck Garwin. I'll put the mares wherever *he* wants them to go." She knew she sounded testy, but she didn't care. She hadn't realized until now how authoritative Kyle could be. Was this sudden awareness due to her being his wife or because they both knew she was Indian? Well, *Buck* didn't know she was Indian, thank heavens, and he would treat her with respect, she was certain.

After Kyle left her without another word, she entered the barge and surveyed the open-air accommodations her horses must endure for over a week. Other horses were waiting to be loaded, and several goats and a cow as well. Crates of chickens, too, and a surprisingly large number of cats, also in crates. Empty barrels and stacks of wooden boxes were lashed together along the perimeter of the deck.

She tethered Lady next to Legacy and turned to Buck. "Why so many cats? And all those empty barrels?"

He placed his palm on Legacy's hip and then ran his hand carefully along the mare's enlarged belly. "Them barrels are for river water. We keep 'em filled as we go. When we cain't drink whiskey, we drink the Missouri. The whiskey's a damn sight better, I can tell you. But don't you fret, ma'am, the cap'n won't allow any of the crew to get too liquored up to do his job."

"I'm sure that's wise," she said.

"As fer the cats, they's worth their weight in gold at the settlements upriver. We bring 'em in to go after the rats. At the cavalry posts, rats eat the government grain faster than you kin shovel it into the feed cribs. The pesky varmints overrun the barns unless you got a goodly number of mousers hanging around."

"Rats. Of course." She must remember to put cats on her list of necessities once she moved out west. "Buck, I have a small dog traveling with me. I'll be keeping him in my cabin on the Royal Eagle, but sometimes he likes to walk in the woods. Do you think you could accompany me on strolls from time to time?"

"I'd be proud to, ma'am." He slapped the holster hanging at his hip. "Mollie and me will take care of any murdering hostiles that dare show an eye around us."

"Mollie is your pistol, I suppose."

"You bet. Named after a woman I once't knew up in Pierre. She was a killer, too, if you'll forgive me fer saying so. This here Mollie's killed half a dozen Dakotas already, and two or three Comanch."

She had a sinking feeling as she asked, "Comanch?"

"Comanches. Down in Texas. The Dakotas I killed were part of a raiding party above Fort Pierre on the Missouri. They's after my hair, I figured."

Just as she'd feared—more hatred of the Indians. She hid her dismay and said, "I must be confused, Buck. I thought the Indians here were called Lakota, and they were peaceful, friendly to the trappers and other settlers."

"Friendly? Hah, like a nest of rattlers." Buck snorted and spit a dark glob onto the deck beside him; a trickle hung in his beard.

Skye felt her stomach turn again.

He wiped the back of his hand across his mouth. "Maybe years back, they was friendly. Maybe some still are, loafin' around the posts and tradin' their goods. But times are changing. Dakota's the name of the whole territory, but the Dakota tribes live in the part closer to the river; the Lakotas live in the other half out toward the badlands." As he spoke, he raised his hand and made a slicing motion in the air. "Some here, some there. All the same tribe, just different spelling. Easier to call 'em all Sioux. *Sioux* means *snake,* and that fits all them redskins just right."

With difficulty she responded, "Well, I can see I have a lot to learn. Thank you for the information."

"Anytime, ma'am. Anytime. I been in these parts for forty years, seed things change plenty. First the trappers come in, then those American fellows, Mr. Lewis and Mr. Clark. The whole place went from Spanish to French to American and you couldn't tell the difference atall. A Spaniard named Lisa traveled up and down the Missouri back in the twenties, built a fort and established trade, even brought some Sioux chiefs to St. Louis to show 'em to the white folks. A real good show, the way them Injuns strutted around in their feathers and paint. Put 'em up in his own house, like regular people. Later the French sold whiskey illegally to the Injuns and stole the provisions granted them by treaty. Made a big profit selling the goods and set themselves up real fancy here in St. Louis."

Skye saw nothing in all this that would endear the Europeans to the Indians. Quite the contrary. "And the Indians?" she asked politely.

"Just moved around, taking their squaws and their tepees with 'em. Kept after the buffalo, and got real feisty when they learned to ride horses—plumb bold, you might say. Fighting and raiding just for the fun of it."

"Really," she said under her breath, hiding her disappointment over Buck's disparaging remarks. She decided to change the subject. "Are there no cattle ranchers in Dakota? Besides Mr. Wyndford, that is?"

"Not up north. Not yet, but they'll come. Wyndford's got the jump on them that's coming, that's a calcified fact. And that ain't all; they say Kyle Wyndford's as clever and shrewd and crafty as any lobo wolf."

Clever, shrewd, and crafty. Skye hadn't seen him in quite that light before. She was discovering many more facets to Kyle Wyndford than she'd dreamed existed. Skye's doubts about her hurried marriage ballooned inside her. She needed time to learn more about him, but now she would have to wait until they reached Dakota. "So, Buck, you think Mr. Wyndford will prosper?"

"All he has to do is keep out the Injuns and the sodbusters. Run enough head to make a profit and get them safely to market. Once the government sets a price on the Dakota land, makes the place an official territory, he'll have first crack at owning some of the finest cattle country in America, at rock-bottom prices. Guess he knows all that, though. You a friend of his, ma'am?"

She wasn't sure how to answer. All of Buck's information was swirling through her head. She was suddenly aware of how ignorant she was of everything going on out west. She couldn't blame her father for not knowing about all these events. Even though he had grown up in Dakota, he'd been in Scotland since he was eighteen. And when he lived in

Dakota, he had been an outcast to both Indians and whites. "I'm an acquaintance of Mr. Wyndford's, traveling with his ailing sister-in-law. 'Tis my first trip west, and I'm eager to learn all about it. I might want to live in Dakota someday."

Buck's brows shot upward. "You, ma'am? Not alone, I hope."

"Naturally not. My father is . . . well, he was born in Dakota and will be establishing a ranch. My mother will be here, too."

Buck shook his head. "Speakin' direct, ranchin' out west could be foolhardy unless you got an army of fast guns working for you. Or unless Mr. Wyndford will take on the task of being your protector."

"An army? My goodness, do you really think that's necessary?"

"Beggin' your pardon, I surely do. Wyndford's got a fine spread up at Wind River. Got an experienced vaquero out of California to run the place, got thirty, forty hands, all of 'em armed. His vaquero, Reyes Pacheco, is as tough as they come, the best cowman I ever come across. I worked for him on a drive two years ago."

Her head was reeling. So Kyle had his own small army and a hired foreign mercenary to lead it. The whole idea was astonishing and very disconcerting. What was more unsettling was how her own family could expect to survive—without an army to protect them.

"Here, Miss Mackinnon, is two carrots for the mares. I keep a supply of apples and carrots in that tow sack over there."

She accepted the carrots Buck handed her and fed them to Legacy and Lady. Absently, she watched the vegetables disappear amid loud popping and crunching. "Thank you for the carrots, Buck. I know the girls appreciate them." She stroked each soft nose in turn.

The barge's high-pitched whistle sounded a warning.

"I must be getting back to the *Royal Eagle*," she said. "We'll be leaving soon."

"Sure nuff. The *Eagle* will head upriver, then the barge will move out. May not have to tie up till tomorrow morning, if Cap'n Belt does a good job maneuvering through the night. First leg of the river's not so bad. Later on, Old Misery is tricky as the devil's grin."

She stepped gingerly toward the wharf, being careful to stay out of the way of the sweating stevedores who were hauling aboard the last of the boxes and barrels and one more crate of calico cats. Once she and Buck had gained the dock, she paused. "Buck, is this journey dangerous? Really dangerous?"

"Well, the truth is—"

"Could we have long delays? Mrs. Wyndford isn't well, you see, and we are in a bit of a hurry to get her home to Wind River."

"Sure wish't I could say the trip's safe, Miss Mackinnon, but it truly ain't too easy. Boats hang up on sandbars, get sunk by floating timbers, attacked by hostiles, and sometimes when the boilers overheat, they just blow to kingdom come."

She stared at him. "Oh my."

"Don't fret, ma'am. Most packets get where they're headed. By and by."

Her throat tight, her mind dazed, Skye hurried back to the *Royal Eagle*. Before she reached her cabin, the vessel's horn blasted in the afternoon air and was answered by the shrill toot-toot from the barge. Soon they would be underway, creaking slowly against the muddy tide like an aging trapper leading his worn-out mule onto a familiar trail one more time.

She stopped to gaze once more at the city. Worry? Of course not; why would she worry? She was only traipsing off into unknown country, accompanied by a dying woman and a man who was a dictator, the lord of an empire wrestled from the native people, a man to whom she was secretly married. She had three horses, a dog, and gold to buy land that might take an army to defend—and wasn't for sale anyway. Why on earth would she be worried?

She climbed to the deck outside her cabin and stood gripping the railing as the crew began untying the ropes from their moorings. She had no idea what was going to happen—but she was on her way to the American West.

⫸ Chapter 27 ⫷

Kyle stood by his old friend, John Roux, the *Royal Eagles*'s pilot, and took another puff from his cheroot. Beyond the stern of the lumbering packet, the city of St. Louis was disappearing around the bend of the Mississippi.

Kyle had made the trip seven times during his years in America. Whenever possible, he had traveled with John Roux. Roux was the best pilot working the Missouri, in Kyle's opinion, and Captain Belt was a hell of a fine captain. Despite the shabby appearance of the *Royal Eagle*, Kyle had confidence in the boat's ability to make the voyage safely to Vermillion.

At the moment, however, Kyle's mind was not on either his past voyages or the one just beginning. His thoughts were filled with Skye Mackinnon. Skye was his wife, even though she was upset over his views of the Indian problem. Seeing her move around the boat in her modest dress and straw bonnet and receiving nothing from her but coolness was sheer torture. She was hurt and angry, and somehow he must make amends. To go forward in life without her beside him, after what they had shared together and knowing how precious she was to him, was unthinkable.

If only the Indians hadn't murdered Blanton. Kyle had tried to adopt Melissa's forgiving attitude, but he had failed, largely because of the views of the white men he'd encountered since coming to Dakota. In fact, all across the United States, the prevailing view was that Indians were primitive and should be moved out of the path of civilization's progress. Personally, he had never given the matter serious thought. In Dakota, he had expanded his brother's ranch at Wind River and had made excellent profits by his sacrifice, determination, and hard work. He had never killed an Indian nor banished them from his range. They were allowed to cross safely on their way to the trading posts on the river. True, he kept armed cowhands, but as a result of that, he'd never had any trouble. He had heard how deadly the Sioux on the warpath could be. A show of strength could prevent a tragedy—and with Pacheco and his vaqueros working his range, he had been confident he could avoid any confrontation.

But Kyle knew he had trouble now. Not from savages, but from a bizarre twist of fate that was forcing him to reconsider his long-held convictions about the Indians. He was in love with a woman who carried the blood of the Lakota Sioux, a woman whose father was a mixed-blood planning to establish a ranch near his. He had offered to help Mackinnon and had married Mackinnon's daughter.

Kyle knew the Mackinnons would likely be scorned by every white in the area. On the other hand, now that he had married Skye, he could envision a joint operation between Mackinnon and himself, two ranches with common interests, working together to create excellent profits for both families. No one would dare insult a Mackinnon because Skye was his wife.

He blew a puff of smoke between his lips and ignored the constant clanging vibration made by the *Eagle*'s engines. He mulled over the problem with Skye and tried to think things through with a clear head and with as little emotion as possible. What would her life be like as his wife at Wind River? He could provide a comfortable home, cozy in winter, spectacularly beautiful in summer. They shared an interest in animal breeding and love of the land. He knew without doubt she would enjoy life at the ranch. He felt safe from Indian attack with Pacheco and his men on duty. With Melissa as a companion, Skye would have female companionship. The two ladies could visit the post at Vermillion and get acquainted with the handful of white women there, and of course, Badger would keep things stirred up around the house. And every year or so, he could take Skye on visits to St. Louis and New Orleans. Children would come soon to occupy her time, and their lives would be busy and productive. Eventually, Dakota would become a territory, maybe even a state someday. All in all, he saw a good life ahead for them—if they could work things out between them.

But if the Mackinnons struck out on their own without guidance and protection, disaster could befall them before they had a foothold in Dakota. If Fletcher Mackinnon had some fantasy about connecting with his Indian people, he could face serious disappointment. And if the Sioux caused trouble, Kyle felt sure that federal troops would soon be sent to stop their harassment of the white settlements and to protect American expansion along the Missouri. Where would the Scottish laird stand in all this? Where would his loyalties lie? Assuming, of course, the man still lived.

He flipped his cigar butt into the water. His decision was made. Skye was his wife, and he loved her. She had loved him yesterday, and he was certain he could regain her trust, if only he could help her to see his side of the situation.

"How's the current, John?" Kyle asked, gazing across the river at an approaching barge.

"Running pretty high this week," the pilot replied, without taking his eyes from their course.

"Do you plan to run after dark?"

"Might tonight if we get a full moon, but not much after that. I'll pull in at Johnson's Wood Yard south of the Osage tomorrow night."

"I suppose you got your usual mates, and old Flipper George selling liquor and doing the cooking."

"Indeed, we have a full complement of crewmen overseeing the roustabouts. Plenty of hands to get us upriver. Not many passengers, though. Just a few trappers going on north and a preacher headed for Vermillion."

"No women besides my two ladies?"

"One. A whore whose passage is paid by three of the men going to Pierre. You know the rules, Kyle. A woman is a woman aboard a packet. The whore will be treated like a lady till she gets where she's going. No doodling during the trip."

"I know, John. All passengers are equal on the Missouri."

John flicked him a glance. "Rarely get women, you know. Your sister-in-law must have been the first white woman to travel to Dakota."

"I'm sure of it. She's had quite an adventure coming to the American West." He shook his head. "But it's taken its toll on her, I'm sorry to say."

"So—what about the other lady? Damned if she isn't the prettiest girl I've seen in a dozen years. She's nursing your sister, is she?"

"She's Mrs. Wyndford's traveling companion." He would have given half his fortune to announce that Skye was his wife, Mrs. James Kyler Wyndford, but then how would he have explained why she introduced herself as Miss Mackinnon and treated him like he carried the plague?

"She must be as spunky as she is pretty," observed John. "Looks a bit . . . well, a bit Indian, if you'll forgive my observation. But guess she's some type of Scot I'm not familiar with."

Kyle stared at the passing scenery, the dark blue ripples that would soon show signs of the mud sweeping in from the Missouri, the small settlements and farmhouses beyond the shoreline, the cottonwoods and marshland lining the river's edge. Thinking about John's comment, he wondered how he would feel if he did introduce Skye as his wife. Would he be ashamed to slip an arm around her shoulders and say, "Yes, my wife is part Lakota Sioux. Amazing, isn't it?" He would do it, of course, and eventually get used to it. But it wouldn't be easy at first. And if Skye sensed his discomfort over it, would she be hurt once more? How would she deal with her husband's feelings about the natives who were part of her heritage? Could he change? For her sake, he must try. Thinking of her being insulted sent angry waves to the pit of his stomach. No one would insult Skye in his presence or he'd have their hide. Hell, he knew it would happen, probably plenty. He might as well get ready to bust his knuckles raw in defense of his wife.

Completely miserable, Skye lay on her bed in the gloomy darkness. The thumping and clanging and rattle from the engines and paddle wheel had made conversation with

Missy difficult, and now sleep was impossible. The mattress was filled with corncobs and the sheets with invisible bugs. The heat was stifling with the door closed, but after Skye glimpsed the rough-looking crew, she decided to keep it bolted throughout the night. She was concerned over Missy's labored breathing and the spells of intense coughing during the past hour.

Earlier that evening after dinner with Missy, she had sat alone on the deck so she could watch the passing scenery. Naturally, she had watched for any sign of Kyle, but he was nowhere to be seen. After dark, the vessel slowed to a crawl. Twinkling lights dotted the shoreline and the glow from the freighter's lights was plainly visible. Despite the clamor and the tension of her day, she found herself yawning and heavy-eyed. After all, she had slept very little last night after her disagreement with Kyle.

But now, in her lumpy bed, she discovered that sleep wouldn't come. She tossed restlessly, her mind filled with doubts and fears she had ignored during the daylight hours. Every throb of the steam engines carried her further away from civilization, away from everything familiar and safe. She was ashamed of her cowardice when she considered the courage of the lady in the bed next to her. Melissa had made this journey ten years ago when things were even more primitive and unsettled than now. On the other hand, Missy had been in the loving embrace of her new husband, a man of equal fortitude and determination. Skye felt horribly alone for the first time since she'd left her island home. She was suddenly a misfit and an outcast. If the Indian people were as aloof and unfriendly as everyone said, how could she communicate with them and befriend them as she'd always planned? She found herself longing for the comfort of Kyle's arms, remembering the way she felt safe and cared for when he held her. She threw back the sheet and wiped her moist forehead. A mosquito buzzed beyond the netting, a *giant* mosquito from the sound of it. Thoughts of Laurel's warning about getting the fever from mosquitoes entered her mind. Sighing, she pulled the sheet up under her chin. Better to sweat in misery than to die of the plague.

Hot tears formed under her eyelids. She covered her eyes

with her forearm. *No,* she thought, clamping her lips, *I will not be defeated. I will see Dakota and fulfill my pledge to my father. I will confront Kyle's prejudices and make him see how wrong he is about the Indians. Then we can put this problem behind us and restore our love.*

Sometime later, she drifted into an exhausted sleep, only to be awakened by a crash that nearly threw her from her bed.

The room was light; the packet was shuddering after the initial jolt. Across from her, Skye saw Melissa sitting bolt upright, her mouth framing a silent scream. Beyond the door, men were shouting. Skye heard a second loud rumbling from beyond the stern.

She jumped toward Melissa but tangled herself in the mosquito netting and tumbled to the floor between the two beds. Her heart racing, she ripped apart the gauze and rushed to unbolt the door. Flinging it open, she blinked in the morning sunlight. Below her, men were running across the stern deck, shouting at each other and pointing down the river. She saw that the freighter behind them was also stranded, listing slightly to starboard and thrusting angry steam from its chimneys. Men on the freighter were shouting back at the crew on the *Eagle.* Both ships were caught as the river flowed past them on either side.

Abruptly, Kyle came running up the steps toward her. Shirtless and in his stocking feet, his hair rumpled and his face showing a night's growth of beard, he stared at her. Momentarily, she forgot her own dishabille, the fact that she wore a flimsy gown with the ribbons open from her neck to her breasts as a result of last night's battle with the heat.

"Are you all right?" Kyle demanded, his brow knitted with concern.

"I'm fine. What happened?" she asked breathlessly.

"Hit a sandbar; both boats are jammed. How is Missy?"

Skye stepped back against the door frame. "All right, I believe."

Kyle brushed past her and leaned over Melissa. "Don't worry, Missy," he murmured gently. "We're just hung up on a sandbar. Nothing unusual. Just Old Misery up to her usual tricks."

Skye clutched the gaping neckline of her gown and slipped back into the room. Reaching for the sheet to pull over her, she was aware that Kyle had turned his attention to her. His voice held more tenderness than it had since their afternoon in each other's arms. "The danger is over, Skye. But I expect Captain Belt will want all the passengers to go ashore to lighten the load. A skeleton crew will man the spars and get us off the sandbar. All in a day's work on the Missouri."

"You mean we must all disembark? Now?" She felt a tug on the hem of her gown. Looking down, she saw that a forgotten MacLard was shivering and cowering at her feet. She picked him up and faced Kyle while using MacLard to shield her breasts.

Kyle's eyes absorbed her before he spoke. "Come to the yawl as soon as you're dressed," he finally answered. "Passengers and crew will row to shore. But the captain might allow Melissa to stay aboard." He looked fondly at Missy, who was resting now against her pillow. "After all, Melissa darling, your feathery weight shouldn't prevent the *Royal Eagle* from lifting off the sandbar." With those parting words, Kyle left the cabin.

Skye took a deep breath, only now realizing she'd been barely able to breathe while Kyle stood so near with so much of his magnificent body bared to her view.

Focusing on Missy, she said, "If you're sure you're all right, I'll dress and do as Kyle asked. Hopefully we'll be on our way again soon."

Melissa smiled weakly at her. "I would prefer to stay here if Kyle can arrange it. But would you bring me some fresh water before you go?"

"Of course." Skye released a squirming MacLard so he could visit his paper in the corner, then she slipped into her clothes from yesterday. In minutes, she had dressed, given her hair a token brushing, and pulled on her boots and hat. When she went outside, she was surprised to see the evacuation of the steamer was well underway. She hurried down the steps to a makeshift concession stand she'd spotted yesterday where gentlemen had been standing in line to buy whiskey to fortify themselves for the trip. She found a pitcher of water and poured a mug for Missy, then delivered it at once.

"Thank you, Skye," Melissa said. "Kyle will be back soon, I'm sure, to check on me. I'll be comfortable, and I do hope I can stay aboard."

Skye watched Missy take a long drink. She didn't like the idea of leaving her here alone, but if the boat was safe and the only remaining crew was working diligently at prying the *Eagle* from the sand, Missy would be better off here than sitting in weeds on the riverbank. "We can keep an eye on the cabin from the shore," Skye said. "We'll be within earshot."

"Yes, that's fine." Melissa had finished her drink and was already looking tired.

Skye fastened MacLard's leash to his collar and led him down the steps to the railing just above the water. The yawl was returning, having disgorged its half-dozen passengers on the bank less than a hundred yards away. The river was flowing sluggishly, and the crossing would only take minutes.

She saw Kyle coming toward her. He was dressed in his clothing of yesterday, which included his broad-brimmed hat and the Colt revolver strapped at his hip.

"Let me give you a hand, Skye," he offered.

"Aren't you coming ashore?" she asked, noticing that he had reverted to her Christian name.

"I'm staying aboard to help with the spars. That way I can be near Missy if she needs anything."

"A good idea. Will this take long?"

"Who knows? We've got to get both vessels moving. Could be thirty minutes or two days."

She gasped. "Two days!"

"Closer to a couple of hours is my guess." His eyes swept over her, than settled on MacLard, who was wagging his tail enthusiastically over the unexpected outing. "Take care of yourself," he muttered, as if suddenly reluctant to ask her to do his bidding.

"We'll enjoy dry land," she responded, also staring at MacLard while her heart cartwheeled inside her.

Abruptly, Kyle reached out his hand and rested it on her shoulder, forcing her to look up at him. "Thank you again for helping Missy" was his simple statement, but she read much more in the heated look he gave her from the shadow of his hat brim.

Aware of the inflaming effect his touch had on her senses, she stepped away and picked up the dog. "I'm glad to be of help," she replied just under her breath.

Kyle yelled at the roustabout manning the yawl. "One more passenger, mister."

Taking Kyle's hand, she eased herself down into the boat and sat in the last available space. As they pulled away from the *Eagle,* she found herself face-to-face with a woman whose mound of red hair and dangerously low-cut purple satin dress was startling, to say the least.

"Good morning, miss," the painted woman said with a broad grin. "Guess we'd best get acquainted since we're the only females going ashore. I'm a whore. Are you?"

⇥ *Chapter 28* ⇤

Pardon me?" Skye exclaimed.

"I said, are you a dove like me?"

"A dove? I'm not quite sure I understand." Skye gaped at the grinning lady whose breasts threatened to erupt from her dress with every movement of the boat.

The woman leaned forward to pat MacLard, causing Skye to catch her breath at the extreme likelihood the woman's bosom would soon be exposed to every man present.

"Only three kinds of women go west," the woman said, straightening up in the nick of time. "Whores, trappers' wives, and once in a while a missionary lady, but those saintly types don't last long. You're so young and such a looker, I didn't figure you for a missionary, and I ain't seen you with one of the gents, so I guessed you wasn't no wife."

Despite her embarrassment, Skye was amused. The choice she'd been given was extremely limited. "I'm none of the three types you described, ma'am." She held out her hand. "I'm Miss Skye Mackinnon, and I'm a *rancher*. I'm going out west to look for land."

She heard men's voices murmuring around her as the "dove" looked at her in surprise while giving her a hearty handshake. "Well, I'll be . . . fancy that. A lady rancher. No man atall?"

"My father will soon join me. Oh yes—I travel under the protection of Mr. Kyle Wyndford."

The blowzy female tossed back her head and guffawed. "Well, why didn't you say so in the first place? I understand about *protection*. Got three gents protecting me right now." She rolled her eyes to her left, then picked a tooth with the edge of a bright-red fingernail. "Name's Sadie Glick," she said. "But you can call me Sadie. Everyone does."

Skye had never met a real live whore before, and she found the experience titillating. "Very well, Sadie. Tell me, have you been out west for very long?"

"This is my second trip. I've spent more time in the yawl going sideways on the river than going upstream. Shallowest damn river in the country. A body's blamed lucky to get where she's going in one piece. But if you gotta go west, you gotta go west! Ain't no hems or haws about it. Just get in a steamer and go. How come you want a ranch out there anyway? Nothing in Dakota but rocks and wind and buffalo and Indians. Oh, I forgot, you're with Mr. Wyndford. Some say he's crazy to run beeves with all those savages roaming around, but I reckon he's made himself a wealthy man. Or so I've heard." She winked. "Never heard it from *him* directly, mind you, or collected in person any of his money, though I wouldn't mind a bit. He's got a lady he sees regularly in the settlement near Fort Pierre. At Miss Sylvia's saloon. A place called Tarnations. But Mr. Wyndford doesn't keep her exclusively. So that means you and I might have a chance with the gent." She broadened her grin. "If you decide against ranching, come on up to Pierre and spend some time. There's not much there but the fort and Miss Sylvia's, but that's better'n what's at Vermillion." She gave Skye an admiring look. "You'd do right well, Miss Mackinnon, if you'd put on a little more weight in certain places."

Skye had listened to Sadie's prattle with a mixture of amusement and dismay. "Thank you, Sadie, but I don't suppose I'll join you." Her humor was tempered by the news of Kyle's personal "dove." She was learning more about the gentleman than she wanted to know.

The boat nosed into the sand and several men reached to pull it as far up on the bank as possible.

While climbing out of the craft, Skye continued to dwell on Sadie's remark about Kyle's "saloon lady." She straightened her skirt and hat and gazed back at the *Royal Eagle*. The steamer looked serene, sitting quietly in the midst of the current, as if it had gotten stranded on purpose just to catch its breath. Shading her eyes, she looked downriver where the freighter sat at a slight tilt. A raft was making for shore, loaded with crates and boxes.

Excusing herself from Sadie's company, she unleashed MacLard and walked along the riverbank to intercept the raft. Perhaps her new friend, Buck, would be coming ashore and could give her a report on her horses.

Sure enough, she saw Buck with three other men. He was carrying a crate of cats who were complaining with noisy meows and hisses.

"Buck!" she called. "Hello there!"

"Hey, Miss Mackinnon. How you be?"

"I'm fine." She greeted him on a rocky spit along the riverbank. "Well, we didn't get very far, did we?" she said, smiling.

"I'm not surprised," he answered, putting the annoyed cats on the ground. "Old Misery likes fer us to appreciate arriving at our destination—once't we get there. Plumb joyful, I can swear."

"So I've learned. How are my horses?"

"Doing fine. They've made friends with a goat that belongs to Reverend Meyer."

"A minister on board?"

"Yes'm. Reverend Barry Meyer. He's going west to save lost souls."

"I haven't had time to get acquainted with the other passengers." She tapped her cheek. "Although I did meet Sadie Glick just a minute ago." She spotted his grin beneath his whiskers.

"Sadie, the soiled dove. A *lady,* though, as long as she's on the *Royal Eagle.*"

"Of course. She was very friendly. She told me all the gossip."

"She would know it, that's fer blamed sure."

Skye looked at the river. "The raft is returning to the freighter."

"It's going back for more cargo. Got to lighten the boat to get it unstuck."

"Maybe the horses will be brought ashore. I would be pleased to exercise them."

"Nah. The crew won't unload them unless they have to. Lotta trouble dragging the big animals to shore. Horses don't like the raft, so we usually have to swim 'em. Get's everyone sopping wet and it's a mite risky, too. We've lost horses when the current grabbed 'em."

"Oh dear. I wouldn't want that to happen."

"They'll probably unload the little milk cow, though. I thought if the cats had some milk, they'd settle some. They surely don't take to being in a crate."

"Poor things," she said, kneeling to reach into the basket and stroke an unhappy kitty. "But I guess they'll have a great time chasing rats when they get where they're going."

"You can count on it."

"I'll help you feed them, Buck. I'm good with animals. That's my dog over there in the bushes."

"Better keep an eye on the little fella."

"He'll keep an eye on me, I'm sure."

"Tell you what, Miss Mackinnon; I'll round up someone to milk the cow and you can feed the cats. Would that suit you?"

"I'd be delighted. But *I* can milk the cow. I can put a

stream right into those cats' mouths, and we won't even have to take them out of their crates. They might run away if we did."

Buck's eyes rounded and he put his hands on his hips. "Well, I'll swan . . . that beats all. A lady who knows how to milk a cow."

"I've been milking cows and goats since I was three," Skye said, pleased to be of use. "I was raised on a farm in Scotland, you see."

"Goldarn, Miss Mackinnon, would you marry me?"

She laughed at the twinkle in Buck's eyes. "I'm flattered you would offer, but I must decline. Look, here comes the cow." She watched the nervous animal being carried across the river until it was forced off the raft and led through the shallows. "Where shall we set up the dining room, Buck?"

"How 'bout over there under them cottonwoods? Should be cooler in the shade. I'll get you a box to set on. Then I'll go back to help the boys pry out the freighter."

In minutes, she was settled comfortably at the cow's side, with three crates of cats close to the cow's bulging udder. She was pleased she hadn't lost her knack as she aimed the liquid at greedy, open mouths. Laughing, she watched the cats roll in delight at the white stream, guiding it with their paws toward their tongues.

She was so engrossed, she didn't hear the footsteps behind her.

"You are a most amazing lady, Skye Mackinnon."

Looking over her shoulder, she saw boots, then muscular thighs, and then a broad chest, until finally she met the amused, steady gaze of Kyle Wyndford.

Withdrawing her fingers from her slippery chore, she wiped them on her skirt and carefully rose to her feet.

"Don't let me interrupt you," he said with the glimmer of a smile. "I find the sight enchanting. You're a talented lady."

"Just wanted to keep my hand in," she replied, keeping her tone light.

His smile faded. "We need to talk, Skye."

"Aye. I suppose we do." She would have liked nothing

better than to move into his embrace this very instant and feel his lips close over hers. But she had to keep her wits about her and not let her heart rule her mind.

"We don't have much chance to be alone," Kyle noted. "I think we should take advantage of this delay."

She looked at the cats, who were quietly licking milk from the bottom and sides of their crates. "I guess that chore's done. Where can we go?"

"How about that grove of cottonwoods?"

She walked with him to the grove and found a seat on a large, flat boulder not far from an eddy in the river.

He took a seat on a smaller rock and faced her. "Skye, I wanted you to know I was not being frivolous when we took our wedding vows. I loved you then—and I love you now. We can settle our differences, I'm sure."

"I love you, too, Kyle. But I do have my pride. And I wouldn't be happy being married to someone who thought I was inferior in some way or that my father was some kind of savage."

He grasped her hand. "Of course not. I've told you how I feel about you. And when I meet your father, I'm sure we'll get along fine. But you must understand how it is out west. There have been wars and killings and brutality on the part of both Indians and whites. It's been going on for years, and some people have strong feelings against other races."

"I can't help what other people feel. I've had a chance to learn what you're saying is true. I'm disappointed that even nice folks like Buck Garwin are full of prejudice. But the important thing is what *you* feel."

"I won't lie to you," he said in a low voice. "I have carried a load of hatred in my heart since I found my brother's tortured body. I don't know the Indian people well and have made no effort to get acquainted. I can't promise miracles, because old prejudices die hard. But I do promise to try."

She felt herself weakening under his intense gaze. "I . . . want to believe you. I want to help, if I can. But I've also learned we're strangers in many ways. You're a different man, now that we've arrived in the West. I have to get used to a new Kyle Wyndford."

"Time will take care of that. I know I can win your confidence and your respect."

For a moment or two, she sat listening to the splashing river, the wild bird calls, and the drone of a bee. She believed in his love, but would he change his attitude toward the people whose blood she carried? Could he? If he couldn't respect her as a Lakota, how would that affect their future together when they would be living surrounded by the native people? Finally she sighed and tilted her chin. "I suppose we'll have to see, Kyle. I do agree we need time. But the first thing we must do is make it safely up the Missouri to your ranch."

He nodded and rose to his feet. "That's fair enough—and all I ask for now. I must get back to the boat. It's being inched forward without too much difficulty. We should be able to get underway within the hour."

His manner soothed her aching heart. She wanted his unqualified love more than anything in the world, but love must be a gift, freely given. She watched him walk away along the riverbank, then stop to converse with several of the men. Sadie Glick sidled up to him at once and giggled loudly. There was nothing subtle about Sadie, Skye thought. To her surprise, Kyle laughed and patted Sadie's backside. For an instant, Skye felt jealousy spurt inside her, but she quickly controlled it. Kyle Wyndford was a hearty, red-blooded man who had spent a third of his life in this wild land far from his cultured home in England. The polished gentleman she had met in New Orleans had another side to his nature that she'd only just begun to know. Sadie's revelation about Kyle's light-o'-love must be added to the growing list of new facts she was learning about the lord of Wind River.

Standing, she brushed the pebbles from her skirt. She must find MacLard and prepare to return to the steamboat. Tugging down the brim of her hat, she walked toward the nearby trees where she'd last seen the terrier. "MacLard! Come here, you rascal. This is no time to hide." She had seen him just before she and Kyle had their visit. Hearing rustling in the brush up ahead, she pushed her way through the weeds. "MacLard!" she called again. Then she whistled loudly.

She breathed a sigh of relief when she heard him yapping just ahead. "Come here, MacLard. Come here this instant."

Parting the thick leafy branches, she gaped in astonishment. Facing her, only feet away, was a tall, well-built man dressed in leather. His face was sculptured bronze framed by hair that was as silken and black as liquid obsidian. His buff deerskin shirt was trimmed with fringe, and around his neck, he wore eight or ten strands of multicolored beads. Crystal earrings dangled from his ears and a single feather was laced through strands of his hair. A bow was slung over one shoulder beside a pouch of arrows. Tied to his waist were the limp bodies of two rabbits and one squirrel.

In his hands, he held MacLard.

Skye bit back a scream. This man was an Indian, not *half* Indian, but a full-blood native of the American wilderness. He scrutinized her without the slightest suggestion of emotion or curiosity. He just stared unmoving, holding the dog, who had also grown quiet as if he sensed he was held in the grip of some alien power.

She must say something before he disappeared taking MacLard as hostage.

"Hello." She wasn't sure if she had actually made a sound or if her lips had only formed the word. She tried again. "Hello—sir. I believe you have my dog. He's very special to me, so I would appreciate your returning him." To emphasize her request, she held out her arms toward MacLard.

For an eternity, the Indian fixed her with his black gaze. She had no idea if he understood what she wanted. "Please." She dared step toward him. "Please give me back my little dog." She motioned toward MacLard.

"Trade." The single word was deep-throated and unyielding.

She stopped walking. Trade. Of course, the natives loved to trade. But she had nothing of value with her. Frantically, she felt in her pockets, but they were empty. Her hat. Yes, maybe that would do. She pulled it off and held it out.

He shook his head.

"But—I don't have anything to trade." Desperately, she

tried to think what to do, what to say. "Wait. My boots."
She leaned over to point to her riding boots.

His eyes narrowed as he considered this offer, then finally
he nodded.

With her heart racing, she sat on a fallen log and tugged
off her boots. They were her favorite pair, but that mattered
little. She held them at arm's length, but when the man
reached for them, she pulled them back and pointed to
MacLard, who was starting to squirm.

"I will trade for the boots," the Indian said in clear
English and put the dog gently on the ground.

MacLard dashed to her and she tucked him under her
arm. When she handed the man the boots, he took them and
gave them a careful inspection.

She found her courage now that MacLard was safe and
decided to make the most of this first meeting with a person
of pure Indian blood. "Pardon me, but I haven't met an
Indian before. Could you tell me what tribe you belong to?"

Her question seemed to intrigue him. He stared at her
with sudden interest, making her wonder about her bold
question. Maybe one didn't ask an Indian such a direct
question. Maybe his tribal identity was a secret. She thought
with increasing concern of Buck's warning—shoot 'em first,
ask questions later. She took a backward step and then
noticed a very slight smile had touched the corner of his
lips. He raised one hand, extended his fingers and placed it
in front of his throat.

Dear heaven, what did this mean? Was he thinking of
slicing her throat? Not *his,* she would warrant.

"Sioux," he said softly. "Da-ko-ta."

Her breath caught. The Indian wasn't threatening at all.
The sign he'd made signified his tribe. "Dakota," she
echoed, and smiled at him. "Friend."

"Yes. Friend." He held up her boots and returned her
smile with a warm one of his own.

The shot came from behind her.

She spun in horror and saw two of the steamship's
crewmen with pistols raised; one man's gunbarrel was
smoking.

"No," she screamed. "The man is friendly!" She turned

back to see that the Indian had disappeared. Thank heaven he wasn't killed. She ran toward where he'd been standing. MacLard was barking hysterically and struggling in her arms. Holding him fast, she stared through the underbrush. Some distance away, she heard the limbs cracking as the man escaped the attack. When she looked down, she saw her boots on the ground where he'd dropped them. They were splattered with blood. "Oh no," she whispered. "He wasn't going to harm me." She grabbed the boots and whirled to face the two crewmen.

"Damn it, Hank, he got away," one of the men said. "Winged him, though."

"You're mighty lucky, lady. That was a wild one, if ever I saw one."

She marched to the men and glared into their faces. "You fools!" she snapped. "How dare you shoot someone who wasn't bothering you in the least? We were having a conversation, that's all."

The man with the smoking gun gaped at her. "Conversation? With a bloody savage? You got sawdust for brains, woman? This ain't no trading post out here. An Injun in these parts could be as wild as a wolf and twice as mean."

"Some may be, but that particular Indian was my *friend.*" She could see by the looks on their faces that she had no chance of convincing them. Her blood boiling, she stomped away toward the river, heedless of the rocks and stickers tearing at the stockings covering her feet.

She heard one man growl to the other, "Indian lover, that one. Or stupid as a maggot. Too bad—she's a damned good-looking woman."

"The pretty ones are uppity like that sometimes. I think she's a friend of Sadie's. Do you suppose she's a whore?"

"Gawd, I hope so. I could sure fancy taking some of the starch out of her."

Ignoring the insult, she strode toward the rowboat.

She was confronted by several men racing toward her. Kyle was in the lead, his pistol gripped in his hand.

"Skye—what happened?" he demanded. "We heard a shot."

She held up the bloody boots. "Take a look, Kyle, at the

handiwork of one of the *civilized* white men. 'Tisn't my blood, but a Dakota's, whom I had just met and was speaking to as a friend. But I'll wager my blood is much the same color." Pushing past the startled onlookers, she climbed into the yawl and took a seat at the back. Someone would row her to the *Eagle* soon, she was sure. In the meantime, she would work hard to keep from exploding.

⊰ Chapter 29 ⊱

Kyle jammed his pistol into his holster and watched Skye's retreat to the yawl. His relief that she wasn't harmed outweighed his concerns over her anger, and he found her blazing Scottish temper both tantalizing and beautiful. He didn't know exactly what had happened just now, but he couldn't blame anyone for taking a shot to prevent Skye from being harmed. Maybe the Indian had been more dangerous than Skye realized. When she calmed down, she would see the reason for what happened.

He suppressed a grin as he watched her climb into the yawl and sit primly on the rear bench with MacLard clutched in her arms. Her hat was askew, her sable hair drifting around her shoulders. Remembering how she had looked when she was busy with the milk cow, with her hands pressing the liquid toward the scrambling cats and her cheeks dimpled in laughter, he knew he loved her beyond anyone or anything he'd ever known. He felt he'd made progress in their relationship. At least she had indicated she would give him time to work on this problem with the Indians. If she could somehow meet him halfway, he was sure this difference of opinion could be settled amicably.

Behind him, the two crew members were explaining to the crowd about the shooting.

One said, "She was standing there, too scared to move, I reckon. There was that big Indian buck, all decked out, and carrying weapons. He already had her boots off."

Kyle spun at those words.

Sadie laughed. "Maybe she likes those redskinned braves. Some ladies have a taste for red meat."

Kyle strode toward the group. He couldn't hit a woman, but he'd sure like to knock that whore on her behind.

The crewman howled. "That's a good one, Sadie. I do think she's a whore, so maybe you're right. No wonder she was downright frosted when I scared him off."

Kyle landed a hard blow to the man's chin, knocking him backward to land in a crumpled heap under a bush.

"Hey, you're out of line, Wyndford," shouted the man's buddy. "That fellow you just punched might've saved the woman's life. And Sadie here told us the girl was her friend, and might be on her way to work up at Tarnations Saloon in Pierre."

Kyle grabbed the man's shirt collar and yanked him off his feet. "You're dead wrong, mister. And so is Sadie. *You're* the one who's out of line, and Sadie wouldn't know a *lady* if one came down on a cloud from heaven."

A heavy hand clutched his shoulder and twisted him around to meet a hard blow to his chin. The first crewman had recovered and was boiling mad. Kyle staggered but recovered quickly and waded into the bricklike fellow, driven by all his frustration and anger. In minutes, the fight was finished, and the foul-mouthed, no-good roustabout was unconscious in the weeds. Kyle wiped traces of blood from his lip and nose and addressed the gaping onlookers, who were enjoying themselves thoroughly.

"Get this straight, all of you. Miss Mackinnon is a lady, something most of you have never seen. Her father is a titled lord in Scotland, and this is her first visit to America. She is traveling with me and my sister-in-law. And if I hear one more word sullying her reputation, I'll come after the bastard with a gun instead of my fists. And that includes you, Sadie Glick." He walked toward the yawl, but a couple of the crew were already rowing it back to the *Eagle*. All he saw was Skye's back and the pink ribbons of her bonnet floating in the breeze. He prayed she hadn't heard the insults. The poor lass had enough to deal with defending her Indian blood, without having to explain she wasn't a prostitute.

Skye spent the next two days, which were rainy and overcast, reading, making notes in a journal her mother had given her as a parting gift, and watching over Melissa. The hours were long and the constant noise of the engines and the stench of smoke and engine oil added to her discomfort and sense of doom. Missy was more uncomfortable than ever. Skye doubled the lady's dosage of medication, but that only made her sleep hours at a time. Missy was terribly ill, Skye knew, but she had deteriorated so swiftly, it was frightening. Skye had pleaded with Melissa to reveal to Kyle the diagnosis of the physician in New Orleans, but Missy had become frantic and begged her not to say anything. Not until they got to Wind River. For now, Skye would respect her wishes, but if Missy grew any worse, Skye decided Kyle must be told

On the positive side, the cabin boy who brought their meal trays said the two boats were making good progress. In two or three days, they would arrive at Vermillion in Dakota. The *Eagle* would continue on to Fort Pierre and points north before starting its return trip down the Missouri.

Late on the morning of the fourth day out, the sun broke through the clouds, and the air was crystalline, freshly washed, and invigorating.

Skye saw to Melissa's needs, then strolled out to the deck to observe the passing scenery. In places, the river had cut deep bluffs, which blocked the inland view from the steamer. In other spots, the banks were more gentle and sloping, and Skye glimpsed undulating empty prairies stretching endlessly to the farthest horizon on both sides of the Missouri. Pulling up a chair on the stern deck, she popped up her parasol and absorbed the view, wishing vainly that the belching smoke didn't obscure the beauty of the panorama. Within the hour, she saw her first buffalo drinking at the riverbank. The passing steamers seemed not to disturb them in the least, and she marveled at their massive, shaggy bodies. She was relaxing and trying not to let her thoughts dwell on Kyle, which they had a strong inclination to do, when a door opened on the far side of the deck and Sadie Glick approached.

"Finally got some sunshine," Sadie observed. "Mind if I join you?"

"Not a bit; please do," Skye offered, glad for any diversion.

Sadie pulled up a deck chair and arranged her wide-brimmed hat to protect her lily-white skin from the sun. "Guess I'd better start by apologizing, Miss Mackinnon. I'm lucky you're still speaking to me."

"Oh? Why do you say that, Sadie?"

"Well . . . I got things a mite crooked the other day. Confused, you could say. I thought you was more or less a whore like me, that you were traveling with Mr. Wyndford as his mistress. I didn't know you was a lady."

Skye was disconcerted by Sadie's sincere apology. Why should Sadie be upset over what a stranger thought of her? And yet the woman appeared truly disturbed. "Don't worry about it, Sadie," Skye said gently. "I suppose some would call me a lady, but I don't think of myself as special. And I make it a practice not to throw stones at people whose moral behavior is none of my concern. You were friendly to me, and that's the important thing."

"But I said some pretty bad things." Sadie lowered her eyes and twisted a silk handkerchief in her hands. "Didn't mean to cause a fight." She looked up hastily. "But it wasn't all my fault."

"What fight?"

Sadie's plucked eyebrows lifted. "You didn't know about the fight?"

"No. I've been staying in my cabin lately."

"Well, sometimes the crew does misbehave. They have a hard lot, you see. Working for their grubpile, without much dallying."

"They do look a rough sort."

"The West is a hard place, ma'am. But hardship is the warp and woof of life, so they say."

"I'm sure that's true. Now what's this about a fight?"

"Your friend, Mr. Wyndford, got into it with one of the crew. He punched the man who shot at the Indian."

Skye stiffened. "Really? Mr. Wyndford did that?"

"Quite a sight, I'll swear. Seeing a rich man like him rolling in the dust like any other hothead."

Skye was astounded and impressed that Kyle would fight in the defense of an Indian. "I'm sure Mr. Wyndford was justified. The shooting was a terrible mistake. The Indian turned out to be friendly, and I don't believe that crewman cared in the least that he shot an innocent man."

"I didn't know what happened between you and the Indian, but it caused a rip-roaring fight."

"Is that so? I didn't see it."

"You were already headed back to the steamer, had your back turned to the shore. I must say, I rightly admire a gentleman such as Mr. Wyndford who isn't afraid to bloody his hands on a cocky lowlife. All things considered, I'm lucky Mr. Wyndford didn't set me on my arse or toss me into the river. I said some pretty awful things. That's why I wanted to apologize to you."

Skye was fascinated and oddly moved. "I'm amazed that Mr. Wyndford would be so fair-minded toward a native—and come to my defense," she said softly.

"Why, there was a mighty ruckus, right there in front of us all. The roustabout said . . ." Sadie hesitated and appeared distinctly uncomfortable.

"Go on, Sadie. I don't mind. The man didn't know me or anything about me."

Sadie looked again at the twisted handkerchief. "Well, the crewman thought you was a fallen dove like me. I guess that was my fault for making myself so friendly to you. And I went along with what he said and added my own two bits."

Skye patted Sadie's sleeve. "Don't feel badly. I'm glad we made friends."

"Anyway, the man thought you was one of us doves, and

he said so right out loud. Said you might have wanted to . . . ah . . . have a romp with the Indian. Said he had your boots off."

Skye gasped. No wonder Kyle had lost his temper. This was far worse than she'd expected. She had experienced a fascinating exchange with a real American native, and as a result, the two of them had been insulted and the poor Indian shot and perhaps badly wounded. "What a terrible thing to say or think! The man deserved a beating."

"He got one, sure enough. I thought Mr. Wyndford was going to pound him to a pulp."

Skye sank back in her chair, imagining what Kyle's reaction must have been to this insult to his wife's reputation. Not that the crewman knew she was Kyle's wife. Not that *anybody* knew. Nevertheless, the remark was unforgivable. "I'm glad Mr. Wyndford hit the fellow, but I hope Mr. Wyndford wasn't injured in the fray."

"He was cut up a bit. That fellow was stout, built like a buffalo. But your friend knocked him sky-winding before the fight was over. When we came back to the steamer, the man's friends had to carry him to the raft."

For several minutes, Skye sat gazing blindly at the riverbank. Kyle had fought for her honor and she found that extremely gratifying. In doing so, he had also punished the man who had wounded the Indian. She found that very encouraging. Whatever else Kyle might be, he was no coward and he was a man with high ideals. He was also very sure of himself. Some men might have come straight to her door to show off their heroism and brag about their wounds to win her favor. Kyle was above such ploys, she concluded. He knew what kind of man he was and had no need to prove it to her, to himself, or to anyone else. She had to talk to him as soon as possible.

"Sadie, have you ever looked after someone who's sick? I mean, just making sure they had whatever they needed and took their medicine?"

"Lots of times. We girls take good care of each other."

"Then I have a favor to ask. Mr. Wyndford's sister is quite ill, but she sleeps most of the time. If I were close by, could you sit in her cabin for a while? You would be paid, of course."

"I'd be happy to do that, even without pay."

"I need to have a private talk with Mr. Wyndford, if he can find the time. And we would insist on paying you."

"Glad to help." She gave Skye a sly smile. "I'd even spend the night, if you like."

Skye felt her cheeks burn. "No, I don't think so."

"Just name the time."

"Maybe this evening, when things are quiet."

"How about right after we eat the scraps of dinner they serve us?"

"Fine. Just come to my cabin. If Mrs. Wyndford is resting comfortably, I'll steal some time away."

Kyle had spent much of the day in his cabin going over his accounts, then taken dinner with John Roux. With the sun fading and a cooler breeze lifting off the river, he strolled along the deck toward Missy and Skye's cabin to see how they fared.

He was surprised to see Skye approaching, a warm smile on her pretty lips.

"Good evening, Miss Mackinnon," he said pleasantly. "Is everything all right with Missy?"

"She's asleep, and I've arranged for Sadie to sit with her awhile. I had hoped we might have some time together."

His heart sang. This was indeed a refreshing change in Skye's manner.

"Come with me," he murmured and slipped his arm through hers. "I know a nice spot to sit and watch the sunset. Nothing would please me more than to share it with you."

Like furtive children, they settled on the planks behind an empty cabin on the top deck. Kyle folded his legs and held his wife's hand.

"Do you think Missy will mind being looked after by a— soiled dove?" Skye asked.

"I think Melissa will accept what she cannot change. Besides, she isn't aware of Sadie's reputation."

"But knowing the way Sadie loves to talk, the secret will be out before long."

Kyle laughed and slipped an arm around her, luxuriating in her presence and in the idyllic surroundings, as the boat made its clanking, puffing way upstream.

Silently they watched a new moon rise above the eastern riverbank; the evening star hung like a jewel above, as if tempting the golden sliver to pursue it across the sable sky. The breeze was sweet with the scent of wild roses and honeysuckle growing along the riverbanks.

Finally Skye said, "Kyle, I heard about the fight. I want to thank you for your defense of my honor, and especially for punishing that man who shot the Indian."

"The man was way out of line—in a number of ways." Kyle leaned against the pilot house and wished with every fiber of his being he could make love to his wife. He held her in the crook of his arm, aware of every feminine curve, curves that he had been so fortunate once to possess. He had left his homespun shirt unbuttoned to the cooling air. Skye's small hand, soft, gentle, and trusting, rested lightly on his bare chest. Inhaling the fragrance of approaching dusk, he laid his hand over hers. "Are you comfortable, Skye, my lady?" The lilting tone in his voice belied his deep feelings.

"Aye, James Kyler," she whispered. "But I'm drugged with lethargy. I feel like I'm drifting in moonglow, weightless and floating on a midsummer night's breeze in Scotland."

He looked down at her tousled hair, the tip of her nose that showed signs of sunburn. "And now *you're* the poet, my lass."

She moved in his arms and gazed up at him. Her eyes were warm and inviting, deep green the shade of a primeval forest in shadow. "I do love you, Kyle. Tonight I love you with my whole heart."

"Tonight?" he queried, one finger tracing the tip of her ear. "And what about tomorrow? And the day after?"

Her fingertips touched his chin. He hadn't bothered to shave today and he wondered idly if his stubble of beard would offend her.

"Why worry about tomorrow, my lord of Wind River?"

His hand moved over her shoulder and found its way to the swell of her breast. "If you don't believe in tomorrow, then perhaps you don't believe in yesterday."

She was silent for a time. "We *are* our yesterdays," she said at last. "We can forget much of our past, but it is always a part of us. And not only *our* past, but our ancestors and *their* past, as well. We ride the wind of our lives, unaware of what we owe our parents or our grandparents—and so on back into the mists of time."

"Damned if you aren't a philosopher as well as a poet, my darling."

"Kyle, that is what I believe. That's why I take pride in the blood ties I have to my Scottish, my English, and my *Lakota* ancestors. I exist because of them, because they lived and loved. Whatever I am, I owe to those who have gone before me."

He caressed her body, paying homage with his touch. "Do you believe we were fated to belong to each other? That the gods planned for our spirits to be joined?"

"I can't answer that. Not yet."

"Why not? You must admit our marriage was a twist of fate and our union as profound and joyful as any could be on earth."

"I do admit that. But as I said, that is part of our past. We have it forever, and now we have tonight. Everything in our future is still a mystery."

He brushed her hair with his lips, found her temple, and pressed his lips against the spot where silken wisps of dark hair met the cool smoothness of her flesh. "The *future* may be a mystery, but my love for you is for eternity. There is no mystery in that."

She gazed at him, a shard of moonlight highlighting the bridge of her nose. "Love is like the Missouri, Kyle. Beautiful, useful, and filled with hidden dangers. We'll follow its path—and we'll see what our future holds."

He tried to decipher her subtle implication. Men spoke plainly; women spoke in riddles. All he knew was that he held heaven in his arms, but that he mustn't hold too tightly or somehow it might escape him.

An accordion accompanied a gravelly voice from the other side of the freighter, managing to sift though the chug-chug of the engines.

"To the west, to the west," came the plaintive song. "To the land of the free! Where the mighty Missouri rolls down to the sea."

"That's Buck," Kyle explained. "Knows all the old songs, I do swear. Verse after verse, some sad, some lively. Guess the crusty gent's in a sentimental mood tonight."

Skye laid her head on his shoulder and made no attempt to move her body away from his exploring hand. Lovemaking was out of the question here in plain sight, but he was pleased she was allowing his caresses. The relaxing of the wall between them boded well for their future together.

"I like Buck," she murmured. "He's taking good care of all the animals. They're doing well, in spite of their confinement."

"Buck is a wise fellow. He's been traveling these parts longer than anyone. If he gives you any advice, you'd better take it."

She stirred and moved slightly away. Kyle wondered if he'd said anything that disturbed her. Had she murmured something about Buck's disliking Indians? If so, she was probably right; Kyle supposed Buck felt like all the other white men out west—but he didn't want that controversial subject coming up tonight when everything was so perfect. He figured he could save that devilish problem for Skye's mysterious tomorrow.

Skye hadn't realized how exhausted she was or how comfortable she would be in Kyle's embrace. And she certainly hadn't expected to fall sleep with the constant clanking of the boilers and Kyle's arm as a pillow. But sleep she did, as soundly as a newborn babe.

When she stirred, she was first aware of the stiffness in her neck, then gradually she roused and realized Kyle was also asleep, holding her tenderly in his arms. It was still dark; she had no idea what time it was or how long she'd been sleeping.

Feeling dreamily contented, she considered what lay ahead for her. Soon they would arrive in the tiny settlement called Belleview to take on wood and supplies, then they would continue on their last leg toward Vermillion. Wind River Ranch headquarters was a couple of hours' ride from Vermillion Trading Post. Soon, very soon, she would see the country she had dreamed about for so many years.

Skye had loved the stories her father told her when she was young, stories of the majestic West of America, the endless fertile plains, the Indians who rode fearlessly on horses like his stallion, Spirit Dog, men who tracked the great herds of buffalo and who lived in a culture as rich as any he'd seen in Scotland. Different from the Scots', but deeply satisfying to the Lakota part of his soul. He had explained he had not been allowed to be a part of their society, but his feelings toward it were warm and wistful.

Lately, however, Skye had wondered if her father had been realistic about his memories of Dakota and his early life there. Often she had seen him gazing out to sea, a melancholy expression on his rugged face. She knew he had missed his distant homeland, but she also felt sure he would never have left Skye if things there hadn't deteriorated so badly that he was afraid his family would starve.

Her father's words were uppermost in her mind as she gazed skyward where the stars had faded, but dawn was not yet in evidence. *Remember my Indian name, White Arrow. Find a well-watered stretch of valley land. You are Lakota, as I am.* She looked at Kyle's face, his chin shadowed with bristles, the planes of his jaw strong even as he slept. What would happen when the two most important men in her life came face to face? Except for his green eyes, her father had the looks of an Indian warrior. How would the most powerful rancher in Dakota, who avoided the natives, come to terms with the proud Lakota laird of the Mackinnons? And where would *she* fit into this clash of wills? If the worst should happen, she could be emotionally ground to bits between these two masculine forces full of pride and misunderstandings.

A whistle from the *Royal Eagle* shattered the night air.

Skye sat up; Kyle jerked awake.

A crewman peered around the side of the wheelhouse and called to them. "Belleview around the bend."

The *Royal Eagle* eased toward the landing with the freighter close behind. The first blue glow of morning was spreading in the east beyond the empty rolling hills.

"Kyle, I'm going to see about Missy and relieve Sadie."

"Good idea. I'll stop by my cabin, then join you there."

When she quietly pushed open her cabin door, she knew at once there was trouble. Sadie was sitting on Melissa's bed, holding a lantern in one hand and Missy's arm in the other. MacLard wagged his tail, but made no sound. The cabin was stuffy and held a peculiar odor. *Blood.* Skye recognized the pungent smell and rushed to stare into Melissa's white face.

⊰ *Chapter* 30 ⊱

Missy . . ." Skye breathed the name as she leaned over the pale, unmoving figure of the woman who had become her dearest friend.

When she received no response, not even the flutter of eyelashes, she turned to Sadie. "When did she become like this?" she whispered.

"About thirty minutes ago, the poor thing began tossing and turning. I started to go looking for you, but she kept holding my hand. She was in an awful lot of pain, Miss Mackinnon. I helped her take her medicine. After that, she went to sleep. She's been like this ever since."

Skye touched Sadie's arm. "I'm sorry you had to go through this, Sadie. I shouldn't have left her. I knew she wasn't doing well." Skye stared dismally at the white face against the pillow. "We've just docked at Belleview. I don't suppose there's a doctor, but at least we can get her into a real bed, maybe find some help for her."

"I'll be glad to help anyway I can. But I do need to get on to Pierre. If I leave the steamer now, I may not get there for another month. I surely need the wages from the summer travelers—if you understand what I mean, ma'am."

Skye nodded. "Of course, you must go on upriver. You've done more than your share already and I won't forget your friendship."

"I wouldn't brag too much about being my friend. Just keep it to yourself and I'll understand."

"You're very thoughtful, Sadie. Why don't you go along and get some rest. Mr. Wyndford will be here any minute and we'll take his sister-in-law ashore. I do hope there's some sort of inn."

"There's rooms above the trading post. Middling clean, I reckon. Good-bye, Miss Mackinnon. This sick woman here has a great affection for you. I can see why."

Skye felt her throat tighten. "She talked about me?"

"Oh my, yes. Said you was the finest young lady she'd ever met. That you had spunk and common sense, and that you would someday marry her brother-in-law. She said she had prayed for that for weeks now and hated to die without seeing it. She wants to see her boy, too. Badger, she called him." Sadie stared at the figure on the bed. "In my opinion, she ain't never going to see much of anything again."

Skye reluctantly agreed. Watching Sadie disappear around the corner, she noticed the cobalt sky was diffused with pink. Chimney smoke drifted upward to greet the lightening sky; a rooster crowed, dogs barked. Tiny Belleview was beginning to stir.

"Skye . . . is that you?"

She hastened to Melissa's side. "Aye, Missy. I fear you've taken a turn for the worse."

"I know. But that nice lady helped me. She tidied me up and gave me my medicine. She held my hand until I slept. I'm feeling better now."

"Melissa, we must have a serious talk."

"Yes, dear."

"Let me do the talking, and you must listen."

"Of course, child." Melissa's voice was barely audible, but she gave Skye a sweet smile.

"Melissa, I must insist we tell Kyle the truth about your condition. We've docked at Belleview and we can take you ashore and make you more comfortable."

Melissa half raised and grasped Skye's arm. "No," she gasped, her voice heavy with alarm. "I'm not leaving this boat. Not until we reach Vermillion."

Skye sighed and placed her hand on Missy's. "Please don't upset yourself. Kyle will be here shortly and you can discuss it with him. But, Melissa, it isn't fair not to tell him how sick you are. He has a right to know."

Melissa collapsed against the pillow. "I suppose so." Her sunken eyes fixed intently on Skye. "I will agree to tell him, but I will *not* leave the steamer until I get home. I must see Badger; I must."

A knock came on the door, then it was opened slightly. "Skye—Melissa? May I come in?"

Skye pushed Missy's hair back from her moist forehead. She hadn't noticed how gray Missy's hair was until now, much too gray and thin for a woman her age.

"Prop me up, please, dear, and hand me a cup of water." Skye promptly took care of Melissa's requests.

With a smile of appreciation, Melissa said, "All right, Kyle, you may enter."

Skye stood aside as Kyle walked into the cramped cabin. Seeing his frown, she said quickly, "Missy had a bad night, Kyle. Sadie sat up with her and has gone to her cabin to rest."

Kyle's brow furrowed as he took a seat on Skye's bed opposite Melissa. Absently, he stroked MacLard, who had jumped up to sit beside him. "I'm deeply sorry, my darling," he said to Missy. "Are you better now?"

Melissa took a sip from her cup and gazed at Skye.

Skye nodded encouragingly and gave her a firm look, the kind one gave a child when a difficult task must be done. "Would you prefer for me to leave you alone for a time?" she asked gently.

"No, not at all," replied Melissa. "You might as well be in on the telling."

"Telling?" Kyle asked, and glanced at Skye.

Melissa gripped her cup in front of her as if it gave her strength. "Kyle, my dear. This is not easy to say, but Skye is right; you must be told."

Skye saw him blanch, his lips clamp.

"I don't want to make a fuss, but the doctor in New Orleans told me I would soon me reunited with my husband—sooner than I expected, I'm afraid."

For several heartbeats, Kyle sat staring at his sister-in-law. Skye was certain he was shocked to his core. She wished desperately she had some way to comfort him, but this was one of those times in life when pain must be faced and worked through with whatever courage a person could muster. Later, she might be of help. But now, he must accept the worst possible news from a woman he loved deeply. Skye had trouble holding back her own tears, but she absolutely had to if she was to remain in the cabin. She swallowed two or three times, grateful she wasn't required to speak.

Finally Kyle was able to mutter, "Are you sure? Nothing can be done?"

"Nothing," Missy said, finding strength from some invisible source. "I've known for weeks, so I'm used to the idea. I'm not afraid, Kyle. I know Blanton is waiting for me. But . . . I'm sorry for you and . . ." Her lips quivered. "For Badger."

Skye clamped her hand over her mouth. Tears were starting, despite her best efforts to prevent them.

Slowly, Kyle sank to his knees by the bed and opened his arms.

Melissa put aside the cup and moved into his embrace.

The seconds crawled by as the first touch of morning sun filtered through the dingy glazing over the window. Men were shouting outside as work began to supply the steamers. Inside the cabin, there was only silence as these two people who had endured so much faced this one last challenge together.

Skye leaned against the door frame, her heart aching as she thought of slipping away and leaving Kyle and Missy alone.

239

But before she could leave, Kyle sat back on his heels and raised Melissa's hand to his lips. "Your courage puts me to shame," he said softly.

Pain tore through Skye's heart when she saw the moisture on Kyle's cheeks. She'd never seen a man weep before, certainly not a man as powerful and brave as Kyle Wyndford. The sight was so deeply moving, she felt herself grow lightheaded from the sheer emotion of it.

Through a veil of mist, she watched Melissa smile and reach out to touch Kyle's face with her fingertips.

"My dearest brother-in-law—oh, let me say *brother* in these last days—I'll allow you your grief and consider it a tribute. But only this once. I am not going ashore at Belleview. I will *live* to reach Wind River. That I swear to you. I will see my son and the hills of my home. I will be buried next to Blanton. Soon, I hope, because I am truly very tired, my darling."

Kyle cleared his throat and sat on the bed. "If that is your wish, Missy, that is what will be done." For the first time, he turned to Skye. "We should be in Vermillion in a couple of days. I'm afraid I must call on your help, Skye. But I stand ready to do anything I can—anything at all."

Her heart turned over with compassion when she saw the bleakness in his face. "I won't leave her, Kyle. Nothing on earth will take me from her side again."

Missy lay back once more. "Now you two, I told you I don't want any fuss. We'll continue our trip as we started, and I want nothing more said about my condition. I hope that I will have a chance to visit with Sadie again. I do believe she's one of the most entertaining ladies I've met since I lived in Dakota." Her sly smile revealed she knew the truth about Sadie Glick's checkered past.

Missy's impossibly courageous quip was more than Skye could bear. "Excuse me," she mumbled and left the cabin. Standing by the railing overlooking Belleview, she buried her face in her hands and wept, releasing some of the wrenching sorrow that had built up over the past several minutes.

When Kyle arrived at her side, he put his arm over her

shoulder and stood for a time in silence. Regaining her self-control, Skye slipped her arm around his waist.

"I can't believe it," he said at last. "She's always been a tower of strength, the way she rose above her grief for Blanton, refused to give in to hatred and prejudice against the Indians, lived in a sod house at Wind River and raised her son without ever complaining about the hardships of it all. I honestly don't know what I will do without her."

Skye couldn't look at him. But she gave him a hug and leaned against him. "You're strong, Kyle. And when she's gone, her strength will enter you because she will send it to you from above."

She felt his eyes on her. "Do you really believe that?" He asked the question like a youngster in Sunday school, wanting to believe, but not at all certain of such glorious miracles.

"I'm absolutely sure. Also I know your brother, Blanton, has sent you strength. Now you will have a double gift when the two of them are reunited."

Releasing her, he gripped the railing. "I need more than strength, Skye. I need wisdom. I need to tear certain terrible images from my brain. I need to purge my heart of anger and bitterness. I don't know if that's possible. Not yet, anyway."

"Why not?"

"Because I can't stand to see Melissa suffer. I hated the people who tortured and killed my brother, who caused her such sorrow. If I had Blanton's murderers in my power right now, I would kill them without mercy."

A shudder ran through her. Would he ever be able to forgive and forget what happened all those years ago?

"For now, I must concentrate on Melissa's needs. If only I can get her home . . ." Unable to continue, he gave her a pat and walked back toward the cabin.

Looking down, Skye saw that MacLard had slipped outside and come to sit by her feet. She picked him up and held his warm, shaggy body against her breast. She was sure the dog sensed trouble and sorrow in the atmosphere. She found it a comfort to hold him close and scratch behind his large, furry ears.

⊰ Chapter 31 ⊱

For three days following the stop at Belleview, Skye had one purpose and one purpose only: Melissa Wyndford's comfort.

Eating and sleeping little, she kept a constant vigil at Melissa's bedside. Kyle looked in often, but she was barely aware of his presence. She had only one brief respite the first day when they steamed out of Belleview. Sadie Glick had stopped and insisted she take a breather on the stern deck. But after that day, Skye had not left the airless cabin for any reason.

Melissa's strength was ebbing quickly. The woman often cried out in pain, despite her effort to be uncomplaining. Whatever was destroying her was cruel and grisly and refused to be held back any longer, even with increased dosages of medication.

Skye lost track of time, of night and day, of whether the steamer was making any kind of progress. She knew only that Missy was most at ease when she tightly gripped her hand, when she wiped her sweating forehead, and when she massaged her tortured body. At last, after helping Melissa through a particularly dreadful night of suffering, she revealed to her that she and Kyle were married. Missy asked no questions about the event, and her gentle smile was ample reward for giving away the secret Skye shared with Kyle. Skye explained that they had waited to make the announcement, hoping that the Mackinnons would be together for that special occasion. She received Missy's blessing and knew the lady would die happier knowing that her brother was a married man.

Early the fourth morning out of Belleview, Skye roused

herself from sleep to the sound of silence. Complete and utter silence, except for the splatter of raindrops on the tin roof of the cabin. No clanking vibrations, no chugging of the engines—no rasping breath from the woman an arm's length away.

Jumping up, she bent over the motionless form. MacLard raised his head from his usual place at the foot of the bed. Sometime during the dark early morning hours, Skye had given Missy her medicine and a drink. Then she'd dropped in exhaustion onto her own bed.

"Melissa," she called softly, adjusting her sleep-blurred vision toward the inert woman.

"It's all right, Skye, darling," came the low masculine voice from the corner of the cabin, causing her to turn in surprise. "My precious Missy is in Blanton's care now. She's happy and at peace."

Appalled, Skye leaned close to Melissa. To her horror, she could detect no sign of life, no trace of breathing, nothing but an unnatural stillness in the lady's body. She placed her hand on Melissa' forehead. Cold, dry, lifeless.

"No," she choked. "She can't be—dead."

Out of the shadows, Kyle moved to stand beside her, to put his arm around her, to hold her tightly against him. "She went away soon after I arrived. About thirty minutes ago."

"But . . . Kyle, you didn't wake me. I wanted . . ." Skye was stunned, then pierced by agonizing pain deep in her heart. "Oh, Kyle, she wanted to die at Wind River." Tears flowed down her checks as she struggled with the reality of Missy's passing.

"I know. She and I spoke about that at the last."

"You spoke with her? And I didn't hear you?"

"My darling Skye, you were so very exhausted. There was nothing you could do. I was with her and she was content. She even said she was glad her son hadn't seen her in such a state. She said . . ." He coughed to clear his throat. "She said she would see him soon from her home in heaven. She asked me to look after him. But she knew she had no need to ask that. And Skye . . ."

Wordlessly, she gazed at him.

"Thank you for telling her we are married. She was very pleased."

Skye rested her head against Kyle's chest and cried in unashamed sorrow. She had known Melissa Wyndford for such a short time, but she had felt a bond with the lady from the beginning. Why did Missy have to die, when she was needed so much, by her son, by her brother-in-law, and by Skye, as well? Skye felt that Missy was the one person who could have been her dearest friend in the years to come, but she had been stolen from her, as if a thief had arrived in the night and taken her away.

For several minutes, she gave in totally to her misery, then she regained control and thought of Kyle.

Moving from his arms, she tried to see his face. He was gazing at the window with unseeing eyes. His cheeks were dry, and he appeared to have accepted the inevitable with stoicism and courage.

"Kyle," she murmured, "what will you do now?"

"We're at the dock at Vermillion. At least one of her last wishes was granted. She's home. I'll send for Reyes and tell him to bring Badger. I want to tell the boy myself what has happened. Then we'll move her to Wind River."

Suddenly weak, Skye sank to her bed. She watched Kyle bend over Missy, but she closed her eyes so she wouldn't see his farewell kiss. To witness that would have sent her into spasms of sobbing. When she looked again, Kyle had drawn the sheet over Melissa's face.

He spoke in a voice devoid of feeling. "I've vacated my cabin. Why don't you gather your things and you and MacLard go there to rest and wait for the wagon from Wind River."

She nodded her agreement.

"Skye, I've said before how much I appreciate your help with Melissa. I have no words to express my feelings at this moment. You were sent to us, to Melissa and me, like an angel straight from heaven. My emotions are spent this morning, but you must understand how much I love you and have allowed you to become a part of me, a part of my existence."

Skye wiped tears from her cheeks. "Thank you," she

whispered. "I'll say good-bye to Missy and go to your cabin for a while."

Leaning near, he cupped her chin in his hand and kissed her forehead. Without speaking again, he walked out into a steadily falling rain.

She sat for a time, trying to gather her strength. She must pack the few personal items she had taken from her trunk. She must tidy up after MacLard and see that he received some scraps for breakfast. She must take her leave of Missy, then find her way to Kyle's cabin.

Standing, she pushed back her hair. Her mouth tasted like sand, and her clothes had been slept in for more nights than she could remember.

In a few minutes, she had repacked her trunk except for one clean dress. She left the door open to allow the fragrance of the rain shower to fill the enclosure and chase away the odor of death. Squaring her shoulders, she promised herself a new beginning, built on Melissa's example of faith and fortitude. And also on the strength of her own Mackinnon and Lakota roots. She said a short prayer over the covered body, then gathered a confused MacLard and hurried through the rain to the other side of the cabin area. Below her on the boat, the roustabouts and the other crew members were gathering at Flipper George's table, where coffee and food were being offered.

She ducked under the overhang of the cabin roof. To her surprise, a tall man was climbing the steps toward her, a man she didn't recognize.

"Miss Mackinnon?"

"Aye. I'm Miss Mackinnon."

"I'm Reverend Meyer. Reverend Barry Meyer. Mr. Wyndford sent me to find you—and to look in on Mrs. Wyndford."

Skye placed MacLard on the deck and held out her hand. "I'm happy to meet you, Reverend. I suppose you've heard, then, of our loss."

"Indeed," the man answered. "I didn't know the lady, but her fine reputation is well known in Dakota. I'd be honored to say a few words over her."

"I'm sure she'd be pleased about that, sir. She was as good

a soul as ever I knew, and she'll find her way to heaven with no trouble at all. In the meantime, please go to her. She's in the forward cabin."

He doffed his black felt hat, causing raindrops to fly from its brim. "Anything I can do for *you,* young lady? I understand the steamer will be tied up here for a day or two. I'll be staying at the post in Vermillion."

"I'm fine, Reverend Meyer. Just very tired after all we've been through. Please excuse me so I may freshen up before the wagon comes from Wind River."

"By all means. We'll speak later at a more convenient time." He gazed skyward. "Rain and death. They do go together. I'll ask Mr. Wyndford if he will need me for the services. I'm just passing through, you understand. Spreading the gospel wherever and whenever I can."

"I'm sure he'll be obliged, Reverend, although I can't tell you what plans he will make for Mrs. Wyndford's burial. Her husband is interred on the ranch, I believe, and she will certainly want to lie next to him. The couple had a hard life, but they will now rest in peace together."

"So I've heard. He was murdered by savage redskins years ago, I know. Now the two are safe in the arms of God." With a sympathetic smile, he left her and disappeared around the far side of the cabin.

A pinprick of anger penetrated Skye's grief as she entered Kyle's small, barren cubicle. Even the preacher called her people savage redskins. Wasn't there anyone in the whole of the American West who wanted to give the Indians some compassion and understanding, some respect, for heaven's sake?

Kyle stood in the pilot house, staring at the thick black clouds and listening to the broken dripping of rain on the metal roof. Melissa had died so quickly that he hardly believed it was real. This homecoming after so many weeks was nothing like he'd anticipated and dreamed of. Beyond the gloom, he saw the outline of the trading post on the bluff above the river. Lining the riverbank were log and sod warehouses built to receive the goods brought to the post by the American Fur Company boats, and then by Indians from their villages in the wilderness. Beyond the trading post stood a row of shops that included a barber and bathing shop, a general store, a room that served as church and schoolhouse, and the office of the trading company officials. Close by were the barns and livery and the quarters provided for the few families who had accompanied the men west. Beyond the settlement during several months of the year, tepees were set up by the Indians who had brought in their trade goods. Not much of a town by civilized standards, he thought.

Kyle had never been concerned about the condition of the place before, as long as supplies were at hand for Wind River and someone was available to teach the four or five children some book learning. But today, with the rain washing away the color, concealing the beauty of the surrounding hills and valley, and turning what served as a street into a muddy swamp, he had to wonder what Skye would think of such a dismal place. He had looked forward to showing off this American West, to allowing Reyes to throw one of his California-style barbeques in honor of his guest. Melissa would have been delighted to oversee the occasion and introduce Skye to what passed as social life in this sparsely populated land. And Badger, of course, would have been his usual boisterous self, no doubt, creating mischief at every turn and capturing Skye's kind and loving heart with his winning ways.

But now, nothing was as he'd hoped. Why would any woman choose to live in such a place? Then he remembered that Melissa had chosen to stay—because of her love for her husband. Would Skye be willing to make such a sacrifice for him? What had he to offer her but loneliness and hardship? His love, of course, but was that enough to make such a woman happy, a woman like Skye, who had grown up in a castle, raised by a laird and a famous, well-educated mother, surrounded by friends and companions?

He considered Elizabeth Mackinnon. Surely she would hate Dakota after her life of travel and books, London and Edinburgh and New Orleans. Men were fools to think of bringing women to places like this. Fletcher Mackinnon was a fool, Blanton had been a fool, and now *he* was as big a fool as any. He wasn't the man Skye had met in New Orleans and found attractive enough to accept his courtship. He was a westerner, a rancher, a rough individual who had made it a point to ignore the native people she had admired all her life. He had been born into a noble family in England and could call upon refined manners any time he liked. But his blood and his soul were American now, and he had found a valley magnificent beyond all others on earth, a place that his heart now called home. Would Skye learn to love it as he did? He didn't know. He just plain didn't know.

"Hey, you old buzzard!" A youthful voice shouted at him from the gangplank.

Startled from his musing, he stared through the heavy mist.

"Doncha see me, Uncle Kyle? Over here!"

His heart lifted from its black doldrums. "Badger? Is that you, lad?"

"Right here, sir. I rode ahead of Reyes. Just couldn't wait to see you and Mama. Where is she, Uncle? I got a real nice present for her."

⊰ Chapter 32 ⊱

In Kyle's cramped cabin, Skye bathed herself in tepid water and stared into the cracked mirror tacked to the wall. She looked ghastly. Her face was pale and her eyes were sunken and lined with purple shadows.

She put on her clean dress and her bonnet and went outside, with MacLard trotting beside her. The rainstorm had passed, leaving the air fresh and pungent with the smell of newly washed earth.

Walking to the starboard side of the boat, she took her first clear look at Vermillion. The settlement was larger than

Belleview, but much more rustic than she'd expected. Still, the air was bracing and the surrounding countryside inviting.

The trading post was situated on an oxbow of land, created by the conjunction of the Vermillion River with the curving Missouri. Behind the clustered buildings rose steep brownish red cliffs, and flanking them stretched a verdant prairie occupied by several dozen Indian tepees. Near the Indian village were fields of corn, tall and abundant as the harvest grew near.

The roustabouts had unloaded most of the crates from the *Royal Eagle,* and several yards downstream, the freighter was also being unloaded. Leaning against the railing, she saw boxes and crates being carried to the dock by the crew. The milk cow was already ashore and being led toward a pole barn near the village. In her desperate efforts with Melissa the past few days, she hadn't given a thought to the horses traveling behind on the freighter. She no sooner had started to worry about them when she spotted Buck leading Diamond Dust toward a holding pen. Behind Buck and Dusty walked Kyle with Raven; behind Raven came a young boy leading Spirit Legacy.

Could that be Badger? Skye's heart filled with sympathy. Poor lad. How manly he looked with his rough western clothes, high-top boots, and wide-brimmed hat. He was a miniature version of his Uncle Kyle. She could tell even from a distance that he was expert with horses as he calmed Legacy and placed her in the pen where the mares were temporarily confined.

That should be *her* job, she chastised herself, not left to a boy who had just lost his mother to a tragic death.

"Come on, MacLard," she urged. She ran down the gangplank toward the open grassy area where Kyle and Buck and the lad stood together.

MacLard barked happily at his sudden freedom and headed for the nearby trees.

"Hello," she called and waved as she approached the threesome.

In unison, the two men and the boy swept their hats from their heads.

"I hope you're feeling better, Miss Mackinnon," Kyle said, returning to a more formal address in this public setting.

"A bit, thank you. I'm ready to attend to my duties." She glanced at the boy.

"Hello, ma'am," he said with no sign of shyness. "I'm Montgomery Wyndford, but I'd rather you called me Badger like everyone does. I surely thank you, ma'am, for all you've done for my mother lately. Uncle Kyle told me all about how good and kind you were to her."

For some reason, the lad's simple words, so mature and brave for a child no more than nine, tugged at her heart. He must be feeling miserable, but his solemn blue eyes were unwavering and his words suggested he was thinking of her rather than feeling sorry for himself. Instantly, she was enchanted with the lad. He must have inherited Missy's thoughtfulness and the Wyndford strength.

She extended her hand. "Hello, Badger. You don't need to thank me. I loved your mother and did whatever I could to make her passing easier. Your uncle was at her side and her last thoughts were of you. I can see why she was so proud of you."

Badger blinked and slapped his hat back atop his straw-colored, shoulder-length hair.

She looked closely at Kyle and saw his gaze, full of love and pride, fixed on the boy. Kyle's ravaged expression had eased somewhat, and she thought his comfort must be due to Badger's presence. These Wyndford males were quite a pair, she decided. Two of a kind, from the same mold, just about twenty years apart in age. If Kyle Wyndford had ever dreamed of having a son, he should consider his dream had come true. Not like he would have wished, but the fact was, he now had a boy to raise who was his spitting image. She turned to Buck. "How are the horses?"

"Did jus' fine, Miss Mackinnon. All four. I'd keep a close eye on Spirit Legacy in a few weeks. That foal is filling out her belly aplenty."

"Stop by often, Buck. And thank you again for all your care during the voyage."

"I gotta git busy," Buck said. "Gotta make sure those

kitty-cats are delivered to their new owners. I wanta say one thang, Miss Mackinnon. If those kitties live to be a hunderd, they'll never git such a feedin' as you gave 'em. I've seen some fancy milking, but you surely win the prize."

Smiling at Buck, she shook his hand. "Good-bye, Buck Garwin. I do hope we meet again someday."

As Buck headed toward the freighter, she and Badger both looked at Kyle, anticipating his directions on what to do next.

"Reyes has already started for the ranch with the wagon," Kyle explained. "He has Melissa—and the trunks, of course. If you're ready, Skye, we'll saddle Dusty and Lady. Badger has his own pony tethered behind the barn. Are you ready, Badger?"

"Yes," the boy said quietly. "See you at home." Pulling down his hat brim, he walked with a firm stride toward the barn.

"He's a fine-looking boy," Skye said. "And very brave."

Kyle watched Badger until the boy disappeared around the corner of the barn. "He took it well. Maybe too well. No tears at all. I guess he's still in shock—as we all are."

She touched his sleeve. "He's going to need you, Kyle. But you're aware of that, I know."

Before Kyle could respond, the sound of a horse galloping along the road opposite the settlement caught their attention. Badger was riding at a furious pace toward the northeast.

Kyle nodded. "That will help. A breakneck ride along the ranch road. I imagine he'll let those tears go when no one will see them."

She started toward the pen, holding the mares and doing her best to conceal the moisture forming in her own eyes. "I'll get Lady. Buck left the saddles handy."

"I'll help you." Kyle started to accompany her.

Over her shoulder, she said, "No, please. I'd rather do it myself just now. I really do need to get busy." She was relieved to see Kyle turn and head toward the barn to get the stallions. She allowed a few tears to fall, then wiped her face with her hanky and blew her nose. Following the courageous example of Melissa's family, she wouldn't allow herself to break down again.

Once astride Lady, she felt better. She placed a delighted MacLard across the saddle in front of her and led Spirit Legacy at her side.

Leading Diamond Dust, Kyle trotted Raven out of the barn and joined her. "This isn't the way I'd hoped it would be when we arrived at Wind River," he said, regret heavy his voice.

"I know. Please don't worry about me. I'm sure you have a lot on your mind."

He gave her a long, studied look. "Forgive me if I seem distracted. I'll make it up to you, Skye. I want you to love this land as I do. Things will be better in a few days, and we'll explore the country as I promised."

She smiled across at him. Sitting on Raven, Kyle was a head taller than she was on the small mare from Skye. "I'll make myself at home, don't you worry. Maybe I can spend some time with Badger. I was pretty rough and tumble myself when I was growing up. I might show him some games I played on Skye when I was about his age."

"He'd like that, I'm sure. Normally he's so full of beans and loaded with energy he barely has time to spit. But today . . ."

"He's astonishing," she said sincerely. " 'Tis easy to see he inherited great courage and has been properly raised."

For the next half hour, they jogged in silence along the narrow path, little more than a dirt trail between tall grass. The breeze was gusty and the day warm as the sun reached its zenith. The huddle of houses and low-slung buildings that made up the town of Vermillion was quickly left behind and they rode across a rolling plain that stretched from one horizon to the other.

Skye had expected vast distances, but nothing in her wildest imaginings had prepared her for this awesome landscape, the grass so tall it would reach the horses' bellies if they left the trail. Behind her, the Missouri was a twisted brown ribbon; soon, a second river came into view, smaller with water the color of coppery red wine.

"The Vermillion," Kyle said. *"Vermillion* means *red.* The earth here has a reddish mineral that sifts into everything: the river, the wells, the stew pot, our clothing. I hope it's healthy, because I've drunk enough of it in my lifetime to turn *me* into a redskin—damnit." He stared at her. "I'm sorry, Skye."

"Your apology is accepted. Old habits die hard."

Just as she finished speaking, they topped a low hill, and in the midst of another expanse of prairie, she spotted a small herd of bison grazing at the foot of the highest point of land she'd seen since they left Vermillion. The soaring mound was an eye-catching landmark, perhaps unimpressive compared to the snow-topped Cuillin Mountains on Skye, but quite distinctive in the grasslands of Dakota.

"Kyle, the land is spectacular. So open, so fresh and clean—and so *much* of it." With one hand stroking MacLard, she absorbed the scene, the windswept sea of grass, virtually treeless and stretching for eternity, the silence broken only by the shrill call of birds riding the summer thermals beyond the next hill, the almost spiritual grandeur that made one speak in whispers.

"'Tis unbelievable," she murmured. "The whole Isle of Skye would fit comfortably in this place. Those birds." She gazed skyward. "They're huge. What are they?"

"Turkey vultures. They must have spotted carrion beyond Spirit Mound."

"Is that large hill Spirit Mound?"

"Yes, it's the highest point north of Vermillion. An Indian burial ground in the old days, they say. The Lewis and Clark expedition camped nearby and used the hill to survey the surrounding countryside."

They continued along the path for another half hour before she spoke again. "This land," she began. "No one lives on it? No one owns it?"

"Not yet. The federal government is struggling with the problem of what to do with its newly acquired property. The first step is to get the Indian tribes to cede lands to the United States in exchange for guarantees of land elsewhere and for trade goods. In the West, the cattle must compete with the buffalo for food and put on enough weight to survive the harsh winters. Thousands of acres and many head of cattle are necessary to make ranching profitable. Personally, I never would have thought of taking on such a challenge. But once I began managing my brother's ranch, I caught the fever, and I knew I was born for the task."

She relaxed in her saddle. "I can understand those feelings, now that I've seen this place." She felt her enthusiasm catch fire once more. "Aye, Kyle, my father was right after all. He must have been thinking of this land when he stood on the shores of Skye and gazed west. 'Tis like a vision of paradise. Surely there is opportunity for people here, whether they be Indian or white. Everyone can share in the abundance."

She was twisting in her saddle, absorbing as much of the scenery as possible, when Kyle halted once more at the crest of a hill. "Home," he announced huskily. "Wind River Ranch."

Skye reined in and gazed at the idyllic setting spread before them. Here the Vermillion River made a horseshoe bend in the emerald valley. At a spot above the river stood a two-story house built of rough-hewn logs flanked at either end by tall chimneys made of river rock. Though dwarfed by the awesome scenery, Wind River Ranch headquarters had the appearance of solid permanence and prosperity.

" 'Tis so lovely," she whispered, her voice filled with awe. "I never saw a more beautiful place on this earth. Not even Strathmor on Skye."

He gave her a half smile. "Surely not *more* beautiful than your castle above the sea. Only beautiful in a different way."

"Aye, that's true. But for a farmer or a rancher, this place must have no equal on earth. Not even Texas."

He chuckled. "Not even Texas. I agree."

She wiped perspiration from her forehead with the back of her gloved hand. MacLard was demanding to be put down, so she leaned over to ease him to the ground. "I'm glad to be here. And I can see why Missy wanted to come here at the end of her life."

"Well, the poor darling made it, thank God. Shall we go see to things?"

"Of course." She put Lady into a trot, keeping Legacy trailing close behind. Yapping in excitement, MacLard dashed beside them.

Raven snorted at the increased pace, but as they rode down the hill, kicking up clods of earth, the stallion swiveled his ears and showed signs of impatience.

"Raven knows he's home," Kyle called to her.

In minutes, they covered the distance and arrived at the stable. A squat, dark-skinned man ran out of the barn to meet them. "Welcome home, Mr. Wyndford," the man said politely. "Sure sorry about Mrs. Wyndford."

"Thank you, B. J. This is Miss Mackinnon. She has two mares, one soon to foal. Put them in the south corral. Also, find a clean stall for the blue roan and put Raven in his regular stable," Kyle instructed. "Where is Reyes?"

"Waiting for you, sir, in your office. He just come in a short time ago with—"

"Yes, I know." Kyle paused. "Where is the wagon now?"

"Back of the big house. Señor Pacheco, he took Miz Wyndford inside. Then we hauled in the trunks. But they's sittin' in the middle of the hall, sir. We wasn't too sure where you'd want 'em."

"That's fine, B. J." Kyle turned to her. "We'll leave the horses here and walk on over to the house. God knows what shape it's in after my long absence. Reyes's wife, Pilar, keeps the house, but she had no idea when I'd return or under what tragic circumstances."

Skye dropped from her saddle, retrieved a panting MacLard, and walked along a rocky path toward the back of the house. Despite her sorrow over Missy, she was fascinated with the sight of the charming log structure set in a thin grove of cottonwoods and framed by two enormous pines. As they approached the low wall enclosing the back area of the house, she noticed a vegetable garden in full summer production, and bordering the path, low-growing rosebushes filled with red and white blooms in their summer glory.

"Those were Melissa's pets," said Kyle. "The roses. She brought some cuttings years ago from England. I didn't think they'd survive, but they were hardy, like her. *Hardier*

255

than her, I guess," he added sadly. He opened the door at the top of wooden steps.

Skye entered a cool, dark paneled hallway, distinctly masculine and heavily pine scented. The floor was polished pine and the ceiling soared above the second level. A newel post at the foot of the steps was six feet tall and its top was elaborately carved into the shape of a walnut. At the bottom of the stairs sat her trunk.

Kyle trailed behind her until she faced him.

"What do you think?" he asked, his face strained and sad.

" 'Tis a beautiful home, Kyle. You must be very comfortable here."

"We have been these past four years. In a day or two, I'll show you where we lived before I built this place: the sod hut that Melissa and Blanton lived in when they first came to this valley."

He gazed at her so intently and for so long that she grew uncomfortable. She broke eye contact and looked down at the terrier held in her arms. "Is it all right for MacLard to come inside? He's well behaved, but I don't want to break any rules."

"Of course." Kyle reached out to scratch behind MacLard's ear. "Badger keeps all kinds of varmints in his room. Even had a pet snake once. You'll find most westerners live in close proximity with animals of all kinds."

A door slid open off the hall. A lanky, deeply tanned man whose boots and spurs echoed in the stillness of the shadowy entryway stepped out to greet them. "Señor—welcome home. My deepest condolences, Señor Wyndford."

Kyle shook the man's hand. *"Gracias,* Reyes. This is Miss Mackinnon. She'll be visiting for a time. She was my sister-in-law's companion—and she is a very special lady. Miss Mackinnon, this is my ranch manager, Reyes Pacheco."

Kyle's warm expression when he introduced her started a glow deep inside her. It was the first stir of happiness since she had awakened this morning to learn of Missy's death.

"I'm pleased to meet you, sir," she said. "My family had a farm in Scotland, so I know how much Mr. Wyndford counts on you."

Reyes lowered into a courtly bow. *"Buenas dias, señorita."* He cut an impressive figure in his Spanish bolero jacket with a froth of white ruffles displayed from neck to waist. Skye had never met a Spaniard before, but her first impression was extremely favorable. His wife must be very special to have captured such a handsome man.

Reyes turned to Kyle. "I have placed Mrs. Wyndford in the downstairs bedroom. Pilar will begin preparations as soon as she has opened the guest room for Miss Mackinnon."

"Thank you, Reyes." Kyle looked at her. "Would you like to rest?"

"Aye, I surely would," she answered gratefully.

"Then allow me to show you to your room."

She climbed the stairs at Kyle's side. When they arrived at the upstairs landing, he directed her to the left toward an open door. "Your room is there," Kyle pointed out. "Missy's bedroom adjoined the guest room. I am in the right wing, and Badger has taken over a downstairs room. Easier to accommodate his wildlife menagerie."

She entered the room and was greeted by a surprising sight. Dusting the frame of a newly opened window was a slender Indian woman, her skin copper brown and her ebony hair twisted into long braids hanging to the center of her back. The woman stopped her work and gave them a slight bow with her eyes cast downward.

"Hello, Pilar. This is Miss Mackinnon. Skye, this is Pilar Pacheco. She and her daughter will tend to your needs."

With MacLard starting to wiggle beneath her elbow, Skye gave Pilar a warm smile. "I'm happy to meet you, Pilar—and I don't need a thing just now but a pitcher of water and a few hours' rest." She looked up at Kyle. "And my trunk, whenever 'tis convenient to have it brought up."

"Then I'll leave you and tend to critical matters. Pilar can arrange for food to be brought up if you're hungry. We'll have dinner tonight at seven in the dining room." His eyes briefly reflected tenderness. "Welcome, my lady Mackinnon. I hope you will make yourself completely at home at Wind River."

She felt her cheeks blush pink, knowing without doubt that Pilar was observing them closely. She also knew Kyle was wondering when they could announce their marriage and begin to live as man and wife. "I'm sure I will be comfortable," she said softly.

Kyle walked out of the room and down the stairs.

When Skye put MacLard on the floor, the dog immediately sat at her feet as if wondering what he was to do in these new surroundings. "Thank you for airing the room, Pilar. It's quite lovely." She gazed around at the spacious bedroom, which was luxuriously furnished. The four-poster bed was polished mahogany and was almost certainly imported from abroad. A wingback chair was pulled up near the wide window, where crisp white drapes fluttered in the warm afternoon breeze. The entire impression was one of quality, charm, and comfort. Skye was amazed such a place could exist in the American wilderness.

A girl of about six rushed into the room. Instantly recognizable as belonging to Pilar and Reyes, the beautiful child held up a handful of roses to Skye.

"For you," she said, her blue eyes alight with curiosity. "Badger said you were a real nice lady."

Skye was enchanted. Taking the bouquet, she smiled at the little girl. "I'm Miss Mackinnon. Thank you for the roses."

"I'm Dulcinea. My daddy is the boss of this place." Her pride shone from her face.

Pilar stepped forward. "Dulce, your daddy is *not* the boss. Mr. Wyndford is the boss. Now, go find a jar for the flowers, *niña.*"

Skye observed the graceful Pilar, struck by her rich coloring and distinctive bone structure. She boldly asked the question uppermost in her mind. "Your husband is from California, I've heard. Are you Spanish, Pilar? Or perhaps Indian?"

Pilar's replied solemnly, "I am Lakota Sioux from the Teton tribe."

Skye's heart raced. "How wonderful! We might even be related. You see, my father is half Lakota, also from the

Tetons. His mother was a princess, the daughter of Chief Blue Eagle. I'm eager to meet the Lakotas, especially a woman named Ola who raised my father when his mother died in childbirth. Of course, she may not be alive."

Pilar stared at her for several seconds with expressionless Indian eyes. "Ola. Yes, she lives. Ola Moon Deer is my grandmother."

⇥ *Chapter 33* ⇤

Loup Leveque lay on his belly in the damp earth and cursed under his breath.

Last night, he had seen the arrival of the steamer, *Royal Eagle*. At dawn, he had left his camp outside Vermillion and taken up his position atop Spirit Mound. From here he could see the trail leading from Vermillion to Wyndford's ranch headquarters. If Wyndford had arrived on the steamer, he would travel this road toward home.

Leveque couldn't miss seeing him.

Shortly before noon, Loup saw two riders jogging along the trail, leading two horses behind them.

Crouching in the grass on top of the sacred hill, Loup watched the riders moving below. One was Wyndford; the other, the Mackinnon woman.

The woman rode astride expertly, shoulder to shoulder with Wyndford as if she were equal to the man. No squaw should be so bold. He hated her as much as he desired her. And he would have her, too, force her to her knees, bend her to his will—before he killed her. Loup was absolutely certain the gods had delivered her into his hands to compensate for the terrible injustice done his own Lakota father by the girl's half-breed sire.

He slunk away toward the back of the mound, then scurried down the side so he wouldn't be spotted by the pair. He had seen all that was necessary. Earlier, he had watched in silence as the manager of Wind River had driven the ranch wagon down the road. Loup had no inclination to confront the infamous Spaniard or the small army of cattlemen employed by Wyndford. Now that Wyndford and the girl had arrived at the ranch, he must formulate a new plan for their capture that would ensure his own survival.

Loup knew he must get Wyndford away from his armed ranch hands by luring him alone into Indian country. He muttered to himself as he threw his leg over the blanket of his spotted pony. "You know I'm out here, Wyndford, you white bastard. I'm just waiting until the right moment to spring my trap. And the perfect bait is riding at your side."

After Kyle had seen Melissa lowered into her grave next to Blanton, he had invited the dozen guests back to the house for refreshments. His grief made him feel like he walked in a fog, plodding forward, lifeless inside. Missy had been the spirit of Wind River. Only now did he fully appreciate all she had done while he spent the past nine years working the cattle, building the headquarters, and traveling when necessary to do business in Louisiana. If he had known she was dying, he would have told her how he felt, how much he admired her, thanked her for all she had done. Seeing the sincere outpouring of grief by the five ladies at the funeral and the downcast eyes of all his hands, he realized how much Missy had been loved by everyone who knew her.

But what shattered his heart was Badger's straight back and dry eyes. The boy must be devastated, but with a face as solemn and stoic as any adult, he had showered a handful of rose petals onto his mother's casket as it was lowered into the ground. After the service, Badger had thanked Reverend Meyer and moved about among the guests, acting as host in the same way Missy had been the hostess during the functions held at the ranch throughout the years. Kyle was extraordinarily proud of the lad and couldn't help wondering where this sudden maturity had come from. He was ashamed he hadn't been as well acquainted with Badger as he had thought.

According to Missy's will, Badger was now half owner of Wind River Ranch along with Kyle. He must consider how best to guide the boy's future, making sure he received a good education and preparing him for the future of Dakota, soon to be a territory, and someday perhaps a state.

And then there was Skye. He watched her move around the shadowed house, staying in the background and working closely with Pilar to make certain everything was as it should be. He knew everyone was extremely curious about her but would not inquire too deeply on this occasion. With Missy's service behind them, he would give his attention to solving their differences. Soon he would ask her how and when they should announce their union. Maybe she would like to have a small ceremony, a proper wedding, planned in advance.

But today, the poor lass looked exhausted. He wanted to give her plenty of time to recover, both mentally and physically, from the draining events of the past week. He himself had urgent need to spend a day or so with Reyes checking on the stock. He hoped Skye was not determined to wait for her parents' arrival before she acknowledged their marriage. If so, he would have to tell her what he knew about the uprising in Tangier. He couldn't imagine what she would do then. Maybe head for New Orleans on the next packet.

The day dragged on endlessly into the lingering summer twilight. Finally, when the last wagon of mourners left for Vermillion, Kyle entered the parlor and poured himself a stiff brandy, then crossed to the window overlooking the back porch.

There, in the fading light, he saw Skye talking with Badger. The two were leaning on the rail surrounding the corral; they appeared deep in conversation. Their hand motions indicated they were discussing the mares who were penned in the enclosure. Skye had said she would strike up a friendship with the boy. Now she was making that beginning. Lord, how he loved her, how he needed her. Would she be willing to take on a husband and a growing boy as well?

Without Melissa here to guide her, to be female company for her, she might find Wind River Ranch an intolerable place to call home. He knew only too well how long and lonely the winter nights could be, with the countryside waist deep in snow and nothing stirring in the white, frigid night but a pack of wolves tracking a weakened cow. It was a great deal to ask of a girl not yet twenty.

Cloaked in gloom, he tossed the brandy down his throat and sank into his favorite leather chair.

He stared absently at the painting above the mantel of the Wyndford manor house in Northamptonshire. Faraway, long-ago memories filled his mind, memories of his older brother, memories of Blanton and his sisters, memories of his parents, who had always seemed like strangers, aloof from their children. He recalled especially the greenness of the earl's estate, the enormous trees and the river bordering the property. He didn't miss it, never had, but not to have any family of his own created an emptiness he hadn't expected at this point in his life. There was only Badger, who was not old enough to be considered a companion.

He looked up to see Skye entering the parlor. Immediately, he rose to greet her.

"May I join you for a minute, Kyle?" She looked tired, but her lips were set.

Already on his feet, he pulled out the comfortable rocker that had been Missy's favorite. "I'm glad to see you. We haven't had a chance to visit privately since we got here."

"The services were lovely," she began. "Everyone loved Missy, and they gave her a fine send-off to heaven."

"Yes. Reverend Meyer did a good job. Missy would have been well pleased."

"Pilar prepared a wonderful feast."

"You helped, too, Skye. I'm very glad you've made yourself at home at Wind River."

" 'Tis a lovely place. I can see why you're so proud of it."

"Is there anything at all you need, lass?"

"Nothing. Pilar has seen to everything. By the way, I learned that Pilar is Lakota. Who knows? She and I might even be related."

Her announcement took a minute to register in his leaden brain. Somehow the idea of his wife being related to the Indian woman who cleaned his house seemed very peculiar. "Related?" he muttered. "Oh yes, your Lakota ties. I see."

She gave him an odd look. "You don't seem especially pleased."

"Pleased? It's quite a coincidence, I suppose."

Skye's expression grew tight. "Did you even know Pilar is Lakota?"

"I knew she was Reyes's wife."

"But you didn't inquire about her Indian heritage?"

He heard condemnation in her tone. He was in no mood tonight to be made to feel guilty over the servants. "I admit I didn't. But I'll speak with her about it at the next opportunity."

Skye gazed toward the window, where darkness was mercifully bringing the day to an end. "I don't want to interfere, but I must point out that Missy loved Pilar and Dulce and felt they were like her own family. She introduced Pilar to Reyes and encouraged the match; she assisted at Dulce's birth."

"How did you learn all this? So soon?"

"I spoke at length with Pilar yesterday. She was reluctant to tell me anything of a personal nature, but I drew it out of her."

"No doubt you did," he said, with grudging admiration.

"Pilar is a full-blood Lakota from the Teton tribe. You knew *that*—didn't you?"

He pulled a cigar from his pocket. "I knew she was Indian. Reyes's wife. What else did I need to know?" He reached for a match from the table, feeling Skye's disapproval like the jab of a dozen needles.

"You might like to know that Missy taught her to speak English and encouraged her to become a Christian and be baptized before she married Reyes, and that Dulcinea's middle name is *Melissa,* and that sometimes Pilar visits her Lakota people when they're camped nearby."

Kyle sat up stiffly. "She what?"

"What I'm saying is that Pilar has been far more than just

a servant in this house. She has been invaluable to the success here. I hadn't intended to bring this up tonight, but I won't sleep a wink unless I speak my mind. Pilar is a bright, caring woman. A *Lakota* woman. She will now be running the household. But she's *afraid* of you."

He stared across at her. He had been in charge of Wind River for almost ten years, but he had missed a great deal going on right under his nose. It had taken Skye Mackinnon just twenty-four hours to discover his neglect and make him feel guilty about it. "So Pilar is *afraid* of me. That's hard to believe. Granted, I may have paid little attention to her, but I left the running of the house to Melissa. I swear to you, I've never given Pilar any reason to fear me."

"Not intentionally, I'm sure. But your dislike of the Sioux is no secret. I don't believe Pilar would have stayed a minute in your house if she hadn't been in love with Reyes, then married him. She won't speak to her husband about her hurt feelings, because he might be inclined to leave your employment, and she knows how happy Reyes is as foreman of your ranch."

Leaning back against the soft leather, Kyle took time to light his cigar and mull over Skye's accusations. It was true he distrusted the Sioux, and he had never bothered to inquire about Pilar's ancestry. Maybe he hadn't wanted to know but had found it easier to accept her servitude without concerning himself that she was Indian. "I consider myself chastised," he said between puffs on the cheroot. "I'll have a talk with Pilar, express my gratitude for all she's done. You're right about her taking over more responsibility around here. I will need to discuss that with her and increase her wages accordingly."

Skye scooted to the edge of the rocker. "That's a good beginning, but you'll need to give her more than money, I'm thinking. What you must give her, and what she deserves but will not demand, is your *respect.*"

Kyle was abruptly vexed at Skye's needling. He was exhausted, he was depressed, and he needed comfort rather than advice on how to run his ranch. "I've agreed with you, Skye. But I also intend to forbid her to go to the Indian camps without my permission."

Skye's expression turned cool. She rose to her feet, forcing Kyle to stand as well. "I'll say good night, sir. May I inquire as to when I may begin looking for my family's property in this area?"

"Not for several days. I'll be busy riding with Reyes, checking on the beeves scattered across miles of range land. After that, I'll show you the place I originally thought would be ideal for your headquarters."

"I know the place," she snapped. "Missy showed it to me on the map. I believe it's located on a creek not far from Spirit Mound. A nice level plot with some shade trees."

"That's it. We'll go there when I've completed my urgent inspections with Reyes."

She smoothed back her hair. "I'm eager to do my scouting. My parents might arrive soon. I must remember why I came west in the first place."

He stepped near her, his cigar forgotten in his hand. "Just promise not to ride out alone. It's always dangerous, even for armed men. Don't forget about Loup Leveque."

"Leveque? I thought you said he had probably gone for good."

Caught in his own lie, he hesitated. "I suppose he has, but I can't be sure about that. Promise you won't leave the headquarters unescorted."

"I have no plans to do so," she responded. Then her lips softened. "Kyle, I'm tired and so are you. I'm going to my room and get a good night's rest. In a day or two, we'll have more time to talk things over."

He put aside the cigar and put his arms around her. Her very closeness was like balm to his aching heart. "Good night, lass. Yes, we will talk. Very soon, my little wife." He couldn't resist calling her that. It was a gentle reminder of all they were to each other and all they had shared.

She raised her face and kissed him tenderly, then moved away. "My deepest sympathy on losing Melissa," she murmured with genuine feeling. "Good night."

Observing Skye's exit, Kyle shook his head. He had wanted desperately to feel her warmth and her affection, to take her to his bed and hold her through the night. This business about the Lakotas kept popping up like a persistent toothache. And now Skye had aligned herself with Pilar. Hell, he hadn't mistreated Pilar in any way, ever. He had agreed to try to change his ways. But Skye must also try to understand the reality of life in the West.

⊰ *Chapter 34* ⊱

During the night, Skye awoke shaking with fear and drenched with sweat. She had been dreaming that she was running across the plains, but the grass tangled her ankles and kept her from making any progress at all. Behind her, Loup Leveque, his scarred face exposed, his mouth twisted in a lecherous grin, gained on her with each passing second. She screamed for Kyle, but he couldn't hear her. He was riding Raven Duke at a fast clip up ahead, but he never turned to see about her. Kyle disdained her, she was sure of it. When she stumbled and fell to the earth, a snarling, vicious Loup, now more wolflike than manlike, loomed over her. She tried again to scream, but no sound escaped her lips.

Sitting up in bed, forcing her eyes wide to dispel the terror of her nightmare, she thought of her parents and wished they would hurry to Wind River. She longed for her mother's comfort and advice. And she needed her father's strength and wisdom. It was a while before she was able to calm her nerves and go back to sleep.

She arose at daybreak but found she was not the first person abroad at Wind River Ranch. Pilar was in the kitchen, Dulce had gone to gather eggs for breakfast, and Badger was in the corral inspecting the new equine arrivals.

Skye was sorry she had spoken sharply to Kyle last night. What she had said was right, but she should have chosen a better time. She and Pilar had formed an immediate bond after they discovered their common heritage. Kyle must learn right away his wife would befriend whomever she pleased, whether white or Indian.

Wearing a full-sleeved cotton blouse and her riding skirt, she joined Badger at the corral. "Good morning, Badger. You're up bright and early."

"Yes'm. I'm mighty curious about these mares. And the silver stallion. They surely have a different look from my uncle's racing stock."

She greeted Lady and Legacy with a hug around each neck. "This is Spirit Legacy. She's in foal to my father's wonderful old stallion, Spirit Dog. He died shortly before we left Skye, but you can see he passed on his light gray coloring. We hope Legacy will pass them on to her own offspring."

Badger gave the plump mare an admiring once-over. "Where's your black pup, today, Miss Mackinnon? He's a feisty little fellow. Never seen such a short dog with such a large head and big ears."

"He's a Skye terrier. And if he finds out your name is Badger, he's likely to chase you till he brings you to earth. He was bred on my island to dig up varmints. That's why he's so long and low to the ground. Of course, the breed's been mostly just a pet for years, a favorite of English royalty."

"Royalty. You know my pa was kinda like royalty back in England."

"Aye. I know the Wyndfords have an earldom."

"Uncle Kyle says you're royalty, too. Your pa is a *lord.*"

"He was a laird on the Isle of Skye. But we left Skye and I've sold our castle to my cousin in New Orleans." She smiled warmly. "And MacLard is happy as a piglet this morning begging scraps from Dulce. I believe he's found a true friend in the lass."

Grinning, Badger ran a hand along Legacy's swollen belly. "That Dulce is a scrappy girl. She looks sweet like her name, but you should see her ride my pony. 'Course, she's an Indian, and they can ride like they was part of their horses."

The reference to Indians made Skye pause, but she plunged on. "Did your uncle also tell you *I* am part Indian? Part Lakota like Pilar and Dulce?"

She knew from his startled look that Kyle hadn't passed on the information about the part of her heritage that was not exactly British royalty.

"Is that a fact?" Badger asked.

"A true fact. My father is what some people out here call a half-breed. His mother was an Indian princess, so he is royalty from two cultures. Now what do you think of that?"

She watched Badger's brow knit in concentration.

He said, "I think that's fine." He lowered his voice. "You know, my uncle doesn't like Indians because of what they did to my father, but my mother told me Uncle Kyle was wrong to carry hatred inside. She said not all Indians are bad, and sure enough, she loved Pilar and Dulce. I guess I love them, too. They don't seem like savages to me."

Skye took a huge breath of relief. Thank heavens, Missy's wisdom had won out with her son over Kyle's prejudice. "Your mother was correct, Badger. My very own mother told me there is good and bad in all races of people. I'm sure our mothers were right in their views."

He smiled shyly, his tanned cheeks becoming rosy. "I'll tell you a secret, Miss Mackinnon, if you promise not to tell my uncle."

"I promise, Badger."

"I'm going to marry Dulce when we grow up. She'll make a fine wife."

Skye hid her rush of pleasure. "That's good news, laddie. I hope you'll invite me to the wedding."

Badger laughed heartily, almost bouncing his straw hat off his head. "Now, tell me about that silver stallion, ma'am. Do you think he will throw that color if we breed him to one of the light-coated mares?"

"Let's go ask him," she suggested cheerily.

The two entered the barn and found B. J. cleaning stalls and filling the feed bins for the eight animals eagerly awaiting breakfast.

"That Dusty is one fine horse, Miss Mackinnon," B. J. called. "Most gentle stallion I ever met."

"He is, indeed, B. J. I'd like to saddle him for Badger to ride."

"Yippee," cried Badger. "I'll get the Spanish saddle Reyes gave me for my birthday. That will surely look smart on Dusty."

Within minutes, Skye was standing in a field near the barn, enjoying the warm sun, the sweet smell of the fresh morning wind off the prairie, and the sight of Badger cantering Diamond Dust in an excellent display of horsemanship. At the far end of the grassy field where a line of willows interrupted the landscape, he abruptly leaned over the horse's neck, reined him in two tight circles, then kicked him into a sprint back toward Skye.

She applauded in approval as he halted in a cloud of dust and bits of grass. "Wonderful, Badger. You handled him expertly."

"He's a wonder horse, Miss Mackinnon," Badger called breathlessly. "I've never seen a horse turn so fast. Must be the way he's built."

"Dusty is a quarter racing horse," she explained. "Built for a jump start and a swift getaway. But I noticed he pivots in place as fast as my short-coupled mares."

Badger slid from the saddle. "You know what, Miss Mackinnon, this horse is born to herd cattle, not just to be a racer."

"Why, you're a genius, Badger Wyndford. I knew that all along, but I didn't think anyone else would notice until I showed them."

"Have you herded cattle in Scotland?"

She laughed merrily. "Not really. Our island was so small, with a mountain in the middle, that the cows couldn't go far. And we had dogs to help us round them up when need be."

"Dogs? Sakes, I'd like to see that kind of dog."

"They help us with the cows and the sheep. Someday maybe you can visit Scotland and see them work."

"Good morning, Badger, Miss Mackinnon. Looks like we have a warm day in store."

Skye turned at Kyle's pleasant voice.

"Uncle Kyle, this stallion is the best I ever rode for

chasing beeves. Maybe we could cross-breed him to my Indian pony. I think they'd produce fine stock for the ranch."

Kyle nodded toward Badger. "Perhaps. But Diamond Dust belongs to Miss Mackinnon, so you'll have to discuss stud fees with the lady." He gave her a searching look.

"You have forgotten, Kyle, that I offered Dusty to you. I owe you a great deal for your assistance. I'll give you and Badger the stallion, if you'll allow my mares to visit from time to time."

"You don't owe me a thing, Skye," he said gently. "It is *I* who owe you."

"Aw, come on, Uncle Kyle. Say you'll take him."

Skye smiled at Badger's urgent pleading. "I'm sure your uncle will accept my gift. Won't you, Kyle?" She fixed him with a look that said he must.

His gaze held admiration and pleasure.

"Breakfast," came a call from the kitchen door.

Kyle laughed as Badger flipped Dusty's reins over a railing and dashed toward the house. "He's still a growing boy, I'm happy to see," he said.

"Aye. With a full life ahead of him," she responded pleasantly.

"I've already had breakfast, Skye. I'm meeting Reyes right away and we're heading for the north range. We'll be gone several days."

Her bright spirits faded. She had hoped they might have time together before he left. "I understand," she said through a false smile. "I'll stay busy learning procedures here at the ranch while you're gone. I'll just trail after Pilar, if I may."

"Of course. Walk me to the barn?"

Skye fell in step beside him until they entered the musty shadows. B. J. was nowhere in sight, and she was suddenly acutely aware of the virile, rugged man walking beside her, his snug leather breeches, his open-neck shirt, his wide-brim felt hat shadowing his face. He wore scuffed boots and spurs this morning, and his treasured six-shot revolver was tucked into a holster on his hip. He was undeniably a working rancher today, quite different from the polished

English nobleman she had first met in New Orleans. The sight of his chiseled profile, the leathery scent of him, the knowledge that he was master of everything surrounding them, sent rational thoughts winging and her blood racing through her veins. She knew without doubt he hadn't brought her into the barn just to pass the time of day.

Reaching a stall holding a bay stallion, he stopped and turned to her. As he gazed down at her, she felt his power and blatant desire envelop her as if it had life of its own. His arms encircled her and drew her against him, making her a willing prisoner in his embrace. She felt the ripple of muscle under his shirt, and with a beleaguered sigh, she raised her hands to his shoulders. Closing her eyes, she awaited his kiss, but instead, felt his hands encircle her waist as he lifted her from the ground. For a heartbeat, he held her against his length, then he sat her on his knee. He had propped his foot on a stack of hay and now balanced her as if she were a child. With one arm around her back, he cupped her chin with a crooked finger. For what seemed an eternity, he studied her, his expression solemn and heated. "There is danger all around us, Skye," he murmured. "Keep those Scottish wits in place while I'm away, lass."

Before she could respond, he bent to kiss her as he moved his hand up along her spine and settled it between her shoulder blades. Her arms went around his neck; her palms felt the solid muscle of his shoulders as she returned his kiss in full measure. Pressed against him, she gave herself to his lips, aware only of his magnificent body, the hard, inflexible thigh under her hips, the pressure of his chest against her breasts. Fire met fire, and passion locked with passion. The world and all its pettiness dissolved in the magic of the moment, and she gloried in his need for her. Slowly, while his mouth captured hers and his tongue toyed with the delicate flesh of her lips, he leaned her backward, arching her body to conform to his, cradling her until his mouth moved downward to tease the hollow of her throat. Like lightning, jagged shafts of desire pierced through her body, scorching her inner being, driving her to cling to him in unashamed pleasure.

Gradually he straightened, bringing her up with him,

perching her once again primly on his knee. "I'll miss you," he said huskily. "I love you, my darling Skye."

How could she resist him when he looked at her with such intensity, filled her mind with thoughts of the intimate love they had once shared, sending doubts and hesitation sailing into oblivion? She was about to say *I love you, too,* when he lightly kissed her lips and set her on her feet. *"Adios, chula mia,"* he said grinning.

His devilish charm captivated her. This work-hardened, worldly, brave-hearted man who was years her senior, a man who controlled an empire in the vast Dakota wilderness, a man who was respected in some circles and feared in others, seemed nothing more than a mischievous, teasing youth. "What does that mean, *adios, chula mia?"* she asked, happy to allow him his boyish display of linguistic skill.

"Adios means good-bye." He tapped the tip of her nose with one finger and stepped away to open the stall door.

"And the other—*chula mia?"*

"Ask Reyes," Kyle quipped, reaching for his tack. "He has taught us all to speak Spanish, or at least the words we need to communicate with the summer ranch hands from Texas."

Inching back, she watched in silent admiration as he saddled the bay. He tossed over its back an exquisitely tooled California saddle; a rawhide rope was attached by a thong to the pommel. Behind the saddle, Kyle fastened a bedroll.

"Ah-dee-oss," she mimicked as he swung onto the horse and gathered the reins.

Kyle touched the brim of his hat. *"Buena suerte,"* he said, smiling, and cantered from the barn, leaving her with shafts of dust-filled light dancing around her.

She gazed after him, waiting for her heart to slow its wild rhythm, until he was out of sight. There was no denying she was utterly smitten with the man. Then she strolled down the row of stalls until she came to Raven Duke, who was peering alertly over his stall door.

Holding her hand near the stallion's nose, she curled it to resemble a muzzle so he would sense something horselike

and familiar about her. He nickered and allowed her to
stroke his jaw. How lucky Kyle was to have saved the horse
from Loup Leveque. Where was that terrible man? she
wondered idly, leaving the barn to have her breakfast and
begin her day as Pilar's trainee.

Three days after Kyle's departure with Reyes and a group
of cowhands, Skye stood in the kitchen helping Pilar cut up
ta-lo, or beef leavings: hocks, hoofs, neck, and guts, which
were made into stew. Then she took a turn thickening the
juice with corn meal.

"Pilar, the soil here in Dakota is perfect for crops," she
said, stirring the pungent gravy. "I marvel at the garden
behind the house. Why, I could almost see those vegetables
growing before my very eyes. And the prairie grasses, the
hay and rye, flourish in such abundance it takes my breath
away. I can't wait for Kyle to show me the place my family
might own someday." Standing in the heat of the kitchen,
working beside Pilar like hired help, Skye had never been
happier or more certain the decision to come to Dakota was
the right one.

Pilar placed an iron lid on her stew pot, then said
abruptly. "I'm going to see Ola. Will you come with me?"

Skye stopped stirring and stared at her. "Your grandmother? Ola?"

"Yes. I have learned that she and her band of Lakotas are
following the buffalo west along the river that the white men
call James. The Lakotas will not return here again this
summer, so I must go now."

"How far is it? How long would we be away?" She was
thrilled at the prospect of finally making contact with her
father's people. She had dreamed of this for years, and now
the opportunity was at hand. She had promised Kyle not to
go alone into the wilderness, but with Pilar to guide her, she
wouldn't be alone but safe with a Lakota native.

"A few hours' ride. We could leave soon and arrive at the
camp at midafternoon. We can spend the night in Ola's
tepee and return tomorrow."

Laying aside her wooden paddle, Skye wiped her hands

on her apron. "We must surely go, Pilar. Who knows when I will have another chance to learn about my father's tribe? Do you think Reyes will be angry? Or Mr. Wyndford?"

"Reyes is accustomed to my visiting my people. Mr. Wyndford might be angry, but perhaps he won't know, if we say nothing to anyone about our going."

"But—what about the house? The duties? Who will look after things? What about MacLard?" Skye glanced at the terrier, asleep on his back in a patch of sun, his four paws skyward and his plump belly soaking up warmth.

"Mr. B. J.'s woman will be here. She came from Vermillion yesterday and is at his quarters now. She has done this before when Mrs. Wyndford needed extra help. Dulce will help, too."

"Then 'tis settled. When do we leave?" She pulled off the apron and folded it into a drawer.

"The *ta-lo* is ready. I will leave the pot covered on the stove for the hands to find. Also the biscuits and the strawberries." Pilar looked pleased with her secret plan. "We won't be missed—and we'll be back at work by tomorrow afternoon."

Skye flew up the stairs with an awakened MacLard yapping at her heels. At last her dream would come true. Entering her bedroom, she opened her trunk and removed the bear-claw necklace. She stood before the mirror of her dressing table and put on the necklace, then she pulled her hair into two matching hanks and bound them with pieces of rawhide. The face looking back at her, with its naturally rich coloring darkened by recent days in the sun, was as Indian as Pilar's—almost. Skye's cheekbones were less prominent, but the flesh across them held the same coppery undertone. Her hair was midnight black, gleaming with just a suggestion of soft waves as it fell below her shoulders. Her green eyes would betray her at once as a "breed," but that couldn't be helped. On the other hand, the thong, with its gleaming claw resting against the smooth, florid skin of her collarbone, looked as natural there as if she were a native, the relative of a proud warrior, and a Lakota woman, the same as Pilar.

ᵛ Chapter 35 ᵛ

There is the camp. There—along the river," Pilar called.

Skye had found the ride under a flawless diamond-white sky exhilarating beyond any she had ever experienced. Freedom. Free as the wind with neither a rock nor a tree nor a sizable hill to interrupt fanciful flight. Alternately jogging and cantering beside Pilar, she felt Lady's unrestrained pleasure in release from her confinement in boats and barns. Not even on the Isle of Skye had either she or her horses raced through such endless vistas with nothing to slow or halt their progress but their own will or fatigue. For over two hours, they had ridden due west, startling the occasional rabbit or field mouse and skirting a slow-moving herd of buffalo on a nearby plain. Pilar pointed out clumps of brush and weathered stacks of rock that marked the trail to the James River.

Along the way, Skye had taken her first look at Kyle Wyndford's stock: large, lanky cattle with long, curving horns like their Texas cousins.

Halting beside Pilar on a low rise above the river, she saw two dozen or more tepees along the tributary. The buffalo hide lodges were surprisingly tall, imposing even from a distance. Several were decorated with colorful designs, and most had smoke curling from the opening at the top. The settlement appeared serene in the afternoon sun.

"Will your people be surprised to see us?" she asked Pilar.

Pilar smiled at her from where she sat astride her spotted pony. "They know we're coming. They have watched us for a long time."

"Oh? I haven't seen a single Indian until now."

"They know," Pilar said simply.

As they trotted down the gentle slope, a shirtless, bronze-skinned man wearing leather breeches and strings of bright beads ran out to meet them.

Skye held back while Pilar rode to the man and talked to him briefly in the Lakota tongue. Several times, Pilar motioned in her direction, evidently explaining her presence to the scout. Finally, the man waved the two of them forward, and he jogged back toward the tepees set up along the riverbank.

Skye rode at Pilar's side, as fascinated by the sights as if she were passing through the streets of London. She saw only half a dozen men and one or two women seated at cooking pots or working on buffalo hides. They glanced up but appeared unconcerned with their visitors.

Pilar explained softly, "I asked permission to go at once to Ola's tepee. Most of the men are hunting, but something special is happening today among the women."

"Are your parents here, Pilar?"

"My parents died long ago. I was raised by my aunt until I married Reyes." She smiled proudly. "He paid a great price for me to my aunt and uncle. Four horses, a rifle, and five pots of pony beads. We were married twice. Once in my village, and once by the priest of my husband's Catholic religion."

They reined in at a tepee and tethered the horses in its shade.

"Wait here," ordered Pilar. "I will greet my grandmother. Then I will come for you, if she agrees to see you."

If she agrees. Until this minute, Skye hadn't considered the possibility of being turned away by the Indian woman. Standing beside Lady, she straightened her hat and fingered the bear claw. The minutes dragged by until she feared there must be some problem.

She located a pail of water and offered a drink to the horses, then continued to wait, aware there was nothing else she could do, now that she had come so far. What if Ola wouldn't see her? What if Ola remembered nothing about

White Arrow? What if the old woman's memories were ones she preferred to forget?

At last, Pilar ducked out of the tepee.

"What happened?" Skye asked, afraid of the answer.

"All is well," Pilar quickly responded. "But she is a very old woman, and I had to explain many things to her."

"Does . . . does she remember my father, White Arrow? Does she remember Chief Three Bears or his son, Siyaka?"

"You must ask her yourself. I will wait outside while you visit her. Then we will go to my cousin's lodge. Today, the quilling society will gather to initiate a new girl. I will suggest that you be an honored guest."

"That's very kind, Pilar, but I would be happy just to sit and visit with Ola in her tepee."

Pilar shook her head. "She is ill and sleeps much of the time now. After your visit, she will need to rest. Later, you will eat with her and make a pallet for the night. I will visit my cousins."

Swept with anticipation, Skye nodded.

"Go inside," Pilar said. "I will wait by the horses in the shade."

With her heart thudding, Skye squatted and entered the shadows of the tepee. After the brightness of the sunshine, she paused until her vision cleared. At first, she saw no one, then gradually she made out the form of an elderly lady, reclining on a buffalo robe across from the entrance.

"Ola? May I approach you?"

"Yes. Come near. I am blind, but I would like to touch the daughter of White Arrow."

Scooting across the cone-shaped enclosure, which was scented by pine needles smoldering on stones in its center, Skye knelt at the old woman's side.

The dark eyes were open, staring sightlessly; the woman's face was covered with wrinkles; her hair was white and smoothed back from her forehead like strands of spider webbing. But her mouth was smiling and her expression euphoric. She raised a bony hand, the fingers extended.

Skye grasped the hand and guided it to her own cheek.

The fingers gently explored the lines of her jaw, her nose,

her forehead, moved along her neck and finally rested on the bear claw at her neck. Skye knew then that Pilar had told her about the amulet.

"White Arrow earned the bear claw when he was only a boy."

"You remember that?" whispered Skye.

"As if it were yesterday. He was about ten years, and he came home from the hunt with the skin of a bear he had taken in the far mountains."

"He must have been very proud," Skye murmured, trying to picture her father as a child, an Indian growing up among his mother's people.

"He was proud at first. He told me he hoped the conquest of the powerful bear would earn him a place of honor in our tribe. But the chief's son, Siyaka, was jealous, and told lies about White Arrow. Before long, White Arrow was handed over to the whites to be raised as one of them. I begged Three Bears to keep the boy, but White Arrow's mother had been dead for a long time, and the boy's father was a white fur trapper from a faraway land. Siyaka made certain that Chief Three Bears disposed of White Arrow."

Skye shook her head at the sad story. "I know what happened next. My father ran away from the white settlement and lived alone until he was nearly eighteen; then he went to a gathering of the Lakotas to challenge Siyaka. He won the combat, but then was condemned by the chief to be burned alive."

"I saw that. I wept, but I knew White Arrow had chosen death above living with dishonor. I was sure he would die, until suddenly his white father came and saved him, then took him away across the great sea."

Skye picked up her thread of the story she had heard as a child. "White Arrow took the Christian name of Fletcher Mackinnon, married my mother, and soon I was born. He was a well-loved laird on our island of Skye, equal to a Lakota chief. But often he gazed west across the water. This past year, when so many of our people left the island to make homes elsewhere, he decided to return to his native land here in Dakota."

The old woman raised to one elbow, her eyes wide as if

she struggled toward a vision. "He is coming? White Arrow is coming?"

"Aye, he is coming—or so I firmly believe. My mother will be here, too, and we'll make our home near the Vermillion River. The land is vast and fertile, and we will build a house there."

Ola lay back and closed her eyes. Skye saw a trace of tears escape their recesses.

"That is good," Ola whispered. "But there is an evil one among us."

Skye leaned close. "Really? Who?"

"Siyaka is dead. He was banished from the tribe for telling lies and for cowardice against the enemy. Old Chief Three Bears disowned him, sent him away. Many years later, a man who claimed to be Siyaka's son came to our village north of here where we have our permanent lodges. He said his name was Brave Wolf, and he is half Lakota and half white. He uses the French name for wolf—Loup. And I don't think he is brave. He wants to sit at the council fires, but always he is turned away. I have not seen him, but it is said by our men that evil is carved into his face."

Skye's breath caught and she sat back on her heels. "Loup Leveque. I know this man."

"Beware the wolf half-breed. Tell all your people what I say because he brings great danger." Skye decided not to tell Ola she had already encountered Leveque. Or that he had recognized her as the daughter of the man who had caused his own father to be disgraced. Fear nibbled inside her. "Thank you, Ola," she murmured. "I understand many things now. I will be on guard against Loup Leveque. And when my father comes, I will warn him, too."

Ola's words were barely audible. "That is wise. Very wise."

Skye reached to stroke the withered arm resting across a blanket. "You raised my father, and you loved him. As long as we live, you will always be cherished in his memory and in mine."

A single tear found its way along the ridges of the woman's cheeks.

"You speak very good English," Skye said gently.

"I learned at the same place as your father," Ola murmured. "From the white missionary at the trading post at Brown's Valley in the land of the Yankton."

"I've heard there are many Yankton Sioux in this part of Dakota."

"There are many, but all the land belongs to the Great Spirit. My Lakota tribe has come here to hunt buffalo and to communicate with their Yankton cousins about the Paha Wakan at the place the whites call Spirit Mound."

"Spirit Mound? The hill above Vermillion?"

The woman's hand shot out and encircled her wrist. Her grip was scratchy and painful as she squeezed tightly, but Skye made no move to pull away.

"Do not go near Spirit Mound. There is great danger there."

"But . . . from what? It looks like a beautiful place, the highest in the entire countryside."

"The Paha Wakan—the little people—inhabit Spirit Mound. Anyone who goes there tempts disaster. Anyone with white blood who disturbs the spirits of the little people will surely die in some terrible way."

"What do you mean, little people?"

"For as long as there has been memory, the Paha Wakan have lived there. They are devils in human form, with very large heads, who are less than two feet high. They carry sharp arrows with which they are skillful, and they will kill anyone who becomes their enemy."

Skye was enthralled. The little people were well known in Scotland, and Ireland as well. Perhaps the Celtic imps were not so deadly, but they were known to be full of devilment. "Go on, Ola. I'd like to hear more about the little people of Spirit Mound."

"They were sent by the Great Spirit when the Indian people were killing too many animals for their own use. To take revenge, the Paha Wakans drove the animals out of the country and many Indians starved for want of food. But after many prayers and sacrifices, the Great Spirit was appeased and permitted the animals to return. If the people should destroy too many animals, the Wakans will once again drive the creatures away, never to return. No Indian who knows the secret of the Paha Wakan will ever set foot on Spirit Mound."

"Then I will never go there," Skye agreed. "Never. And I will tell my family and friends they must only kill what animals are necessary for their survival."

Ola released her wrist. "Where do you stay until your father comes?"

"At a ranch headquarters called Wind River. An Englishman runs many cattle on the prairie there."

Ola put an arm across her forehead. "I have heard of this man. He is the first white man to bring his own animals here from far away."

"I believe he is a good man, Ola. But unfortunately, ten years ago, a band of Lakotas murdered his brother. He has not been friendly to the Indians since that time."

"Yes. I heard the story. Those Lakotas returned to our country with the scalp of a white man. They were proud of what they had done, but the chief was very angry that they had killed a stranger who had not been our enemy. He banished them from the village, and for many years, they lived in disgrace."

"Is that a fact? My goodness, I must tell my friend, Mr. Wyndford, about that. It could make a difference in his feelings toward the Lakotas."

"The Indians and the few whites who have come here live in peace. I do not know if it will always be so. But we have learned to enjoy the treasures of the white man—beads, salt, kettles, and shooting sticks. The women decorate the buffalo hides with quills and beads and trade them for many fine things at the posts along the river."

Skye remembered she was not to tire Ola. "Aye. I've seen some of the beautiful handwork at Mr. Wyndford's house at Wind River. Ola, I must go now. I am invited to the women's quilling group. But I will return to eat and sleep in your tepee, if I may."

Ola held up her hand. Skye took it in both of hers.

"You wear your father's token, the bear claw," Ola said hoarsely. "Tonight I will give you a Lakota name, which will always be yours. While you are with the women, I will have a vision and choose your name. Since your Lakota grandmother is with the Great Spirit, she will have to communicate her wishes to me in my vision. Go now, and allow me to dream."

Spellbound, Skye made her way from the tepee. She blinked in the brightness, then found Pilar still waiting beside the horses.

"Did it go well?" Pilar asked.

"Very well," Skye said, shaken by the experience. "Ola told me all about my father's fight with Siyaka. She will give me my Lakota name tonight."

Pilar smiled with pleasure. "For a person with white blood to be given a name is a great honor. Ola is very wise. And she loved your father as if he were her own son."

"I felt a strong bond between us, Pilar. How sad that she is blind. Is she unable to sit or walk? Do you think she's seriously ill?"

"Very ill. Yes, I think she suffers, but she won't show it. All of the old ones come to this time when they must suffer and die."

"True, we all must die, but the suffering could be helped. I have medicine at Wind River that Mrs. Wyndford didn't use. I think it only relieves pain, but I would like to bring some to poor Ola."

Pilar frowned. "I don't know if she would take the white man's medicine."

"But the Indians have learned to accept some of the white man's ideas. Treasures, Ola called them. We could bring the medicine and offer it to her caregiver before the tribe leaves this area."

"Yes, we could try. Then Ola could decide what to do if her suffering becomes very great. Now, we'll go to the tepee where the women have gathered. They will be pleased to meet the daughter of the famous White Arrow."

Later that night, after a fascinating lesson in the art of quilling hides, given by a friendly, giggling group of young women, Skye sat before Ola's fire and listened to a blessing in the Lakota tongue of her father's people. When Ola patiently switched to English, Skye learned about the history of the Teton Lakota Sioux and their land in the north, close to the sacred Black Hills. Finally she said, "The earth is bountiful and we are surrounded with the blessings of the Great Spirit. I see great hardship in the years to come, a struggle between the white man and the people of Wakan Tanka. You have come from far away, Skye Mackinnon, and you are needed to walk a path of wisdom and peace to show how two races of people can join their blood and grow greater because of the blending. Therefore, I have chosen Morning Song to be your Lakota name. You have lived in the white man's world, but you are one with the Lakota because of White Arrow. You are like a new day dawning— a joining of ancient blood. You bring hope for peace between the races. Your strength and knowledge are very precious now, and in the dangerous years to come. Your path will not be easy. But I believe you have the courage to show the way to all the people, white and Indian."

"Morning Song. Thank you, Ola. 'Tis a fine name. I will try hard to do as you say."

"Now I have a gift for you."

Skye was suddenly concerned that she had brought nothing to Ola. If only she hadn't rushed away so unexpectedly. "Ola, I have nothing for you."

Ola smiled. "You have given me great joy; that is your gift. Now—this is for you." She took a necklace from the folds of her sirt and held it up. So different from the menacing bear claw, the necklace was an intricate design of colorful beads. Not fragile, but feminine and finely made.

"How beautiful," Skye sighed.

"Do not wear it now—only after you return the bear claw to White Arrow. Then this necklace will be your token of your Lakota legacy."

Carefully, Skye put the necklace into her pocket. "I'm so grateful, Ola Moon Deer. I will treasure it always."

Skye couldn't prevent a few tears escaping her eyes and moistening her cheeks. They were not from fear or sadness but from the sudden connecting of her Indian past to her Indian present. Ola had given her the precious gift of her legacy, and the challenge lay before her, veiled in smoke, but waiting for her in her future. Covering the bear-claw necklace with one hand, Skye vowed silently never to remove it until her father came to claim it.

Sensing that Ola must now rest, Skye made herself comfortable on a buffalo skin in the last glimmer of the central fire and thought of her new identity as Morning Song. Or was this an *old* identity that had been waiting for her in this place, for this exact moment in time, to unite her with her Lakota Sioux ancestors? She felt she had become whole, where once she was splintered into two parts. White and Indian. Now she was not half of each race, but a unified blend. Her future path would not be easy, she knew, but one she would walk with pride and endurance. She fell asleep to the haunting sound of a flute and the occasional cry of a night bird.

Kyle arrived at the ranch in a state of complete exhaustion. He and the men had ridden hundreds of miles, checking the herds scattered from one end of the range to the other, driving strays back to water, and skinning some beeves who had died by one means or another.

He strode into the ranch house and went straight to the kitchen and dipped a ladle into a bucket of fresh water. The liquid quenched his thirst as he gulped it greedily and allowed it to trickle down his bristled chin and throat.

Replacing the ladle, he took a deep breath and gazed around. Why wasn't Pilar here preparing lunch? Where was Skye on such a scorching day?

He walked back outside and down the path to the barn. Before he entered, he heard horses approaching. Looking up, he saw Pilar and Skye arriving from the west at a fast clip. Enjoying the sight of Skye's rich beauty and her expert handling of her mount, he waited for her to rein in and hand over her horse to B. J. She said something to Pilar, who hurried toward the house. Then she approached him with a winning smile.

"Skye," he said, unable to keep from reaching out to touch her shoulder. "You've been riding with Pilar, I assume. Not too far, I hope." He saw she wore the bear claw for the first time since her arrival at Wind River.

She shoved back her hat and looked at him with a mixture of pleasure and defiance. "I've had the most wonderful experience, Kyle. I accompanied Pilar to visit her relatives at the Lakota camp. I met the woman who raised my father—and I've been given an Indian name."

⊰ *Chapter 36* ⊱

Kyle felt like he'd been kicked in the stomach. "Bloody hell, Skye," he snapped, and removed his hand. "You did what?"

She tilted her chin. "Now don't be angry. You told me not to ride out alone, and I didn't. Pilar goes whenever she can to see her people. They don't come here often, so this was a rare opportunity for me to go to their camp. Surely you—"

He didn't hear the rest of her explanation for the anger exploding in his brain. She had taken a terrible chance, risked her life—ridden abroad after he'd warned her not to. "Skye, you could have been killed! Two women alone have no business riding across country without a male escort. What if Loup Leveque was lurking about?"

Her eyes grew frosty. "I took a rifle and Pilar had a pistol. And Kyle, the important thing is, I learned that the Indian people are gentle and inclined to be friends with the white man—as long as their food supply and way of life isn't threatened. I hope you'll visit them, too."

He couldn't help admiring her spirited defense, despite her youthful naïveté. He didn't know whether to shake her or embrace her. The woman saw the world through her own vision of fairness and kindness and idealism. "Truly, Skye," he began more calmly, "you are simply not familiar with life in Dakota, with the dangers and adversities. I will forgive you this one mistake, and I will chastise Pilar for her part in the escapade, but I am responsible for you here, and

I must insist that you not venture beyond ranch headquarters without an armed escort."

She jammed her fists into her waist. "You sound like the king of England, or maybe Bonaparte giving orders to his underlings. I am used to making my own decisions, Kyle Wyndford, weighing the risks and doing what I want to do. My parents have given me free rein since I was a child."

"I'm thinking they should have given you a spanking or two, Miss Mackinnon."

Her mouth fell. "A . . . spanking! How dare you!"

"I dare because your life is at stake." He stepped toward her. "Skye, for God's sake, you must listen to reason."

"I'm sorry, Kyle, but you have let your prejudices blind you to the real goodness of the Indian people. You've made no effort to get to know them, their ways, their thoughts and feelings. You've lived here nearly ten years, and I would wager I know more about them at this minute than you do. My father charged me with the task of exploring this area and finding his relatives. With great good luck, I've just spent a wonderful day and night in the tepee of the woman who raised my father as a boy. Would you have me miss such an opportunity?"

"You could have waited till my return. I would have taken you there."

She frowned at him, her green eyes glittering beneath half-lowered lids. "I could have, but I had a chance to make this visit with someone both familiar and friendly to the Lakotas. Pilar made me feel welcome at the village of her people."

"I think this disagreement has been a gulf between us for a long time, Skye. You cannot base your sudden expert knowledge of the Indians on one brief visit with an elderly woman accompanying a hunting party. Granted, most of the Indians are not killers. If so, no white man would survive at this moment. The Sioux in this area outnumber us a thousand to one. They have horses and rifles and could wipe us out overnight if they so desired. They have chosen to trade with us instead. But there has been trouble, and I see more coming. I don't wish to be caught in the middle of an Indian war with no way to protect my home and family. I must provide safety to every man, woman, and child at Wind River. I love your independent spirit, Skye, but in Dakota, it could cost you your life."

Her hands fell to her sides, and for a second, he thought he'd convinced her. Then he saw her back stiffen and she cocked an eyebrow.

"I do not wish to be a *worry* to you, Mr. Wyndford. I'll try to confine myself to the kitchen from now on—like a good wife."

Damn her obstinance. He would try a new approach. He lowered his voice and touched her sleeve. "Skye, you're not being fair," he said gently. "I want you to have your freedom and enjoy yourself, but this is not Scotland, not even civilized America."

He knew instantly he'd made a serious blunder.

"Civilized! Why, I saw more *civilized* people today in the Indian village than anywhere I've been since I arrived in the United States."

In a quick movement, he placed his hands around her waist and lifted her from the ground. She was light as a kitten, and her shock at his abrupt action kept her motionless, her lips parted in surprise, her hands gripping his arms. He pulled her against him and crushed her lips, causing her hat to fall back and her body to arch against his. For a fleeting instant, he felt her respond, but he knew she was bound to struggle like a wildcat once she came to her senses. Before that could happen, he set her roughly on her feet and released her.

"Disdain me. Rebuke me. Despise me, if you wish, Skye Eugenia Mackinnon. But don't leave the safety of Wind River Ranch without me. If you try, I swear to you, I'll lock you in your room with a guard outside the door." He turned his back to her and headed for the men's quarters. He'd have a word with Reyes about Pilar's traveling at will around the prairie, then he'd give Badger the task of keeping an eye on Skye. He'd prefer to watch out for her himself, but he had a five hundred thousand–acre ranch to run, and autumn was fast approaching. He knew Skye held out hope that her parents would come to Dakota, but his doubts about that increased daily. He decided he must tell her about the concerns he and Blaine Caldwell had that her father might have died in the uprising in Tangier. He hated to worry her, but the truth was, her father was probably dead and would never return to Dakota. She must decide if she wanted to stay in Dakota as his wife—or abandon him and end their secret marriage. Would she consider such a thing after what they'd shared? He was counting heavily on their love to prevent such a tragedy.

Skye was deeply shaken. She rushed to her room, tossed aside her hat, and sat on the bed, holding MacLard close to her breast. During the past hours spent traveling across the magnificent prairie, she had been riding a cloud of joy. Now that she was back at Wind River, she was angry, depressed, and upset. She understood Kyle's concern for her, but he was so demanding that he drove her into resistance. Ola had understood her nature immediately and had predicted she would have a difficult path to walk. Already, Skye knew she was being forced to choose sides in a world torn by conflicts and misunderstandings.

"It's a big problem, MacLard," she whispered, settling among the pillows with the dog snuggled at her side. "Nothing seems clear. Ola said I was fated to come here, to help promote peace and understanding between the Indians and the white man. How can I best do that, MacLard? How can I begin?" She mulled over the problem, then gradually realized that the door had already been opened for the first step. Kyle had offered to go with her to the Indian camp. She thought of his lips on hers, of the fire ignited in her when he kissed her. She sat up. Of course, she had the perfect solution. She had a very good reason to return to the Lakota camp—to take medicine to a sick old woman. Kyle could take her there. Then he would see the gentle beauty of their way of life, the practical manner with which they went about ensuring their own survival, their profound spirituality and respect for their natural surroundings, and maybe then he would understand why some Indians felt threatened by the arrival of the white man in their traditional homeland.

Feeling better with her plan in mind, she left the bed and

looked in the mirror. The sight of the bear claw filled her with pride. This new purpose in her life was titillating and inspiring. "Morning Song." She spoke the name out loud while placing the new beaded necklace into a drawer. She was created from two cultures, but in her, they were well matched. By combining the knowledge and forcefulness of her Scottish heritage with the insight and patience of her Indian forebears, she would bring Kyle around to her way of seeing things. And through his strong leadership in the area, they would be an influence in obtaining peace and prosperity for everyone. With that high-minded thought, she left the room and went downstairs to find Pilar. She was hungry and had much to think about.

To her embarrassment, she came upon a heated argument between Pilar and Reyes. They didn't hear her approach, so she halted and started to turn away.

"I must forbid you to go again, Pilar," Reyes was saying sternly. "I know I've allowed it before, but Señor Wyndford has given orders that you and Miss Mackinnon are to stay at ranch headquarters."

"I understand, but I must see my people when they're here. They'll return to their lodges in the north soon, and I'll have no other chance."

"You *have* seen them. Yesterday and today. It is enough for this season. They'll return next summer and things might be different then."

"I . . . suppose so. But my grandmother is very ill. I doubt if she will survive the winter. And Miss Mackinnon was planning to take medicine to her."

"You know your people won't use the white man's medicine. You've seen your grandmother, and if it's God's will for her to die, then your time with her must come to an end, as it does with all families."

"Yes, but—"

"Pilar, this time I must be obeyed. Mr. Wyndford is very upset with both you and Miss Mackinnon, *querida*. We're lucky I wasn't fired and you weren't dismissed from his service."

Stunned, Skye backed silently toward the stairs. All this was her fault. If she hadn't gone with Pilar, the woman would have slipped back into the house and no one would have been the wiser. Now Pilar was in trouble with her husband and both were in danger of losing their positions at Wind River. It was obvious that Kyle wouldn't go gladly to the village as she'd hoped. He would go, of course, but just to please her. He had kissed her, but in anger, and only to prove his mastery of her. She had to let him know, once and for all, that she had a mind of her own.

For several hours, she stayed in seclusion in her room, puttering with her things and scribbling a few lines in her journal. But writing wasn't the comfort to her that it was to her mother. She was restless and hurt and confused. She longed to have another visit with Ola. What would the wise old woman suggest she do now? She felt trapped for the first time in her life, and she hated the feeling.

The more she considered the conflict, the more she needed someone to talk to about her concerns. Her own mother was far away, and Missy was dead. Ola was the only one who understood her dilemma. She must see Ola and deliver the medicine.

Could she go alone? At least she wouldn't get Pilar into more trouble. But how could she? And what about Loup Leveque? Even if he were in the area, the chances of his harming her seemed remote if she used caution. She could saddle Diamond Dust and ride swiftly to the Indian camp, spend an hour or two with Ola, then return before anyone knew she was gone. Was it foolhardy? Probably, but she couldn't stay a prisoner one minute longer. Resolve turning to action, she laid out fresh clothes and packed the last of Missy's medicine bottles into a leather pouch. She would eat a good supper, then try to get some sleep. Shortly before dawn, she would go to the barn and saddle Dusty. She remembered the way to the camp, and the silver racehorse was sturdy and could outrun any pursuer if need be. She would announce at dinner that she intended to stay in her room all day tomorrow, that she didn't want to be disturbed under any circumstances. If somehow her absence was discovered, she was prepared to pay the price by accepting without complaint Kyle's unleashed anger.

But go she would. Nothing would stop her.

⇥ Chapter 37 ⇤

As light from the waning moon drifted through the open window of the parlor, Badger stirred at the sound of stealthy footsteps. He had spent the night on the sofa, a clever idea, he thought, so he could hear any movement coming from Miss Mackinnon's room.

But he had been sleeping so deeply he hadn't heard her door open or her muffled steps as she tiptoed down the stairs. The squeak of the loose floorboard in the back hallway was what alerted him.

His uncle had suspected the girl might try something like this, and Badger was proud he had been given the duty of watching over her.

Now he must make a quick decision—whether to wake up his uncle or follow Miss Mackinnon. He decided on the latter.

Picking up his boots, he tucked them under his arm and waited for her to leave the house. A furtive glance out the window showed she was headed for the barn. Maybe she was just restless and going for a walk. Or maybe she planned to go for an early-morning horseback ride. She was sure stupid if she planned to do that. Even a simpleton would know better than to ride these prairies alone in the dark. But then, Miss Mackinnon was a foreign lady who didn't know much about Dakota. His uncle had been right to be worried about her. Badger had thought at first that Uncle Kyle might have been sweet on the lady, but sometimes they didn't seem to get along too well. He couldn't understand why his uncle wouldn't love her. She was the prettiest lady Badger had ever seen—*grown lady,* that was. Dulce was prettier than anybody, of course. But Miss Mackinnon knew all there was to know about horses, and Uncle Kyle said he'd seen her milk a cow. She'd make a dandy aunt, he thought, just as soon as she got a little more sense about riding around by herself. Heck, he didn't care if she was part Indian. In fact, he'd trade his pet 'coon and all of next month's desserts to wear that bear-claw necklace of hers for just one minute.

Slipping outside, he stayed out of sight, hiding behind a wagon until he saw her lead the silver stallion out of the barn and along the path heading west. Then he ran like crazy and threw a blanket over his own pony. In minutes he was following her, but he knew she wouldn't see him. He had slung his bow and arrows over his shoulder in case he should need them. He didn't keep a gun handy but he was just as good with the bow and arrow. He wished he had Uncle Kyle's new Colt revolver. Gee, when he was a little bigger, he sure wanted one of those fancy guns. He'd impress Dulce so much she would surely agree to be his wife.

Badger was an experienced tracker. And he could tell right away Miss Mackinnon was not experienced at escaping someone trailing her. She kept a steady pace, heading southwest, never aware he was two hundred yards behind her. All he had to do was to get glimpses of her as she topped each gentle hill. He knew the Lakotas usually camped there when they were on the hunt, so it was easy to figure that was where she was headed—to visit her Lakota cousins. If he didn't need to be so quiet, he'd be singing a good ole song while he jogged along, watching the purple sky becoming light blue, then pink. This spying was easy business. He bet he'd earn double pay from Uncle Kyle once he got back with Miss Mackinnon. But he sure didn't want to be around to hear what his uncle would say to that girl when he caught her. He planned to hightail it out to the range and plug up his ears.

Skye was concentrating on her ride toward the village. The farther she got from Wind River Ranch, the more uneasy she became. The landscape that had been so bright and warm and inviting at midday yesterday took on a mysterious quality in the predawn glow, and the sounds of night birds and the call of a distant love-struck elk were eerie and unsettling. She felt like an intruder in a world where she wasn't wanted and didn't belong. She told herself that her feelings were brought on by twinges of guilt caused by disobeying Kyle's orders. As soon as the sun was up, she would relax as she rode over familiar terrain.

She thought she heard movement behind her soon after she headed her horse down a hill about five miles from the ranch. Twisting in her saddle, she rested her hand on the butt of the rifle at her knee.

Diamond Dust reared suddenly and jumped to one side.

Skye had been looking over her right shoulder when Dusty jerked to the left. She was jolted from her seat, but she regained her balance at the last instant and hauled in the reins.

Dusty whinnied and tossed his head, his thick black mane thrashing.

"What's wrong, Dusty?" she cried. "What scared you?"

"We meet again, Miss Mackinnon."

The man's low voice sent terror streaking through her.

The dark figure had emerged from the tall grass like a predator bringing down its prey. From the corner of her eye, Skye saw the silhouette of a horse about twenty yards away beside a low-growing bush. The man must have dismounted and lain in the tall grass directly in her path. She yanked Dusty's reins and kicked his sides, but the animal snorted and danced in a circle, his bridle firmly clenched in the man's gloved hands.

"Let me go—whoever you are!" she demanded. "If you're an Indian, I am one of you. I'm Lakota. See? I wear the necklace of my father's tribe."

The man laughed, a hoarse, cruel guttural sound. *"Oui,* you are Lakota, the same as I. We are alike, my fine woman. Our blood is a mixture of white and dark. We are bastard children of the earth. We have great power because we are bound to neither heritage but can be whichever one we choose to be."

Leveque. His voice was unmistakable. She could see him now as they circled in the midst of the empty prairie, his scarred face a nightmarish vision from hell. His hair was loose and flowing; his black silk shirt was dirty and frayed beneath a leather vest. His breeches were black, too, and tucked into knee-high black boots. Dressed like this, he was a shadow in the night. She knew with certainty that he had been watching her, waiting for his chance to pounce on her like some evil demon.

"Let me go," she pleaded. "I have gold at the ranch. I give you my word, I'll pay well for my freedom. I'll get the money and slip it out to you, so you won't be seen. We'll get it now before daylight. Please, I beg you . . ." She could see by the whiteness of his grin that she was wasting her breath. He didn't want gold. He had what he wanted right here in his grasp.

He laughed as he pulled the rifle from her saddle scabbard and led the horse toward his own mount. She thought of leaping off Dusty and making a dash for freedom, but she knew how useless that would be. For a minute, she rode quietly, watching Loup's profile beside her. Thinking she saw an opening, she grabbed the reins and yelled at Dusty while pivoting away from Loup.

He dropped the rifle and used both hands to hang on to the stallion's bridle. Digging in his heels, he stopped the animal from breaking loose.

"No you don't, squaw woman," he snarled. He reached up, gripped her arm, then hauled her out of the saddle and threw her to the ground.

She inhaled painful breaths as Loup encircled her waist with one arm and hauled the two of them aboard his horse. She was trapped in front of him. He put his mount into a canter and led Diamond Dust behind, heading toward the prominent rise in the landscape known as Spirit Mound.

Mildly nauseated, Skye was pressed against his body, locked in his powerful arms as they galloped in the first light of morning across the range land. How foolish she had been not to listen to Kyle's warning. How quickly she had fallen prey to their enemy. She realized Kyle had been right when he called her naïve. Loup Leveque was evil through and through and would never set her free. She felt his hatred pumping through his veins as he held her in a painful grip against his chest. Struggle would be useless now; later, she would try to find a way to escape him—even if it meant her death. Something terrible had been instilled in Loup Leveque long ago, by someone who knew the full meaning of the word *hatred*. That someone, she believed, was Siyaka, her father's archenemy when he was known as White Arrow.

Just as the sun rose above the eastern horizon, they halted beside a stunted cottonwood at the base of Spirit Mound. Why here? she wondered. Here, where they could be discovered with little difficulty? Loup could have taken her far into the wilderness. Instead, he was stopping at the foot of this famous landmark, just two miles from the trading post at Vermillion and four miles from Wind River Ranch headquarters. Hope for rescue breathed new life into her leaden spirits.

Loup lowered her to the ground, dismounted, and whipped out a short length of rope and bound her hands behind her. Then he took the scarf from around his neck and tied it over her mouth. She lifted her face, frantically fighting for breath, assailed with the stale odor of his sweat. Rolling her eyes in an effort to see him was a mistake. He yanked off her hat and took a handful of her hair, which she had worn loose around her shoulders. Pulling her head backward, he stared closely into her eyes. "Take a good look at me, Miss Mackinnon." He said Mackinnon as if he cursed the devil. "You will see a lot of this scarred face before you breathe your last."

Paralyzed with fear, she realized how desperate her situation truly was.

"Someone is following us." He spoke so matter-of-factly that she thought she'd imagined his words.

Suddenly his fist shot out and struck her squarely on the jaw. Lights exploded in her brain and everything became fuzzy. When her vision cleared, she was lying on her side, and Loup was nowhere to be seen. Dare she hope he'd done all he intended? Merely to hurt her and frighten her out of her wits, steal her horse and her rifle?

But then she saw he had crouched in the grass several feet away. The horses were tied to a bush. He had his pistol aimed at something, or someone, moving along in the grass, someone coming toward them.

To her dismay, she saw a boy's hat, then a head, appear above the greenery. A child was crawling toward them, carrying a small bow with an arrow in place. Her first incoherent thought was of the little people of Spirit Mound, the Paha Wakan who lived in this mystical place.

But the small being who stood and called her name was no Paha Wakan. It was Badger who had come to her rescue. The sight sent anguish to the pit of her stomach.

After an early breakfast alone in the dining room, Kyle headed toward the stable to saddle his bay. He had spent a restless night and had awakened at sunup when he heard Reyes and the wranglers starting for the eastern range. He would catch up with them before they reached the Big Sioux River, then spend the day checking on the herd browsing through the tall bluestem grass so lush in that region.

Tomorrow, he planned to show Skye the place he thought would make an excellent ranch headquarters for the Mackinnons. During their ride, he would take the opportunity to reveal his concerns about her father's possible death. Then he would tell her how much he loved her. After that, the only thing he could do was let her make her own decisions about their future and that of her parents.

The stable area was as quiet as the house had been. Only the munching of the horses in their stalls and the clucking of a stray chicken that had escaped the roost interrupted the stillness of the morning. B. J. should be somewhere around, but the fellow had a woman guest from Vermillion, so he could be late getting on the job today.

Kyle looked in on Raven, who appeared downright frisky in the cool morning air, then he saddled his bay and rode back toward the house. Something about the stillness made him uneasy. He decided he'd make certain Pilar was up and Badger was all right. Usually, the boy was thunking around the house in his size-ten boots, fussing over one of his adopted critters or loading his plate in the kitchen with eggs and sausage and hot biscuits.

As Kyle started to dismount, Pilar ran out the back door, her braids flying and her hands raised in alarm.

"Mr. Wyndford—wait!" she screamed. "They're gone, both of them. I checked their rooms and they're gone!"

His throat tightened. "What? Who's gone?" he asked, leaning from his saddle to look down at her terrified face.

"Miss Mackinnon. Badger. The boy slept on the couch in the parlor last night. Miss Mackinnon said before going to bed she didn't want to be disturbed today. But she slipped away—and Badger must have followed her."

Kyle rolled his eyes skyward, cursing under his breath. Why hadn't Badger awakened him? He never dreamed the boy would follow Skye into the open range land. "All right, Pilar, I'll go after them," he said sharply. "I know exactly where she's headed."

Pilar was weeping unashamedly. She ground her hands and moaned. "I'm so sorry, Mr. Wyndford. I didn't think she'd ever do such a thing. It's my fault. I'll pray to the Virgin at once—pray Miss Mackinnon and Badger are safe."

Kyle said softly, "Well, you couldn't have known this would happen. I'm more to blame than anyone. I shouldn't have told Badger to look out for her. Go on with your chores, Pilar, and be sure to tell B. J. what's happened. I hope I'll be back with those two scamps very soon." He pulled the Colt from his holster and checked the cylinder. Then he kicked his horse into a gallop and headed toward the Lakota camp.

Skye had no way to scream a warning to Badger. Loup was on him like a raging beast, knocking him to the ground and snapping his bow and arrow into pieces.

Holding the boy by his shirt collar, Loup put a knee on his chest and stared at him.

From where she lay in the grass, Skye could see the fear in Badger's eyes as he gaped at the hideous face so close to his. To his credit, he didn't scream but immediately started to pummel the big man with his fists.

Loup gripped Badger's arms, stood, and pulled him to his feet. "What have we here?" he gloated, digging his fingers into Badger's flesh until the boy flinched and gnawed his lip with pain.

Skye twisted and fought her bonds, to no avail. What kind of animal would hurt a child? She never imagined such evil existed.

Badger glared, then announced, "I'm Montgomery Wyndford. I own Wind River Ranch, and you'd better let me and that lady go right now. My uncle has plenty of men who'll come after you if you hurt us."

Skye's heart broke at Badger's brave words. Instinctively, she knew the lad had said exactly the wrong thing. He shouldn't have revealed his relationship to Kyle. His innocence had left him as vulnerable to evil as she.

Loup cackled with delight. "The gods keep offering me treasures," he said. "I knew I was born under a lucky star."

"Let me go. You're hurting me, mister."

Loup kept his hold on Badger, but cocked his head in thought. "I believe I *will* let you go, boy. I have use for you."

Skye opened her eyes wide, praying Loup would indeed let Badger go. Whatever else happened, the boy must be set free.

"*Oui,* I believe I will send you on an errand. A life-and-death errand."

"What kind of errand?" Badger muttered, looking across at her.

"An errand that will mean life or death to the Mackinnon woman." He shook Badger hard to force his attention. "Do you hear me, boy? Do you understand what I'm saying?"

Badger scowled up at Loup, but nodded.

"That's better," Loup snarled. "I'm going to take her to the top of Spirit Mound. It is my intention to keep her there until Wyndford comes for her."

"He will," snapped Badger. "My uncle will come, and so will Señor Pacheco and the men. If you hurt Miss Mackinnon, they'll kill you. That I swear."

Skye marveled at the youth's courage. Even at this dreadful moment, she couldn't help thinking how proud

Kyle would be of him. She prayed harder than before that he would get away—and not come back.

Loup sneered at the boy. "No, your uncle's army won't come, because you are going to warn them not to. That is your errand, Montgomery Wyndford, and this woman's life depends on your succeeding. Do you understand me?" He shook the boy once more.

"What . . . what do you want me to do?" Badger mumbled.

"Find Wyndford. Tell him he must come here—alone—if he expects to find the woman unharmed. Tell him *he* is the person I want. He is the only white man who has dared to possess the lands of my people. He must be sacrificed—so no other whites will come."

"You're crazy, whoever you are, mister. There's lotsa whites living up and down the Missouri. More coming all the time. The Indians and whites like to trade their goods. Everyone gets along fine most of the time."

Loup moved a hand to encircle the boy's throat.

Skye twisted and jerked and moaned, but could do nothing.

"You're young, ignorant like all whites. You will do as I say, boy. Or would you rather I slit your throat here and now—then hers?"

"All right," Badger choked.

"Good. Then get on your horse and find Wyndford. I'll wait until the sun sets; then, if he has not come, the woman will die. I'll be on top of Spirit Mound, where I can see everything for miles around. No one can slip up on us. I'll wait—but only until sundown. Tell Wyndford exactly what I said. If anyone else comes near, or if he brings help with him, the woman will die instantly. Got that, boy?"

"Yes." Badger looked once more at Skye, then walked to his horse and threw himself into the saddle.

She nodded vigorously, hoping against hope he would understand he was doing the right thing by hurrying away.

Loup watched him closely, then as Badger turned his horse, Loup yelled, "I'm Loup Leveque. Tell Wyndford I'll be waiting atop the hill with his woman."

❧ Chapter 38 ❧

Badger rode to the ranch at full gallop. Flinging out of his saddle, he ran first to the barn, but finding no sign of Kyle, he dashed breathlessly into the house.

Pilar met him in the hall. "Where have you been, Badger?" she cried. "Your uncle is out looking for you."

Badger pulled off his hat and twisted it in his hands. "Which way did he go, Pilar? I've got to find him fast."

"Toward the Indian camp. But he left two hours ago. He's probably there by now. Where is Miss Mackinnon?"

Badger slapped his hat against his thigh. "Blazes, Pilar, some terrible man's got her. Said his name is Loup Leveque. He's so blamed ugly, he could make a buffalo faint. He captured me, too, but then he sent me here to get my uncle."

Pilar crossed herself. "Oh, Jesus, help us. That's the man Mr. Wyndford was so afraid would catch Miss Mackinnon. And now it's happened. Holy saints . . . holy saints . . ."

"I don't think he'll kill her. If he intended that, why would he send me to get Uncle Kyle? 'Course, he's crazy as a rabid skunk." Badger headed for the kitchen. "I'm gonna get me a drink of water, then head after Uncle Kyle. Are any of the men around?"

"Just B. J.," Pilar said, scurrying after him.

"Tell B. J. to go find Reyes and the others. Tell him to bring them back here pronto."

"Yes. I will. Please be careful, Badger. Maybe there's more than one crazy halfbreed out there. More than one *lobo*."

Badger gulped down a cup of water. "I'm headed for the Lakota camp."

300

He was out the door when Pilar called after him. "Where has that man taken Miss Mackinnon?"

"To the top of Spirit Mound. He's waiting there." Badger stopped cold and spun around. "But he said if anyone came besides Uncle Kyle, or if my uncle brought anyone with him, he'd kill Miss Mackinnon quick as a wink."

Pilar gasped and covered her mouth.

"When the men get here, be sure you tell them what Loup Leveque said. From the top of Spirit Mound, he can see them coming before they get anywhere near the place."

Pilar was running toward the quarters. "I'll tell B. J. You ride after Mr. Kyle. Holy Mary, Mother . . ."

Kyle rode his horse slowly into the Lakota camp, expecting to see Diamond Dust at one of the tepees. But there was no sign of the stallion—or of Skye.

An Indian man loped silently beside him. Kyle eyed him, but decided the man would not attack unless he felt threatened. A second native fell in at his flank, but he also padded along in silence.

Too bad, Kyle thought, that his first visit to an Indian village other than the settlement at Vermillion would be under such strange circumstances. For once, he was at a disadvantage. He needed information, and he was at the mercy of the Indians. Glancing around as he ambled his horse through the middle of the camp, he saw order and tranquility. He didn't know what he had expected to find— painted savages dancing in a circle, scalps dangling from every tepee, captives being burned at the stake—but his first impression was that these people were neither savage nor disorganized. Quite the contrary. This hunting camp was clean, colorful, and utilitarian, ideal for the purpose of traveling across the plains in search of game. The main problem was he didn't know who was in charge or whom he should speak to, now that he was here and he didn't see Skye. He wasn't even sure these people spoke English, and to his regret, he had never bothered to learn any of the Indian languages.

He halted his horse in front of the tepee with elaborate

paintings on its exterior. No one came out to greet him, and he hesitated to dismount.

One of the men who had followed him into the camp now stepped forward. "What do you want here?" the man asked. "I am Light Eagle. I have seen you at the trading post. You are the white leader who has brought the long-horned cattle to this land."

Grateful for someone who spoke English, Kyle nodded. "Yes, I'm Kyle Wyndford, owner of Wind River Ranch. I came in search of a young lady who visited here yesterday with her Lakota friend. I thought she might have come again and I must find her at once. But I don't see the horse she was riding. I could have made a mistake about her whereabouts." Until now, Kyle had refused to think anything really serious could have happened to Skye. But now, fear mounted inside him. He tried to think where else she might have gone. Out for an early-morning ride? Exploring on her own? He remembered she had a map showing the place Missy thought was best for her to establish a ranch. Maybe she'd gone there alone in an attempt to prove she didn't need his help. It would have been like her to do that, the independent little fox.

"The woman with the bear-claw necklace visited Ola yesterday," Light Eagle said. "I walked in with her when she came to the camp. She was with the Lakota woman who married the Spaniard."

"Yes. That's Pilar Pacheco."

"The woman you seek is the daughter of White Arrow, the warrior who was half Lakota."

"Yes. She is indeed. She's very proud of her Indian heritage."

"And she is now *your* friend?"

He hesitated before answering. Would being his friend spoil Skye's reputation among the Lakotas? He had no idea what these people thought of him. He lived in a separate world, ignorant of their way of life. Grudgingly, he realized he had been wrong to think total separation between the races was a wise course to follow. He should have listened to Missy long ago and tried to open some communication with the native people. He might need their help now to locate

Skye if she were lost on the prairie. "Yes, she is my friend. Are you sure she didn't come here this morning?"

Light Eagle said, "No, she is not here. If she is lost, we will help you find her. All the men are hunting now; only two of us are left to guard the camp. But we expect no trouble from the Yanktons, and the women here know how to fight if necessary. When the hunters return, if you need us, we will spread across the prairie to search for White Arrow's daughter."

Kyle was deeply moved by Light Eagle's suggestion. He was doubly sorry he had never made friendly overtures to any of the Indians. "Thank you, Light Eagle. I may need the help of your people if we don't find her soon. I do have one question."

Light Eagle waited.

"There's a half-breed who calls himself Loup Leveque who sometimes comes to these parts. He's made threats toward me and my friend, Miss Mackinnon. Have any of your people seen this man recently?"

"I know the man you speak of," Light Eagle responded. "He is evil and untrustworthy. Last year, he came to the Lakota camp and wanted to be welcomed at our fires. But he is cowardly and known to cause much trouble wherever he goes. He has not come here this season. He knows he would not be welcome at our tepees and lodges."

"I must agree with that wise decision," Kyle said, relieved to learn Leveque hadn't been seen. Reaching down, he grasped the Indian's hand. Feeling the firm grip, looking into the dark, intense eyes, he felt a sudden bond with the people who had occupied the land he loved long before his arrival. "Thank you again for offering to help. Consider yourself and your people welcome anytime at Wind River Ranch. I'm sorry I don't have time to pay my respects to Ola, but I'm impatient to find the missing lady."

The brave lifted his hand in farewell. "Good luck. If you don't find her, return to us and we will begin a search of the prairie."

Kyle started back the way he'd come. He was upset with Skye, but when he found her, he would smother her with love, just as soon as he chastised her for taking such a chance. She must have gone exploring on her own to spite him for ordering her to wait for him. He refused to allow thoughts of Loup Leveque to set him into a panic. If the Indians hadn't seen Leveque here or in Vermillion, Leveque was probably a hundred miles away by now. But still, worry ate at him like a hungry pest.

Kyle saw a rider coming fast from beyond the next hill. Putting his horse into a gallop, he rode to intercept him.

Damned if it wasn't Badger. Well, that was one missing person found, he thought with relief. He prayed Badger was coming to tell him Skye was safe at Wind River, pouting because she knew she was in a mountain of trouble.

One look at Badger's bleak face wiped away his hopes.

"Uncle Kyle," Badger cried, reining in his frothing horse. "I'm sure glad I found you. Something awful's happened to Miss Mackinnon."

Kyle's heart stopped beating. "What, Badger? What's happened?"

"A man got her. He's ugly as sin and mean as a crazy wolf. His name is Loup Leveque, and—"

"Good God!" Kyle interjected. "Where are they? Has he hurt her?" Kyle felt his worst fears exploding inside him.

Badger calmed his horse and said hurriedly, "He's got her over at Spirit Mound. He grabbed me, too, 'cause I was following her—you know, to protect her."

"I know, lad. I stupidly put you at risk. But why Spirit Mound? He can easily be found there."

"That's just it, Uncle Kyle. He wants you to come right away. He let me go so I could look for you."

"Damn the villain! So that was the bastard's ploy. He was using Skye as bait to hook a bigger fish. Well, he'll sure as bloody hell get his wish."

"There's something else. Something real important I've got to tell you."

Kyle waited, staring hard into the boy's tense face.

"Leveque said you were to come *alone*. He said if you brought anyone with you or any of your men, he'd . . . he'd . . ."

"He'd what, Badger?"

"He'd cut her throat."

Kyle's jaw tightened. He should have guessed Loup's plan. The man was insane with hatred for the white settlers. Loup Leveque hated *him* especially because he had dared to be the first white man to make his home in Dakota. And now, because of hatred and prejudice, a lovely, innocent girl was the pawn in a deadly conflict that could cause her death. Kyle had to take his share of the blame for what was happening. But an hour ago, at the Lakota village, his personal feelings toward the Indians had shifted. He had made a new beginning with the Lakotas. And the only hatred he had left was aimed at Loup Leveque.

"Go to the ranch, Badger. Some of the men may have come in from work. Explain what's happened and send them to Spirit Mound."

"But Loup said no one else could come there."

"I'll have to take that chance. I'll try to stall Leveque until I can jump him—or until help arrives. The important thing is to get Skye out of there safely. Badger, if things go wrong, if I don't survive and Leveque gets away, tell Reyes to do whatever he must to save Skye. Tell him not to fail, no matter how far he has to go or how long it takes."

"Yes, sir," said Badger, his young voice deep with feeling. "Be careful, Uncle Kyle. I'll ride as fast as I can." He spun his horse and headed back toward the ranch.

"Be still, woman. You aren't going anywhere."

Skye ceased her struggles and sat quietly on the ground. Here atop the gently sloping hill, the grass was dry and sparse and there were no trees at all.

She was bound and gagged in the hot sun. Every minute was an eternity as she watched Loup Leveque working at bizarre preparations for the anticipated arrival of his enemy. The only fortunate thing at the moment was that he was too busy to torment her, molest her, or even give her more than a frequent cursory glance to make sure she was where he'd left her.

Loup had taken time to secure his horse and Diamond Dust in a scrap of shade at the foot of the hill and give them water from a container strapped to his saddle. Skye concluded he planned to use the animals in his getaway.

Then Loup had marched her to the top of Spirit Mound, forced her to sit, and tied her ankles. After that, he had retrieved a long metal stake from his saddle and driven it into the ground at the center of the hilltop. Once he was satisfied the stake was well anchored, he began gathering dead grass from the slopes and arranging it in clumps in a wide circle around the stake. He stopped often to stare at the surrounding countryside, his ears perked for the sound of approaching hoofbeats. After an hour, Loup took up a position facing north and sat as if carved in stone.

Skye began to feel woozy from the heat and the tension. She was surprised Kyle hadn't come and decided Badger must be having trouble finding him. What if Kyle had ridden a long distance from Wind River? What if Badger couldn't find him at all? Loup had sworn she would die at sundown, but when she thought of the circumstances, she realized her chances for survival were not very good. The chances for Kyle's survival were even less if he came to help her.

Another endless hour crept by with no sign of anyone. Suddenly, Loup stood and stared across the empty landscape toward the road leading from Vermillion to Wind River.

Skye used great effort to get to her knees and gaze down the hill. A single rider was cantering along the road, looking like a child's toy from this lofty vantage point. It was not Kyle; it appeared to be an Indian from the settlement.

Loup studied the figure until it disappeared over the northern horizon, then he walked over and scowled at her.

She slumped to her heels and closed her eyes. She mustn't faint, she drummed into her fuzzy brain. Somehow she must stay alert, in case Loup became bored with his vigil and decided to take his revenge on her without waiting for Kyle. She was certain she couldn't stop him from raping her, but she would use her last ounce of strength to fight him.

"You, Mackinnon squaw. You're suffering, I hope. Maybe I put too much stock in Wyndford's wanting to save you. You're a breed, after all. A rich and powerful man like him could find a better woman than you. He knows great danger awaits him here, so maybe he won't come. I figured his pride and arrogance would make him show up, even if he cared little for you. But—maybe I figured wrong."

Her lips were numb under the kerchief; her fingers tingled from lack of circulation. With her hands tied behind her, she couldn't reach the gag.

Loup glanced around, then squatted over her and grabbed a handful of hair and jerked her head backward. She felt the heat of the fierce midday sun burning her face.

He laid the side of one hand across her throat above the claw necklace. "I'm glad you wear your father's token," he said, his voice acid. "When I do what must be done with you, I want the bear claw in my vision. Then I will take it for my own and know my father is avenged for what he suffered at *your* father's hands." He pushed her to her side, letting his hand rest fleetingly on her breast. "Later, I will have you," he said harshly, "after I have made an example of your man, Wyndford. When I am through with him, no white man will come to this land for a hundred years. Maybe never. My act will inspire the cowardly Yanktons to take a stand at last. The Oglala, the Blackfoot, the Mandan—all will see what Loup Leveque has done, and they will take up the battle cry and unite against our common enemy." Then he left her and loped to the crest of the hill.

Skye had had trouble concentrating on Leveque's speech. If he fancied himself some sort of hero or savior, she had no interest in his scheming. Loup was mad with hatred and filled with dreams of his own grandeur. He would never listen to reason from her or from anyone else, she was certain.

Suddenly, Loup raced back toward her from his place atop the hill.

He pulled her to her feet and cut the thongs around her ankles. For a second, she thought she would fall, but he supported her and tugged her forward to look down at the valley. With wildly confused emotions, she saw Kyle riding in from the west. Kyle had come, come to save her from her own foolishness. He must truly love her to have risked so much. And she loved him beyond believing. But what good would their love do them, if they died at the hands of Loup Leveque?

Kyle saw the two figures at the top of the hill. Thank God, Skye was there and able to stand, though he could see she was gagged and at Loup's mercy. He hadn't come up with any kind of plan. He couldn't try a shot at this distance, especially with Skye being used as a shield. If only he could have found enough cover to sneak up on Leveque, he might have overpowered him. But approaching across the open plains had made a surprise attack impossible. Already Loup had seen him and was waiting for him atop the hill. With Skye in jeopardy, he knew he would have to play along with the bastard, try to negotiate Skye's safety. He had a strong hunch that the only thing Loup would be willing to take in trade for the girl was Kyle Wyndford himself.

He halted his mount within shouting distance, wondering why Loup hadn't taken a shot at him by now. Apparently, the man had something else in mind besides instant death.

"Leveque," Kyle called, "let the woman go. We can talk."

Leveque yelled back, "Get off your horse and throw down your gun, Wyndford. Do exactly as I say, and I will talk to you."

A good beginning, Kyle thought, encouraged. Every second he could keep Loup talking would give him a better chance to ascertain the situation. Maybe Leveque wanted money, after all. So far, Loup hadn't killed anyone. The bastard could demand a fortune in Wyndford gold and go anywhere in the world he wanted to go.

"I'm coming up," shouted Kyle. "I'll pay you whatever you ask if you'll release the woman and leave Dakota." As he spoke, he dismounted.

"You must climb the hill toward me. If you don't, I will slit the squaw's throat." Loup held Skye in front of him and flashed his knife in front of her face.

"Don't do it, Leveque. *I'm* the one you want."

Loup put away the knife and brandished a pistol.

"I'm out of pistol range," Kyle shouted.

"But the woman is not." Leveque placed the barrel of the gun against Skye's head.

"Wait, Leveque. I'll make you an offer. If you're not interested, you can do what you please with the woman and I'll return to my ranch. She doesn't mean that much to me—considering she's a *half-breed* like you."

"You took a great chance coming here if that's true," Loup said loudly.

"I didn't come here because of her. I came to settle a score with *you*. You made a fool of me in St. Louis, and you threatened to kill me. But since you have cleverly captured the woman, I'll bargain with you." Kyle had moved several yards up the hill, close enough to see Skye's wide-eyed terror and the pistol jammed against her temple. The sight made his stomach churn with fear, not for himself but for her. All he could think of was getting Skye out of the man's clutches.

"Get rid of your gun," Loup demanded.

"I will—when you let her go. Release her now, or I'm returning to my ranch. This foolish episode is a waste of my valuable time." He despised his words, but he knew convincing Loup of his indifference could help him negotiate for Skye. Also, he was gambling heavily that Loup wanted to kill him more than he wanted to possess the woman.

For several seconds, Loup said nothing. Then he yelled, "I should have known you were a coward, Wyndford. You and your kind always are."

With his heart in his throat, Kyle waved casually toward the two figures atop the mound, returned to his horse, and picked up the reins.

"Wait!" cried Leveque.

Closing his eyes as his breath returned, Kyle stopped and turned back toward Loup. "Wait?" he called. "What for? If you want her, you can have her."

"No. If you come forward and throw down your gun, I'll let her go. You're right, Wyndford, I'm willing to trade her—for you."

Kyle left his horse and climbed halfway up the slope.

"That's close enough," said Loup. "Throw down your gun. Now."

"Not until you turn her loose." Kyle knew that with Skye pressed to Loup's chest, he had no chance for a shot. "Let her go, Leveque, and we'll settle this between the two of us."

Loup hesitated, reluctance vivid in every line of his face and body. Then with one hand, he reached behind Skye's neck and yanked off the thong holding the bear claw. Next, he pulled his knife and slashed the ropes binding her wrists.

Instantly, she tugged off the gag. "Kyle," she choked out his name. Then she stumbled down the hill toward him.

"All right, Wyndford. Come up here," Loup yelled.

"Kyle—no," Skye screamed hoarsely, almost within his reach.

"Get on my horse, Skye," he said firmly. "Show me the courage of your Lakota ancestors."

She paused a few feet from him. He could have touched her, but he knew better than to try while Loup threatened from above them. "Get on the horse, my brave lass. Ride to the ranch. You must live—for Badger." These words could be his last message to her; he hoped she would remember them.

Loup yelled again. "Woman, stay right there. If you take another step, I'll kill you."

"You said you'd let her go, Leveque," Kyle shouted.

"Not until you disarm yourself and come up here."

Looking across at Skye, he said, "His pistol is pointed directly at you. I need to buy time until help comes. I'll try to keep him talking."

"Get up here, Wyndford," Loup demanded. "I can pick her off like a buzzard at this distance."

"Kyle, he'll kill you," she whispered through swollen lips. "I think . . . I think he plans to start a fire on top of the hill, to burn you . . ."

Kyle considered this and realized Skye was right. To sacrifice the owner of Wind River Ranch would send a clear message to everyone that any white man coming to this land risked a terrible death. "Who knows what's in a madman's mind?" he said flatly.

"Don't go up there," she pleaded.

"I have to stall him," he said under his breath. "Badger's gone for help. Keep still until I get up there, then when Loup's distracted, run like hell for the horse and get out of here."

"No more conversation!" Loup howled. "I'm giving you to the count of three to get up here, Wyndford, or the woman's dead."

Kyle gave Skye a brief smile, then started up the hill with his hands stretched outward. As he neared the top, he watched for any sign Loup might shift the pistol away from Skye, but the clever bastard kept it directly on her.

"Stop right there and throw down your gun, Wyndford. Do as I say, slow and easy, or I'll shoot her."

Kyle couldn't gamble with Skye's life. Not when she had a chance to escape. He removed his Colt and tossed it into the weeds ten yards away.

"That's right, Wyndford. Now ease on up here."

Kyle focused on Loup and climbed to the top to face him.

Keeping a safe distance, Loup narrowed his one good eye. "I don't need to kill you to make an example of you, Wyndford. If you'll cooperate, we'll soon have this over with."

He knew Loup was lying, but he had to play along with him. "I'm glad to hear that, Leveque. I'm here. The woman can leave. Now, what do you want with me?"

In a swift movement, Loup stepped forward and placed the pistol against Kyle's chest.

Kyle stiffened and cut his eyes toward Skye, praying she had obeyed his order to run to the horse. To his horror, she was climbing back up the hill as fast as she could.

Skye reached the top and approached them. "Don't kill him," she pleaded. "I'll go with you, anywhere you want."

Loup grinned at her, then hit her across her jaw with the gun barrel.

Kyle leaped at him and felt the gun stab hard into his ribs.

"Stop right there, Wyndford. I don't want to kill you, I said. But I will do it, if you try anything again."

It took all the control Kyle could muster to calm his fury. But throwing away his life wouldn't help Skye. Taking a deep breath, he studied her body crumpled on the ground. Foolish, wonderful woman. He had never known a lady with such amazing courage, but her courage—and her love for him—might have cost both of them their lives.

"What now, Leveque? Our deal's off if you don't let her go."

Loup laughed and moved toward an iron stake at the center of the hilltop. "What *deal,* Monsieur Wyndford? You have just drawn a deuce to my ace, and I'm enjoying my little game. Come over here and sit in front of this pole."

The man was completely insane, Kyle thought, as he walked toward the stake. But insanity was close to brilliance, and Loup had the upper hand at the moment.

"That's right," Loup crowed. "Sit with your back to the post and put your hands behind it."

Keeping his eyes on Skye, who was beginning to rouse, Kyle obeyed. Any chance was gone for him to get them out of this ungodly mess. He didn't dare resist with Skye again at Loup's mercy. His only hope now was to play for time—and pray that Badger had found someone to come to their aid.

Loup bound Kyle's wrists to the stake. From this point forward, Kyle knew his life, and Skye's, was in the hands of fate.

⇥ *Chapter* 39 ⇤

Skye had only one thought when she rushed blindly up the hill: to save Kyle from a terrible death, even if it meant giving herself to Loup Leveque. The blow from Loup's gun sent pain crashing through her and sparklets dancing before her eyes.

By the time her head cleared, she found that her hands were tied once more. Turning her aching cheek to the pungent earth, she sobbed in misery. Kyle would die soon, and she would die later, after Loup had used her for his purpose.

She gazed at Kyle. He was bound to the stake a few feet away, looking at her with a mixture of worry and regret. She had failed him and failed herself. Twisting, she located Leveque, who was close by, piling up dried weeds in a circle near Kyle.

So it *was* to be a fire. And Kyle would be the burnt offering to the insane man's dreams of glory, a symbol of Loup's hatred of the whites.

She inched toward Kyle, her cheeks wet with tears. She wanted to die with him, even if it meant burning in Loup Leveque's fire. From the edge of her vision, she saw Loup keeping an eye on them, but he didn't prevent her from moving to Kyle's side.

Resting against him, she closed her eyes. "I'm . . . so sorry . . ." she began.

"You were wonderful," he said softly. "With my last breath, I'll adore you."

"But I . . . I disobeyed you—again. And I failed to help you."

His smile was heavy with sadness. "I was beyond helping. But you did fail to escape. That's what breaks my heart. But as a courageous and loving woman, you were magnificent. Have no regrets, whatever happens, my precious Skye. And don't give up hope if Leveque takes you away and—and mistreats you. Badger has instructions to tell Reyes to find you, no matter how long it takes or how far he has to search. He will come for you. You're a fighter, as you've just proven. Don't let my death destroy your spirit."

Beyond tears, beyond anguish, she laid her head on his chest, felt his warmth and the beating of his heart. That he should die was unthinkable. She refused to accept the finality of the situation. She raised her face to give him a look of pure worship.

"My poor lass, your lip is bleeding."

His concern for her trivial injury at such a time gave her more pain than any blow. "I love you, Kyle. I will always love you. I hope he lets me die here next to you."

Kyle rested his lips on her forehead. She felt his tenderness and sorrow to the depths of her being.

She sought his mouth and found it. The lingering kiss was as bittersweet as petals falling from a dying rose.

"Very touching," Loup called. "Make that a kiss of farewell." He had begun to strike matches to the stacks of grass piled in a circle around them. Suddenly, he stopped and looked over his shoulder. He muttered a curse and threw down the matches. "Someone's coming. Two riders. I warned you, Wyndford." Pulling his knife, he started toward Skye.

She saw murder in his face, and she threw her arms around Kyle's neck.

A puff of wind rushed across the hilltop, extinguishing the three fires Loup had ignited.

"Damnation," he said, turning back and peering downhill at the approaching riders. Quickly, he sheathed his knife and hurried to rekindle the flames. Kneeling, he blew on each stack until it blazed into life. Focusing on his efforts, he continued crawling from bundle to bundle, striking matches, puffing and cursing.

Skye saw a chance. Getting to her feet, she jumped across the flames opposite Loup and ran to the edge of the mound. "Help!" she screamed. "Up here!" All she could see were two horses arriving in a cloud of dust at the base of the hill.

Loup sprang toward her through the smoke-filled air. He tried to pick her up, but she kicked and fought with every ounce of strength in her body. Loup couldn't pull his pistol with her struggling in his arms, so he shoved her toward the spreading fire. "To hell with both of you!" he yelled.

Tumbling across Kyle's legs, she saw Loup whip out his gun, then suddenly gape wide-eyed beyond them. With another curse, he turned and fled toward the far side of the hill and disappeared over the rim.

"Get away, Skye!" Kyle yelled. "Get out of the fire!"

Coughing, she frantically scooted with her back toward

Kyle and began searching desperately for the ropes binding his wrists. "I'll try to get you loose!" she screamed. She located the knot, but with her own hands tied, it was too tight for her to work open.

"Get away, Skye!" he shouted, tugging against the stake.

Sweat and tears and smoke almost blinded her as the snapping flames touched the hem of her skirt.

Another sound reached her—a cry like that of an enraged beast.

Staring through the thick smoke, she saw a vision rising from her past, or from some long-ago dream of her Lakota ancestors. An Indian warrior was running toward them, his hair flying, his broadsword hoisted overhead, his voice calling a fierce warning in the tongue of the Lakota Sioux.

She believed death was coming to claim her.

The warrior lifted her, carried her away from the fire, and rolled her in the dirt to put out the flames around her ankles.

"Save Kyle!" she screamed, but wasn't sure it was her own voice she heard.

The Indian grabbed his sword from the ground and leaped back across the flames. In several seconds, he reappeared with Kyle running beside him.

Kyle dropped beside her and locked her in a fierce embrace. His face and hands were smudged, but he seemed uninjured.

Her hands still bound, she kissed him long and deeply, tasting a bitter mixture of blood and ash and tears.

When the kiss ended, she lay weakly in his arms, stunned and exhausted after the sudden escape from death. With her eyes blurred and stinging, she looked at the man who had saved them. Her words of gratitude caught in her parched throat.

"Darling—Skye—let me," Kyle murmured, reaching to untie her. He worked on her bonds as he spoke to the Indian standing over them. "We're grateful, sir," he said. "You saved our lives. Who are you?"

"Fletcher Mackinnon," announced the large, handsome warrior. He looked every inch a Lakota. Kneeling, he opened his arms toward Skye.

"Papa!" she cried, recovering from her shock. The moment she was free, she rushed into her father's embrace.

Kyle watched in surprise. Skye's father, the laird of Mackinnon, was here? Apparently so, and it was a miracle indeed—a miracle well deserved by Skye. He didn't know if he himself qualified for the miraculous, but nonetheless, he would take such good luck whenever it came along.

With an arm around his weeping daughter, Fletcher said, "Doesn't appear much has changed in Dakota since my youth. The day I left, *I* was the one about to be roasted alive."

"How'd you find us?" Kyle asked.

"I was escorted by a young lad who said his name was Badger. I insisted he stay out of sight until it was safe to come up."

Badger dashed forward to join them. Breathlessly, he said, "When I got to the ranch, Uncle Kyle, nobody was there but Mr. Mackinnon. Are you all right?"

"You did fine, Badger. And yes, I'm quite all right."

"I spotted Loup Leveque, too," Badger announced.

Kyle stiffened. "Where? Did he see you?"

"Heck no. He was riding that gray stallion like the devil was on his tail. Heading west."

"Diamond Dust," Skye said still snuggled in her father's protective arm.

Kyle noticed the blackened hem of Skye's skirt and the burns on her ankles and hands. He said to Fletcher, "Skye has been hurt. I don't know how badly. Will you take her to the ranch and see that she's cared for?"

"Of course."

"But Kyle, where are *you* going?" Skye asked.

"After Leveque. If I don't catch him now, he'll make trouble again for sure." Behind him, the flames that had roared around the stake were dying for lack of fuel.

"Please don't go. He's crazy."

"I agree with my daughter, Mr. Wyndford," Fletcher said. "Let *me* go after him while you take Skye home. I'd be happy to avenge this outrage."

Kyle got to his feet. "Sorry, sir, but I can't give you that pleasure. I have a personal score to settle with Loup Leveque." He stepped to the crest of the hill and stared at the horizon. "I'm betting Leveque is heading for the badlands if he can ford the rivers between here and there."

Badger interjected, "You can ride the stallion, Uncle Kyle."

"Which stallion, Badger?"

The boy grinned. "I rode Raven Duke, since my pony was clean wore out. I didn't think you'd mind, and Raven's the fastest horse we own. He's tied to a bush down below the hill beside Mr. Mackinnon's good-looking stallion."

"Good. I'll ride him." Kyle went back to lean over Skye and give her an affectionate smile. "Looks like we'll find out at last who's the faster—Diamond Dust or Raven Duke. My money's on Raven."

She reached up for his hand, but he didn't want to chafe her burns. Instead, he dropped to one knee and framed her face with his palms. "I love you, my darling Skye. Take care of yourself and I'll be back soon. I know you're in safe hands."

Her brow furrowed with concern. "Please be careful, my husband. I'll be waiting for you."

Startled, he gazed at her, allowing the word *husband* to echo in his mind. He leaned and kissed her moist forehead, feeling the heat from sunburn and possible fever, then feather-kissed her lips. Hiding his worry for her behind a smile, he said, "Your father is a hero and a gentleman. I'm looking forward to getting better acquainted with him, once Leveque is out of the way."

He stood and shook hands with Fletcher. Hell, the man could have been a full-blood, he thought, except for those green eyes. "Your timing was perfect, Mackinnon."

"Glad to oblige, sir."

"Take good care of her. She's very precious, as you know."

"Aye. Her mother will help. She's waiting in Vermillion, along with Cheyne Sinclair."

"Sinclair?"

"He helped me to escape from the Turks, then escorted us here. He said he had always wanted to make a trip west. Do you have weapons?"

"I hope to retrieve my revolver from the hillside." After a wave toward Skye, who was reclining on one elbow, he made his way down the slope to the spot where he'd thrown the Colt. Fletcher and Badger came with him. Their first search was futile, but then Kyle saw a gleam in a patch of grass. The gun was waiting, and he shoved it into the holster on his hip.

Walking toward the horses, Kyle slipped an arm over Badger's slender shoulders and drew him aside. "You were very brave today, Badger. You acted like an man. If something should happen to me, I know Wind River will be in good hands."

Badger nodded. "Don't worry, Uncle Kyle. I'll soon be grown, and I want to be just like you."

The boy's words touched him deeply. "I appreciate that, but I've made my share of mistakes—especially about the Indians. I learned a lot today about these people, and I expect to learn much more. They've done some bad things, but they have grievances, too. Get to know them, Badger. Make friends with the native people of this land. At least treat them fairly. Your mother wanted this, and so does Skye. I've learned my lesson the hard way. You can benefit from my mistakes."

"Yes, sir."

They arrived at the horses, and Kyle gave Raven an affectionate pat. The animal appeared fit and full of energy as he tossed his head in pleasure at seeing his master.

Kyle swung into the saddle—Raven's racing saddle, he was glad to see.

Fletcher stepped forward. "Take this," he said, handing him his double-edged broadsword. "The Mackinnon claymore goes with me wherever I go. 'Tis a weapon that brings me good fortune. Use it against your adversary. That way I'll have a part in the bastard's punishment. According to your housekeeper, he is the son of Siyaka, an old enemy of mine. I want to be with you in spirit when you take revenge."

Kyle accepted the weapon and leaned to again shake Mackinnon's hand. "Thank you, my lord Mackinnon, for what you did today. I'll never forget it."

"Not *my lord*. I'm in America now and done with titles. I'm a mixed-blood Lakota Scot, with plenty of hard times ahead."

"You'll do just fine, Mackinnon. I hope I can be of help."

"By the way, if you don't mind my asking, why did Skye call you husband?"

Kyle gathered the reins. "That's a long story, sir. I'm just happy she said it. No doubt she'll explain to you and Mrs. Mackinnon."

Kyle put Raven into a canter, relishing the familiar feel of the powerful muscle and sinew beneath him. Loup had a half-hour head start, but Badger had said Leveque was running his mount at a full gallop when he left Spirit Mound. That meant he would use up Dusty's quarter-horse sprint in a very short time. Raven was a distance runner, and Kyle was certain he could overtake the blue roan.

If he guessed right about Loup's whereabouts, he would find him and settle this contest once and for all. He would be back at Wind River before this day ended—or he would be dead.

᷃ Chapter 40 ᷄

Loup forced the mighty blue roan stallion across the plains, slapping it brutally with the slender walking stick whenever the animal began to slow.

Although he figured his scheme to kill Wyndford in a symbolic sacrifice had probably succeeded, he was furious he hadn't had time to escape with the Mackinnon woman. He hadn't planned to kill her, not until he'd used her the way he'd dreamed of for weeks, ever since he saw her in St. Louis. He hoped she had died on Spirit Mound, but he had stupidly failed to bind her ankles, so the chances were good she escaped the fire. If she survived and stayed in Dakota, he might yet have a chance to abduct her.

But the woman had no knife, so she could not have cut Wyndford free in time to get away from the flames. When people heard about the fire and that the white invader, Kyler Wyndford, had been burned alive by a Lakota, the message would be clear: disaster awaits any whites who come to Dakota to establish a home.

Loup eased his pace when the horse stumbled in a prairie dog hole. It wouldn't do for his mount to break a leg and leave him on foot. He was disappointed that the animal, who looked like it could run forever, was already tiring.

Loup thought of his shock when the sword-wielding Indian had suddenly interrupted his sacrifice. He'd never seen such a warrior before. The man wasn't dressed like an Indian, but his face and hair made his heritage plain. And the man spoke in the Lakota tongue. Everyone knew Wyndford had no friends among the Indians. Who would have come to his aid? Loup thought of the legendary little people of Spirit Mound. He had never believed the place was haunted, and certainly the native who had rushed to help Wyndford today could not be described as small. But there had been a mystical hellish quality about the warrior, especially viewed through the smoke and crackling flames. Whoever he was, he had been too late to save Wyndford. The fire had been leaping around the couple when Loup made his getaway. If Wyndford hadn't been roasted alive, he would die a slow and agonizing death from burns.

Within the hour, Loup came to the James River. He had been careful along the way to skirt any Indian villages. Here he could cross easily with the horse because the river was sluggish during August after a rampage earlier in the spring.

Dismounting, he led the exhausted animal into the stream and made his way to the far bank. A grove of willows and cottonwoods lined the shores, offering shade and a place to rest and fill his water containers before riding toward the Missouri, where he'd camp for the night. Tomorrow, he would cross the central lowlands on his way to the badlands in the west, to the Black Hills, sacred to all the Sioux tribes. He wasn't known among the people there. He couldn't pretend to be a full-blood, not with his mother's features prominent in his face, but he should be able to join with others who hated white men as much as he did. From that craggy and inhospitable land of soaring stone towers, of furnace-like heat and bitter cold, he could enflame hatred toward the whites as never before.

Kyle kept Raven Duke moving at a steady canter across the rolling plains. At this pace, he knew the stallion could travel for hours, his huge lungs and great heart displaying the careful breeding of the English thoroughbreds that had no equal in horsedom.

The best spot to ford the James lay south of the Lakota village. He figured Leveque would try to avoid confronting the people who disliked him and at the same time take the shortest route toward the safety of the badlands. Kyle knew that if he guessed wrong, he could miss Leveque entirely. But somehow he believed he had been spared from the flames for the sole purpose of cleansing the earth of such a foul creature as Loup Leveque.

A few minutes' ride east of the river, he saw fresh horse dung beside the trail and tracks that looked as if a horse had stumbled in a prairie dog hole. He was sure those large hoofprints belonged to Diamond Dust. For several minutes, he rested Raven and tried to think like Loup Leveque. Loup's horse was tiring. They were both hot and thirsty and needing to rest. Where would Leveque take refuge for a time before heading on toward the safety of the badlands?

The James River was two hundred yards away, wide and muddy and shallow. Both banks were lined with trees and underbrush.

Kyle had hunted here several years ago, and he knew there was a shady clearing, flanked by a large rock outcrop on the opposite side. In fact, only a mile downstream from here, he'd found Blanton's mutilated body. He knew this area well.

He entered the trees and walked Raven slowly toward the

river. Stopping in the shade, he dismounted and found a secluded pool and filled the crown of his hat. Then he carried a drink to his horse and made certain Raven was well secured and out of sight. If he encountered Loup and killed him, he would be back for Raven. If he lost the fight, Loup would come looking for an extra horse. At least Raven wouldn't be left here to die.

He checked his pistol, then took Mackinnon's sword from the saddle. Years ago in the English army, he had excelled at swordplay. But with today's modern weapons, he hadn't expected to ever need a sword again. Still, it felt good in his hand, balanced and deadly. He could almost feel the fiery courage of ancient Scottish clans flowing into his soul, a gift from the Mackinnon laird.

Moving to the river, he checked the position of the sun. He estimated it was between five and six o'clock, with plenty of daylight left to do what had to be done. He pulled off his shirt, then unbuckled his holster and held it aloft along with the claymore as he slid quietly into the water. In minutes, he had reached the far shore and entered the trees.

Moving west, he took a diagonal path that would put him near the boulder above the clearing. If he had guessed wrong, this entire effort would cost him valuable time, but he had to take that chance. Sooner or later, Leveque would have to stop and rest. It was unlikely the clever bastard would build a fire, so finding him during the night would be impossible.

Kyle crept slowly through the tall grass, being careful not to step on a branch or dislodge a stone as he approached the boulder.

Someone coughed.

His heartbeat quickened. Damned if he hadn't outsmarted the wolf after all.

From beyond the clearing, he climbed up the boulder, then crawled forward until he could see below. Diamond Dust was grazing beneath a tree. Leveque was leaning against the trunk and appeared to be dozing in the late-day heat.

The urge to shoot him without warning was strong, but

Kyle couldn't bring himself to commit cold-blooded murder, even if it was against someone as deserving as Loup Leveque. He rose to one knee and took aim. "Good afternoon, Mr. Leveque. No doubt you're surprised to see me."

Loup leaped to one side and ducked behind the horse. Fast as a darting lizzard.

Kyle fired, but the bullet lodged in the tree. He dropped to his stomach and shot twice more at the figure skulking through the underbrush. He heard Loup moving in the grass. He raised up to take another shot, but Loup fired his pistol from behind a sycamore.

Diving to the boulder, Kyle heard the bullet whiz by his ear. He wriggled off the boulder and dropped to the forest floor. Leveque's single-shot pistol was no match for the Colt.

A breeze rustled the leaves high overhead. Far across the plain, a mountain jay cried. No other sound disturbed the late-afternoon sun filtering through the trees.

Kyle held his breath and listened. He knew Loup also watched and listened.

"You've taken your shot, Leveque," he shouted. "Give yourself up and you will live."

A twig snapped. Kyle spotted a moving shadow. He fired, but the bullet ricocheted off a stone and thudded to earth.

"You're trapped, Leveque. Give yourself up and I won't kill you. I give you my word."

"I've learned never to take the word of a white man," called Leveque from his hiding place.

Kyle ducked behind a tree and inched toward the voice. With great stealth, he circled behind Leveque until he was sure he could jump him. Then he moved into sight with his pistol ready. "Don't move, Leveque," he ordered.

Slowly Leveque turned to face him, his face a mask of hatred.

"It's over," Kyle said flatly. "Get your horse."

After a long pause, Leveque rasped, "You win this hand, Wyndford. Do you swear you won't kill me if I go with you?"

"I could have killed you when I first spotted you, but I'm no murderer. If you'll agree to go to Vermillion as my prisoner, I'll take you to the authorities. You'll get off lightly, since my wife and I escaped the fire."

More seconds passed. Finally, Loup said, "All right. I'm unarmed."

With his pistol ready in one hand and the broadsword in the other, Kyle entered the clearing and strode toward Leveque, whose gun lay at his feet. In Loup's hand was the slender walking stick Kyle remembered he had carried in St. Louis.

"You are the victor, after all, *mon ami.* I am entirely at your mercy."

Kyle holstered the Colt.

In a lightning movement, Loup snapped the stick through the air like a whip. A sheath flew from it, revealing a gleaming slender foil. Loup sprang at him, the ten-inch stiletto headed for his heart.

Kyle sucked in his breath, and as if he had rehearsed for years, swung the claymore with his left hand toward the leering face of Loup Leveque.

The stiletto slid past his ribcage, stinging his flesh. Instantly, he was covered with a spray of blood.

Loup Leveque's blood.

Kyle's stomach turned when he saw he had sliced through Leveque's throat. The man was dead before he hit the ground. Standing over him, Kyle collected himself while wondering where such twisted hatred had come from. Thank the Lord, it was over.

He removed the bear-claw necklace from Loup's bloody neck and tied the body over Dusty's saddle. Tomorrow, he would take Leveque to Vermillion for identification and burial. He was surprised how little pleasure he took in the man's death. The man's father, Siyaka, had sowed seeds of hate, and this was the harvest. It was like destroying a mad dog, merely something that had to be done to make the earth a safer place.

He led Diamond Dust back across the river, retrieved Raven Duke, and started toward home.

* * *

Skye's face was bright pink, her lips were peeling, her palms were bandaged and useless for any valuable work—but her concern was only for Kyle.

After a painful ride from Spirit Mound, she had spent the afternoon in bed visiting with her parents, while her mind constantly strayed to what might be happening to the man she loved more than life itself.

"Lie still, sweetheart. I know how you feel, but you must get some rest." Elizabeth stroked her daughter's arm. "I'm confident God won't let that terrible man hurt Mr. Wyndford."

Skye wasn't so sure. Loup was smart and mean and would kill Kyle if he had the chance. She was furious with herself that she hadn't insisted her father go with Kyle. She could have managed to travel home with Badger. "Tell me again, Mother, about the Caldwells." She would try to concentrate on something pleasant.

"Laurel is busy preparing for her voyage. She'll go to the Mediterranean, then travel to the Isle of Skye to claim the castle at Strathmor. I told her to find your dear friend Rosie, that Rosie would help her get acquainted on the island. Not that Rosie is a social equal of Laurel Caldwell, but Laurel insisted she wanted to be friendly with all the locals. She's not a bit snobbish for one so young and beautiful. I'm delighted she'll occupy our old home."

Skye rolled over on the sheets, searching for a cool spot. "Laurel would hate to see how I've ruined my complexion," she said, trying to take her mind off Kyle. "I was careful as could be, then today I was cooked." She paused. "Almost *burned,*" she added with bitter humor.

"Oh, darling, try not to think about it. After Mr. Wyndford returns, today will be only a bad dream. I learned years ago to put aside unpleasant memories as much as possible. I found that writing a book about Fletcher and our adventures was very helpful. Maybe you would like to write one, too."

Skye sighed deeply. "I wish I could, Mother, but I have tried and the words won't come. I start, and then something else I want to do pops into my head, and I'm off to do it."

Elizabeth smiled with understanding. "Full of energy.

Too spirited to sit still. Well, the Lord makes all of us different. People have different likes and dislikes, different skills and skin color. That makes life more interesting, I always say."

"May I come in?" came a voice from beyond the bedroom door.

"It's Mr. Sinclair," Elizabeth said. "Do you feel like seeing him, lass? He's been down at the barn with Fletcher this past hour, but he promised to stop in to say hello."

Skye sat up and plumped her pillow. "I'm feeling far better than I look. Of course I'd be happy to see him."

Cheyne Sinclair entered, carrying a bouquet of yellow goldenrod and pink thistle blooms from the prairie.

He was more handsome than she remembered, Skye thought, accepting the flowers and giving him a grateful smile. "I'm pleased to see you again, sir. It's very kind of you to come so far to help my parents on their journey."

Cheyne doffed his hat and gave her a courtly bow. "Entirely my pleasure. I wanted to see the American West, and I won a small fortune on the *Mississippi Belle* en route. I hope you're not in pain, Miss Mackinnon."

"Very little, thank you. And it's *Mrs. Wyndford* now, I'm proud to announce."

"Is that a fact? My heartiest congratulations."

"I must also thank you for saving my father's life, Mr. Sinclair. My parents told me the whole story this afternoon. How you sailed to Tangier and rescued him during the uprising, how you brought him and his Arabian stallion to New Orleans."

"A man worth saving, I do swear," Sinclair said, grinning. "We fought our way out of the Kasbah, and your father took down half a dozen rebels with his broadsword, while I fired but one pistol shot."

"I'm eager to see the new stallion," she said, trying to remain polite when she wanted only to listen for the sound of a horse approaching under the full moon.

"Your mother rode him here from Vermillion. A more beautiful sight I never saw."

"You flatter me, Mr. Sinclair," Elizabeth said.

"Nay, ma'am. You sit a horse as well as anyone I've ever

seen. You should claim the Arab for your own, even if it is a stallion."

Elizabeth was laughing when footsteps sounded in the hall. "Perhaps that's my husband now," she said. "I'll ask him to give me the Arab, and we'll find out how much he truly cares for me."

Without pausing to knock, Kyle Wyndford strode into the room, the jangle of his spurs punctuating the thud of his boots on the wooden floor. He was stained with blood, and his eyes were underlined with dark circles. He had the beginning of a beard and his hat was rumpled and pushed back from his forehead. He brought with him the aroma of horse and smoke and earth.

"Kyle!" Skye cried, sitting up.

He crossed to the bed and raised Skye's bandaged hand to his lips while absorbing her eyes. Then he placed the bear-claw necklace in her palm and said quietly, "I recovered your necklace, my darling. I apologize for taking so long."

As she held out her arms to draw him to her, she was vaguely aware that her visitors had slipped from the room. Her hero, her husband, was hers alone.

Kyle lost track of time with Skye folded in his arms. He lay on the bed as the lantern flickered and an owl hooted beyond their window. He was fully clothed atop the quilt, but he was content to hold his love and kiss her warm forehead and the tips of her small fingers peeking from beneath their bandages. He had told her the story of his visit to the Indian village and of how Loup died. He described how swiftly Raven had carried him on his mission and how he had thought constantly of her as he rode toward home.

She touched his stubbly chin. "I'm happy you saw the Lakota camp. Were you well received?"

"Indeed I was," he said softly. "The warrior offered his help—and that of his men. I saw serenity and tradition and glimpsed a way of life I knew nothing about. I was wrong to hold such prejudice against the Lakotas for so many years. Missy told me, and you told me, but I was too stubborn to learn until now. I assure you, things will be different after today."

"Ola told me that the warriors who murdered your brother were banished forever from the tribe. She said they're all dead now."

For a long moment, he absorbed this news. "Then Blanton is at peace—and so am I."

"But I was wrong, too, not to listen to your advice. I have much to learn about living in the West." She leaned up to press her lips to his chin.

"We'll learn together," he murmured.

Tipping up her face, he captured her eyes, deepest green in the shadows. Then he sat on the edge of the bed and pulled off his spurs, then his boots, then his shirt. He heard her soft laughter behind him as he snuffed the lantern, leaving them with only the moon to light their way.

⤜ Chapter 41 ⤐

Come along, Dusty. You surely do need a bath. We'll wash off every trace of ole Loup Leveque."

Skye was fully recovered from her ordeal on the crest of Spirit Mound and was eager to take part in ranch activities. For next week, they planned a barbecue, a horse show, and a fiesta to celebrate her marriage to Kyle and to say farewell to her parents and Cheyne, who were starting back to New Orleans. Her mother and father had known at once that they would make their home in the place Missy had chosen for them. But it was too late in the summer to start building a house or bringing in stock. The Mackinnons had toured the area, then decided to winter in New Orleans with the Caldwells and go to Texas in the spring to buy their foundation herd for their new ranch in Dakota.

Skye had slipped away this morning to bring Diamond Dust to this secluded pool trapped between cascades of water and hidden by a thick stand of willows. Kyle had shown her the lovely spot yesterday on an early-morning ride, an oasis in the windswept plain surrounding it.

In the privacy of the brush, she had pulled off her blouse and skirt, her boots and stockings. She kept on her filmy chemise and petticoat and her Lakota necklace at her throat. The winds of autumn were not far from arriving, Kyle had explained. Already, snow was falling in the high country. This might be her last chance to bathe in the sparkling water and soothe her sunburned face and throat. But she had learned a hard lesson. Today, she had told Kyle exactly where she was going and how long she would be away. He had given his permission, since the falls were only half a mile from the ranch and safe from any intrusion.

"Come along, Dusty. If you stand under the falls, I can give you a good brushing." She waded into the pool, luxuriating in the cool, refreshing water on her warm skin. As they made their way toward the cataract, Dusty lifted his nose and snorted in pleasure. The water swirled around his flanks and finally covered his back, but he had no trouble walking beside her.

Maneuvering the horse partially under the splashing waterfall, she stood with her toes in the mud and her breasts submerged in the water and began grooming his silvery coat with the stiff brush she'd borrowed from B. J.

"Don't move," she instructed the stallion, holding on to his halter as she swam around to the far side, letting the plunging shower pour over her head and upper body. Spotting a yellow bloom that reminded her a bit of the wildflowers of her homeland, she picked it and tucked it into her sopping bodice. Then she moved around the animal's high rump, stroking briskly and humming to make certain he wasn't frightened. How docile he was, like a gentle pet dog who enjoyed the care and attention of a trusted master.

Dusty's sable tail was floating on the surface, and she ran her fingers through it to smooth out any tangles and remove traces of dirt.

"You'll be beautiful for the fiesta, Dusty, if you behave yourself. We'll show the guests your lightning turnaround. I know they'll be impressed. You mustn't worry a minute over letting Raven catch up with you last week. You were bred for sprinting, not distance racing, and you wanted Raven to overtake you anyway." Skye tread water until she got back to her starting point and began working on his mane. She was so busy enjoying herself under the azure sky, she didn't hear the sound of a body sliding into the pool behind her.

Large hands went around her waist.

She gasped and sucked in a deep breath as she was pulled under and swirled to face her assailant.

Her husband, his eyes open, his lips smiling, his lithe body entirely naked, was holding her at arm's length.

He drew her through the liquid and kissed her deeply, then they floated to the surface, where she sputtered and pretended to be annoyed. Laying the brush on a rock, she scolded, "How could you scare me so, Mr. Wyndford? I thought a wolf had me."

"Not this time, Skye Eugenia. Only a fox in wolf's clothing."

"Clothing? I don't see a stitch," she teased.

"What you see is a *man,*" he answered, his lazy smile inviting her admiration.

Laughing, she tossed back her hair and ran her hands along his dripping shoulders above the water.

He bent to kiss her throat below the beads, then strayed to the swell of her breasts, which were bobbing near the surface. He stood like a mountain, trapping her as if she were a rushing river in his arms. His tongue toyed with her nipples, which were plainly erect under the soaked gauze of her bodice.

Delicious shudders of excitement crept through her. Closing her eyes, she smiled up at the sun and wrapped her legs around his hips, feeling his hardness pressing against her femininity, open and vulnerable beneath her drifting underskirt.

His movement pushed her through the water before he

could claim her, but her back bumped against Diamond Dust's side, and she was held firmly in place.

Kyle smoothed out her long hair with his fingers, letting it drift on the bubbling water and mingle with Dusty's mane.

She lay back across the quiet stallion's smooth hide and relaxed to receive Kyle's thrust.

One hand held her hips; the other cupped her buttocks to steady her. Kyle possessed her forcefully, then rocked her in a sensual rhythm known to lovers since life began. The sensation of his entry beneath the blue-green fluid sent a jolt of delight racing through her body. With her palms along Kyle's ribcage, she used Dusty's solid back as leverage to respond to Kyle's demanding maleness and let him carry them both to the heights of pleasure. Crying out her release, she clung to him and drifted in his embrace, the two of them one, pledging themselves wordlessly to the pure joy of their union, here in the pristine purity of the crystal pool.

Smiling, she lowered her feet into the soft floor of the pond, and discovered Kyle hadn't dislodged the yellow flower. She removed it and tucked it behind his ear.

"Goldenrod," he murmured as his lips brushed her cheek.

"Kyle," she whispered, "I've been wanting to ask you something."

"What is it, lass?" he said idly, caressing her.

"I never learned what *chula mia* means. I'm curious."

"My pretty one," he said tenderly, and kissed her parted lips. "Ah, Skye, my own true love. Will you remember this day when the snowflakes fly in January?"

"I will carry the memory deep in my heart," she responded with a sigh. "The vision will warm me, no matter how cold the temperature may be."

"Mrs. Wyndford," he whispered, "my Lakota lass, you have captured my very soul."

Dusty swished his tail impatiently, whipping their faces and splattering them with a spray of water.

Laughing, Skye and Kyle ducked together under the surface of the pool.

≈ Epilogue ≈

The scent of beef cooking in earthen pits, mingling with the aroma of fresh-baked bread from Pilar's kitchen, wafted through the early evening air. Above the Vermillion River valley, a new moon rose to transcend the stars splashed across the velvet heavens.

In the courtyard behind Kyle Wyndford's log home, a makeshift wooden platform had been erected to serve as a dance floor. Surrounding the platform were torches and lanterns, giving light to the immediate surroundings. Long tables held a feast for the revelers. Near the dance floor, Reyes Pacheco, accompanied by three of his musically inclined California vaqueros, played a fandango with more vigor than skill. To the rhythmical clapping of the onlookers, a laughing Skye Wyndford whirled in the arms of her husband, whose execution of the Spanish dance left no doubt he should continue as a cattleman rather than join a gypsy troupe.

As the last vibrating note echoed across Wind River Ranch, Skye bowed to acknowledge the applause of the gathering, the two dozen settlers who had come up from Vermillion and guests of honor—her parents and the enigmatic Cheyne Sinclair.

The music softened into a love song as Fletcher and Elizabeth Mackinnon took the floor to join the newlyweds in a romantic waltz. Over Kyle's shoulder, Skye gazed with pride at her father, dressed now in a black broadcloth suit, but with his open-necked shirt displaying the bear claw of his mother's people. Already, Fletcher Mackinnon was becoming a legend in Dakota. He had saved Kyle Wyndford from a fiery death, and he was the type of man who could tame the raw land of the American West.

Soon, to the delight of the onlookers, Badger took Dulce by the hand and led her in a stiff-legged maneuver along with the others. Dulcinea's full ruffled skirt above polished kidskin boots made a perfect foil for Badger's Spanish charro suit of black leather with silver piping.

Cheyne Sinclair gallantly paid tribute to Pilar, the lady responsible for the evening's feast, by leading her expertly in the waltz. At an invitation from Kyle, the rest of the couples filled the dance floor. Never before had such an occasion been seen in this wilderness outpost near the confluence of the Missouri and the Vermillion Rivers. The winter ahead would be harsh and demanding, both at the trading post and on the plains; but for tonight, hardships were forgotten as the celebration continued under the stars.

The day had been wondrous and unforgettable. During the afternoon, some of the finest horseflesh ever seen in Dakota had been on display. First, Kyle Wyndford rode Raven Duke across the corral while the gathering cheered their host atop his gleaming black stallion. Next, Reyes rode his West Indian Spanish jennet, showing off the incomparable smooth gait that had been bred into the best of the ambling horses of the New World. To climax his act, Reyes spun his lasso in ever expanding circles that encompassed both himself and his prancing horse.

Skye put Diamond Dust through his paces, the blue roan pivoting in powerful turns as his diamond coat shone like the jewel for which it was named. Fletcher Mackinnon stunned the crowd by riding bareback on a spotted horse and piercing a target with an arrow while he leaned beneath the animal's neck, Indian style. Then, to top off the spectacle, Fletcher showed off the stallion he had recently obtained on the Barbary Coast as he circled the arena on the blood bay Arabian, its delicate nose and flared nostrils, long and gracefully arched neck, and flowing tail almost touching the ground making it surely the most elegant horse the audience had seen anywhere in the West. The show ended with enthusiastic cheers and applause.

Soon after, as the guests drifted toward refreshment tables, B. J. hurried to the spot where Kyle and Skye chatted beside an ancient cottonwood.

"Look who's coming, Mr. Wyndford. What do you think about that?"

Skye was astonished to see a band of Indians riding into the area—men and women, and horses pulling several travois. Kyle hurried to greet them, then announced to one and all that his new friends, a Lakota hunting party, which had been camping near the James, had taken up his offer to attend the fiesta. Skye was thrilled to see them and introduced the women she'd met at the quilling society to everyone present, the girls' shy laughter making up for language barriers. The only cloud on the occasion was the announcement that Ola had passed away a few days earlier. Fortunately, Fletcher had been to visit the elderly woman several times since his arrival. Everyone agreed that Ola had died happy because she had been reunited with the boy she raised so many years ago.

Sometime before midnight, Skye held a tired MacLard under her arm as she bid the guests farewell and watched the horses and wagons disappear down the road.

Badger ran along the path from the barn, calling to her. "Come quick, Auntie Skye. Come to the barn. Where is Uncle Kyle?"

Skye hurried after him and was quickly joined by her husband.

Entering the enclosure lighted by a single lantern, Badger led them to the stall occupied by Spirit Legacy.

"Lookee there. Just look at that," said Badger in a hushed tone.

Skye stood arm in arm with Kyle and gazed misty eyed at the tiny colt struggling to get to its feet. Legacy nuzzled her newborn, then stood aside to see if her son had the strength and will to live.

In minutes, the foal was on its spindly legs and nursing, proving without doubt he was a sturdy survivor. The wet colt was as shiny and black as obsidian.

"He's perfect," Skye said with a sigh. "His daddy, Spirit Dog, would be very proud of him."

Badger hung over the stall railing. "Will he be black, do you think? His mother is as white as a mourning dove."

"No, he won't be black for long. Just you watch. By the

time he's three, he'll be the color of a rain cloud. When he's ten, he'll be nearly white like both his parents. Spirit Dog was a rare gray-white stallion my father took from America to Scotland. Now Legacy has brought the breeding and the color back to America."

"What'll you name him, Auntie?"

"I haven't decided. What do you suggest, Badger?"

"You could call him Skye Legacy, after you and his mama."

"Good idea, lad," Kyle interjected. "He's both Scot and Lakota, uniting European and Indian bloodlines. He's the first of many I expect to be born at Wind River. Do you agree, Skye?"

"Indeed I do," she said, smiling at the double implication in Kyle's words. "Skye Legacy he will be."

On that late summer night, peace rested a serene hand on the green river valley of Dakota.

⊰ Author's Notes ⊱

By 1840, the young United States was flexing its muscles and beginning to probe deeply into its recently acquired territory known as the Louisiana Purchase. Following in the footsteps of the Lewis and Clark expedition of 1804, the "West" was mapped out by the Army Corps of Engineers with the goal of promoting westward expansion. The day of the mountain man was nearly finished and the beaver trapped out. American entrepreneurs were sending steamboats up the Missouri into land referred to as the public domain, and by 1834, Congress had passed three hundred and seventy-five land laws to control and encourage settlers and land speculators.

The push was on toward America's Manifest Destiny.

On the western edge of the tide stretched Dakota, containing well-watered grassland with some of the richest soil in the entire West. Occupying Dakota were the Mandan and Sioux Indian tribes. But by 1837, the Mandan nation was obliterated by smallpox.

In Texas, the cattle business was beginning to boom, and men with imagination and courage saw the possibilities for profit in the fertile north. Only huge herds of buffalo and the Sioux stood in the way. The stage was set for a terrible conflict with an inevitable outcome.

But in 1840, the time period for *Skye Legacy,* peaceful trade between the whites and the Indians was still taking place. Very few whites lived in the territory. I chose to create a true pioneer, James Kyler Wyndford, who would use as his role model the empire builders of Texas whose cattle operations were flourishing. Kyle had the ambition, the courage, the stamina, and the prejudices of the cattle barons of the time. It would take a high-spirited and beautiful young woman who was both Scottish and Lakota to capture his heart and lead him into a new and enlightened way of thinking. I hope you enjoy their story.

Krista Janssen

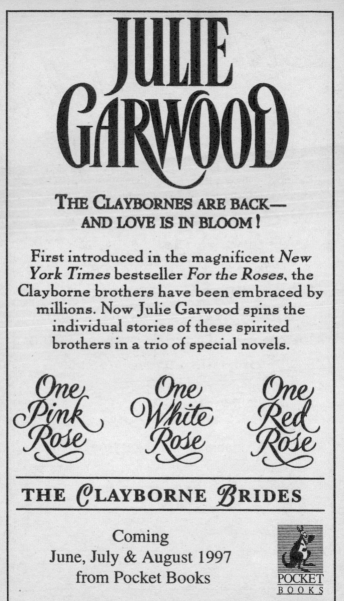

JULIE GARWOOD

THE CLAYBORNES ARE BACK— AND LOVE IS IN BLOOM!

First introduced in the magnificent *New York Times* bestseller *For the Roses*, the Clayborne brothers have been embraced by millions. Now Julie Garwood spins the individual stories of these spirited brothers in a trio of special novels.

One Pink Rose *One White Rose* *One Red Rose*

THE CLAYBORNE BRIDES

Coming
June, July & August 1997
from Pocket Books

POCKET BOOKS